WITHDRAWN

SONG OF EDMON

ADAM BURCH

47NORTH

Published by 47North, Seattle

www.apub.com

ISBN-13: 9781477805350
ISBN-10: 1477805354

Cover design by Adam Hall

Printed in the United States of America

This book is for my family—my mother and father, Ben and Marcy, and my sister, Lindsay.

MOVEMENT I: EFFLORESCENCE ÉTUDE

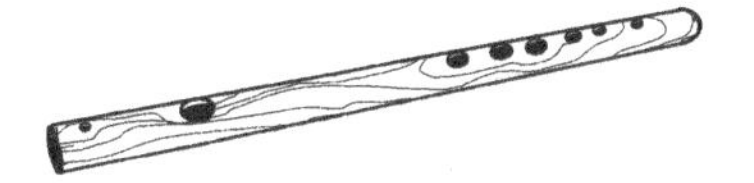

CHAPTER 1

First Lyric

My father strides into the island manse the day I am born. The same day, the heavens burst in the skies above us. The whole planet is abuzz with the news—the Fracture Point has exploded in space and opened a new pathway for our planet. But the islanders don't realize that. They see only fire in the sky. They still hold on to their ancient beliefs.

"It's an omen," they say.

My father pulls me from my mother's arms in spite of her cries. Protestations of an island woman mean little to the great Edric Leontes. He bolts from the birthing chamber to the balcony. He holds me aloft to the brightness of the star of Tao, making certain all the strategically placed camglobes hovering around us capture the moment in pristine high-definition aquagraphic. Then he proclaims to the sea, the sky, and all the ancestors old and newly ascended, "This is Edmon, the son of Leontes. Let all behold and claim, 'The son is greater than the father!' He is a leviathan!"

My father knows how to exploit an event for personal gain. He makes this ordinary moment, the birth of an unremarkable child, history. On this day, on the Isle of Bone, on the Dayside of the distant planet Tao, my birthday is written in the ledger of our people's history. It is the nineteenth day of Wu Chen, 8227 by Tao Reckoning, 1234 Post Fractural Collapse. Augurs deem the date auspicious to please him, and the exploding Fracture Point only confirms their announcement. My father—Edric, Patriarch of House Leontes, Nightsider, and a giant of a man seemingly carved from granite—is a king in all but name. His shoulder-length flaxen hair whips in the wind as he makes his proclamation over his firstborn son.

It is the last time he makes predictions regarding my destiny.

You see, I am not a leviathan.

I am nine when my mother and I are summoned by the emperor himself. It is the day after the Combat, the yearly killing games on Tao, an occasion for great celebration. I'm washed and polished, my dark hair slicked back and pulled into a thong. My mother has adorned us both in the finest linens of Bone.

"The island people were here before the Great Song," she tells me. "We go back to the time of the Elder Stars. Never forget that, Edmon." She hugs me tightly.

I don't understand all of what she says, but it makes me feel proud to be who I am.

To me, she looks stunning, her mocha skin smooth and luminous against the cream of the linen. Her hair is pinned up high with inky tresses cascading down her back. She looks like a queen, even though she isn't one . . .

"Cleopatra was born a commoner on Bone," Gorham, the old musician and village elder, told me one night a few months earlier. "She was the daughter of a fisherman," he whispered in my ear as the guests entered for the Eventide feast. "But she was the most beautiful girl on our island. Still is."

Bone is one of the many small islands that dot the surface of the green seas of Tao's Dayside like freckles. Here, amid white beaches and limestone cliffs, the sun never sets. Eventide sees the streets empty as islanders escape from the sweltering heat. Almost the whole island comes together at our house atop the summit. The shades are pulled low to simulate the setting sun of Ancient Earth. Family and friends gather in a circle with drums and flutes, strings and voices. Everyone plays. Everyone sings. Even the shy ones are part of the dance.

"Beauty on Tao is always revered, always given power," Gorham continued.

My mother finished greeting the guests, raised her hands, and signaled for the drums to beat.

"Cleopatra's mother, your grandmother, was an important voice in the Eventide song, and so your mother, too, was given a voice at council meetings."

My mother entered the circle of guests to dance. She twirled her body in rapture, and I saw in that moment the girl she must have been before I was born.

"Then Edric Leontes came. He was deeded this island by the High Synod when he won his second Combat." The old man's voice turned sour. "The Nightsiders pretend our land is theirs to give. He was smitten with her beauty and some say her arrogance."

Fire alit in my mother's gaze, and there came something primal and aggressive in her movements as the drums beat.

"Their love wasn't the kind that lasts forever, Edmon, only the kind that survives until they tamed each other." He nodded. "He built this manse for her and for you."

I did not know how to react to these words then. I didn't remember meeting my father when I was born, but I listened to the punctuated shot of the drums and watched how my mother held the final pose of her dance, balanced on the tips of her toes. Not a single person in the room took a breath. Then she fell back to earth, releasing the moment. The crowd cheered, and so did I, filled with pride.

My thoughts return to our meeting with the emperor . . . and my father. *What will he be like? Will he be proud of me when he sees me?*

My mother is like a sea siren, fierce and strong, readying herself for a contest. "We're to look our best," she snaps. I feel her tension. This is an important occasion, but it's more than that. There is danger in this meeting.

We make our way down narrow, winding stairs. They lead from our manse atop the high limestone cliffs through a sleepy town of white adobe dwellings with azure-tiled roofs. We take this path daily to the white beaches, where I collect shells and we bathe in the great Mother Ocean.

On this day, however, a giant mechanical monstrosity awaits us at the docks. Its shiny black carapace hovers over the sea. A sonic engine hums, raising the thing on a cushion of sound. Spindly, articulated claws reach into the cerulean island sky. They will hold the massive metallic balloon when it inflates to carry us toward Meridian, the capital city of Tao.

"A sondi." I whisper the name for the sonic dirigible. I've seen them in the aquagraphic storybooks but never in person. It looks like a dead sand beetle lying on its back. Suddenly, I'm filled with dread.

"Your father thinks this is a great honor that Old Wusong affords him." My mother's voice is caustic. "But we'll not be brushed aside. You're Edric's first son. You're his heir. He wants you strong? Show him strength."

Be strong . . . does that mean do what I'm told or speak my mind? I wonder.

A boarding ramp extends from the carriage to the docks. A thick, muscular man in a navy-blue, military-cut uniform lumbers down. He is grizzled and scarred. His massive, hairy left arm ends in a puckered stump where a hand should be. The sight of it makes me gasp with sudden shock. His lips curl in disgust as he takes in our appearance.

Is there something wrong with the way we are dressed?

"Lady Cleopatra." He nods. "I'm to escort you to the imperial palace." He gestures for us to board the sondi.

"Alberich," she says curtly. "Just like Edric to send his pet fish to do his bidding."

He bristles at the insult but steps aside as my mother strides past him up the ramp, her gaze tilted proudly upward. I follow, eyeing the man suspiciously.

We sail over the Northern Sea. The horn of the sondi blares, and the carriage shakes. I peer out the porthole to look at the island receding from view. From the air, it looks like a sharp, white sliver against the blue-green of the ocean. Maybe that's how she got her name—the Isle of Bone.

My mother squeezes my hand. I'm scared. I don't want to say a word out of turn or give the emperor cause to throw me to the fires of the Pavaka. Every year following the Combat, children with birth defects are incinerated in large burning cauldrons.

"This is how the Nightsiders of Tao keep their race strong and pure," the droning voice of the aquagraphic instructional had relayed.

I didn't believe it to be true, but my mother confirmed that the practice was real. "Barbarian Nightsiders! Islanders do not murder their young because they are imperfect. We embrace our differences." She held me close, wiping the tears of terror from my cheeks. "You are the scion of a noble house of the Pantheon, the firstborn son of Edric Leontes, the leviathan. No one would dare discard you."

I felt the comfort of her breast against my face, but I couldn't shake the feeling that she was not telling me the entire truth. *I am different.* I feel this way now as I watch through the porthole the sky turn from a deep cerulean to a pale violet as we sail across the latitudes.

"Tidal lock," the gruff man, Alberich, grunts. "The light never sets on the Dayside, Lord Edmon, due to an asteroidal impact early in the star system's formation—"

"I know," I respond smugly to my father's seneschal. It's a big word that means he is in service to House Leontes but is something more than just a servant. "The force of the asteroid disrupted the planet's rotation on its axis. It's why the Dayside always faces the star and why the Nightside is always dark."

"I see you have not kept the boy completely ignorant, Cleopatra. Will it be enough when the emperor questions him?"

The emperor . . .

I suck in my breath, and my mother grips my hand more tightly.

"Approaching Meridian," the pilot's voice cuts in over the loudspeaker.

Alberich unstraps from the harness and stands. "Come," he says as he strides toward the cockpit.

My mother and I follow. I stand on tiptoes behind the pilot's chair straining to get a peek. Meridian—the capital city, Tao's only city, the first city I've ever seen. Monolithic skyscrapers of metal and glass rise from the earth like black claws, silhouetted against purple. Fireglobes blink in an array of colors, and aquagraphic screens display advertisements and images of fighters in the arena. Screamers howl as riders sail on their sound engines skirting the tight corners of the angular buildings. I've never seen land like this before. It stretches to the horizon as far as I can see.

"The Nightside of Tao is landlocked," Alberich offers. "Our ice and dirt is as much as your ocean."

My eyes go wide at the implications. The massive buildings are everywhere. Even my mother, who has been to the capital once before, seems impressed.

So many people! I think.

"The Dayside is always light. The Nightside is always dark. The Twilight Band is where the light and the dark blend. Meridian is the megalopolis that spans the vertical equator of the globe. Here there is just enough light for the strongest civilization humanity has ever known to flourish."

"The most arrogant and self-righteous humanity has ever known, you mean, seneschal," my mother says derisively.

The sondi arcs over wharves and harbors as the Northern Sea meets the land. Just as the Twilight Band is the habitat of the Nightsiders, the Eastern, Western, Southern, and Northern Seas are really one great Mother Ocean, where the many islands of Tao sustain the small population of Daysiders. The water is divided merely by name according to which way to sail toward Meridian.

I point to several large conical pyramids on the horizon. "Those are farms, aren't they?"

Alberich nods. "Very good. Ninety percent of the planet's food is grown hydroponically in such farms."

"The surfaces of pyramids are solar collectors," I recite from a lesson. "I read in the aquagraphics that they open?" No sooner do I ask it than the cones swivel and blossom like flowers, panels splayed to the sky.

"There is just enough solar energy in the Twilight Band for their collectors to harness the star of Tao," Alberich says.

"What are those?" I point below. The cityscape is pitted with giant metallic shafts, dug into the earth's crust. Lights blink from their gaping maws.

"Arcologies." He nods at the giant pits. "Communities drilled into the earth, housing tens of thousands."

"The underclass." My mother's voice is calm, almost sad. "That's where your father was born and bred."

Alberich tenses at my mother's words. I'm confused by them as well. I always understood my father to be a noble. "Isn't Edric the

Patriarch of House Leontes, the newest noble house in the Pantheon?" I ask.

"Yes, because he won the Combat. Twice," she affirms. "It's a feat that lifted him from ignominy, made him more beloved than any man since the Great Song. It raised him even higher than Alberich, who was once the scion of a noble house himself. Isn't that right, Alberich?"

The stocky man scratches at his bristly iron beard. "You know the history, my lady."

"I know you called for mercy and chose servitude instead of imprisonment or an honorable death." The big man remains silent. "Edmon, the reason your father is the most admired man on Tao is because of how far he had to climb. It's why I admired him, too. He was born a commoner, like those of us from Bone. Never forget where you come from," my mother whispers to me, "even if your own father forgets where he does. That is where Lord Leontes lives now."

She points to two large glittering scrapers of glass and steel. They stand like monoliths surveying lesser troops of an army. A neon sign flares in my retinas—Wusong Palatial Towers. The imperial sigil of the sea monkey flashes across the enormous aquagraphic screen that runs between the two.

A giant tube snakes around the base of the buildings and continues through the city. Tributary tunnels radiate from the main tube. I can hear the supersonic whoosh of a train as it exits one tube and enters another.

"A train?" I point.

"The Banshee Rail," Alberich corrects.

"Do we get to ride?" I ask.

"The name Leontes is noble now." He shakes his head. "Nobles live in the towers and ride the skies in screamers or sondis. Plebeians dwell on the city surface and travel rail—"

"And the underclass live in the arcologies," I say. I'm starting to understand.

The sondi swoops lower, and an entire section of the palatial towers hinges open, revealing a docking bay. The sondi balloon deflates and floats in, and the carriage gently touches down on the dock. Alberich leads us down the boarding ramp.

"The other scions will arrive shortly," he says.

My mother nods. She holds her chin high as another sondi enters the bay.

"Mother," I whisper, "what are other scions?"

This next sondi is much larger and more ornately painted than the one we traveled in. The carriage's silver hull shines like some sort of bullet shark of the deep. The ramp lowers, and a pair of uniformed guards exit. They take up positions at the bottom of the ramp. A man wearing a frilly kimono follows and plants himself between them. His hair has outrageous curls above a puckered face with lips too large. "The concubine Lady Zabeth Tandor of the Tao-Trans Corporation and her daughter, Lady Lavinia Leontes," he announces with a flourish.

Lady Lavinia Leontes?

The delicate and porcelain-skinned Lady Tandor daintily steps to the bottom of the ramp, adorned in a lacy, lavender gown. A small girl in identical dress stands at her side. She has her mother's pale, flawless skin and eyes the most entrancing shade of violet I've ever seen. Her hair is raven dark, which is highly unusual for the uniformly blond-haired Nightsiders. The color is even deeper than that of the islanders, but her skin has never touched the sun of the Dayside—I'd bet my life on it. She would be beautiful but for the extreme sense of superiority that rolls off her in waves. She curtsies alongside her mother.

Everyone is dressed so ornately. Our island linens stick out like tillyfish in a pack of makos.

Humiliation sends blood to my cheeks.

Alberich bows, and Lady Tandor extends her hand. The grizzled man kisses it. She pulls it away as if she would rather it be touched by a soiled rag. "My lady," he grunts.

"Where's my husband?"

"Lord Edric is preparing for the ritual."

Lady Tandor lets out a sigh of exasperation.

Edric is her husband? I thought my mother was the only woman who belonged to him, but that can't be true if this painted lady claims to be his wife, too.

Lady Tandor does not look at my mother. "I see Edric has invited all his whores to the proceedings then."

"Whores are paid, Zabeth. Therefore, theirs is the mark of pomp and finery." My mother's eyes skim Lady Tandor's ostentatious gown. "Wives are those that bear heirs. That's a lovely dress, though." Her voice drips sarcasm.

Lady Tandor scoffs. "It appears that after this ceremony, both of us will be little more than old laundry."

What does she mean, old laundry?

I steal a glance at the little girl with the violet eyes. Lavinia looks back at me with the curiosity of a predatory bird, then turns away as if I'm a speck of dust not worth her gaze.

Another sondi enters the chamber. It's the color of burnished copper. The boarding ramp extends, and a curvaceous woman with auburn hair exits. Holding her hand is a toddler—a girl, maybe three years old. The child's undoubtedly beautiful, even at this young age. Her face, however, is covered with so much paint that she looks like a clown to me.

Alberich bows and kisses the auburn-haired woman's hand. "Lady Tamara Calay, welcome."

The woman smiles broadly, and so does the toddler by her side. Lady Calay turns to the others. "Cleopatra. Lady Zabeth."

My mother smiles stiffly. Lady Tandor doesn't even acknowledge the newcomers.

"Now that you're all here"—Alberich breaks the discomfort—"you're to follow me to the main hall for the christening."

The christening?

Moments later, we are packed into a pneumovator car that rockets us to the apex of the tower.

I will see my father for the first time, I realize. *I must look brave. I must look strong. I must make him and my mother proud.*

Lavinia catches me balling my fists and puffing out my chest. She snorts. My face turns bright red.

I'm ignoring you! I think.

The giant double doors open. The imperial throne room is huge, packed with people dressed in finery. They flank a lavish red carpet with gold embroidery that has been laid upon the marmoreal floor. I'm shoved forward next to Lavinia. Our procession remains in tight formation as we walk down the carpet toward the giant sea-ape throne raised upon a dais. The shades of the room have been opened to let the orange light of the half-lidded sun spill in.

"Edric's children. Look at them!" I hear whispers from the sea of blond-haired nobles. "He's just an island blackhead, see!" One points.

My skin may be light, but my hair is like a Daysider's, thick and dark. *They think I'm disgusting,* I realize. *They think I'm different.*

"Pay them no heed," Lavinia whispers next to me without turning. Her violet gaze remains ever forward. "They know that we are their betters, no matter the color of our hair."

I nod, taking courage from her words. "Right," I say.

"Well, at least I am their better," she adds, undercutting me.

My father stands at the foot of the dais. I recognize him from the aquagraphics—Edric Leontes, the leviathan. I swallow, feeling like I have a rock in my throat when his ice-cold eyes pass over me. He looks so handsome and stern. His silvery hair is pulled back and braided around his shoulders. His granite face glows with pride.

A wizened old man in green and gold robes sits upon the throne behind him. His wispy hair is covered by a pointed cap, and his eyes are narrowed slits. The tails of a gray mustache flow down to his chest. In a gnarled hand, he holds a cane of darkest cocolao wood. It's capped by a silver dancing monkey, the sea ape, sigil of House Wusong. His eyes turn to us, and I feel my pulse quicken with fear.

"Don't be frightened," Lavinia hisses. "Old Wusong isn't like the emperors of the past. The Great Song, Tao's founder, may be his ancestor, but the emperors ceded their authority to the High Synod in 815 P.F.C. when the Empress Boudika was forced to abdicate. This emperor never even entered the Combat! You probably didn't know that, stupid."

"I'm not frightened," I lie. "And I'm not stupid." Still, I'm thankful for the uneasy ally. Lavinia might think the emperor does not have the power of the emperors of old, but as Alberich stops the procession, I can't help but feel that we're in the presence of a threat.

We reach the foot of the great throne, and the seneschal bows deeply. My mother has her hand on the small of my back directing me, so I follow suit and bow along with everyone else. I feel dreadfully out of place and ill prepared.

"Concubines and scions of House Leontes," Alberich announces, then joins the ranks of the Leontes guard flanking the hall.

"Lady Zabeth Tandor of the Tao-Trans Corporation and my daughter, Lady Lavinia Leontes." Edric gestures to the cold porcelain woman and her daughter with the violet eyes. The emperor nods as Lady Tandor and Lavinia step forward. They curtsy.

"Lady Tandor," the old Patriarch croaks. "Your father's manufacturing ensures the Banshee Rail connects all of Meridian. Your sondis and screamers let us reach the farthest Isles of Tao with ease. The honor is mine."

"Thank you, Old Wusong. My father hopes that you will see fit to grant him a deed to expand his leases past the Twilight Band and into the Nightside. We also hope the High Synod will revisit our family's petition to enter the ranks of the Pantheon . . ."

The emperor waves a gnarled hand. "Twelve families for the twelve regiments. Four high seats for the Great Song and his generals. No more. No less. That is the tradition."

Lady Tandor nods but does not give up. "Surely times change, Old Wusong. House Leontes was added . . ."

"House Leontes was an exception." He nods at my father, mildly annoyed. "When House Tandor presents a two-time champion of the Combat, your family's petition may be reconsidered. For now, the imperial house abides by all decisions of the High Synod."

Lady Tandor purses her lips but bows her head in deference. The old man grins wickedly. I see his teeth are all painted black. The look is terrifying. My mother squeezes my hand, silently warning me not to make a sound.

"A christening is not the place for politics," Old Wusong croaks.

"Forgive me, Grand Patriarch. I thought such events were about not much else." Lady Tandoor smiles in return.

Old Wusong cackles. "Perhaps! Though, some of us are more skilled at subtlety."

He turns his slitted gaze upon the girl at Lady Tandor's side. "Lady Lavinia. What a pretty little thing you are." Lavinia steps forward and curtsies. "*Lady* Lavinia. So wonderful you have received such a noble title. Though neither your father nor your mother was actually noble born."

I can't pull my gaze from my father, his handsome features, his fearsome stature, but now I see him clench his jaw at the slight. This is the second time I've seen the emperor suggest my father's ascension was anything but providence. *The emperor likes to diminish him,* I realize. *Edric could snap the old man in half! Why doesn't he?*

Once I asked my mother about Edric. She told me, "He's stronger than anyone on this world, Edmon, yet feels he must forever conquer a society that views him as unworthy. He tries to be like them. They love him, but they will never fully accept him. Daysiders learned this lesson long ago—only be yourself. Do you understand?"

Now, I understand. Edric wasn't born of the nobility. He grew up in the arcologies. And, like me, he doesn't want to be different.

My sister's voice snaps me back to the present. "Nobility isn't blood in your veins, Grand Patriarch." She startles everyone by challenging the old man. "It's the blood you can spill from your enemy."

The old man's shrewd eyes narrow. "Explain yourself, my lady."

Edric steps forward to interrupt, but the emperor taps his cane, stopping my father in his tracks. The whole room is on edge. If he doesn't like what Lavinia says, I don't know what will happen. They could throw her to the fires of the Pavaka. My father, the man I've heard is stronger than all others, is powerless to do a thing.

"It should be obvious to someone of your intelligence, Grand Patriarch." Lavinia's fine brows arch. "History is written by the victors. And victors can say whoever they want is noble."

"How old are you, girl?" Old Wusong rasps.

"Thirteen, Grand Patriarch."

My mouth drops open. I feel my mother squeeze my hand again, so I stay quiet. Lavinia is so petite, I thought she was my age. I'm shocked by this revelation.

Old Wusong strokes his wispy mustache. "What do you know of victory in battle, my lady?"

"Conflict isn't merely physical, Old Wusong. Every interaction is a battle. An exchange of words for instance."

Another moment of silence hangs thick. Anyone who speaks this way to the Grand Patriarch of the ruling houses of Tao must be insane.

The man breaks the silence with a full belly laugh. "Thank you, my dear, for such a formidable lesson!" The old emperor addresses my father. "This one is clever and cunning, Leontes. She will make a fine addition to your household."

"Lavinia has already served as one of my scriveners, Grand Patriarch," Edric says. "I hope she will continue to serve me through marriage to another great house."

"Do you have someone picked for her?" My father moves to answer, but Old Wusong cuts him off. "Be mindful that she always has meat to chew. Hunters are dangerous when hungry. Especially those who kill with their tongues." The old man laughs. He turns back to Lady Tandor. "A pleasure, my lady."

Lady Tandor and Lavinia step back in line with the rest of the coterie.

My father clears his throat. "Next my—"

Old Wusong stamps his cane, cutting Edric off again. My father's glacial eyes flash.

Everyone has someone they serve, I realize. *Even my father.*

"Step forward," Old Wusong says, beckoning Lady Calay and her doll of a daughter. Lady Calay gracefully bows before the shriveled old man. Her child does the same. "I am Lady Tamara Calay of House Angevin, here to serve you, Grand Patriarch," she says.

"Beautiful and compliant," Old Wusong muses. "What more could one want in a companion?"

I feel my mother stiffen at my side. Lady Tandor practically sneers at the word *compliant.*

"And who is this little figurine you bring, my lady?" Old Wusong asks.

"This, Grand Patriarch, is my daughter, Lady Phoebe Leontes." Lady Calay nudges her daughter forward. The little painted doll curtsies.

"How old are you, Phoebe Leontes?" Old Wusong leans forward.

"I'm three, Grand Pat-arch," the little girl says.

"Do you like chocolate, Phoebe?" Old Wusong grins.

"What's chocolate?" she asks innocently.

Old Wusong snaps his fingers. A steward emerges from the bevy of bystanders and kneels before the girl. He holds in his hands a little square of a rich brown color.

"Our new friends, arrived through the Fracture Point, have provided us with this delicacy. I'm told that the substance is manufactured according to a recipe of Ancient Earth." The hall murmurs at this bit of news.

My ears prick up at the mention of travelers and Ancient Earth. All my life I've dreamed of traveling to the different planets of the known universe. The Fracture Corridors, a series of interconnected cracks in the dark matter of the cosmos, make it possible. I hope someday I'll see the stars, too. Not through the drowning lights of Meridian twilight, but through the portholes of a real rocket looking straight into unfiltered black.

Be here and now, Edmon, I admonish myself. Still, chocolate. Something so small and silly opens my mind to a world of possibilities.

Old Wusong waves Lady Calay and her daughter back into line. "Now, Leontes, your son. Your first son," Old Wusong beckons.

My mother gently nudges me front and center. We bow low before the throne.

"Cleopatra Muse, how could I forget your exotic beauty?" I feel rather than hear an arrogant laugh hidden within his words. His eyes glide over my mother with a thirsty look, and I see my father's hands flex open and closed with suppressed rage. The muscles of his forearms writhe, making the leviathan tattoos that snake along their length undulate. These tattoos are the mark of a Patriarch of the Pantheon. In my mind, I see a deep ocean and a battle between the sea dragon and a demonic, grinning sea monkey.

"Many of us Nightsiders find your island people very attractive. I myself took a Daysider to bed on more than one occasion. Though, I never sired a child by her." The emperor laughs.

"A wise ruler embraces all her people, Daysider and Nightsider." My mother nods deferentially to Edric upon the dais. "But my island name is of no great import, Grand Patriarch. It's my son's name that will be remembered."

Old Wusong's narrow gaze falls upon me. I feel his look bore into me, through my skin, past my rib cage, to my heart. "What's your name then, boy?" he asks softly.

My mother's hand grips my shoulder tightly.

"You know my name," I blurt, startled by the pressure. The crowd breathes a collective gasp. "I'm his son." I point to the tall, pale warrior on the dais. My father's eyes widen. Lavinia, behind me, suppresses a giggle.

How could I have spoken so insolently? To Old Wusong? My cheeks are hot with embarrassment. My eyes dart back and forth over the pale faces of the murmuring crowd. They are all staring at me, whispering, laughing. I want to run home, dive into my bed, and cover my head with my pillow, but there is nowhere to escape. I am trapped.

My gaze is pulled to a pair of steel-gray eyes in the crowd. They behold me not with derision but calm curiosity. The eyes belong to a boy, my age or thereabouts, dressed in a smart, black uniform. His skin is the color of alabaster. On his head is a silver circlet, and underneath, his thick, straight hair looks like molten flame. He returns my stare with a slight upward tilt of his chin conveying a sense of expectation.

I deserve to be looked at, it seems to say.

Strange. In this moment of utmost crisis, I find an anchor of calm in this boy. I have the unsettled feeling I am gazing into a distorted mirror, an alternate version of myself looking back.

Old Wusong surprises the crowd by not skipping a beat at my insolence.

"I do know your name, boy. When you were born, your father made much of it to everyone. 'A worthy son and heir,' birthed on the day the heavens opened with the Fracture Point. 'A child of destiny,' he boasted. But he has not said your name lately. Perhaps there's nothing more to say about you?"

I stay silent, not sure how to respond to this information. *My father no longer speaks my name?*

"What say you, son of Leontes?" The old man leans forward on the sea-ape throne.

I'm nervous, scared. I've already embarrassed myself. The old man is frightening. I wish I could fly to the stars where people know the secrets of chocolate and kind words.

"Look me in the eye, boy. Didn't your father teach you that?" Old Wusong says acidly.

"He has not taught me much of anything, Grand Patriarch," I say quietly. "I'm told I met him the day I was born, but I don't remember it, and I've not seen him since. You say he no longer speaks my name?" Coldness tinges my voice, a bitterness I didn't know was there, but I am not dissuaded. This time, I don't look away. My mother's hand behind me, Lavinia's encouragement not to be frightened, the calm gaze of the strange fire-haired youth, somehow all push me forward. I become someone else in this moment.

"You try and scare everyone, old man. But you don't scare me. Why should I do what you or anyone else says?"

"Edmon!" Edric shouts. His pale eyes are terrifying.

The audience bursts into a shocked hush of confusion and fear. *I am going to die,* I realize. My lower lip quivers. I bite down on it, causing the metallic taste of blood to enter my mouth.

Old Wusong slams his staff to the marble floor, silencing the hall. My heart pounds.

"You said he was not a warrior yet, Leontes. Yet he dares speak like this to the descendant of the Great Song," the emperor hisses through black teeth. "Your father is a great Combat champion, Edmon Leontes. Will you fight in the games one day?"

"No. I'm a musician!" I declare.

The emperor stares for a moment and then laughs hysterically. The audience joins him.

"Are you sure, Little Leontes?" the emperor asks through his gut-wrenching scorn. "It looks like you have more fight in you than you think!"

The crowd chortles at the jest.

"Lord Julii's son's not much older than you." The emperor points to the boy with gray eyes and hair of flame. "He's already fighting in the children's bouts. What do you think of that?"

I clock this—*Lord Julii's son.* "Good for him!" I exclaim defiantly. "But he's not better than me at the flute."

The audience laughs harder.

"Can he ride a dolphin or catch fish? I know the sirens' calls and the pattern of whale migrations. I've even taken a boat past the breaks myself to see them!"

With each mention of my accomplishments, the audience only laughs more. All of them do, except one—the boy with red hair. His perfect features remain placid, though his eyes flash.

There is danger there, I realize. His body tenses under his black-caped uniform.

"Those are very important things, indeed." The emperor grins sarcastically.

"They matter on Bone," I say with conviction, but I fear I'm grasping for purchase on a slope of derision, and only find myself sliding farther down. "They matter more than fighting . . ."

Old Wusong taps his cane for silence, and the effect is immediate. Something I've said causes him to lean forward.

"Why is that, Little Leontes?" he asks shrewdly. "Why do these things matter more than fighting?"

"Because . . ." My voice quivers. I notice camglobes hovering around me. I see the irises within their silver orbs dilate as they record everything I say. I glance at Edric furious in his silence, yet he says nothing against the will of the emperor. *This is the answer,* I realize.

"Old Wusong, my father fights, but he's never come to Bone to see me. He's supposed to rule there, but doesn't know anything about what matters to the people. How can he rule that way? He won't, and he never will. Edric is supposed to be the strongest warrior on Tao. He won the Combat twice. You're just an old man, but somehow you know what matters to these people. There's something you know that he doesn't, and it has nothing to do with fighting."

I should just shut up, but I don't. I feel anger as I understand what I say for the first time. "My mother told me the High Synod gave him the right to own Bone, but what right did they have to give it? Because they are fighters? A bully fights people who are weaker than him. And cowards do whatever stronger people tell them to. My father is both."

I repeat words my mother has spoken aloud a hundred times, but I've never connected them like this before. My father stares hot daggers.

"And so are you, Grand Patriarch," I add.

The crowd gasps. Alberich and his armored guards tighten their grips on their swords and pikes.

"A bully *and* a coward, Little Leontes?" Old Wusong's voice is so calm I know there is deadly anger in it. The whole court is watching—my taunting sister, my imperious father, the boy with the red hair, the old man on the throne, and the silvery camglobes that hover around my face like buzzing insects. A lump wells in my throat so big I can barely swallow. Instead, I shrug with a casualness I do not feel.

"And what are you, young Leontes, that you can speak these words to me, the emperor of Tao?"

He is about to end me with a word.

"You're right. I'm nobody," I say quietly. "But what I've said is the truth."

His eyes search me, looking for something deep inside. I don't know what. He turns to my father after a long beat. "This is the one you want to discard?"

Discard?

"You think he's too weak for the patricide?" Old Wusong croaks. "He's impudent but undeniably brave. Though I know how fathers see only what they wish to see. I know that all too well."

He turns back to me, and I hear his bones creak. "Little Leontes, you have been honest with me. I'll be honest with you. It is sometimes necessary when you're a leader and a man to hurt others. Other times it is necessary to not risk your own life, to stay alive. Especially when you are a Patriarch who must choose a man for his daughter. Your bravery has convinced me this day."

He has a sly look in his eye. *This is all some sort of game,* I realize. Old Wusong snaps his fingers. A small figure, robed and veiled, is trotted out from behind his throne. She's attended by two older women, faces painted, dressed in kimonos. Old Wusong reaches over and lifts the veil from the little figure. "My daughter, Miranda Wusong," he pronounces.

The girl is excessively plain. Her eyes are passive. My initial feeling upon seeing her is discomfort.

"Do you like your betrothed, Little Leontes?" Old Wusong asks. He grins, black-toothed.

He said I'll marry his daughter? The camglobes hover close to my face.

My father's knuckles go white as he clenches his fists. The muscles in his jaw twitch. *The emperor's game is for my father, and I'm caught in the middle,* I suddenly understand. *This was not supposed to happen, but something I said changed things. Somehow, my words allowed the emperor to win and my father to lose.*

I smile and try to respond politely. "I don't even know her, Grand Patriarch."

"True, Little Leontes. In our world, though, one does not always have that luxury."

The hall breaks into a collective "ah," acknowledging the wisdom of the old man. I think they're just happy the danger seems to have dissipated.

"You see why it was necessary that you and I got to know each other?" he asks.

He made me stand here and answer his questions because I'm to marry his daughter? I feel humiliated, but I nod because an adult is telling me I should understand.

Old Wusong's wispy eyebrows arc in suspicion. "Are you being honest now, Little Leontes?"

"No, I'm being like my sister," I respond. "Clever."

Old Wusong breaks into a crooked smile. "No, you're being something quite different, Edmon." The name sounds alien on his withered lips, but it's the first acknowledgment that I'm not just my father's son. I'm my own person. "You're being unpredictable. Such a quality, if it doesn't kill you, perhaps will save your life one day."

Then he casually waves my mother and me away as if we are mere gnats. My turn has ended. Mother and I step back into line with the rest of the Leontes coterie. She grips my shoulder, and I feel her fear. The image of the fiery Pavaka cauldrons flashes in my mind.

I catch sight of the red-haired boy from across the room. He tilts his head at me and nods. It's a gesture of respect, I think. *Have I made a friend this day or an enemy?* I wonder.

The old emperor raises his arms to address the crowd. "Today we will welcome a future Patriarch to the Balance. So, I can think of no more fitting occasion to make this announcement. Dr. Jou . . ."

He gestures to a man dressed in the green and gold colors of House Wusong. His hair is clipped short, and he wears spectacles on an aquiline nose over a pencil-thin mustache. "People of Tao!" Dr. Jou begins. "For the last nine years, the Scientific Institute of House Wusong has monitored the Fracture Point that repositioned itself and opened much closer to the planet . . ."

"Yes, yes." The old man on the throne waves his hand impatiently. "Get on with it, Doctor."

The scientist tries to regain his composure. "The institute has the pleasure to announce that this Fracture Point, well within our solar system's gravity, will now provide a new, direct route to a planetary system known as Lyria."

Lyria! A new planet? No, a whole planetary system.

"Lyria." It sounds strange as I whisper the word.

Old Wusong stamps his cane, and the science doctor steps into the background. "As a gesture of good faith between our world and our new interstellar neighbor," the emperor croaks, "House Wusong has officially invited emissaries from Lyria to this sacred ceremony. The first off-worlders to set foot on Tao in the almost seventy years since my predecessor expelled all outsiders."

The crowd murmurs. Several men, strangely dressed, step from the throng. They look ragtag in their flight suits and worn leathers. An older man with dark skin like a Daysider and strange reddish hair bows before the Grand Patriarch. "Old Wusong, I'm Captain Ollie Rollinson, of the UFP ship *James Bentley*," he says in a warm, gravelly voice.

He gestures to the men at his sides. "My first officer, Mr. Stephen Sanctun." The captain indicates a lanky man with a scraggly beard, dressed in a hodgepodge of color. A tall black hat stands upon his head. He removes it, revealing a bald pate framed by a frazzled horseshoe of sandy hair.

I stare intently. This is the first time I've ever seen a true bald man before. Baldness was bred out of the Tao gene pool long ago.

"And his son." The captain points to a lanky, pimply-faced teenager. His arms and legs look way too long for his body in the knee-length coat he wears.

"We bring news from Lyria and from Elia Lazarus of Lazarus Industries regarding a unique trading opportunity." Rollinson smiles.

They look strange, unkempt and bedraggled, but also so free. I long for that feeling in this moment.

Old Wusong nods. "Welcome, and thank you for the gifts you've brought us. After today's festivities, we'll most gladly receive the news of our newest friend and business partner."

The captain and his crew seem confused for a moment before they realize they are dismissed. They quickly shuffle back into the crowd.

"And now," Old Wusong says, addressing the entire hall again, "the new heir to House Leontes . . ."

The great heavy double doors of the hall swing open. Light streams into the room and silhouettes a tall, slender figure. I am swept aside to the flanks with the others to make way.

The sound of a harp rings. The figure strides gracefully across the walkway. It's a woman, willowy and blonde, a Nightsider. Her lean muscles are powerful in their stride. As she glides, her head never dips or rises but remains perfectly parallel to the floor. *No man could move like this,* I think. Golden tresses cascade down her back.

"Try not to stare," Lavinia whispers.

My stomach twists with embarrassment. "I think that's what she wants," I hiss back.

Lavinia tries appear as if she's bored, but neither of us can miss the boy who follows at her heels. He's perhaps four or five, dressed smartly in the navy-blue military uniform of House Leontes. Silver gauntlets and a ceremonial gorget flash in the twilight. A small cape trails each step of his shiny black boots. His skin is pink and perfect, his face round and flat with bright blue, curious eyes. They sparkle as they take in everything around the room. His head is framed by soft curls, the color of spun gold. He looks like a young, innocent version of Edric, I realize.

The woman steps onto the dais beside my father. His chiseled face beams at her and at the boy who follows behind her.

He did not look at me that way.

"Olympias of House Flanders," Old Wusong rasps, almost wryly. "Your beauty is staggering, your gait as true as any Jian sword dancer."

Two retainers emerge from behind the throne to help the old Patriarch stand on his creaky bones. Several more camglobes are released from the crowd. They hover around the dais to record the impending speech.

Has all of Tao heard what I said to the Grand Patriarch? I feel so stupid.

Olympias nudges the boy before the emperor. He bows. Old Wusong leans forward. "Tell me your name, child."

"I am Edgaard Leontes, son of Edric the Leviathan. I present myself before Old Wusong for his es-es-es—"

"Esteemed," his mother whispers in the boy's ear.

"Esteemed judgment."

"Very good, Edgaard," the emperor croaks. "Do you swear to uphold the Balance? To serve the Pantheon and the people of Tao with strength and justice?"

"I do." The boy nods.

The emperor sprinkles water from a small bowl across the boy's brow. I feel like I want to cry. I don't know why. "I bless this child, from Zhu the fire, from Gong the earth, from Mazu the water, and Shangdhi the air. May he embrace the light and the darkness. May he conquer all enemies before him and within him until he returns to the embrace of the ancestors. In the name of the Balance."

"In the name of the Balance," the crowd chants.

The camglobes hover. Edric steps forward and proclaims before all of Tao, "This is my son, Edgaard of House Leontes. Let all behold him and claim, 'The son of Leontes is greater than the father!' Edgaard Leontes is a leviathan. He is my heir!"

The crowd erupts in applause. I see the red-haired boy looking inquisitively at me from across the room, gauging my reaction.

I have a new brother, I think.

"Why are you clapping?" Lavinia's cold voice prickles the back of my neck. "You've just been disinherited, fool."

CHAPTER 2

Duet

"No!"

The shout rings through the chamber. The crowd turns as my mother pushes her way to the center. She stands before the throne of Old Wusong in defiance.

"No, my lord." Her dark eyes flash.

Guards move to arrest her, but the emperor gestures for them to step back. "Speak, Daysider," he says calmly, "and pray that I don't remove your tongue for your insolence."

"I am Cleopatra Muse, the daughter of Ishtal, who was chieftain of the Isle of Bone before you Nightsiders came and claimed land that wasn't yours," she states with bold disobedience. "You sent this man, Edric Leontes"—her arm flings out and points accusingly at my father—"and I was given a choice. Refuse him, and blood would be spilled on Bone, or accept, and should I bear a son, he would be named the heir of House Leontes. I did my duty. I bore a son for Lord Edric, and now he reneges on his promise and names this *second* son his heir? Old Wusong, descendant of the Great Song, I demand justice!"

There is murmuring among the crowd, but I'm too stunned to look at their faces.

My mother had me only to save her people?

From her words, I understand for the first time that her relationship with Edric was not a willing one.

"Is this true, Lord Edric?" The emperor turns to my father.

Edric's muscles ripple beneath his navy robes and silver breastplate. "Words were spoken, your majesty. No written contract was ever made." He and my mother lock eyes. Hers are dark pools of fire. His are glacial ice.

"Words spoken to a Daysider are as effervescent as the surf." Old Wusong waves dismissively. "You have no claim, woman. I have designated your boy consort to my daughter because of his bravery, in spite of his heritage. Your son, though eldest, is a half-breed, and Lord Edric has made his choice. Be content with what you have been offered this day."

My lips quiver at the word *half-breed*. The entire audience laughs at me and my mother. We are humiliated. Still, she does not back down.

"Then I renounce your claim to the Isle of Bone and to my son. Edmon and I will leave, and you will never again return to our shores."

Edric steps forward. "You will not take my son, nor my land from me, woman." His voice is soft and deadly.

Suddenly, it seems they are the only two people in the room.

"What do you care? Why abandon him for so long? He will learn our ways and find his own path."

"There's only one path before him now. He will marry the imperial heiress. You will not defy me or the emperor." My father closes the distance to her. "I've let you keep him from his heritage for too long. Look at the tillyfish." He scowls in my direction. "*I can fish. I want to be a musician,*" he says, mocking me.

I feel hot tears in my eyes even as the audience guffaws.

"Your ways won't make him what he needs to be," Edric says coldly.

"What he needs to be is nothing like you—ashamed of your low birth, crawling before the likes of these sycophants to a withered rag of an emperor. Leviathan? No, worm. You disgust me."

There are gasps from the crowd, then a pregnant moment of stillness.

Rage ignites in Edric's eyes. He grabs my mother violently and backhands her.

I'm frozen in place, not comprehending what's happening. Old Wusong sits coolly indifferent on his throne. The crowd nods at the proceedings with silent assent.

Move! something inside me impels.

I run to her, but I'm yanked back by the collar of my shirt. The grizzled man, the seneschal Alberich, pulls me to him. He smells of metal and sweat. I stare at his puckered stump that wraps around me and pins me to him.

"Boy," he says gruffly, "this isn't for your eyes."

"No!" Edric snarls. "He must watch."

He rips the fabric of my mother's white linen dress, tearing it from her shoulder. She rakes her nails across his face. The scratch cuts him open. He bleeds but isn't deterred. He smiles a shark-toothed grin. My mother raises her hand again, but he grabs her wrist. She tries to slam her knee to his groin. He casually turns aside, deflecting the blow.

My father finishes stripping the dress from my mother's smooth, mocha body. Her naked breasts quiver as she's exposed for all to see. She wants to cover herself, I can tell, but resists the urge. She stands proud, arms at her sides, eyes burning defiantly. My father wears a look of admiration as he meets her gaze. The moment doesn't last long, though. He knocks her to the floor. She kicks at him. She claws. She struggles. It's no use. My father is too big, too strong. He knows how to hold her down. Edric's leviathan tattoos dance.

I clutch at Alberich, even though he frightens me. I try to hide myself from the violence. He grabs my head with his good hand and turns it, forcing me to watch my mother scream as Edric's fists slam into her. On the dais, the blonde woman, Olympias, stands imperiously. Her son, Edgaard, my brother, begins to cry. He tries to hide his eyes, too, but his mother forces his head toward the scene, just as Alberich forces mine.

A hand reaches out and clasps my own. Lavinia. She holds it tightly but never takes her eyes off Edric. Her eyes narrow with hatred for the man we both call father.

"Monster," she whispers.

Finally, Edric stands, flexes his muscles like a bull seal, and slowly backs up the steps, returning to his spot beside the emperor. My mother, bloodied and alone in the middle of the floor, grabs the tatters of her garments and swaddles herself in them.

Alberich releases me, and I run to her. She does not look at me. She seems lost in some other world. I don't know what to do or say. But when she stands, she releases a carefree laugh through a deformed mouth.

"That was nothing, Edmon. He thinks to shape you with his notions of pain, but you are stronger than that, aren't you? You will forget what you saw here today."

"Yes, Mother." I nod. She takes my hand, and alone we walk toward the grand double doors, our heads held high. It's the first lie I've ever told her.

I will never forget what I saw this day.

I will kill Edric for what he has done.

Our sondi docks on the shores of Bone. I sprint down the boarding ramp.

"Edmon! Edmon, wait!" my mother cries.

I don't heed her. I don't care. She is too injured to follow. My chest is thick with hurt, my face strained with the effort of keeping the tears within. I run past the docks and up the narrow, winding roads. I race by the white adobe villas and shining azure roofs. It's afternoon, time of the midday nap. There are no people in the streets. An old woman opens a door, and I duck into an alley. I don't want her to see my dirty tear-streaked face. I feel just like what Lavinia called me—a fool.

I am a fool. I'm worthless.

The uphill climb through the town slows my run to a trudge. I finally reach the edge of the manse grounds high on the cliffs. I wanted to go somewhere no one would find me. Instead, all I've done is return to the only place I know how to get to: home.

Fool. Lavinia's voice still echoes in my head. *Monster . . .*

I don't enter the house but skirt the grounds to the edge of the cliffs. The sea sparkles below me, aqua green with white-capped tips. A crevice between two large rocks looks like it can get me closer to the edge, so I climb through the crack. There's a hidden path just beyond. It leads to a shelf that juts out from the cliff wall a little lower down. I scramble down the tiny trail, skidding on graveled limestone. If I slip, I'll tumble into the waves below. My chest pounds. I want to die, but when faced with actual death, I'm petrified. A strange feeling.

I make it to the shelf and collapse on the edge, my legs dangling out into space. I pick up a stone and toss it angrily over the side of the cliff, expecting to hear a splash. I wait, but I don't even hear the stone land, I'm so high up. I stare at the horizon where the white-hot sun never sets, and the world seems too big for me. I lie on my back and let hot tears stream unabated down my cheeks.

You've just been disinherited, fool.

You will forget what you saw here today . . .

My thoughts are a tumble of despair. All I wanted to do was meet my father and impress him. Now, I hate him more than anything.

"Hey!"

A high-pitched shout startles me, and I scramble to my hands and knees. There's a feral creature sitting on a rock above me. My heart leaps into my gullet.

No, I realize. *It's no creature at all, but a girl.*

I try to stand, but I slip and fall forward onto my stomach. My chin smacks the rock. It breaks open bleeding. The gravel gives way beneath me, and I slide over the edge of the shelf. My hands claw for purchase, my fingernails tear into the stone, and my feet dangle over the edge of the long drop into the bright green sea.

I'm going to die. I don't want to die!

The girl springs forward, dives, and clutches my wrists before I fall over the edge.

"Help me, stupid!" she shouts. "You're heavier than you look!"

My feet kick, trying to find purchase on something, anything that will help me climb back up.

"Stop!" she shouts. "Look at me! You need to calm down. If you keep kicking, you'll pull us both over the edge. Relax."

Her words are confident and calm. I stop thrashing and hang limp while she strains against the dead weight of my body. Her feet spread eagle against two boulders on opposing sides preventing me from going over.

"Take your right foot and lift it as high as you can. Search for a hold that you can step on."

"I can't!" I shake my head.

"You can. Because you have to. What's your name?"

"Edmon."

"I'm Nadia. Edmon, if you don't want to die, lift your right leg."

I slowly do it. My toe finds purchase. "I got something!"

"Good. Now, on the count of three, push with your right leg. One, two, three!" she shouts.

I push with my leg as Nadia pulls. As I slide on my belly over the lip of the outcropping, the bit of rock I just pushed off breaks free from the cliffside. I scramble to higher ground while Nadia looks over the edge, watching the rock splash into the sea below.

"Whoa!" she exclaims. "You almost bought it."

I huddle against a large boulder that doesn't seem to be moving anytime soon.

"Bought what?"

"The kelp farm," she says. "You're not too smart, are you, little boy?" She hops on top of a rock and squats, gazing down, inspecting me. "Or too good on your feet."

No wonder I took her for a wild creature.

I stand just to prove her wrong and slip on the gravel as I do. I grab the boulder again to steady myself. She laughs. It makes me angry.

"I am Edmon of House Leontes. You had no right to sneak up on me! And I'm not little!" Even to my own ears, I sound like a petulant toddler.

"How old are you?" She laughs in my face, and for the first time, I really notice her. She's maybe a year or two older than me. She has dark skin and bright mahogany eyes with flecks of green in them. Her dark brown hair falls in tousled strands across her oval face. A little mole on her cheek is the only mark on her otherwise unblemished skin. She's pretty. All of a sudden, I feel nervous and tongue-tied.

"Nine!" I say with mock bravado.

"You sound two," she retorts. "Anyway, I'm turning eleven." She says this as if it means she wins. "And I just saved your life, Edmon of House Leontes. I've been coming here since I was six. So this is my spot. And I can do whatever I want."

"This is my island. It belongs to my father, Edric Leontes, who was granted the deed by the High Synod after winning two Combats! That means I own everything on it." I try to use the words I've learned since the audience with the emperor to sound smart, but next to this girl, a commoner with no fancy educational equipment, I feel dumber than a stick in the sand.

Nadia snorts derisively. "People can't own places."

"Don't you know anything?" I counter.

"I know lots of things," she says archly. "Like how to not fall off a cliff. In fact, I'm the best climber on Bone," she boasts. "I can crimp a snag on any crag you see on this island. The whale's tooth, the siren's hump, the manta face. I even crack-climbed the high fathom."

I have no clue what any of these things are, but I don't want to let her know that. "Who taught you that?"

"My brother, Yanoa," she says sadly. "He was taken to Meridian by the emperor's men and forced to participate in the Combat."

I thought competing was always voluntary. I've never heard of them forcing people like Nadia's brother before.

"I'm also an excellent dancer," she adds before I can get a word in. "Hey, if you own this island, does that mean you own me, too?"

"I don't know. I guess so. At least my father does."

"And you own everything your father owns?"

Honestly, I'm not sure. I'm not sure of anything anymore. I've been disinherited. I still don't even know what that means exactly.

"Nobody owns me!" Nadia shouts. "One person can't own another. I climb where I want, and I dance when I want."

"You don't know anything. Have you been to Meridian?" I ask.

"You have?" she jabs back.

I nod.

"But you're a Daysider?" she asks.

"I don't know what I am." I slide to the ground, my back against the rock. "My mother's a Daysider. My father he's . . . not."

"Oh." Realization comes to her face. "You're telling the truth. Edmon Leontes . . . you're the half-Nightsider who lives in the mansion." She points to the top of the island a little way away. "I've heard of you, but you don't usually come into the town to play."

She lowers herself from the top of the boulder and bends down. She looks at me more closely.

"You were crying?" she asks.

"No, I wasn't!"

"You were," she says. "You are!"

"I don't want to talk about it." What I really want is someone to tell everything to.

"Fine. Don't tell me." She walks away.

"Wait!" I shout, and she turns back.

I tell her everything. I tell her about Alberich and the sondi flying over Meridian. I tell her about seeing a city and twilight for the first time. I tell her about the throne room, Old Wusong, Lavinia, and Phoebe. I tell her about the Fracture Point and the strangers, a new place called Lyria and chocolate. I tell her about the curious boy with red hair. I tell her about Olympias and about Edgaard, my brother, the new heir of House Leontes. Finally, I tell her how my father beat my mother in front of everyone as they laughed.

"That's it. That's all there is."

The star of Tao shines hot above us. It's a second or two before either of us speaks.

"Do you hate Edgaard?" she asks.

I should hate him, shouldn't I? He took my place, but he's just a boy with a smiling face. How can I hate a boy I don't even know?

"It's not his fault."

Nadia nods. "I think your father would want you to hate him."

"What do you mean?"

"If you hated him, wouldn't you want to prove that you should be the heir and not him?" she asks.

"I guess," I say slowly. "How would I prove that?"

"How do you think?" asks Nadia.

My father said that there was only one path before me, that the island would not prepare me for what I needed to know.

"The Combat?" I think it out. "If I hated Edgaard, I'd want to prove that I'm better. I'd try to be a fighter like my father wants, and I'd enter the Combat."

"If you win, you'll join the College of Electors and might be voted into the High Synod. That's how Edric founded House Leontes. That would earn his love and respect. Is that what you want?" she asks.

"No," I answer. "I hate him. Not Edgaard. I hate my father. I'm going to kill him someday."

"Maybe that's also what he wants?" Nadia suggests. "If you hate your father and want to kill him, he wins," she says solemnly. "He wants for you to be a fighter, a killer. That's not balance."

"I don't care!" The words burst out of me. "What he did to my mother—"

"He should be punished," she cuts me off. "But not by you."

"Why not?" I ask curiously.

"I don't think you want to be like him." She stands, head tilted to one side. "What is it you want to be, Edmon Leontes?"

Her question catches me off guard. I just stare at her dumbly for a moment. It's the same question the emperor asked me.

"I want to be a musician. But I don't think music is something that people think is useful."

"Who says?" she asks defiantly.

I shrug. "Old Gorham has taught me to play quarter and eighth notes. I can play an upbeat. I try to practice scales. None of it is useful. It doesn't help catch food or clean the house. What good is it?"

"Well, why do you want to be a musician?" she repeats, not letting it go.

Again, I'm not sure what to say. I stop thinking and just blurt out, "Because I'm good at it. Because it's beautiful. Because it makes me feel good. Because maybe it makes other people feel good, too. One time, I played, and my mother danced. The whole crowd cheered. I love to play, and people love me when I do."

"You think that's not useful?" The wind brushes strands of hair across her mahogany eyes. "I'd like to see you play sometime." She turns to leave.

"Where are you going?" I ask.

She walks up the path. "Home, Little Leontes," she calls back, mocking me with the words of Old Wusong.

"Don't call me that!" I snap.

She laughs. "You don't own me. I can call you whatever I want."

She disappears between the crevices in the boulders at the top of the path.

"Hey!" I hear.

I turn back to see her head peek through the crack. "If you aren't your father's heir, you should be who you want to be instead. Maybe I'll see you here tomorrow?"

Then she's gone.

For the first time in the whole day since I left Bone and returned, I'm happy. I feel free again.

It doesn't last.

CHAPTER 3

Counterpoint

For three years, I live in blissful ignorance of the machinations of my father and the Pantheon. Days are spent swimming in the ocean and fishing. When I was little, my mother taught me to read, but it never seemed as fun as watching aquagraphics. Since my trip to Meridian, though, I devour everything I can. I want to know everything, not only about my world, but about the many worlds of the Fracture that were only hinted at by those strange travelers. I love the legends and myths of the Daysiders. I ask for more. I read during afternoons when others take their naps. My mother finds tomes for me from off-world, histories and fictions of other places, other times. *The Pirates of Nonthera*, *The Lost Anjins of Miral*, *The Prosperan Countesses*, *History of the Chironian Civil War* are some of my favorites.

Nadia and I meet by the cliffs almost every day. I tell her about the books I've read. She tells me the news of the daily market. We talk about Old Wusong and the day of the christening often. She makes me describe the strange visitors from off-world over and over again. We dream about where they came from. We invent new people and new planets as a game to pass the time. I tell her what I've learned from my reading, how the great scientists think that our universe is only one of an infinite number of universes, shaped like amoebas that sometimes touch or bubble off from one another.

She says I'm an idiot.

"Everyone knows that in the beginning there was just the Chaos Sea. The universe burst forth from a giant egg, creating the sky and stars. Then the ancestors were born who whisper into the wind of all things."

"Well," I say. "They do think that the dimensions of hyperspace are like a roiling sea, and universes are like foam bubbles constantly forming and springing up. Most universes probably don't have life. The only reason we know this one does is we're here to observe it."

"That seems self-centered." She sighs, unconvinced. I shrug, but she's adamant. "Some things just are, with or without you."

"Scientists think black holes might hold entire universes inside of them," I say.

"Next time you're in a black hole, let me know!" She punches my arm.

She is thirteen, still a tomboy, all knobby elbows and knees, but several centimeters taller than me. It might as well be a mile. I blush at the touch, even though it's a punch.

We watch silver streaks of rockets burn through the atmo overhead. Even though Nadia says I'm an idiot, I know she, too, dreams of flying beyond the day sky.

We're told the rockets carry men heading to the deep Nightside where it's so dark and cold it'll freeze your bones. That's where they drill for minerals and ore. Nadia and I sometimes talk about where we'd go if we stole a rocket. The cracks of the Fracture could take us anywhere in the universe.

"If you leave, won't you be afraid you won't be able to find your way home?" she asks one day.

"No," I say simply. "If I was lost, I'd never have to worry about my father ever again."

I change the subject. I ask her to show me how to scale the boulders. She's been showing me the intricacies of how to climb sideways. She calls it traversing. Sometimes I feel like that's what she and I have been doing, just moving sideways instead of up. That's okay, though. I'm happy and would stay like this with her forever if I could, best friends just moving sideways.

—

A week later, I'm in town with Mother when I see Nadia manning a cart in the market. She stands with a small, kind-looking man selling fish. Mother stops by the cart and asks the man if she may buy some dried octopus. The man gives her a price, and Mother haggles. I look at Nadia, but she won't meet my eyes.

The haggling becomes heated.

"Surely you don't expect me to pay ten. This is clearly a third-rate specimen."

It's not an insult my mother gives. It's just the island way of doing business.

Nadia's eyes are still glued to the ground. *Have I done something wrong?*

"Mother," I interject. "Give him double."

Both adults stare at me, shocked. My mother's brow furrows.

"This is the best fisherman on the entire isle," I say.

"How do you know that?" she asks incredulously.

"Because Nadia is my best friend. She saved my life," I reply, and indicate Nadia, though she's looking at the ground.

Mother looks at me curiously. I've kept my time with Nadia secret. I don't know why. I guess I figured she was a confidante, someone I could tell everything to, even the things I can't tell my mother.

Cleopatra turns to the fisherman. Her face is not exactly the same as it was before her horrific beating, but she is still beautiful, and she still commands respect.

"This is your daughter?"

The fisherman nods.

"Is what Edmon says true?"

"Yes, m'lady," Nadia replies, eyes downcast.

My mother hands the fisherman double his asking price. "For the finest fisherman on Bone."

The fisherman bows and accepts the payment. He pulls the octopus from the clothesline, wraps it in cloth, and hands it to my mother. We amble up the winding road toward our home. I wave goodbye to Nadia, but she stares in the other direction.

As the Eventide feast commences, the shades are pulled low to mimic night, and the fireglobe is placed in the pit in the center of the floor. My mother presides, welcoming the guests. She sits at a high table and discusses politics and gossip with the other islanders. I smile at the woman she is, fiercely proud of her people, a leader.

Then it begins with the beat of a drum. Flutes and pipes sound. Strings take up the melody.

Gorham has been teaching me the flute, but I can play the drums and strings, too. Singing is actually my favorite, but Gorham says that if I can make an instrument sing like it is my own voice, my true singing will become deeper than the ocean and rise higher than the Elder Stars. So I practice my flute with focused determination.

"Feel the rhythm," he instructs as always. "Melody first. Make the tone as pure as you can, unchanged. Then change it. Find variations."

I try it on the flute.

"Your song is part of the whole. Listen to the others. Complement them."

I try to find a harmony that will balance what the others are playing, but I can't seem to find the right notes. I start to play something different, something underneath the whole of the music. Before I can ask Gorham what I am hearing, though, someone shoves me out of the circle. Taken by surprise, I smack into the wall behind me, the wind knocked out of me. My flute clatters onto the flagstones. I snatch it quickly. I look up, fuming, and come face-to-face with Nadia. Her eyes are fire-hot coals.

"What did you do that for?" I ask.

"You know what for!"

This is the first time I've seen her attend the Eventide feast. I'm pleased, but also utterly confused; the closeness of her body near mine creates a strange sensation I've not felt before. "What?" I blurt.

"My family doesn't need your charity. We may not be as rich as you, but we have pride." She jabs her finger into my chest.

"It wasn't charity." I fumble my words.

"We're just as good as anyone, especially some half-Nightsider." She starts to walk away. Her hips seem different somehow, wider.

Why am I staring at her as she walks? I shake my head to snap myself out of it.

"Just remember who pulled your clumsy butt up off the cliffs," she adds as she turns back.

"I was just . . . ," I mumble. "I was just trying to thank you."

She stares at me like a hooked lumo-fish. "Oh," she mutters as she stalks off.

I trudge back to the circle of musicians.

"Trouble with your girlfriend?" Gorham asks with a sly smile.

"She's not my girlfriend!" I respond a little too vehemently.

"She seemed upset."

I explain to him what happened in the market. He nods. "I don't get it!" I confess with exasperation.

"Edmon," Gorham intones, "everyone has their weaknesses. If someone mentioned your father—"

"I hate my father!" I cut the old man off.

"If someone mentioned him," he goes on, "you might feel upset even if what they were saying came from the intention of helping."

"I wouldn't get mad if they were trying to help," I insist.

"You wouldn't?" Gorham arcs an eyebrow at me. "What if this girl didn't know you were trying to help? Making your intention clear is all you can do. Many think of you as the lord of the isle."

Lord of the isle?

"Many, in comparison to you, have very little. Maybe to this girl, it seemed you were showing off, playing the bountiful lord by being kind to a poor islander."

"But I wasn't!" I insist.

"Did you make that clear to her?"

"I think so," I mutter.

"That's all you can do." He beats his drum. "Now keep playing. Day's end is only just beginning."

I make the notes sound pure like Gorham instructed. It still doesn't work. They sound shrill rather than clear.

"Try what you were playing before," he suggests. "Find your own tune. Make it work with the other musicians' notes."

I start again. I glide underneath the main song. My tune punctuates the rhythm of the drums. There's sadness to it that maybe wasn't there before, but it makes the main melody sound richer, more intricate.

"Yes!" Gorham exclaims. "You've found a counterpoint, Edmon. Very good."

The song goes on through the night. I can't help but feeling, though, that I didn't find a counterpoint at all. Rather, a counterpoint found me.

The next day, a sondi lands on the shores. The town is buzzing over the arrival, but for me, a deep fear like a clenched fist squeezes my belly.

My father.

I don't go to the docks. I don't want to see him.

Why is he here? What could he want?

Nadia finds me at the cliffs, gazing at the Southern Sea. She sits beside me. The warm breeze blows our hair as we listen to the crashing waves.

"Hey," she says. "You didn't come to the docks this morning."

"I didn't." My voice sounds lifeless.

"I'm sorry," she says tentatively. "About last night. I didn't mean to be so angry. You were trying to help. It's just—"

"It's fine." I cut her off.

A silence sunders us. I should just let it be.

"I don't know if it's worse for you or me," I say. "You're ashamed of your family, but mine is ashamed of me."

"I am not ashamed of my family!" Nadia's eyes flare.

"I didn't mean . . . sorry." It's all I can manage. I keep making mistakes it seems.

"Your mother isn't ashamed of you," she says.

"Not her," I concede. "But House Leontes, my father, and everyone who carries the family name."

"You think they count more than she does?" Nadia asks.

Maybe.

"Your father hasn't summoned you or visited Bone in three years. He has another son. Why should you care about what he thinks? If your father is ashamed of you, he's the one who shouldn't count."

"You were wrong," I say. The gulls caw in the distance. She looks at me. "You said that my father wouldn't return for me." My voice is tinged with bitterness.

Nadia shakes her head. "No. I said that you are free to be your own person whether or not your father returns. I never said he wouldn't come back."

She stands and walks away. Over her shoulder, she adds, "Besides, your father wasn't on the sondi that landed. It was a big man with a metal hand. And a red-haired boy he brought with him."

A red-haired boy?

"What?" I turn, but she's walked off.

There's only one red-haired boy I know of. *Is it the same one? The one from the christening?* I run back up the path toward the manse.

"Phaestion of the Julii," Alberich's voice rings out as I burst into the foyer. I stop cold as everyone turns to me.

My mother waits on the staircase flanked by her handmaids. She nods at Alberich. "What brings the scion of House Julii to the shores of Bone?"

"Lord Edric and Lord Chilleus of the Julii invoke the tradition of fosterage," grunts Alberich. "Phaestion will remain here as your guest; he'll serve as regent. Your son, Edmon, will be his companion."

"I see." My mother's voice is cold. "Unfortunately, it is not Edric's right to command here."

Alberich sighs as if he expected this. "My lady, you know that it is. Edric is the ruler of this island, entitled by the High Synod—"

"The people of Bone were here long before the High Synod, long before the Great Song, long before any Nightsider set foot on planet Tao and pretended that one could own the land. Bone does not recognize—"

"Bone recognizes the soldiers of House Leontes."

There is a beat of silence as my mother simmers. "It's my understanding that in the tradition of fosterage, the hosts will receive equal hospitality in return," she responds.

"Edmon will leave for Meridian in a quarter cycle's time and receive the tutelage of House Julii's private academy," Alberich says.

My mother's face turns to stone.

"M'lady, I remind you this is a great honor. House Julii is one of the four High Houses, descended from the generals of the Great Song. They hold many seats among the Electors, including their traditional seat on the Synod."

"I'm aware of the political status of the Julii," my mother replies acidly.

"Edmon will receive an education of the finest order, an opportunity he wouldn't otherwise have on Bone. I will oversee the boy's tutelage in combat training."

"Instruction? In martial skill? Why would he need such an education, Alberich?" she asks, her voice edged with anger.

"M'lady?"

"If Edmon's no longer considered Leontes's heir, why should he leave his island home for schooling in Meridian? How does this serve Lord Edric? Edmon is a forgotten son. Let him remain forgotten."

Phaestion's gray eyes turn toward me with dispassionate appraisal, gauging whether I'm worthy.

He was there that day. He knows I'm not the heir of my house. Why should he bother being here?

His features are so symmetrical, and his eyes are so innocently piercing that I feel like some kneaded clod being placed under a microscope.

"Phaestion's the highest ranked fighter of his generation. One day, he'll enter the arena and continue the illustrious name of House Julii. Edgaard, the Leontes heir, is yet of an age to offer companionship, but

Edmon is. Edmon is the son of the only two-time champion ever. The honor for both sons is mutual."

What a sham! I feel like laughing. My father sold House Julii on the premise that since I'm his son, I've inherited the same fighting skills he has. When Phaestion realizes I've never even thrown a punch in my life, I'll bring dishonor, embarrassment, and even more humiliation to myself.

Edric must have known that. When I fail, I'll receive much worse than a quiet exile here on the isle. What will happen to my mother?

"Fosterage is commonplace among the houses. Youths bonded by it are more than brothers. They are companions."

Alberich is no longer asking.

"You've not answered my question, seneschal," my mother persists.

"Edmon is betrothed to Old Wusong's daughter. Though he is not the heir, he still must serve his Patriarch."

There is a cold beat. Mother knows she must accept the red-haired boy into our home and that I must accept him as my friend. Then we both realize that I'll be gone in three months for an "education."

"Welcome, Phaestion of the Julii." She looks at the red-haired boy. "This is my son, Edmon Leontes."

I step forward.

"I know who he is," the boy interrupts with a casual indifference. I've never been spoken to before in such a dismissive way.

"I'll be back tomorrow to begin their training," Alberich says.

"Training?" My voice cracks. My mother glances at me.

I've given it away! I can't fight at all. This game is over before it's started.

"I'll find lodgings in the town proper and return before the start of daily hours to instruct Phaestion and Edmon together."

"Then be a good servant and run along," my mother says.

Alberich suffers the insult admirably and simply bows and takes his leave.

I can tell that my mother is tense, afraid for me. Edric may still intend for me to compete in the Combat when I come of age. Starting the training now, however, seems absurd. At twelve, I'm significantly behind almost every other noble boy my age. I'd be no match for someone like Phaestion.

What chance do I have?

Then it occurs to me. *Maybe my father hopes I have no chance? If I'm thrown in the ring, I'll be torn apart. He'll be free of me, and he can marry my brother to Old Wusong's daughter.*

Mother exits with her handmaidens, and I'm left in the foyer alone with the red-haired boy.

But if that's the case, why bother training me at all?

Phaestion and I stare at each other for a beat. He's impossibly overdressed in a crisp black uniform and a purple cloak. The silver circlet around his head flashes as he looks down at me over the bridge of his small, perfectly straight nose.

"Well?"

He expects me to say something. I'm not sure what.

"Well . . . what?" I respond more sarcastically than I intend.

He cocks his head to the side. He looks like he's computing whether I'm mentally deficient or merely rude.

"Gather my things and show me to my room, of course," he says and strides confidently toward the hallway, leaving me with several metallic cases of luggage to carry. I consider ignoring his order, but I know that my mother will admonish me for leaving his things in the foyer. I pick up the heavy metal boxes and drag them on the floor behind me with a dark scowl on my face. *I may carry his things, but that does not make me his slave.*

I find him looking at a small guest room at the end of the hall.

"You just expect me to carry your bags for you?" I demand, exasperated.

Again he cocks his head to the side. "Yes," he says, effortlessly. "You're now one of my companions."

The way he says *companion* sounds as if it's a title like *servant.*

There's more to this fosterage custom than I'm aware of.

"Is this where you sleep?" He nods toward the small guest room.

"No. I sleep there." I point a few doors down.

The red-haired boy turns on his heel and walks into my room. I follow, shocked that he's simply entered my quarters without permission. He stands in the center of the room, gazing out the large bay windows. "Is it always this bright?" He shields his eyes from the Tao sun.

"Shades," I call out. Shutters slide across the windows. "Globes," I follow up. The warm orange of the fireglobes ensconced in the adobe walls bathes the room in soft light.

"That's better." Phaestion nods.

"Your eyes aren't strong enough for the isles," I mock.

His gaze narrows. He isn't sure if he's being purposely insulted. "My night vision's much stronger though, Daysider."

I ignore the taunt. "Shades are mechanized to do a gradual fade to mark the diurnal schedule of Ancient Earth."

"Primitive." He nods.

"Primitive?" I'm getting angry.

"Ancient traditions are stagnant in the face of the thousands of different worlds we will one day reach once we have explored the Fracture beyond Lyria." He's showing off. His haughty tone is clear—*my ways are stupid.* I clench my jaw.

"I train to stay awake for forty-eight hours at a time," he goes on. "I can fight with only half an hour of sleep if I need to."

"Big deal," I retort. "Can you fish? Do you know how to row? Or rock climb? I've climbed the whale's tooth, the siren's hump, and the manta face. I even crack-climbed the high fathom."

In truth, I've climbed none of those things. Nadia is the climber. I have two left feet. I'd mention my prowess at music, but I remember the reception that got at the christening all those years ago. Still, there's no way I'm being out-boasted by this boy. Even though he seems impossibly more handsome and strong than I.

He strolls the perimeter of the room. *My* room.

"I'm not impressed by any of your island hobbies," he says simply.

"Of course you aren't. You can't even see in the daytime." I snicker.

He holds my gaze placidly. "Do you read?"

"Of course," I say, thrown off balance.

He picks up the aquagraphic tablet on my desk and taps it. The gel screen leaps to life. "*The Chironiad*?" His eyes widen with surprise.

"Yeah?" I respond sullenly.

"My father is named after the hero of the story, Chilleus."

He places the tablet down and picks up a model rocket that my mother purchased from a Meridian trader.

"You like space travel." It's not a question.

"Yes."

This is my room. These are my things. He's acting as if he owns it all.

"That's important." Before I can ask why, he says, "Where do you sleep then?"

"Bed," I call out a little more forcefully than I intend. A thin bed panel slides out from the wall just a few inches over the floor.

"So low to the ground?" He sits on the panel. The gel cushion forms to his body. "Interesting. This will do. Thank you." He smiles simply.

"What do you mean?" I don't understand.

Again, he cocks his head to the side. Everything he does seems so graceful and absent of guile. It's as if I'm the one who isn't following the rules, not him. It's maddening.

"I mean this will do for my quarters," he says.

"Your quarters?" Heat rises to my cheeks.

"Surely." He stands and grabs one of the heavy metallic cases. He presses a thumb to the identifying lock on the luggage. One case snaps open. He pulls out strips of metal and begins assembling them.

"Where am I supposed to sleep?" I ask.

My eyes are glued to his task, fascinated by what he's doing.

"I don't know," he answers calmly. "Maybe the guest room down the hall?"

He finishes assembling the instrument. He connects a taut string from the bottom to the top.

"What's that?" I ask, my anger momentarily forgotten.

"A compound bow," he says, stretching his arms while gripping the string, testing the tensile strength of the wire. "You've never seen a bow before?"

I shake my head.

"I suppose that's normal for your kind."

He pulls out a case holding thin metallic tubes with featherlike things attached to the ends. "Sonic arrows," he says as he holds one up. "You shoot them. The sound blast of a well-placed arrow can bring down a whole regiment."

He thumbs another case open, revealing a sword with an ornate handle. It's sheathed in smooth black synthetic leather.

"A sword!" I exclaim. I've seen my father carry one in aquagraphics, but nothing like this, not up close.

"A siren sword," he corrects. He whips the blade from its scabbard with a whisper. "Rapier and dagger," he adds as he pulls out a smaller matching knife from the case. He practices against his shadow, moving the blade with lightning speed and precision. Thrusts, pivots, and graceful, flowing retreats. It's like watching a ballet. "My father had it crafted for his first son, Augustus."

"His first son?" I ask.

"It took armorers twenty years to make the long blade in the forges of Albion. Another five for the dagger." He holds the long tapering blade out for me to admire. It's ringed by an intricate silver handguard with an ivory handle. "I'm the heir of House Julii now, so my father gave it to me."

"What happened to Augustus?" I ask.

There is a long silence, too long. I start to shift uncomfortably.

Suddenly the sword sings! It sounds like a woman, a siren. He twirls the blade. The sword calls out a melody. The dagger hums, too, in harmony.

"It's singing!" I'm in awe.

Phaestion smiles mischievously. "The alloy's a rare substance that reacts to the vibrations of the body. The metal vibrates at the same frequency I do. When it touches something or someone . . ." He looks around. "Throw me your pillow."

I grab the pillow from the bed and toss it in the air. Phaestion thrusts; the pillow explodes. I'm hurled back by the concussive blast. I shake my head and open my eyes. Burned pillow foam lies scattered all over the floor.

"Sorry." Phaestion shrugs. "I'm still learning the fine tuning."

"That was outstanding!" I'm giddy.

"Want to hold it?" he asks with a lopsided grin.

I nod. He slowly hands it over. My fingers wrap around the handle.

Fire runs through my body. I scream in pain as the sonic vibrations of the steel ignite my flesh, my bones. I drop the sword and collapse to the floor, teeth chattering.

Phaestion laughs.

"That wasn't funny!" I yell. I turn to storm out of the room.

"Wait!" he yells. "Edmon, I'm sorry."

I stop in my tracks. He seems sincere.

"It takes years to master the vibrations. I couldn't hold it the first time, either," he admits.

"But you knew it would shock me!" I say.

"I thought. I didn't know. People have different affinities. Each sword is tuned differently. The siren steel comes from special meteor ore. Not everyone can use it. These happen to be my signature."

"Your signature?" I'm still fuming.

"The thing I'm known for—my combat specialty. Your father was known for the spear. Did you know that?"

I shrug. I guess that's why the Leontes guards always carry those silver pikes.

He puts the swords away. He pulls out a shining silver disk from a case and slides it over one arm. He quickly assembles metallic tubes into a long, fierce-looking spear. He thrusts deftly, demonstrating, before he places the spear and shield in the corner.

"I've seen all of Edric's fights. Even the death matches from the Under Circuit. I like the spear and shield, but not as much as the swords." He nods. "Spider-weave body armor and polyceramic shields will make ballistics obsolete against our armies in the next war. It will be a new age of individual skill on the battlefield, glory returned to modern fighting."

"What war?" I ask. "Tao doesn't have armies. No one threatens us. What do we need armies for?"

He smiles. "You know Chilleus and his foster brother Cuillan used spears and shields mainly. Of course, they were in Anjin mech suits."

"The characters from *The Chironiad*?" I ask.

"Our ancestors were expert with them," he goes on. "That's where you get your name, right? Leontes? The Anjin pilot who held off a thousand invading ships against Miral with just his squadron of mechs?"

I don't really know. I shrug.

He looks at me suspiciously for a beat, as if it's impossible that this is something I don't care about. "I need some sleep."

"It's just after the midday rest," I say, confused.

He flashes another placating smile. "It's going to be a long day tomorrow. I need to conserve energy. You should, too."

He disrobes. I look away. It's not like I haven't seen nakedness before—it's hot on Bone. We have to wear light, loose clothing—but he does it right in front of me, so casually.

The red-haired boy's skin is smooth and pale without a mark on it. He's lean and muscular, even at this age. It makes his frame look angular, designed. He stands as confident as if he were armored for battle.

This is what a boy is supposed to look like, I can't help but think. Not like me, gangly and uncoordinated.

"Where do you keep your clothes?" he asks.

"My clothes?" I repeat.

"I'm not going to walk around in my Julii uniform. If I'm to rule here someday, I need to live as you do," he says simply.

What does he mean, rule here?

"Dresser," I say.

Drawers pop out from the wall. Phaestion crosses to them. He pulls out a linen shirt and holds it up.

He smiles. "You can go now." He delivers the command with the ease of someone who is never disobeyed.

Instinctively, I take a step toward the door, then stop myself.

This boy has shown up unexpectedly, to my house, tells me to carry his luggage, comes into my room, claims it for his own, and belittles me and my customs. He struts naked in front of me, takes my bed and my clothes, and dismisses me without thought as if I'm his servant.

I am not his servant.

He looks up and realizes I haven't left. He cocks his head to the side, as if daring me to speak.

"I come and go as I please," I state boldly.

He holds my gaze, saying nothing. I stand there for another awkward beat. I could demand that he leave my room, but what if he refuses? I certainly can't force him.

He sits, watching me.

"What do we need armies for?" I ask again. I don't know why I ask that. It's just something to say.

He thinks. Then he says, "Alexander the Great—do you know who that was?"

I shake my head.

"Alexander the Great was from a small country of sheep herders, but he and his army conquered the known earth. Rome was a small city state that became a Republic then a whole empire. Genghis Khan and his tribes of horsemen conquered even more. Small places with great men made small people into great armies, up to the time of Conn the Magnificent and his first Anjin mechs of the Miralian Empire. Every time there was conquest, it brought trade, new ideas, and inventions. They made civilization evolve to new heights. Humans soar on the wings of our violent nature. There's no other way."

He sounds like he's repeating something from an aquagraphic. I feel something horrible and ominous inside.

Run as fast and far as you can, it says.

"I'll see you tomorrow," I say. I back out of the room, trying to make it seem as if I'm in control, that it's totally my decision to leave. The door slides shut behind me.

"Were you impressed?"

I spin around at the sound of the voice. *Mother.* She stands imperiously in the hallway.

"Did the little killer impress you with his weapons?" she asks coldly.

My mother has never talked to me this way before. She sounds angry, cruel. I look down, ashamed. I *was* mesmerized by the red-haired boy and his shiny weapons, if the truth be told.

She kneels in front of me. Her finger gently lifts my chin. Her gaze is soft again.

"The ability to kill someone doesn't make you a leader, and it doesn't make someone great," she says. "There's nothing great about dying or taking a life. Remember that tomorrow?"

I nod. I hope I do.

CHAPTER 4

Continuo

The sun blazes high in the blue sky as Alberich leads us down the cobbled streets through the town. I carry Phaestion's cases slung on my back.

Whispers echo from doorways. "House of the Julii . . . Little Lord learning to fight . . ."

My face flushes with mentions of the "Little Lord." After the incident with Nadia in the marketplace and now the whispers that surround us as we walk, I feel keenly how I am different. I live on the high hill. My skin is pale. I'm not a fisherman, nor do I fit in with the Nightsiders. The red-haired boy makes me carry his things, like a servant.

I don't belong anywhere.

We arrive at a narrow patch of white gravel and sand surrounded by large boulders where the foam of the sea licks the edge of the land. Alberich stakes several practice spears and swords into the earth.

"The Great Song's army wandered the Nine Corridors for a decade before they found planet Tao. Ten years passed in the vacuum before Supreme Bushi Tamerlane Song finally stepped on the Twilight Lands as an emperor. He swore to uphold the Balance that his masters had forgotten. What is the Balance?"

Phaestion immediately parrots an answer. “Elder Stars illuminate only because there is darkness. A warrior can know righteous cause only because there is evil. Heart to thought, thought to voice, harmony rises from discord. This is the Balance.”

The grizzled seneschal nods. “Without shadow, there cannot be light. Song’s men were warriors, but with no war. They had thrown off the yoke of slavery their masters placed on them, but what was their worth without conflict? Without trial? They created the Combat: the ultimate test of strength, speed, and intelligence.” He says it with pride. “Contestants compete throughout the year in sparring matches until the end-of-the-year final. Twelve spots for nobility, one for each house of the Pantheon, twenty-four for the underclass. The one who survives the arena lives to rule. Both of you as scions of noble houses are fated to compete one day.”

I am to be forced to do this? My heart begins to pound.

Phaestion only nods, not only aware of his fate, but determined to meet it with deadly confidence.

“Phaestion,” the seneschal commands. The red-haired boy steps forward. “Pick your best weapon.”

Phaestion pulls a long trident and some sort of net out of his cases. My eyes narrow. These are not his “best weapons.”

“Retiarius.” Alberich nods. “Very well. Come at me.”

Phaestion looks puzzled. Alberich scowls. “Edmon, Phaestion, I’m not your friend. I’m here to teach you. You will call me Master. If you don’t learn, you’ll end up dead. If you end up dead, I end up dead. Therefore, if you don’t follow my instruction, you’ll be punished.”

“Yes, Master,” Phaestion says without hesitation.

My voice is a beat behind. I feel totally out of place.

“Come at me!” Alberich commands.

Phaestion feints with the trident, then swings the net, trying to trip the big man. Alberich merely uses his large trunk of a leg to tear the net from Phaestion’s grasp. Phaestion refuses to let go. He rolls with it.

The metal-capped stump of Alberich's hand slams into the sand where Phaestion stood a split second earlier.

The red-haired boy draws into a crouch. He thrusts the trident forward. It almost catches Alberich square in the back, but the big man spins away deftly. His hand springs out and grabs the shaft of the trident. He yanks it, but Phaestion holds on. The boy flies into the air and releases his hold on the shaft. He somersaults midair and lands on Alberich's shoulders. He wraps his arms and legs around Alberich's throat.

A choke hold!

Alberich rears back and slams Phaestion into a boulder. The boy gasps and drops like stone to the earth. Still, he refuses to give up. He reaches for the net, but Alberich kicks it from his reach. He touches the captured trident to the boy's throat.

"Hold!" he calls.

Phaestion immediately stops and stands.

"Good," the big man says. "But you waited too long to release the trident midair. Sometimes letting go sooner will give you openings."

Phaestion nods.

"Now show me your weakest weapon," Alberich commands.

Phaestion pulls the siren sword and dagger from his cases. He flourishes both weapons and crouches like a cat. Alberich smiles and beckons the boy forward.

If Phaestion was a phenom with the trident, he's inhuman with the swords. He twirls them with incredible speed. Siren steel glints in the sunlight, but Alberich dodges every stroke. Phaestion's brow furrows with concentration. He increases the speed of his attacks. Alberich uses the metal stump of his missing hand to parry the sword as he spins away from the dagger's thrusts.

Phaestion leaps onto a boulder and ricochet-jumps off the rock. He brings the blade of his sword stabbing down. Alberich's eyes widen as he ducks under the blow, but not quickly enough. The razor-sharp metal slices open his muscular back in rivulets of crimson. Alberich ignores it and barrels into Phaestion's legs midair. The red-haired boy tumbles end over end and hits the sand with a thud.

"Hold!" Alberich calls out. "Very good, Phaestion, but that was definitely not your weakest weapon."

Phaestion cocks his head to the side in that way I'm beginning to recognize as belonging to him. "There's no weapon that I'm weak with, Master." He puts his fist into his palm and bows.

After what I've just witnessed, I believe him.

Alberich nods. "Let your enemy think you're weak where you're strong. Cloak weakness in strength. Still, you did not follow my instructions to the letter," he admonishes. "First kata. Now."

A hint of anger flashes across Phaestion's gray eyes as he picks up his swords and begins practicing in the air.

"Edmon, choose your strongest weapon."

I freeze. Holding Phaestion's siren sword was the first time I've ever even held a weapon, much less a weakest or strongest. With hesitation, I approach the spears and swords the seneschal's staked into the earth.

What am I going to do?

"Be quick about it, boy!" Alberich commands.

I hastily grab a spear and a shield from the sand.

My father was an expert with the spear. Maybe I will be, too?

I heft the spear in one hand and fumble to tighten the shield to the forearm of the other. I try to place my legs in a wide stance as I saw Phaestion do.

"Begin," Alberich commands.

I'm more afraid of what will happen if I don't try, so I thrust the spear forward, but it's half-hearted, weak. The big man easily bats it aside, knocking it from my grasp. I immediately back away, expecting him to pummel me to the ground or at least end the farce by shouting, "Hold!"

Instead, he gestures for me to pick up the spear. I kneel slowly, watching him, unsure if this is a trick.

"Again," he commands.

This time I thrust with more surety. Still, the big man dodges easily and slams his stump into my shield. I'm knocked into the sand, unhurt but stunned. He takes a step forward, and I scramble to get up. He comes for me again. I run out of the way. This appears to be a successful tactic. He lunges for me, and I scurry from his grasp.

"You're quick when you stop thinking and just act," he grunts. "But you can't win by running, Edmon."

I can't win at all! I want to scream. *Why bother trying?*

He rushes forward. I thrust the spear. He brutally knocks it away. He punches both arms into my shield, which I raise just in time to save myself. I hunker down behind the barrier. Blow after blow I suffer as he continues to pound relentlessly. I am a nail being hammered into the earth. Finally, he rips the shield from my arm and tosses it aside. I scramble away. I barely make it a meter before he clutches the scruff of my neck with the claw of his good hand.

"I yield!" I shout pathetically.

"Is that what you are going to do when someone tries to take your life from you? Or the lives of your family?" he asks scornfully. "Yield and hope that they take pity on you?"

No, damn it! Don't cry. Do anything, but don't cry!

I look over to Phaestion. He looks away. My humiliation is painful even for him to watch.

"Maybe you aren't worth keeping alive then," the seneschal says. He lifts me into the air. He smacks me against a boulder and pins me there as he chokes me. I can't breathe. I struggle.

"You are not fit to be a son," Alberich growls.

Blackness comes for me.

"Stop!" someone far-off shouts. "You're killing him!"

Then there's nothing but the singing of the sirens.

A cry of pain—mine? The fingers on my throat release. I gasp for air. I run with all my might to get away, but I run directly into Alberich. We tumble in the sand. He claws for me. From somewhere deep inside, somewhere primal, a scream arises and bursts from my mouth. I attack for my life. I claw and kick. I punch and bite. I fight with every fiber of my being to survive. My knuckles grow slick with blood. A hunk of meat comes away in my teeth. I don't stop. Something caged inside me has been set free.

Suddenly, I'm hurled to the ground. I continue to claw, but one arm is pinned, then the other. My chest is compressed under the weight of something heavy.

"Stop!" I hear the shout. Phaestion comes into focus on top of me. "Stop!" he shouts again. "You're going to kill him if you don't stop!"

I stop thrashing, and he slowly gets off me. I sit up, dazed. The cloud of rage that had descended upon me has lifted. I look at Alberich. He lies unmoving, blood soaking into the sand around him.

Have I killed him? I taste the iron tang of blood in my mouth.

Run, boy, run! I need to get out of this place. Anywhere. Fly to the stars.

I jump to my feet.

"Wait!" Phaestion calls out behind me. "He needs help!"

I sprint uphill and don't look back. Through the town. I don't stop. I run to the only place where I'm safe—off the path and through the cracks of the two boulders. I tumble down the rocky path that overlooks the Southern Sea.

She is there, Nadia, as if she knew I would come. She stands at my approach.

Doesn't she know I need to be alone?

"Edmon?" she calls out.

I try to answer and can't. My adrenaline worn off, I realize I'm in terrible pain. My left arm screams. My throat is scratchy, my voice almost gone. I collapse.

"You're hurt!" she exclaims.

She comes up underneath my arm to support me. I wince at her touch. The next thing I know, I'm on my back looking at the sky. Tears stream down my face.

I always seem to be crying. The world just seems such a hateful place.

"What happened?" she asks.

When I calm down and can breathe again, I tell her of the arrival of Phaestion and the commencement of my training. I finish with my assault on Alberich. I tell her she was wrong, that my father will never let me go.

There is a beat of silence between us. Then she says solemnly, "The midday rest is almost over. We need to get you back."

"I can't go back, Nadia," I implore.

"Wrong." She stands and lifts me up from the ground. "If I've taught you anything when we practice climbing, it's that you don't give up when you're slipping. You hold fast and think it through. This isn't over. Not by a long shot."

She's so resilient. Like my mother. Every challenge placed before her, she meets with strength. It occurs to me—

Girls are stronger than boys. They have to be.

"Alberich got what he deserved. They'll have to leave you alone now," she reassures me.

I lean on her, and we hobble up the path. We sneak into the manse, where the shades are pulled low for the midday nap. I direct her down the hallway. She pauses by the doorway to my room.

"Is this it?" she asks hesitantly. "I've been to the Eventide feast a few times, but I've never seen where you sleep."

"That room isn't mine anymore." I point toward the guest room a few doors down, and she drags me to it.

"Bed," I call out.

The platform ejects from the wall. She stares wide-eyed at the unfamiliar technology, but lays me gently on the gel mattress.

"Why did you let him take your room from you?" she asks.

"I don't want to talk about it, Nadia," I groan. "I just want to sleep and never wake up."

"Talk about what?"

We turn to see Phaestion's pale, lithe form framed in the doorway.

"Go away," Nadia snaps, her dark eyes burning. "He doesn't want you here."

Phaestion ignores her and steps into the room anyway. He approaches the bed. Nadia bars his way. His gray eyes hold her gaze as he calmly hands a jar of something to her.

"What is it?" she asks.

"Tissue regenerative. Rub it on his wounds."

Nadia looks at him distrustfully but takes the jar. She kneels by the bed and peels the shirt from my torso. My entire left side is discolored, black and blue. She rubs the salve on me. I wince. The ointment is cold then extraordinarily hot on my skin.

"It burns," I say.

Phaestion nods. "The engineered bacteria absorbed by the skin help repair damaged cells. You'll be less afraid of getting hurt from now on because you know the pain is only temporary."

"The best of Tao's scientists don't have this kind of medicine!" Nadia exclaims with wonder.

Phaestion smiles enigmatically. "My father's hired many off-worlders. This salve comes from Nonthera. If we want to be a strong house, a strong nation, a strong people, we have to learn the strongest ways. Even if they aren't our own."

"Even if those ways come from the Daysiders?" Nadia scowls. She massages the ointment into my skin.

I feel better. A lot better. I sit up in the bed.

"Don't forget his ribs," Phaestion says.

Nadia purses her lips. She doesn't like taking orders, especially from this highborn know-it-all, but she follows his instruction. The stinging subsides, and then all I feel are Nadia's hands. We haven't touched like this before. I feel a stirring below, and I don't want her to stop. I blush.

"That's enough," I say more harshly than I intend.

She backs away and folds her arms across her chest.

"Feel better?" Phaestion asks.

I nod.

He pauses. "You've never held a weapon before." It's a statement, not a question. I look away, ashamed. "I already knew," he says simply. "Your father never entered you into competitions. If you were worth anything as a fighter, he would have."

"Then why come here to train with me?"

"I remember the day of your brother's christening, as do all in Meridian. They played the aquagraphics of you telling off Old Wusong for days and days. You're famous. Probably the only scion almost as famous as me." He shrugs.

I'm famous? The camglobes recorded everything that day, I realize. *Still, if he knew I couldn't fight, why request this fosterage?*

"People think you're strong. You're to marry the emperor's daughter one day. They think you could be emperor. A strong emperor, maybe even like the Great Song. I suppose I thought having you as a companion might be fun."

"Glad I could amuse," I respond acidly.

Nadia smirks at my sarcasm.

"You may have no value as a training partner, but that doesn't mean you have no value at all." Phaestion arcs an eyebrow knowingly. "Just don't hinder my progress," he says as he heads for the door.

"Considering Alberich's dead, I don't think that will be a problem," I mutter.

Phaestion looks back over his shoulder. "He's not dead. You ran off, so I dragged his body from the beach myself. He's really heavy, you know. My family shuttled in a healing tank from Meridian when I arrived. He's recovering in your servants' quarters. He should be fine in an hour or so. I was careful when I stabbed him."

"You stabbed him?" I ask, shocked.

"He was choking you." He shrugs. "He might not have killed you, but I wasn't ready to take the chance. So, I stabbed him."

I bite the inside of my cheek in anger. "This whole time I thought I had—"

"You ran off." He shrugs again.

Nadia shakes her head in disgust, but when Phaestion smiles at her, something changes in her expression. My stomach turns. *Does she like him? This boy stole my room, saved my life, and now steals Nadia?*

Suddenly, my mother is in the doorway. She pushes past Phaestion and kneels by the bed. "Edmon!" She clutches me. "What happened? Did they hurt you? My baby, are you all right?"

I want to cry into her arms, but over her shoulder, I see Phaestion staring curiously. He tilts his head as if calculating what this embrace between mother and son could mean.

It may be a weakness, I realize. *I must no longer be a child if I'm to protect her and be his equal.*

I gently but firmly push my mother away from me. "Mother, I'm fine."

"Edmon—"

"I'm fine," I say more forcefully. "You should go. The Eventide feast will start soon. They'll need you to help prepare." I try to sound as adult as I can.

Her face registers shock and hurt, but I push my guilt aside. A firmness sets over her features. I think she understands.

I must no longer be a baby. I must be Edmon of House Leontes.

"You're right, Edmon. I'm down the hall if you need me." She turns quickly, her hands rubbing her eyes as she leaves.

I stand to face Phaestion. I feel different, not afraid anymore. We stare each other down, each waiting for the other to make a move.

"You're lucky," he says. "You have a mother."

I don't know what he means by this, but before I can ask, a drum beats.

"The Eventide feast," Nadia says, diffusing the tension. She grabs my hand. "Join us, Nightsider. You might learn a thing or two about what it means to be an islander."

She pulls me toward the music. Phaestion follows.

—

The music is in full rhythm when Nadia pulls me into the room. Gorham catches my eye with a gap-toothed grin. He plucks out a twangy rhythm on his sampo guitar. Without missing a chord, he reaches into a basket and tosses me a small wooden flute. I catch it midair. Nadia gives me a little shove into the center of the ring. "Show them what you got, Edmon!"

I look back toward the doorway. Phaestion leans against the frame.

He came here with all of his weapons, all of his haughtiness. He thinks his people's ways are superior and that my gifts are worthless. This is my arena, I think. *Let's see how he feels when he's not always winning!*

I bring the flute to my lips. The other instruments pick up my cue. I lose myself in the beat. I play a riff. Gorham mimics on the guitar. The drums punctuate our call. Then I pull the flute away, and I do something I've never done in the center of the circle. I sing.

I call out a line, "We, the islanders, have a home!"

The circle responds, picking up my call. "We, the islanders, have a home!"

"Yes, we call it the Isle of Bone!"

"Yes, we call it the Isle of Bone!"

"You can't take me across the sea!" I shout.

"You can't take me across the sea!"

"'Cause I be where I be!"

"'Cause we be where we be!"

The guests burst into an exultant cheer. They clap with celebration. Someone lifts me up on top of their shoulders. I'm floating on a wave of hands that pass me overhead. I see my mother standing, her smile broadening on her lips as I am carried. I find myself placed down on the edge of the circle where Nadia stands. She cracks a crooked grin. I beam back at her.

She gave me the courage for this, I think. *She and my mother.*

I glance at the doorway, but Phaestion has vanished.

Later. It's dark in the hallway and the noise of the last guests echoes through the corridors. I'm near the servants' rooms in the basement levels. Maybe I shouldn't be here, but I want to see if Alberich is really alive. I hear his gruff voice coming from a door at the end of the hall.

"My Lord, he's not without talent. He's your son, after all."

I hear my father's voice in response. "Don't honey your words, Alberich. Had the Julii boy not been there . . . But for the emperor, I could still send him to the Pavaka."

I peek through the doorway. Alberich, a bandage wrapped around his abdomen, converses with my father via aquagraphic. A large tank full of yellow gel like Phaestion's healing ointment sits in the corner.

"I've no need to flatter, my lord," Alberich replies. "It was your son who injured me. A child of twelve, who has never fought before. Considering his lack of experience—"

"This fosterage was a mistake," my father interrupts. "That bitch, Cleopatra, no doubt objected?"

"She still claims Bone does not recognize the deed granted you by the Synod."

"But she recognizes I could send in my soldiers and declare martial law." My father laughs. "It's by my grace that they live free as they have." His voice softens for a moment. "Tell me, is she still beautiful, Alberich?"

"She is still beautiful, my lord. And strong."

"Good," he says almost kindly. "That is very good . . ." His voice trails off. Then Edric returns to his hard self. "Train the Julii boy. Teach him well, and he may remember the debt when he claims the title of Patriarch."

"And of Edmon?" Alberich asks.

"You know what's intended. If he's not strong enough to complete the ritual . . ."

The screen winks out. I back from the doorway, intending to sneak off unnoticed.

"I know what he intends, Edmon." Alberich's graveled voice catches me. "But what do you intend?"

"You tried to kill me" is all I can say.

"And you survived." He seems pleased. "Every creature has within him the will to fight, from the fiercest shark to the meekest minnow. Conflict is in the nature of all things. You can be strong, but only if you use the violence within. And you did."

I stare, not knowing what to make of this.

"I'm commanded to train Phaestion. If you choose, I'll see that you receive equal attention."

I say nothing because I truly don't know if that's what I want.

"Edmon, I can't replace the years you haven't trained. More importantly, I can't replace desire. Your father anticipates your failure. He's made your brother his heir, but beware: you're the elder. Others may use your status to weaken House Leontes. You'd be wise to become strong enough to make your own choices whether that means fighting or not."

Others may use my status . . .

With the arrival of Phaestion on Bone, I'm beginning to understand who he means.

I think on his words and say, “The meekest minnow does not choose to fight the mako who hunts him. He has to because that’s the way it is. Still, he will lose. Does struggling gain him anything?”

—

After returning to my new room, I find Phaestion waiting for me.

“What do you want?” I accuse more than ask.

“How do you do it?” he fires back.

“Do what?”

“The music?” He looks almost desperate.

I lie down on the gel mattress. “It’s music. It’s nothing special.”

“How can you say that!” He leaps at me and pulls me to my feet. His strong, sculpted hands wrap around my arms. I struggle, but he’s too strong. His gray eyes bore into me. “They love you!”

“Let me go!” I say.

He releases me. I rub my arms as blood flows back into my limbs.

“I have to know how. How do you make them love you?” He paces the room frantically.

“I’m told you’re the best fighter of this generation. Even the emperor said you were competing when you were only five. Surely, the cheers of an arena are enough. They love you plenty. Leave me alone.”

He looks at me dead in the eye. “They love me like an idol, but not as one of them. You sing with their voice. Do you understand the difference?”

“No,” I say. “You’re in my room. Get out.”

“Teach me to play like you play.”

“I can’t.” I lie back down and roll over, turning my back to him.

Then something occurs to me . . .

Two can play.

“What if I teach you? Will you teach me?” I ask.

“What do you mean?”

"I teach you to play. You teach me to fight," I propose.

"You want to fight?" The mask of innocence is stripped from his face. I see him for real now: shrewd, tactical, competitive, calculating.

"You need me. I need you," I say. "And you'll give me back my room."

"Don't press your luck." He grins.

"If you want my help . . ."

He turns to leave. Then over his shoulder, he says, "Perhaps this was meant to be after all, Leontes. Chilleus had Cuillan. Phaestion and Edmon."

The Chironiad again. Cuillan was the foster brother, some said lover, to the hero, brilliant Chilleus. They were the closest of friends, but Cuillan betrayed Chilleus for a woman. They ended up on opposite sides of the civil war. In the end, Chilleus bested Cuillan in mortal combat. He held his brother's broken body in his arms and wept after he delivered the deathblow.

"What about my room?" I ask.

"Sorry. It's mine now." He smiles and walks out the door.

I lay my head back against the gel.

How can I beat him? I wonder.

Slumber takes me. Chilleus had his Cuillan, but both ended up dead.

CHAPTER 5

Magia

Months pass. Intense months. Laborious months. Days are spent on the sands drilling—sprints on the beach, standing on one leg for hours. I sit and watch Alberich and Phaestion duel. I want to practice, too, but the techniques and moves Alberich teaches are far beyond me. Alberich sees my frustration and, as recompense, forces me to punch rocks. The pain is blinding but quickly over with use of the salves and treatments Phaestion imports from Meridian. I heal so completely I'm able to endure it all over again on the morrow.

My mother circles the confines of her room like a caged shark. She wants to lash out but can do nothing for fear of repercussions. It comforts her little that I actually begin to enjoy the training. Instead, she assures me that she's planning something.

"The other islands—Rock, Shell, Conch, Leaf—they tire of rule by their Pantheon overlords, too. We will rally. You won't be taken to Meridian. I promise."

I've never seen her like this before, standing over maps, talking with the other villagers about trade. She's like an ancient battle commander discussing sieges, politics, and tactics. It occurs to me that she's more like Edric than I ever realized.

I just nod in agreement to her statements, but fear she can't stop my leaving. If she defies Edric, nothing will prevent his wrath. The technology of Meridian and the Pantheon is far beyond anything we have on the islands. We are not strong enough to defy my father. I'm not strong enough to defy him yet.

I will find a way to protect her if she rebels, I think. *Patience. One day I will be full grown. Then . . .*

Phaestion and I steal away for private sessions. He breaks down what Alberich teaches into simpler techniques I can learn. Eventually, I spar with him. He yawns, parrying the thrusts of my sword using only one arm. The second I admire his skill is the second I'm knocked onto my back in the sand.

"It's dangerous to respect one's opponent," he says. "Honor and admiration may be savored only after your enemy is beaten."

Alberich will occasionally catch me practicing a move that he knows I didn't learn from him. He'll correct my form before giving me some other task that will wear me out.

Nadia spies on us once. She climbs the rocks above our makeshift arena on the sands.

Phaestion admonishes her. "You break our concentration."

"I can fight as well as anyone!" Nadia fumes.

Phaestion grins rakishly. "You can. He can't." He jabs his thumb at me. "Don't distract us."

Nadia stays away from our practice but blames me for the exile in the few moments we still meet on the cliffs.

"Little Lord can't bear to have a girl watch him," she taunts.

I find myself tuning out her words more and more, though. Instead, I stare at her lips and her legs. When she leans down and snickers, my eyes go to the V of her tunic and the narrow shadow created by her blossoming breasts.

When did that happen? I wonder.

I'm pulled from my reverie when her japes segue to her true topic of interest—Phaestion. She wants to know everything about him.

"Where does he come from? What things does he like? Does he talk of any girls back home?"

I tell her with hot jealousy, "Meridian, fighting, and I don't know."

The last is a lie. He talks of girls, but only to say he has many who love him and that seems totally natural. Sometimes I think of myself in contrast to him: my arms skinny, my knees knobby, and my hair dirty and dark. I start to feel that if I was more like Phaestion, my father would love me. Maybe Nadia would love me, too.

—

Daytime belongs to combat, but the Eventide is mine. Phaestion and I practice the notes of songs. We try the flute first, then the sampo guitar. We try singing. I use an aquagraphic tablet to write notation for him. He studies with intensity, but it doesn't come. He plays the flute with too much force, piping a shrill tone. Or he'll try too softly, and no sound emerges at all.

He throws the instrument across the room, shattering it against the wall, his usual calm demeanor devolved to frenzy. "I'll never learn!" he paces, arms gesticulating violently.

"Give it time. You weren't always good at fighting."

"Yes, I was!" he insists. "Like I can see a man's movement and know what he will do before he thinks it. I don't know why."

"You still had to be taught."

"But it wasn't like this!" He pounds a fist against the wall. "Even if I learn it, I'll never be great. What's the point? It won't help me win or conquer anything. It won't help me lead."

"How is fighting supposed to help you do that?" I ask sullenly.

I'm reminded of my audience before Old Wusong. The one thing I'm good at is considered useless. I put my flute in its case now that the lesson is finished.

"Humanity's savageness is what makes it civilized," he answers.

Do all people from Meridian think this way? I wonder.

"Technology, trade, computers, space travel," he goes on. "All are products of competition and conflict."

"So art and music and learning—all those things don't make civilization, too? The sand between your toes, the sun on your face. Don't those things make you happy? Isn't being happy what makes things worth it?" I ask.

"Stretching my physical capabilities, pitting myself against a worthy opponent, and defeating the challenge—that's what makes me happy."

"I wasn't the one who wanted to learn this," I say bitterly. "Just remember to keep your end of the bargain, even if you can't learn."

"You think I can't?" he challenges.

"I know you can't," I say slyly, baiting him.

"Give me your flute," he demands.

"No!" I whisk the case away from his grasp.

"Give it here." He reaches. I pull it away again. The game is on.

"It's mine, and you can't have it!"

Finally, he lunges with a speed I can't match. The flute case skitters across the floor. We wrestle until he bests me. I struggle furiously. "Get off me, Nightsider!"

Calmness comes over him. I try to knock him off, but his skill at positioning is too good.

"You'll always be my friend, won't you, Edmon?" His voice sounds far-off, though his eyes hold me in their grasp.

"Yes," I say confusedly.

He seems somewhere else. His panting breath suddenly calms, and his face flushes.

"I've never met anyone like you before," he whispers.

I feel my heart beating in my chest. He slowly leans down.

What is this feeling?

He presses his forehead to mine.

The gesture of brothers.

More than a kiss, this is the symbol of a bond greater than blood. A bond between warriors. For a moment, it feels like I'm him and he's me and we'll be this way forever. Then he pulls back with a haunted look in his eyes.

"Phaestion?" I ask.

The sound of his name snaps him back to reality. He smiles, carefree again, and helps me off the ground.

Out in the main hall, drumbeats reverberate. Phaestion grabs my hand. "Come on."

The feast brings the dance. I look for my mother, but she does not attend. She comes less and less to the festivities, always locking herself in her chambers with the village elders. They are discussing something secret. She knows the days are running short until the sondi will arrive to take me to Meridian and House Julii. I don't think my mother plans on letting me go.

How can she think to fight them? I wonder. *Do I even want her to succeed in preventing me from leaving if she tries?* That is the greater question that hangs in my mind. *There must be more to life than the simplicity Bone has to offer.*

I watch Phaestion mingling among the islanders, observing. I wonder if my mother keeps me from her plans because she sees the heir of House Julii and I have become friends? Or is it so that if she fails, my father cannot hold me accountable? The music pulls me from my dark thoughts.

I play and sing while Nadia teaches Phaestion to dance. He's actually much better at dancing than playing music, almost as graceful as when he's fighting. They smile at each other. I see Nadia laugh as he tells her some joke I cannot hear. The villagers call for him to take center stage. They clap and sing for him to move his fancy feet as Nadia watches with admiration. My chest burns.

Now he takes the thing that I'm best at from me, too.

"You're as good as him," the old, worn voice says, catching me. Gorham smiles his kindly gap-toothed smile. "In your own way, young lord. You play beautifully. He can't do that."

"But look at him dance. He's so good in so little time. Everyone loves him. Even Nadia," I say venomously. "It's not fair."

"Does the star of Tao burn any less brightly than the star of Lyria?" he asks.

"What do you mean?"

He knows I've mentioned Lyria often. He knows I've dreamed of it, the people, the capital city of Prospera with its libraries and schools and opera houses. Now, though, I'm in no mood for his old-man riddles.

"Loving Phaestion doesn't mean they do not love you," he answers.

I'm not about to give up self-pity so easily. "I've never seen the star of Lyria. How should I know which is brighter?"

"Someday you will, I think, young lord." Gorham grins sadly. "And you'll understand the light from one star does not eclipse that of another. Each star has its own to give."

I try to understand his wisdom but don't allow myself to see it. "If each star shines equally as bright, how do we measure them? There is an objective truth, old man." I turn on my heel and leave, shoving the guilt of my insult aside.

Phaestion and I lose ourselves in the darkness of the shaded house when the feast is over. We skirt through the halls or sometimes we just sit and talk.

One night, he steals some fruit from a kitchen table. We return to his room. He takes three golden sea peaches and hands me six more.

"Watch," he says. He juggles them. His perfect, white hands move with practiced ease.

"Toss another!"

I throw one, and the new peach becomes part of the mesmerizing loop.

"Another!" he calls out.

I do it again, laughing at his preternatural skill.

"Another!"

I stare, incredulous, but I toss it in anyway. It is too many for anyone's hands to manage. A peach drops to the floor, but he doesn't let it touch the ground. He traps it in the crook of his ankle, then tosses it seamlessly back into the loop, creating a new pattern with hands and now feet.

"Another!" he says.

Is he serious?

"Another!" he insists.

I toss it into the mix. He deftly includes it. "I should try this blindfolded next time. Now you!" he says.

"What? No!" I shout.

He throws the peaches at me. One. Two. Three. I manage for a few seconds, and then they all tumble to the floor, rolling everywhere.

He bursts into laughter. "Bed!" he calls and falls on the gel mattress, which slides from the wall. "You should have seen your face!"

"Thanks," I mutter as I chase down rolling fruit. "I've never juggled before."

"Neither have I."

I stare at him in disbelief. He gazes back innocently.

"How were you able to do that then?" I ask.

"It probably has something to do with the way I was born." He lies back on the bed.

What does that mean?

"My mother was a sea goddess," he says very seriously.

There is a moment of deadly silence before he bursts into laughter. Then we're interrupted by a musical hoot from the sea.

He sits up, alert. "What was that?"

"A siren calling for a mate," I respond, annoyed by the interruption. "Don't you know anything?"

Phaestion cocks his head to the side. "Have you seen one before?"

"I've caught glimpses. They usually stay in the depths."

"Let's go." He springs from the bed.

"What?"

"To see a siren."

"It's past Eventide!" I protest.

He grabs my arm. "Gotta train for the unexpected!"

We sneak through the darkness of the house, then out into the light of the never-setting sun.

"Come on!" he hollers as he takes off at a clip down the path.

"Phaestion!" I shout, but all I can see are the soles of his feet licking the air like tongues as he sprints down the path.

A distant rumble sounds. Bloated, cottony clouds bloom on the horizon. A storm is brewing, not far off. If we are quick about it, we might not get caught in it. Then, again . . . I sigh and take off after my rash friend.

I find Phaestion near the shore, not another soul in sight. I'm panting, out of breath. Rivulets of sweat glide down my forehead.

"What took you so long?" He smiles, not even winded from the sprint. "Come on!"

He skips along the sand bar that forms a rudimentary dock and untethers a small canoe from its moorings.

"That doesn't belong to you!"

"Why does that matter?"

I start to protest, but he interrupts me. "Edmon." He puts his hand on my arms. "Your father's Patriarch of House Leontes. Bone is his. As his son, it's yours. By the rights of fosterage, I have the rights and privileges that you do. So it's mine, too. The whole world could be ours between your family and mine and the friends we make with other scions. If you don't start acting like you are worth it, then you never will be."

Nadia wouldn't see things that way, I think. *I wish she were here.*

"What if—?"

"Enough talk." He shakes his head. The puffy clouds in the sky seem much closer now. A siren calls, her mellifluous sound beckoning. "I'm not missing this because you're afraid, Edmon!" He hops into the canoe. "You coming or not?"

I scowl, but I get into the boat just the same.

We paddle out of the harbor on choppy waves. Phaestion's face is beaming. He seems ready to conquer anything. All I feel is the sickening twist of fear. I rev the blast engine, and the sonic pulse propels us through the high waves of the open sea. Phaestion leaps onto the bow. He holds his stance with superhuman balance even as the boat crashes into the breaks. We're quickly drenched with sea foam. Phaestion howls with delight.

"I'll take us around to the north side of the isle!" I shout over the engine. "Once we get within earshot, I'll have to cut the power or risk scaring them off."

We round the island underneath the great cliffs. I spot the nook high up where Nadia and I have spent so much time. I turn off the engine.

"Are they here?" Phaestion asks. "I don't see them."

I hold my finger to my lips, indicating the need for quiet. We slowly paddle to an outcropping of rocks a few kilometers from the isle. A cloud passes overhead and swaths us in shadow.

"Phaestion?"

"What?"

"The weather's shifting," I say with trepidation.

He fires me a look of annoyance.

The boat slides closer to the rocks. We can see them now—three sirens. Their pearlescent bodies shimmer against the green of the sea. One of them throws her hair back in a rainbow shower of anemone tendrils. The filaments dance with an array of color. They're beautiful. Remarkably human and alien all at once. The sound of their call feels magnetic, pulling us toward the rocks.

"Wow!" Phaestion exhales.

The sirens' heads snap up. Their hair flares with violent bursts of color. Their slitted eyes narrow, and their calls turn to shrieks as they spot us. They dive into the water, their shimmering bodies visible just below the waves.

"They're getting away!" Phaestion cries.

He grabs an oar and snaps it like a twig against his knee, creating a sharp wooden stave from one fragment. Thunder crashes, and the sky spills forth a deluge.

"By the twisted star, what are you doing?" I shout above the maelstrom.

He poises the stave above his head.

No! Something inside me screams. I hurl myself at him, tackling him just as he throws the spear. It torpedoes into the water wide of its target.

"What did you do that for?" He throws me off him.

"Why would you try to kill it?" I fire back.

The argument is cut short as the water beneath us roils. The boat rocks like a seesaw, water overflowing everywhere.

"We're tipping!" I shout.

Phaestion presses his limbs to the sides of the boat for stability. "Just hang on!"

It's no use. I'm flung into the air.

"Edmon!"

It's the last thing I hear before I smash into a curling wave. Through darkness, I struggle for the surface. Brine fills my nose and mouth. I flail my limbs, then realize I'm swimming in the wrong direction, down rather than up.

Idiot!

My lungs are on fire. Something whooshes nearby. I risk opening my eyes. It's a siren, her iridescent scales glowing. The filaments of her hair flare out like the snakes of a medusa's mane. She opens her mouth, revealing row upon row of vicious needle teeth. I scream, stupidly releasing all the oxygen from my lungs. Her webbed hands outstretch to grab me.

Suddenly, I'm swept aside. The current carries me in its clutches. Something huge circles below me. The siren shrieks and swims away faster than I ever thought possible, then disappears as if swallowed.

A gigantic green eye opens before me. My head feels dizzy. Blackness clouds my vision. Water fills my mouth.

Hands grab hold of me. I'm pulled up away from the eye. Next thing I know, I'm vomiting seawater into the boat. Phaestion pounds my back.

"What happened?" I cough out.

"I dove in to rescue you," he says over the torrent.

"The siren, the eye," I sputter. "There's something down there!"

An explosion rips the surface of the ocean. A geyser soars into the air, flinging the boat across the waves. A hideous shriek thrums through my entire body as a colossal eel-like creature bursts from the water then dives back down.

"By the twisted star!" My voice is hushed by the awesome sight.

"A leviathan!" Phaestion echoes.

He grabs an oar and paddles furiously. I jump to the blast engine and pull the rev cord. Nothing. I pull again. *Damn the ancestors!*

"Hurry!" Phaestion screams.

"It won't turn!"

The creature circles beneath us then bursts forth from the depths again. His dragon's head breaks the surface, and his great green eyes open. The large pupils dilate with something more than primitive intelligence.

Phaestion brandishes the remaining oar like a sword. His normally sure and steady hands shake wildly.

The creature opens its maw, displaying an incredible array of enormous razorlike incisors. Its shriek knocks us from our feet to the back of the boat. The leviathan bobs and weaves its massive head, following us, a predator toying with its food.

Phaestion stands, but I motion for him to stay back. I don't know why, but I feel something. *This creature won't harm us,* I realize.

The monster's eyes flash. His nostrils flare. I am sucked toward his inhalation.

He's smelling us!

The creature snorts like a massive "humph."

I smell the odor of a thousand fermented sea creatures in his breath. Still, I stand my ground in spite of my terror. The rain ceases. The only sounds are the creaking boat, the waves, the breathing of two boys, and a monster. I raise my hand in some sort of greeting.

"What are you doing?" hisses Phaestion.

I have no idea.

I step forward, my hand centimeters from the enormous snout. Giant tendrils extend from its nostrils like the elongated mustaches of some ancient guru. Thunder crashes, and rain falls once more. The creature shrieks. I'm blown flat on my back as it dives beneath the sea. The splash is tremendous. It smashes against the deck of the boat with incredible force.

"Hang on!" Phaestion grabs me.

We plaster ourselves to the deck as we're hit by a massive wave. It propels us with terrifying speed toward the cliffs.

"We're going to hit!" I shout.

"What do we do?" Phaestion screams.

"Toss me the oar!" I plunge it into the sea like a rudder, trying to turn us.

"It's not working!" Phaestion shouts.

I paddle with all my might against the current, silently cursing my companion for destroying our other oar.

"Brace for impact!" Phaestion screams, echoing dialogue from every space opera aquagraphic we've ever seen.

The cliffs rush to meet us. I keep paddling furiously, my arms on fire. *Here it comes!* Miraculously, our pace slows, and at the last second, the wave dissipates. I reach out with the oar and stab against the rocks, jamming us away from impact as much as I can. We bump into the cliffs with nary a sound. I collapse back in the boat, angry, relieved, and exhausted.

I hear laughter building slowly, and I look up to see Phaestion flop against the hull, giggling with delight. I stare at him as he laughs and laughs and laughs.

Crazy bastard! This is all his fault!

My knuckles whiten on the oar. I stand and glower at him. I raise the oar, ready to smash it on his fiery head. He looks up, points, and howls even harder.

Lightning crashes. I slip and fall on my rear. "Ow," I moan.

Phaestion hoots with joy, and now I can't help but giggle, too.

We're alive. Against all odds, we're alive.

"You should've seen your face!" He holds his sides. "You should've seen your face."

We paddle into the harbor soaked to the bone. It's an easy matter to tie the boat where we found it and make our way through the deserted village. We silently enter through the foyer of the manse, sneak down the hall, slip into my old room, and shut the door behind us. I collapse onto the floor, the whole ordeal having taken little more than a couple of hours.

Phaestion strips out of his sopping-wet linens and dives under the covers of the bed.

"No one's seen a leviathan for over a hundred years!" he whispers excitedly.

"Yeah." I feel numb.

"You just walked right up to it," he continues. "You, who's afraid of everything!"

"Yeah" is all I can think to add.

"How'd you know it wouldn't kill you?"

"I didn't," I say quietly as I strip off my wet linens. I grab a sheet from the built-in closet, wrap myself in it, and lie down on the stone floor.

"We better get some sleep," he says. "There are only a few hours before training."

Sleep comes in fits. I'm plagued by something more than a dream, fainter than reality.

I'm running. I hear the monster's laughter behind me, the leviathan.

"Why run, boy?" His voice vibrates through me.

Then he's in front of me. His dragon face spews noxious fumes from his maw. His great green eyes, slitted, bore into me.

"Why run, boy? You can wait billions of years, but the stars will burn out. Space will go black. Your life, all life, will end."

The truth hits me like a cold wave.

"You will not even be a memory. So why run? Why run from me?"

I awaken with a gasp, sweating.

"Edmon?" Phaestion asks groggily. "Are you all right?"

"A nightmare," I say.

"Tell me?"

I hesitate, but then I tell him everything.

Phaestion nods. "I had a dream I was an orca once. Only I wasn't running. I was swimming at the head of a pod, hunting. Nothing mattered but my prey. Not yesterdays or tomorrows. It felt good to know what I was supposed to do."

I listen to the steadiness of his breath, like a metronome, so clear, so sure.

"They say young orcas kill their own fathers," he adds.

"Why do they do that?" I ask.

"To lead the pod, they must take the old leader's place. The orca is where our ritual of patricide comes from."

"Patricide?" I ask.

"A noble scion becomes a Patriarch when he murders his father and takes his place. Didn't you know that?"

"Oh" is all I think to say.

"What do leviathans do?" he asks.

"I don't know."

We sit for a moment staring into the darkness.

"Thank you for saving me," I add. "Earlier today."

He shrugs. "You're my best friend."

CHAPTER 6

Accompagno

Cycle's end arrives. Alberich stands in the foyer, but this time he's not bringing someone with him; he's taking someone away. Phaestion is next to him dressed in his black uniform and cape, the silver circlet of nobility returned to his brow.

My mother waits imperiously atop the staircase. "You'll not take my son," she commands.

Of course my mother would try something dramatic.

I know that she's been planning with the village elders, sending communiques to Drum, Rock, and Leaf, and whomever else will listen to the whispering of rebellion. But I've been training to fight every day. I'm beginning to understand the strength of these Nightsiders. Even if every island rose up to throw off the rule of the Pantheon, I think they would be crushed.

More than that, I feel different since the arrival of Phaestion. The fosterage has given me a friend and opened a window into a world I'd only glimpsed before. It's the world of my father and of war and of men. I'm curious to climb through, but my mother's rash words threaten to close the window forever. *She should have warned me!*

Alberich sighs. He expected my mother to protest. "My lady, I'm sorry. This is not something you're able to choose."

"Edmon is my son! I'm his mother. By the laws of Bone, you have no right to take him from me without consent."

"Laws of Bone are not recognized by the Synod," Alberich states. "My lady, there comes a time when a boy must leave the comforts of a mother's arms. For Edmon, that time has come."

"Not yet!" Her voice cracks.

A cadre of Leontes guards, with blue uniforms, flashing silver gauntlets, and pikes at their sides, burst into the foyer.

"I'm sorry," the seneschal says. "If you won't let him go, I'll have to take him."

"I'm no warrior," she admits, "but Bone has friends among the other islands—Leaf, Drum, Conch. They have pledged their support. As Bone goes, so do others."

At her signal, islanders, men of the village, appear at the top of the steps. They hold spears and fishhooks, nets and oars. They brandish the tools as weapons, outnumbering the Leontes guards at least two to one. It is a standoff. Nadia is there next to her father, her eyes burning with dark intensity.

She knew about this and didn't tell me?

"You see, it is not just my son, Edmon. None of Bone's sons or daughters will ever be taken by the Pantheon again to feed the thirsty blades of the Combat against their wills."

The air crackles with tension.

"You're suggesting open rebellion with Meridian?" Alberich looks around the room warily, calculating his next maneuver. "You cannot fathom what you would bring down, nor the bloodshed you'd cause. For what? Because a father wants to educate his son? Think, my lady, before something happens that cannot be undone."

"Edmon, come here," my mother says.

Alberich is right. If I go to her, I won't be able to stop the violence, and I'll be taken anyway. I have to show her I am no longer a child. I have to save her from herself. If she's killed, if Nadia—

"Mother," I say quietly. "I want to go."

She looks at me aghast. She glides down the steps toward me. "Is this truly what you want, Edmon?"

I wish I could stay here with her and Nadia and the island and the music. I wish my father wasn't my father.

"It's only temporary," I say. "In the meantime, you and the other islands shore up your defenses. Resisting now won't do either of us any good. Wait until I'm grown, until I'm stronger."

She watches me for the lie beneath my words, then brushes a dark lock of hair out of my eyes. She straightens my linen robes as if to make sure that I look proper for my leave. "My brave little warrior. How did you become so clever?"

"Killing isn't something to wish for lightly," I say. "You taught me that."

There's something more I don't say: *I can't be here forever. There's more waiting for me out there.*

She embraces me, fighting back tears, then steps back, her gaze landing on Phaestion. "Lord Julii, since the fosterage in your house commences, I expect that you'll carry my son's things from here on?"

The barest hint of a smug smile curves on Phaestion's otherwise impassive face. Yet he bows his head with deference and lifts my bags to his shoulder. "It is my honor."

My mother's dark eyes drift to Alberich and become steel. "Tell Lord Leontes he'll regret this coercion."

Pity flashes in the seneschal's eyes, but we walk through the door. We're met by a cadre of black-clad guards from House Julii outside. They salute Phaestion. It all feels so formal. I'm entering a world of pomp and circumstance I've only glimpsed. Phaestion leads the procession down the narrow winding road of the town.

The cadre my mother gathered at the mansion follows. They line the streets and watch in silence. For a moment, I think I see Nadia's face flit through the gathered faces. We haven't said goodbye. I lose sight of her as we reach the sleek black sondi waiting for us at the docks.

I step onto the ramp, but a tug in my stomach pulls me back, and I turn. The faces of all the Daysiders of Bone look at me. I raise my hand to them. They raise theirs. For the first time, I sense that these are my people and I am theirs.

A hand falls on my shoulder. The angular, refined features of Phaestion Julii break into a smile.

"Come on." He laughs. "The capital awaits."

He turns, his cape swirling behind him. I follow.

"Alberich," I say as I strap into my seat. I muster a commanding tone, as if I'm my father giving him an order. "No matter how angry she makes Edric, please see to it my mother is not harmed."

The big man grimaces. "I'll do my best, young lord."

The engines whine. The balloon lifts into the sky. I glance out the window at the whiteness of the stone, the high cliffs, and the green-blue sea. I've said goodbye before, but only for a day, years ago. Not like this. The vista moves past the viewport.

Everything is changing.

The island recedes. I spy through the porthole a tiny ledge jutting out from the cliffside. The spot where I first met Nadia. A young girl stands there, her hair blowing in the wind. She raises an arm. I put my hand against the glass to return the farewell, but I don't think she can see.

The sky turns the color of a bruise. The star of Tao dips on the horizon. It hangs like a lidless red eye. We reach Meridian, the capital. The sondi roars through the narrow avenues of glass scrapers in the southern districts where House Julii makes its home. It approaches a tower with the crest of a massive orca emblazoned on its surface.

"Welcome to your new home," Phaestion says.

"It's gigantic," I whisper.

"Dwarfs even the palace of Old Wusong." He smiles. "The Julii were the first leaders of the High Synod after Empress Boudika was forced to abdicate. Our position allowed us to corner the market on interstellar trade, limited though it was, when the Fracture Point was much farther away. Tao survived because of House Julii, and someday, I'll be Patriarch and inherit the seat on the Synod."

"Provided you win the Combat," I say bitingly.

Phaestion winks. For him, the outcome isn't in doubt.

One of the giant glass panels of the scraper opens to reveal a hangar. Our sondi glides through the port.

"How would Tao not have survived without House Julii?" I ask.

Phaestion gives me a look like I should know this basic history. "I forget, on the island you have no formal schooling. You saw the kelp and algae fields of the Southern Sea upon our approach?"

I nod.

"Those fields and our hydroponics buildings are the source of oxygenation for our atmosphere and oceans. Forests of the Twilight Band were all clear-cut, and minerals within half-lighted zones were mined long ago. Tao needed imports. House Julii was the first to build ships that could ferry to and from the distant Fracture Point. When the High Synod formed, the Julii fleet became the national fleet. Old Wusong may hold the imperial name, but Julii is the name that keeps this place alive."

I think of the Fracture Point changing the day of my birth and the visitors from off-world I saw at Edgaard's coronation years ago.

"With the repositioning of the Fracture Point," I think out loud, "your giant freighters for long voyages are obsolete. Other houses should have been able to build ships much more cheaply and end Julii dominance by now."

Phaestion's eyes go hard.

I've said something wrong? No, I've said something revealing . . .

Then the tension is gone as if it had never been there.

"Competition's good. It makes us stronger."

He's right, but something also tells me that Phaestion and House Julii will do anything to win, even if that means crushing rivals before things get competitive. I wonder if this is why other houses haven't challenged their fleet yet.

Giant tapestries of deep purple line the walls of the hangar, blending ancient heraldry with modern tech. The sondi ramp lowers, and Phaestion leads us down. An ancient man with snow-white hair and a beard waits surrounded by guards adorned in black and purple.

"I've returned, Father." Phaestion bows.

"My son," the old man says kindly. "Was your trip successful?"

Phaestion gestures to me. "May I present Edmon of House Leontes. Eldest born of Combat champion Edric Leontes."

I bristle. *Edric's eldest born.* That's all I am to anyone here. I suppose I need to learn to accept it. I bow. It's hard to believe that this hunched old man, nearly thrice the age of my father, is Phaestion's sire. Even harder to fathom that one day his son will willingly kill him to take his place.

"Leontes's boy." He grimaces. "Your hair is so dark? I thought you were blond."

Phaestion smiles. "You're thinking of his younger brother, Edgaard, Father. This is Edmon."

"Of course," the old man says indifferently.

I chew the inside of my cheek at the mention of the brother who has usurped me. Meanwhile, I can't keep my eyes off the diminutive figure standing next to the old man. He has extremely large eyes of an unnatural shade of blue that peer out from the shadows of his hooded robe. The black pupils narrow like a cat's as he catches me staring.

"Are you a spypsy?" I blurt out. "I've read about space gypsies in my books."

Alberich shifts uncomfortably behind me. Everyone averts their gazes.

"I'm sorry," I say, trying to recover from the outburst. "I've just read a lot about the six clans of spypsies that wander the Fracture, survivors of the great Miralian Empire."

"You seem to know more of such subjects than most on Tao." The man brushes back his hood to reveal a smooth skull. In fact, he's completely hairless—no eyebrows, no eyelashes. It's disconcerting. "I am Talousla Karr. I am a space gypsy, but I am not of the clans."

"Oh" is all I can say.

"Edmon's mother is a Daysider, your grace," Phaestion says, cutting in. "That's why his hair is so dark."

Lord Julii furrows his brow as if searching the back of his memory. "Yes, of course." He smiles at me. "You should be happy here with us, young Leontes. You will be a fine cadet in the academy, in spite of your disadvantage."

Disadvantage? My eyes narrow.

"Come, Phaestion," the old man says.

Phaestion escorts his father from the chamber. "I'll be seeing you around, Cadet Leontes."

What does he mean, Cadet?

The hairless man, Talousla Karr, looks at me with his cat eyes. "I was led to believe your Daysider race was the less intelligent of the two. Perhaps you'll have more surprises for me in the future." Then he, too, is gone.

Alberich looks down at me. "Remember what you've learned. We are precarious guests here, but Edric will still be watching." The seneschal strides off into the building. The rest of my father's guards return to the sondi as it revs its engines.

"Cadet," a tall man in a smart black Julii uniform says. "This way."

I follow the man down a marble hall, his polished boots clacking with every step. The hallway widens. One whole wall is a glass panel. I peer through it into a cavernous space. Scores of boys, all Nightsiders, dressed in black body armor form ranks in the room below. They ready shiny shields on their arms. High-powered pistols rest in their other hands. They fit the pistols into a groove at the top of the shields. On command, they march forward in formation.

Turn, pivot, pivot. Stop.

It's almost musical, I think.

"I am Commandant Vetruk," the man with the pointed face and graying hair beside me states. "I'm the principal of House Julii's Academy. Here you will be trained in the way of the pen and the sword."

"What are they doing?" I ask, indicating the boys below.

"Drilling," he responds. "Exercises are compulsory for all students. Lowborn as well as high." He emphasizes the word *low* as he scans my island garb.

I remember the disdain Nightsiders had for the clothes I wore at the christening all those years ago. I also remember that my father was, himself, a commoner before he rose to claim his titles.

The man's tone is clear—*I'm not worthy enough to be here.*

A pneumovator takes us several floors up to a barracks. The door slides open, revealing several other boys waiting for me.

"Attention!" Vetruk shouts.

Three pale-haired boys dressed in sleek black uniforms stand rigid-backed.

"This is Edmon of House Leontes. He's your new roommate. Edmon, this is Sigurd of House Flanders." Vetruk indicates a large, beefy boy with hair the color of pale straw and a broad face.

"Perdiccus of House Mughal." Vetruk indicates a slim athletic youth with hair of spun gold and large buggy eyes.

"And Hanschen of House Julii." He is the smallest of the three and pale of skin. He eyes me with a furtive gaze. His lips curve in a twisted smirk.

"Prepare him. Teacher Michio's astrophysics lab commences within an hour."

"Yes, Commandant!" the boys reply in unison.

Vetruk turns on a dime and leaves.

"Edmon of House Leontes," begins Hanschen.

Hanschen of House Julii, Vetruk had said. *Phaestion's cousin maybe?*

"Curious they would send us one so lowborn," the boy says, sneering. "Phaestion must have seen something in you if he wants you as one of The Companions."

Companions? I thought I was the only one.

"You should close your mouth, snail guppy," the one with the crazy eyes says.

Perdiccus of House Mughal. Mughal is one of the four High Houses of the Pantheon along with Flanders, Julii, and of course Old Wusong. They're all represented here. All except House Wusong, which has no male heir. It has only Miranda.

Miranda, my betrothed . . .

"Look at his dark hair and raggedy clothes!" exclaims Perdiccus. "You look like a whale-turding Daysider."

"I am a Daysider," I say defiantly.

They stare.

"You must be a good fighter," says the thuggish one, Sigurd.

He steps close, almost a full foot taller than me. He slams his fist into my solar plexus. I double over in pain, gasping for air. Perdiccus howls with laughter and leans against Sigurd as he slaps his own thigh.

"Hurts so much, Sig! Can't stop laughing!"

Sigurd grins, but he doesn't seem amused.

Hanschen kneels and pulls my chin toward his face. "Not a fighter then. You must have some other qualities Phaestion thought redeemable. You're pretty enough."

A chime sounds. The boys collectively sigh.

Sigurd cuts in. "Save the new-fish hazing for Combat practice. We're going to be late for astrophysics. Your bunk is the bottom, snail guppy. Don't cry tonight. I hate criers."

"I'm really scared," I mutter sarcastically.

"What did you say?" The tendons in Sigurd's neck flare like a bull's.

"You're clearly the smartest of the group," I say as I stand.

Damn it! Stop talking, Edmon.

The thug's brow furrows as he tries to discern whether I'm mocking him or not. Hanschen giggles under his breath.

"Shut up!" Sigurd commands. Hanschen quiets, and Sigurd stalks off. Perdiccus bursts into hysterical laughter before following like a hyena eel.

Hanschen lingers for a beat. "That was dumb, snail guppy. Now Sigurd will kill you."

"Would it be different if I'd said nothing?" I hold my stomach.

Hanschen shrugs. "Enjoy your licks while you can get them."

I walk into the classroom wearing the black military suit and shiny boots of a Julii cadet. Teacher Michio motions for me to take a seat next to the other "companions." The kimono that's hastily wrapped about his waist, his smooth pate, and his small stature tell me he isn't from Tao.

Perdiccus kicks the stool out from under me as I sit. I fall to the floor with a thud, and the other boys snicker.

Teacher Michio lets out an exhalation of frustration. "No interruptions, please."

I scramble to pull my stool underneath me.

"Where were we? Ah, yes, the propulsion force needed from a rocket to break Tao's high gravity atmosphere."

Teacher Michio goes on for the next hour about Tao's high level of gravity. He waxes on nuclear fuel production. He drones on about the synthesis of polymers for shuttle construction and the durability of high-grade transparent plastics against cosmic rays.

Sigurd yawns. Perdiccus draws shapes on his aquatablet. Only Hanschen listens intently, but even he doesn't appear to be taking notes. Meanwhile, I furiously write. I don't understand even half of what I transcribe.

Why am I here? I was so stupid to come. I miss home already.

Then Teacher Michio says something that catches my ear. "All matter and energy is created from tiny strings that vibrate."

I think of Gorham and his gap-toothed smile. *Everything is music, Edmon,* he would tell me. *Even the ancestors who have risen to the Elder Stars or those who became one with the great Mother Ocean are a part of it.*

Teacher Michio says the frequency at which everything vibrates creates the matter and energy of the known universe.

Gorham was right! Music is everywhere and everything. The fabric of existence is music.

I'm comforted to know that even here, I can still find the source of the thing I love best.

Then class is over. I follow the others into the hall. Perdiccus stabs me with his stylus in the small of my back. It punctures through the fabric to my skin. The point hits just the right nerve to send my back into a spasm. I collapse to the floor.

"Hurry up, snail guppy," Hanschen says, smirking.

I pick myself off the floor and hobble, trying to keep up. I look out the bay windows. Hundreds of other students are seated in a vast lecture hall below.

"Who are they?" I whisper as I catch up to Hanschen.

"Plebs." He shrugs. "Lowborn."

"They don't take classes with us?" I ask.

"We're The Companions," he says as if it explains everything. "We lead. They follow." He hurries into the next room.

Teacher Croack lectures on genetics. Whereas Michio was most certainly from off-world, Croack looks like the perfect Nightsider with his blond hair and muscular build. The lesson advances quickly from Punnett squares to RNA manipulation. Croack suggests the environment of Tao has mutated the inhabitants, namely us. High gravity evolved increased bone and muscle density. The low light of the Twilight Band forced Nightsiders to develop eyes more sensitive to light.

He recounts the environmental influence on culture. "The Combat and the Pavaka have eliminated weakness and congenital disease, ha-hmm."

He ends all of his sentences by clearing his throat. I find it extremely annoying.

"Strategic marriage between ruling houses has led to an elite class with superior mental and physical capacities, ha-hmm."

It's hard to believe that anyone who encourages a practice like the Pavaka, a ritual burning of babies with defects or disabilities, is considered "superior" in any way.

"The Tao Nightsider is the most perfect human form that has ever existed!" he exclaims.

"And Daysiders?" I ask.

The others gasp at my question.

Croack scowls. "Ha-hmm, Daysiders are born of Tao and share similar traits, hmm, but their race came to this planet sometime after the first human diaspora from Ancient Earth and is of inferior genetic stock. One cannot compare an island Daysider to the sculpted beauty of a Nightsider. Genetics is a complicated science, hmm, but the basic principles are simple. Each person is endowed by their creators with a unique pattern of potential. The Tao Nightsider is the pinnacle of potential." He nods with smug finality.

I believed my father was perfect. Until I met him.

"How do you know?" I ask.

"The Combat." The fact I've even asked annoys him. "Fighting is the art of assessing opponents' strengths and weaknesses. The Electors are even renovating the arena to provide deadly obstacles and puzzles. In a few years' time, the Combat will pit intellect against intellect more than ever, hmm. Body against body, in a fight for survival. The superior live to propagate. It's a natural extension of evolution pushing humanity to its limit, hah."

"The strongest, most capable, rule," Hanschen parrots.

"Not everyone competes in the Combat," I say. "What about those who don't?"

"If you're too scared to wager your life to attain power, then you don't deserve it in the first place." Perdiccus laughs.

"Power? What for?" I ask.

"What do you mean what for?" Perdiccus's crazy eyes widen.

"Why want power? To rule others?" I ask. "Winning the Combat might favor someone stronger or faster, or even smarter, but how does killing make you a better leader? Why not just be free and let others be free in return?"

"Freedom's an illusion," says Hanschen. "We're all controlled by hierarchical social structures whether it's parent and child, husband and wife, house and plebeian, whatever. Strong over weak is the primal law of nature. If you don't choose strength, someone else will."

"Complex society necessitates a system of structure," Perdiccus chimes in. "Tao democracy is based on natural selection because it is intrinsic to humanity."

"Why is intrinsic better?" I fire back.

"Because it is." Sigurd growls, silencing the rest of us. "We are better."

Perhaps I should keep my opinions to myself, but for some reason, I don't care. I feel deep down, they are wrong. "*Because I say so* isn't a valid argument."

Nadia would be proud.

Sigurd stands and looms over me. He's huge, ready to hit me to prove his point.

Hanschen grabs his arm. "Not yet. Soon," he whispers.

"Quiet!" Croack barks. He motions for Sigurd to sit down. "Debate is healthy, ha-hmm." Croack chews on the words. "It challenges us." He turns to me. "But this is not philosophy class, Leontes, hmm. The Combat is mental and physical. It favors strength but also critical thinking, ha-hmm. Our ancestors were warriors, and authority was measured by those who earned it. Strong propagated strong. It has always been thus."

"Just because it's always been, doesn't mean it always should be," I mutter.

"What?" His face grows red at my impertinence.

"What about scientists or doctors? Artists or musicians? Leaders have more responsibilities than fighting. They need to think in ways other than outmaneuvering sword thrusts."

The room bursts into laughter.

"Musicians!" shrieks Perdiccus.

My face heats with humiliation.

"Music, ha-hmm? Yes, we remember your proclamations in front of Old Wusong, Little Leontes"—Croack stands over me—"music won't save you when you have an enemy's knife at your throat, hmm. What will music do? The power to kill is the only true power in the Nine Corridors. Those who have it thrive. That's how humans rose from the muck to spread through the cosmos. Not by music or poetry, but by the ability to be better killers than anything else."

Teacher Michio said all energy vibrates. Gorham said that the universe was music.

What if it is, but it doesn't matter? What if survival is the only constant?

"What about space gypsies?" I ask softly, baiting a trap.

"Ha-hmm, spypsies?" Croack whirls on me.

"Space gypsies practically live their whole lives in micro-g."

Sigurd and Perdiccus look at me confusedly. Only Hanschen nods, following.

Croack shakes his head with frustration. "Your point?"

"Spypsies genetically engineer themselves for space. They have sticky pads on their hands and feet, hairless bodies so air recyclers won't get clogged, and flexible bones for more efficient skeletons. If fighting is the best measure of a man, the Combat might be the standard of perfection on Tao, but how could it be in a different environment, for a different culture, for a completely different type of person? Your rules of perfection are limited at best, arbitrary at worst."

"Gene-splicing is abomination!" Croack erupts. "Changing a genome in a lab is the coward's way to superiority, hmm. Let spypsies trade in their humanity and churn themselves into genetic stew. Let the Combat prepare the righteous of Tao!"

Our time recorders hum. Session has ended. We pick up our aquagraphic tablets and exit as Croack fumes behind us.

Righteous? I think. *He's mistaken. His perfection will not save him. The leviathan in my dream was right—everyone dies in the end.*

CHAPTER 7

Maestro

I stand on the floor of the Julii practice arena stripped to the waist. Sigurd, Perdiccus, and Hanschen are next to me. Around us, other boys, the rest of the Julii Academy, practice with weapons. They're lowborn, the ones I've seen from the bay windows of the hallways above. They drill and march. They practice martial arts against large mechanical automatons with spiked limbs and swiveling torsos.

I feel their eyes on me. I'm the only one in the room with hair duller than gold. They cast furtive glances and sometimes stare outright.

Yes, I am a stinking Daysider! I want to shout.

The only other boy I've seen who isn't blond is Phaestion, but he's not here now.

"What are those?" I whisper to Hanschen and point at the automatons.

"Training tools. They aren't conscious, of course, but they can observe patterns and increase difficulty to challenge our abilities."

I've heard of computers that can think. Most planets abhor them. The Great Song outlawed advanced machines when he arrived with his colonists on Tao. He proclaimed that machine consciousness had degraded human societies. Some historians argue that advanced machines were why the Miralian Empire crumbled. I stare at the mechanical dummies with fascination. Their clockwork gears seem deadly.

"Hanschen!" a gruff voice calls. "Sigurd, Perdiccus, choose your weapons."

Alberich lumbers forward, now dressed in the black uniform of a Julii teacher. I'm glad to see a familiar face, but I tighten my lips, remembering that he isn't my friend. He's merely a trainer and still serves my father.

Hanschen picks up a pair of short swords. Sigurd hefts a giant mace, while Perdiccus leans on a silver trident taken from a rack of weapons.

I reach out and grasp the smooth ivory handle of a katana sword. I've learned the single sword is my best weapon since it's really the only one I can use with any accuracy at all.

"Since my departure at the end of the previous cycle, I trust you've all kept up your training." Alberich nods at each of us. "Today, you welcome a new companion, Edmon Leontes. He will be observing."

"Lowborn," Perdiccus says, coughing.

"Quiet!" Alberich reprimands. "Sequential sparring. No shock vests. Mano a mano, then duo a mano."

Sharp weapons. No shock vests? This is not a child's game.

We touch our fists to our palms and bow with the sign of martial deference.

"Don't worry," Hanschen whispers to Sigurd. "A fight's a fight, no matter what the teacher says." Perdiccus grins.

"What about trio a mano?" asks Hanschen innocently. "There are four of us now that Edmon's joined. Mano a mano. Duo, then trio, right, Master?"

"I've said Edmon will not be participating." The seneschal shakes his head. "He will observe and work on forms."

They all sigh with indignation.

"Master Alberich," Hanschen pleads, "Edmon has to participate. He's one of us now. He can't be a companion without training with us. How do you expect him to command others without the respect that comes from fighting back-to-back?"

My eyes narrow with suspicion. *I'm not one of them.*

"I understand. That doesn't change my decision." Alberich knows he's being baited.

The whole arena watches. There's no mistaking their glances. I feel their contempt, their amused satisfaction. I haven't felt this scrutiny since my audience with Old Wusong. I'm exactly what they expected—a Daysider, weak, not fit. Alberich has confirmed it by not letting me participate.

Hanschen's right, I realize. *They will never respect me if I don't fight.*

"I'll fight." The words leap from my mouth before I've even formed the thought.

"No," Alberich says flatly. "Sigurd, first position."

The thuggish boy scowls and steps forward.

"I said, I'll go first," I repeat.

I step in front of Sigurd. He growls. "I could school you so easily if I wanted to."

"Then do it, bully," I return coldly.

"Quiet!" Alberich booms.

He strides toward me, his voice tight. "Edmon, I know you want to prove yourself—"

"I don't want to," I plead. "I have to."

"These boys have trained their whole lives—"

I take a deep breath. "They're all watching . . ."

It's true. The drills have stopped. All of them are slowly gathering around, like sharks smelling blood. Someone releases a camglobe in the arena. It floats through the hall capturing images, broadcasting them somewhere, for someone, I don't know who.

"They think I'm weak," I confide. "Do you think they'll ever accept me if I don't even try?"

"Edmon, you *are* weak," Alberich states flatly.

His words slam me like freezing water.

"I've done my best to teach you, but you aren't ready. If you think letting them watch you bleed like a stuck seal will convince them, you're wrong. No one respects a dead man. And if they do, you'll be dead anyway."

Death may not care, but they all do. My father does. I do.

I know what I must do—say something so harsh, he won't want to protect me.

"Is that why you called for mercy when my father took your hand, instead of facing your death like a real man?" I ask.

His face pales, then his expression hardens. He walks out of the match circle inscribed on the floor.

I ready my sword. Boys circle the ring, watching. "Mano a mano," Alberich calls out.

Sigurd steps forward, but Hanschen raises a hand. "Save the best for last," he says.

Sigurd scowls but lets Hanschen take position opposite me in the circle.

Hanschen twirls his dual short swords with aplomb.

My katana has greater reach, but Hanschen's blades have a speed advantage. He surprises me. He bats my sword aside quickly with one and slashes with the other. I twist at the last instant. It saves me from certain death, but the edge still grazes my shoulder. I dive-roll, then pop up into a crouch. I whip the katana behind me wildly in hopes I might catch my opponent. Hanschen's too clever for that, though. He stays well outside of the arc of my swing.

I guess we've started, I think.

Hanschen cleans the red of my blood from his blade with a finger. "Daysiders bleed easily, don't they, snail guppy?"

He leaps into the air, raising both of his swords. I'm reminded of my days on the beach drilling, over and over, the lessons with Phaestion, his voice in my ear—

Watch the movement of the elbows, the knees, the shoulders, the hips. Don't be there when they strike. Take the outside angle . . .

I sidestep, raising my blade. I could end this now with a killing blow. Instead, I drag the katana across Hanschen's upper thigh, and his leg opens. He smashes to the floor, howling in rage.

"Submit?" I ask.

He lashes out with his blade, catching my face. Blood fills my vision. I scream, more from shock than pain.

Are my eyes gone?

Hanschen's fist slams into my chest, knocking my sword from my grasp. It clatters to the floor. I clamber to reach it.

A faint voice echoes behind me, "Duo a mano!"

My fingertips scrape the katana's pommel. *Almost there!*

A trident slams down, piercing the back of my hand, skewering it to the mat. I scream as lightning shoots up my arm.

"Uh-unh," Perdiccus taunts.

He lifts the trident, its barbs pulling my arm with it. Perdiccus shakes the weapon violently. Chunks of my flesh tear away.

"Twisted!" He laughs.

"Come here, snail guppy." Hanschen limps to join his friend.

I crawl away. Hanschen lunges and slices my foot open. I lose a toe. I grab my sword in my uninjured hand and swing it wildly. It cuts Perdiccus's hand.

He shrieks and shakes his golden locks. He backs away, sucking on bloody fingers. "I'm hurt, snail guppy," he says. "After we showed you such kindness."

He stabs with his trident again. I roll. He keeps stabbing; I keep rolling. He catches me, spiking my already-maimed foot to the floor. I cry out, and he laughs.

"Trio a mano," Alberich calls.

Sigurd, nearly a head taller than the others, looms into view with his monstrous mace.

"You left nothing for me," he says, admonishing the others.

"We cut the meat," Hanschen says casually, "and left you the bones."

Perdiccus yanks the trident from my foot. My spurting blood paints their chests in swaths of red.

Sigurd's eyes dull as he approaches. I pull myself toward escape.

Why run, boy?

"Come on, Edmon!" somebody in the crowd shouts.

Another echoes, "Don't give up!"

Sigurd smacks the sword from my grasp with his mace. It skitters out of the ring. He raises his weapon again.

I do the only thing I can in that moment. I leap off my still-good leg and fling myself toward them, latching onto Sigurd like a leech. I sink my teeth into his neck, feeling hot, salty blood in my mouth. The thumb of my good hand digs into his eye. I press harder until I feel it pop. He screams.

From the corner of my eye, I see Perdiccus lunge with his trident. I drop out of the way. Sigurd takes the full stab of the barbs.

"Edmon! Edmon! Edmon!" I hear the crowd chanting.

I'm half-dead but emboldened. I know I've no chance. It doesn't matter. I roll toward Hanschen, tripping him. He crashes on top of me. My good fingers find the wound on his thigh. I dig into it, ripping back the skin. He howls, and I push him away.

Perdiccus jumps on me. He slams a fist into my face. I feel the bones in my nose crunch like a bundle of twigs. My fingers find his hair. I grab a fistful and slam his head against the floor again and again until he's out cold.

Sigurd stands. I see him through a bloody haze. Puss oozes from his ocular orbital.

"Edmon! Edmon! Edmon!"

I paint a trail of red as I crawl toward my sword. Before I can reach it, the mace comes down on my leg, smashing it to gelatin. Sigurd raises the club again.

I scream, "Go to hell, you piece of—"

An amniotic sleep. Voices. They slip in from the edge of consciousness. I hear a song, a lullaby my mother used to sing before Eventide sleep. I float on an ocean that stretches forever. Then I find myself washed ashore. It's twilight. I can see the Elder Stars. Something swims out in the music beyond. The monster . . .

You're mine, he says, laughing.

Light blurs in from the edges. I ache all over. I try to move and can't.

"He's waking," says a voice. "It will take him several weeks to function. Perhaps months to fully cope with the changes."

Changes?

"Leave us," another commands. I recognize the timbre. I heard it once in the throne room of Old Wusong.

Edric? I blink, and the chiseled features of my father glower at me.

His voice is ice. "You've survived."

When is he not angry?

"The next time you step into the arena, you won't lose. Do you understand?"

I try to speak, but no sound emerges.

"Prepare the sondi, Alberich. I'm leaving." He turns on his heel, his blue cloak flowing behind him.

Alberich comes into view. "Edmon, I'm sorry," he says.

Then he's gone, too. I close my eyes. I don't know for how long.

When I wake again, I see a flash of fiery hair.

"Phaestion?" I ask.

"Don't try to talk too much," he says. "You've had feeding tubes so your throat is probably a little sore."

"Where . . . ?"

He raises his hand to silence me. "You've been in House Julii's infirmary for almost two months undergoing reconstructive surgery. You almost died."

"You should've let me," I mutter.

I immediately regret speaking. My whole body thrums with a dull ache.

"Funny way to say thank you." He pulls up a chair and sits next to my bed. "Several ribs broken, massive concussion, your legs shattered, hand mangled, and a missing toe of all things." He smiles. "That shouldn't have happened. We usually train to first blood. Fortunately, the match was stopped before any blows landed on your head. I don't know why Alberich let it go on so long."

I can't say I helped him prevent it, but I wonder if the seneschal was motivated to let it happen the way it did.

If I had died, I'd clear the way for Edgaard as heir . . .

"They said you wouldn't last the night. If you did, you wouldn't walk again. Your father wasn't convinced we should try to save you."

Of course he wasn't. I'm weak. They were all right, the teachers, every one of them.

The realization hits me—*I'll never walk again . . .*

I wish I were dead.

"I knew Talousla Karr could repair you, though. Your father refused to pay for it, but it doesn't matter. I always get my way. But he did stay by your side almost every day," Phaestion adds.

"What?" I cough.

My father stayed? Perhaps he was waiting for me to die? I don't think he'll have to worry about me embarrassing him in the ring again.

"Don't worry," Phaestion says. "You'll earn your keep."

"Earn what? I'll never walk again, you said," I answer bitterly.

Phaestion bursts out laughing. "Edmon, didn't I just tell you? I always get my way."

"But my legs." I try to move. Everything hurts. Everything, I realize, *including my legs.*

He lays his hand on my shoulder. "We regrew new bones from osteografts cultivated from your old ones. Talousla Karr oversaw the procedure."

Talousla Karr—the slithering, hairless space gypsy.

"The last surgery was only a week ago. We reinforced the lacunae with a lattice formed from Nontheran spider silk. The engineered cells will eventually replace your whole skeleton. Your bones will be light and virtually unbreakable. Your tendons and muscles will be stronger, too. You will heal from injury extremely quickly. The bad news is you'll be in a lot of pain for the next year or so. A lot."

"Teacher Croack said artificial enhancements are against the law."

"What does he know?!" Phaestion says a little too angrily. "The law doesn't apply to people like us."

"Like us?"

"Laws are for common people with common minds. We create the laws for them."

"You should've let me die," I say again dully. Now, I'm not only a Daysider, but a genetically modified perversion, too.

"Edmon—"

"No!" I cut him off. "This isn't what I thought it was going to be. I thought it was to be you and me together. You said we were companions. Then you just left me with the others. They hate me. The teachers, too. They tried to kill me. Even my own father wants me dead!"

"Edmon . . . ," he starts.

"Get out!" I sob. It only makes me feel worse.

What did I do to deserve this?

Phaestion straightens. "You won't get pity from me. You're better than that."

His words sting.

"I'm different, too," he says.

"What do you mean?" I ask.

His eyes dart around, checking to see if someone is watching or listening.

"You and me, we're alike now."

"You've been . . . enhanced?" I ask.

"Something like that," he says with a small smile.

Most houses of the Pantheon practice genetic selection through arranged marriages. I've learned from my studies that gene-splicing was thought desirable until the animals of Tao were given human genes under the reign of Empress Boudika Wusong. The hybrids wrought havoc upon the planet's ecosystem, and genetic manipulation was outlawed. Boudika was forced to abdicate. Houses caught gene-splicing are immediately expelled from the Pantheon.

The way Phaestion looks, the way he moves . . . his admission means complications for both of us if anyone should find out.

"You won't tell anyone, Edmon?" He stares at me intensely.

"We're illegal."

"No," he says vehemently. "We're better. This is our world."

At this moment, I hate him. "I understand," I whisper through the pain of my throat.

He breaks into a cheerful grin. "That's why I'm not always around," he says. "My schooling's specific. I learn things more quickly than others so it wouldn't be a challenge for me to be in your grade. I still need you, though, Edmon. Just as I need the others. When we grow up, I want us to stay together."

"Why?" My eyes narrow.

Phaestion cocks his head in that quizzically innocent expression. "The houses have fought for generations, each trying to be supreme. What if we worked as one?"

"Why me?" I ask again. "Sigurd's strong. Hanschen's smart. Perdiccus is, well, he's something, too."

"Crazy?" Phaestion smiles.

"They're Nightsiders belonging to the four most powerful families of the Pantheon. I'm none of those things."

"You're right." He nods. "It should be your brother, Edgaard. He's young now, but he'll join us soon. He already competes at a very high level in the youth Combats. Almost as high as me at that age."

I glare at him, not wanting to hear about my perfect little brother.

"You're different," he says, changing tactics. "You like things like music. You're a common person. And the commoners love you. We may need that as well."

"What do you mean?"

"Ever since your meeting with Old Wusong, people all over Tao think you're one of them. They will follow you."

I still don't understand why that makes me valuable.

"You know, they broadcast your fight with Sigurd, Perdiccus, and Hanschen over the nets. A Daysider, with no hope of winning, and they cheered for you. A Daysider? That never happens," he says.

But I didn't win. And winning is all that matters to these people, to my father . . .

Phaestion shrugs. "It's because you never gave up."

We sit in silence for a moment. *Maybe it isn't always about winning,* I think.

"So you'll stay?" he asks.

"Do I have a choice?"

"You can go if you want, but I think you'll stay," he says, so sure of himself.

I think of the torment I've been through and what more will come if I stay.

"I arranged for you to have your own room. You'll still take classes with everyone and train with them, but you'll have your own quarters."

I say nothing.

"You'd leave even if I got you a new teacher?" he asks. He walks to the door. An old man enters at his beckon. He wears spectacles, and his skin is a shade I haven't seen before. He's not from Tao, either.

The man nods to me. "Master Leontes, Master Julii tells me that you're somewhat of a musical prodigy?"

I look at Phaestion then back to the old man.

"I am Maestro Luciano de Coranzo Bertinelli of the Sophia School of Music on Prospera, Lyria. I've trained some of the greatest singers and musicians of a generation there. It would be my honor to continue your musical education. It will be your honor to learn from me."

My jaw drops.

"You'll start catching flies if you keep your mouth open, snail guppy," Phaestion teases.

"Don't call me that. That's their word," I respond harshly, but I close my mouth.

"Then you'll stay?" Phaestion asks.

A music master from Lyria!

"Good," says The Maestro. "My only requirement is that you become the greatest musical talent of this planet."

The Maestro speaks as if he doesn't think that will be difficult. Of course, he's never heard Gorham play.

"I will," I say eagerly. "I promise."

"Told you you'd earn your keep." Phaestion waves casually as he swaggers out of the chamber.

"Very good." Maestro Bertinelli nods. "Shall we begin?"

CHAPTER 8

Molto Allegro

I am bedridden for over a month, but Phaestion comes a few hours every day. It reminds me of our days on Bone when we'd laugh and talk. There are no demands on either of us, nothing between us but our words and dreams. Then my body aches with torturous pain, my bones feel on fire, and he leaves to let me sleep in peace, sometimes for days.

The Maestro also begins his lessons. I lie in bed as he teaches me to breathe and perform simple vocal exercises.

"Do re mi fa so—"

"No, no, no!" The Maestro taps his baton against the edge of a music stand. "Cultivate a round, full sound. Air must come from the belly."

I try again.

"No, no, no . . ."

"But, Maestro, I'm lying down!" I argue.

"That means you have even less excuse. Air from the diaphragm. Not the chest. Like so."

He puts his hands over his stomach and demonstrates.

I try again. For days, then weeks. Occasionally, we stop when the pain in my bones is too great, and I fall into another fitful slumber, the sound of his baton like a metronome in my dreams.

Phaestion is there when I wake. "Fighting any sea monsters in those dreams of yours?" he asks.

I don't tell him about my nightmares anymore, but I do ask him something else that has been on my mind. "When can I speak with my mother, Phaestion?"

He grows quiet. "That won't be possible."

"Why?" I ask. "I need to tell her I'm all right."

"Part of the training," he answers. "We cut ties to our old families to create a new one. Worried parents look over shoulders. We have to learn to rely on ourselves."

"That doesn't mean we can't say hello once in a while. If we aren't training for our families, then what are we doing it for? House before self, says the Pantheon." I use Nightsider logic against him.

"That's the problem with this place, Edmon. Everyone on Tao fights for personal glory then for their family name. So long as we remain a collection of rival, back-biting houses, we'll never be strong. I'm trying to break that. I'm trying to create something greater: a nation. If we stood as one, we could conquer anything."

I hold the gaze of his metal-gray eyes. "Let me speak to my mother."

There is a tense beat.

"For you, Edmon, I'll make an exception."

I sigh in relief.

"You may write letters. They'll safely reach Bone, but I can't allow a response."

"Why?" I grow suspicious.

"I didn't want to say anything—"

"Tell me," I demand.

"That little stunt your mother pulled the day we left for Meridian was only a prelude. The islands are threatening revolt. Your mother is leading them."

"All the more reason I should write her," I plead. "If I tell her I'm all right, she'll be dissuaded."

"I hope so." Phaestion nods but doesn't seem convinced.

So, I write my mother, every day. I tell her I'm fine and that training is hard, but I'm learning a lot, especially about music. I know that will make her happy. I tell her I'm making new friends.

In other words, the letters are full of lies, but I know what is at stake.

I scream as I fall to the floor. "I can't do it!"

"You can," Phaestion says, kneeling by my side. "I know you can."

I want him to reach out, take my arm, and pull me back to my feet. Of course he doesn't. He insists I stand on my own. I grit my teeth and stand with the assistance of the medical leg braces. I wiggle my regenerated toe, amazed that I can feel it. It's a miracle I'm moving at all. I imagine the beat of Gorham's drum. I take a step to the music in my head. It feels like my bones are breaking all over again. I take another step, then another. The drums beat louder.

"You're doing it!"

The rhythm grows in intensity then . . .

"The pain!"

I collapse to the floor. He's right by my side again. His hand reaches out and touches mine. I look into his eyes, and he holds me in his gaze. I feel him wanting to lean into me, but instead he says, "You're amazing, Edmon. You'll be running in no time."

That's how we work for days and weeks. I step more and feel accomplished. The Maestro comes after walking lessons, and we breathe and sing. I feel I'm back to square one learning a completely different skill.

Lessons in biology, mathematics, physics, and history start getting sent to my aquareaders in the infirmary. I begin to feel the strain of being a "normal" Nightsider boy.

"I'm bored!" I shout one day maybe six months on, while trying to learn the lineages of the various houses for history.

Phaestion is practicing juggling.

"Song marries Flanders then marries Wu, becomes Old Wusong. Wusong has a son, but he's killed by Julii, and so Old Wusong's daughter becomes empress, expelling House Angevin because Julii is too powerful to expel, but they are still paladins . . . Who cares?" I blurt.

"It's our history." Phaestion shrugs. "Empress Boudika is pretty interesting, and Hektor the Mako Breaker. Of course, there is the Great Song . . ."

"You care about all this nonsense. I don't. These people are long dead. I'm concerned with where I'm going." I toss the aquareader to the foot of the bed.

Phaestion stops juggling. "Do you want to see how I study?" he asks conspiratorially.

I'm shocked. Phaestion's daily activities are a secret, not just from me, but from all companions.

"Come on." He pulls me out of the bed. I feel stabbing pain shoot up my legs with each step as we run down the hall, but I don't care. I'm too excited. It's the first time I've walked without the medical braces since my accident.

"Where are we going?" I ask, hobbling after him.

"This way!" he calls back over his shoulder.

I meet him in a pneumovator, panting from the exertion. He whispers, "Up." The pneumovator spirals us high through the Julii tower. I'm treated to my first view outside the walls of the infirmary in months. Meridian is dark and majestic as ever in the twilight. I'd forgotten how huge and distant the glass city looks from a high tower. Still, it seems claustrophobic and oppressive to an island boy.

"We're here!" I can tell he's almost giddy to have someone enter his world. I wonder if it's lonely for him, having to spend most of his days away from others his age. The doors slide open on a dark room. A catwalk leads into the center of a vast dome formed of cascading water. It's like being suspended inside a giant bubble.

"What is this place?" I ask.

"My study," Phaestion says. He leads me to the center of the room and calls out, "Lesson!" The entire chamber lights up as one massive aquagraphic. "Historical records mark the fall of the Miralian Empire circa 800 Post Fractural Collapse with the construction of seven arc ships . . ."

The lesson drones much like my own aquagraphic educationals, but this is obviously more impressive in scale.

"Split!" Phaestion calls. Suddenly the aquagraphic dome splits into two lessons simultaneously.

"You're doing two at once?"

"It's more efficient as long as my brain can retain the information." He smiles mischievously. "Split!"

Four lessons play. "Split!" he shouts. "Split! Split! Split!"

Eight. Sixteen. Thirty-two. Sixty-four!

"How many can you do?" I ask, astounded.

"I max out at over one hundred screens," he says as his eyes scan. "Then my retention is diminished."

He's showing off, the bastard, I think.

"This isn't even the fun part. Surveillance. Julii tower."

The aquagraphic lessons blink out and are replaced by images throughout the tower. I recognize students drilling. Vetruk is in his office. I see The Companions in Michio's physics class.

He could just watch us any time he wanted, know everything about us, I realize.

"I see everything that goes on." He nods, confirming my thoughts.

I point to an obscured image on the aquagraphic screen to my lower left. "Why is that one blurred out?"

Phaestion pushes my hand down swiftly. I almost lose my balance on still-wobbly legs. "Those are my father's quarters," he hisses, looking over his shoulders as if we, too, are being spied on.

"What about your mother? Where's she?" I ask. It's something I've always been curious about.

"I told you. She's a sea goddess." He releases a carefree laugh. I stare at him with seriousness, and he suddenly gets very quiet. "I don't have a mother."

For a moment, I see him not as some child demigod, but rather a sad little boy, all alone. I don't know what else to say, so I quickly change the subject. "What's that kid doing?" I ask, pointing to a naked boy in the barracks. His back is to the camglobe, but his arm is moving very quickly.

"Oh that," Phaestion replies with a shy laugh. "It's something with . . . your part."

"Oh," I say, a little shocked. "What?"

"It's hard to describe," he says, stammering. I've never seen Phaestion not quite in control before. "I tried it myself, but I couldn't make it happen like I've seen. I'm told it's because I'm not old enough, but it still feels good. I like watching when others do it."

"What are you talking about?" I ask confusedly.

But his enigmatic smile just returns. "You're not ready yet."

"Who are you to tell me when I'm ready?" I demand.

"Come on!" He grabs my arm.

We return to the hall with the pneumovator, and he pulls me along a maze of corridors and through a nondescript door into a small, pristine, white room. A weapons rack lies against one wall. A strange robotic suit stands in the center of the room, its back opened to the air.

"Is this—?"

"Where I train," he says, finishing my thought.

"It's so small." As impressive as his study was, his training room is equally dull.

"It may not look like much, but it's one of the most advanced physical training systems ever created," he corrects me haughtily.

He steps into the back of the iron suit, and the metal molds close, sealing him inside.

"What does it do, exactly?" I ask.

"Stand back!" Phaestion's voice is muffled by the helmet.

I plaster myself against the wall by the door as Phaestion lumbers toward the weapons rack. He grabs his rapier and dagger, then returns to the center of the room to begin a practice form.

He's not practicing a form, I realize. *He's fighting enemies I can't see.*

"The helmet and suit simulate opponents!" Phaestion calls out.

"Can it simulate anything?" I ask.

"Anything and anyone." He laughs.

All of those images of the Julii students, The Companions, all the footage of old Combats . . . he can access them with this training device!

"The suit can simulate environments," he continues. "Vacuum or increased gravity. Intense cold or heat. And this . . ."

He puts down his weapons. The suit vibrates, slow at first, then faster and faster. The hum becomes intense, uncontrollable. A sonic vibration stronger than any siren. I cover my ears.

Phaestion, inside the suit, screams in horrific pain.

"Stop!" I cry. "Stop, Phaestion, stop!"

The vibrating ceases almost as quickly as it began. The metal peels away softly like the skin of a fruit. Phaestion steps out, panting. He kneels on the floor, and I hobble forward.

"What was that?" I ask frantically.

"I call it the Arms of Agony," he says with a weary smile. "You remember when I showed you my siren swords?"

I remember I tried to hold them and was thrown to the ground, my nerves tingling.

"This suit is based on the same principal, only with the whole body. Talousla Karr invented it for me. It's based on his studies that physical pain unlocks our genetic potential. If we survive, we are molded into something stronger. That was only level one."

Only level one? I take in this disturbing thought. *Pain makes a person stronger.*

Then I have an even worse premonition—*my friend will die trying to achieve some unprecedented level of strength.*

I banish the idea quickly. I don't want to imagine losing the only person I can talk to in this new, weird world I find myself in.

—

The next day, Phaestion tells me he won't visit anymore or help with my therapy. I ask him why, and he simply says that now I can walk without the assistance of braces, and it is time for me to rejoin The Companions. I try to protest and tell him that is still terrifically painful to even move. Our little jaunt to his study has caused me to be bedridden again all morning. He simply shakes his head.

The shift is sudden. I know it has something to do with the fact that I've seen his secrets. I wonder if his father caught me with him. It doesn't matter. I'm to be sent back with the others.

I beg him not to make me go.

"Edmon," he says paternally, "you've already fought all three single-handedly—"

"They almost murdered me!" I protest.

"And you survived. You've nothing to fear. It's they who should fear." He stands.

"What do you mean?"

"You're stronger than they are, and they know it." He smiles. "Besides, if anyone ever took you from me, I would destroy them."

—

I rejoin The Companions on the morrow. My hands shake from fear as I limp into Teacher Michio's astrophysics class.

"Look who has come to join us," Hanschen says slyly.

My whole body stiffens as I remember the edge of his steel breaking my skin.

"He looks stronger than a manta." Perdiccus grins as he brushes a golden lock from his wild eyes.

I try to detect irony in his voice, but his enthusiasm seems genuine.

"If anything he's showing orca pride," Hanschen condescends.

"No," Sigurd interrupts. I turn to the brawny boy who meets my gaze. A regrown pale eye has replaced the one I injured in our fight. "He's a leviathan," Sigurd says.

I gape. *Sigurd, the most brutish bully I've ever known, is actually praising me? In spite of all he believes about his own race's superiority?*

"It's good to have you back, brother."

The high-pitched voice catches me off balance. Behind Sigurd, bright blue eyes framed by golden hair come into view. The square, open face of an eight-year-old boy breaks into a smile.

"Hello, Edgaard," I say, my voice hollow.

My bones mend fully, and soon I can walk without a limp. I feel pain all the time, but I grit my teeth through it. I think to myself, *If Phaestion can endure the Arms of Agony, I can endure this.*

I join The Companions in their sparring sessions a year to the day of my arrival. I am not yet allowed to match since I am still recovering, so I watch from the sidelines.

Phaestion was right. Edgaard is a phenom. At eight, the boy moves with a speed that's almost unnatural. His timing and balance are excellent. It's also no wonder that he's chosen the spear and shield as his weapons of choice.

Adopting our father's signature . . . this is what a son should be, I think.

"Edmon, did you see?" Edgaard comes running up to me after winning first blood against Perdiccus. I try to ignore him and concentrate on the training automaton that jabs me with its mechanical barbs.

"It was a lucky shot, sluggo!" Perdiccus calls as he limps to watch my training, too.

I hate when they look at me, I think. *They're always looking, judging.*

I leap over a spout of flame the training mech blasts at my feet. I feel shooting pain with the movement but force myself anyway. I land with wobbling balance. I feel my ligaments tear with excruciating pain, then almost as suddenly, pull back into taut alignment. *This is the new normal—pain, damage, fast healing.* I hate it.

"Yeah, you were great, Edgaard," I spit out through my concentration. I wish the boy were dead more days than not, but the others look at him almost like a mascot. He tags along on whatever they do, but it's me that he always looks at with a hopeful gaze, wanting some kind of approval. Ironic that all I can see is my replacement, a miniature version of my father.

The training automaton fires a spray of acid. I misjudge the timing, and it splashes my eyes. "Damn it!" I scream in agony and fall to the floor.

"Cease!" Alberich calls out.

Edgaard runs to my side and puts his arm around me. "Edmon, are you okay?"

"I'm fine," I say more harshly than I intend. I shove him off me and stand blinking through the sting. My tears flush out the acid, and I can feel my skin healing the burn already.

"Edmon, what level is this automaton on?" Alberich asks as he inspects the cylindrical monstrosity.

"Chaos pattern," I respond angrily.

I should have been more aware. My stupid brother distracted me.

"Whale turd!" Perdiccus shouts, incredulous.

"I told you to set the machines for repetitive only," Alberich says, castigating me.

"What can I say?" I mutter. "It was becoming . . . repetitive."

"I'm impressed." Hanschen saunters up. "And not just with your recovery." His eyes scan me up and down, like he's picturing me without my clothes. Even though the other Companions have been told not to harm me, they find ways to take liberties, to make me feel less powerful than they are.

"That's enough for the day," Alberich commands.

"I don't think so." I'm sick of sitting on the sidelines. I'm sick of being treated as second rate, incapable of competing. I hate them, yet I want to prove that I'm good enough to be one of them. I'm tired of being injured. I'm tired of following rules. "Automaton: training sequence advanced chaotic. Lethal force, engage."

The gears of the cylindrical metal dummy whir to life, forcing the others back. I dive into attack mode, raising my sword to parry thrusts and cuts from the robot's multiple limbs. Lights flash, and I dive under trip wires that fire from its base. I hold my breath as plumes of neutralizing gases are puffed into the air. I can almost feel a rhythm to the machine, a drumbeat.

Relax into it, Edmon. I feel Gorham beside me pounding on the drum.

Each melodic line may seem like chaos, but layered, they become a symphony, The Maestro reminds me with each tap of his baton.

I slice down with my sword, a final stroke, and suddenly the music ceases. Smoke emanates from the machine. A few of its limbs are bent at odd angles. I've won the sequence. I wipe sweat from my brow. The whole room stares at me with a look of shock.

"That was rip-curl!" Edgaard is the first to break the silence. He can't contain himself. He runs to me and wraps his arms around me.

I'm too exhausted to shove him off. "Yeah, thanks," I mutter.

"Not bad." Sigurd stalks forward, mace in hand. "Of course, training machines aren't the same as the living."

The idiot actually takes a swing at me. My heart thumps in terror for the briefest moment, but the rhythm of his movement is so easy. I have more than enough time to maneuver in front of Edgaard, protect him, and still duck the blow. One, two, three . . . it's like one of The Maestro's carefully crafted exercises. I fire my fist forward, unthinking, and land it squarely into his solar plexus. I feel the give of his diaphragm as he doubles over, gasping for air.

"You're right, Sigurd," I say. He stares at me, eyes wide with disbelief. "Training machines are definitely more difficult."

Out of the corner of my eye, I see a man in a hooded robe, Talousla Karr, nod to me and then exit the training room without a word.

Alberich drills us until we sweat, until we cry tears from exertion. Sometimes we bleed, too, but we are always healed. I cross swords with Hanschen, fists with Perdiccus, and wills with Sigurd. I become one of them, as much as I can be. I am a companion.

Perdiccus is the first to really warm to me. Every session he greets me with a smile and a punch on the shoulder. Hanschen makes a sly comment at someone's expense and then gives me a look, knowing that I'm the only one clever enough to understand without explanation. Sigurd is still dour—he thinks he's better than everyone—but he accepts me, knowing that I've survived his beating. He watches me slowly improve. We will face each other again, I know. Forgiveness is not expected in this Nightsider world. Vengeance, however, is considered inevitable.

My growing abilities gain me acceptance, but I can't shake my feelings of otherness. Outwardly, I mimic their behavior, I jest as they do, I fight as they do, and we compete and push one another. Inside,

I feel that they will never believe I'm equal. I'm born of a race that is considered inferior. Had the surgery not enabled me to hold my own in their deadly games, I wouldn't even be worth their notice. A seed of resentment and hate sprouts inside me, but I shove it down, deep as it can go. *Just try and fit in, Edmon. Do as they do,* I tell myself instead.

Every day I grow stronger. My mind turns to Phaestion. I haven't seen him for months. *Is he watching us? Is he training in the Arms of Agony?* A part of me itches to explore the parts of the tower he showed me, the areas beyond the levels delegated to cadets.

"Edmon, stop daydreaming!" The Maestro taps his baton. "I need your sforzando to crescendo to a full, round note."

"Yes, Maestro."

Music is still my solace, the time when I am truly myself. In all else, I learn to behave as the others do. When cut with an insult, I return their gibes with a laugh, a counter insult, or a punch to the gut when necessary. I keep my mouth shut in classes. I desperately want to fit in with these boys. In music, I can let that drop and just dream and sing.

My mother once told me that my father forgot where he came from while trying to gain acceptance to a world that would always look down on him. *Maybe she doesn't know everything, though,* I begin to think. She has oft told me how the Nightsiders are barbarians, how the islanders came to Tao long before them. She has told me that we are in touch with the Mother Ocean and the rhythms of life far more than they could ever be. It is not us who should be shamed and made to feel lesser. Now I wonder if there is a truth other than her stories.

Teacher Croack talks about evolution and how the environmental and cultural pressures of Tao have shaped its people's morphology. I wonder if there is a possibility that what he says is true, that the Nightsider phenotype is actually more physically and mentally capable than other humans. Might it be necessary to ensure the survival of the human species in the Nine Corridors of the Fracture through the spread of Nightsider genes and culture?

Camglobes hover, constantly observing. They float above our training and circle us when we taunt one another in the sanitizer afterward. They're there just before sleep.

Who is really watching? I wonder. *Is it Phaestion in his study, my father, or someone else?*

I am fourteen, and soon after my birthday, I learn that far more people are in on the show. Phaestion calls us to the throne room and presents us with beautiful blonde Nightsider concubines. One girl for each of us, even Edgaard, and a pretty, young boy for Hanschen. They gracefully walk toward us one by one as their names are mentioned.

My stomach turns at the suggestion that I'm supposed to become enamored with one of these girls simply because I'm told to. I feel embarrassed and ashamed when my concubine comes down the steps and touches my arm. The stirring I feel inside, the desire to grab her and press my mouth to hers, is irresistible and disgusting all at once. I'm almost a man now, and I'm supposed to know so much more about what is happening, but I feel so lost in my own body.

Then all of a sudden I think of Nadia when the girl touches me. I shove her gently and say, "No thank you."

Phaestion is perplexed when I demand to speak to him alone, but before he sends the others away, he plays another game.

"Sigurd." He motions the giant to step toward the throne. Phaestion reaches up, grasps the back of Sigurd's neck, and pulls him forehead to forehead in the gesture of brothers. "You are the only one my equal, the only one I trust to carry out the vision I have. We will share these spoils tonight, you and I, together."

Sigurd grins; the praise he hears undoubtedly echoes what he feels he deserves. I see Perdiccus scowl with jealousy and Hanschen look away. Hanschen knows it's a game, playing favorites and having us compete for Phaestion's affections, but it still cuts him. Phaestion wants us all to be friends with one another, but he wants us to love him more. He bestows praise and affection on one then removes it suddenly, tossing his favoritism to another so easily these days I can't keep track of who is considered the best of us. My love for him sours to bitterness when I reconsider all the moments on Bone and then in the infirmary as merely part of his grand act.

I feel nauseated when one of the concubines escorts my brother, now nine years old, from the room along with the others. Finally, however, it's just Phaestion and me again, at last, after so long. But my heart has become stone.

"Why did you do that?" I ask. "Why are you forcing us to be around these . . . concubines?"

"It's part of the programming, Edmon."

"Programming?" I demand.

"Camglobes record our actions and broadcast them over the nets," he explains as if to a child. "All of Meridian!" He gestures out the large bay windows to the megalopolis. "Of course it's edited, but we're very popular."

"It's our private lives!" I feel my anger growing.

"It generates a lot of revenue from merchants and vendors who want to sponsor the feed. Entertainment is an important source of income for House Julii. It helps the people get to know us, Edmon. You know better than anyone that leaders need the love of their people in order to govern. The programming creates personas that people bond to. When we're of age, they'll do whatever we want because we entertain them."

I can't argue with his logic, even though I feel extremely violated.

"Why haven't I heard from my mother?" I ask suddenly.

It has been months since I've thought of home. My letters have become fewer and less frequent. I guess these concubines and Phaestion's mention of governing have suddenly made me think of Bone and what I've been missing.

"You know your mother's attempted insurrection prevents her from communicating with you. Parental interference isn't allowed—"

"But everything is fine, right?" I regret my tone, but he shouldn't expect me to be his best friend if I only get to see him once every few months.

He puts his hand on my shoulder and says warmly, "Your letters diffused mass violence. You did a great service for your people and for the Pantheon."

I'm still uneasy. "Does my father know about all this? That you record us?"

"Of course!" Phaestion exclaims. "He's proud of you, Edmon."

He's lying.

"You just sent Edgaard off with a girl four years older than him. He's too young."

"He's young," Phaestion says, nodding. "But he's one of us. If he endures the same pains, he certainly should enjoy the same pleasures."

This feels wrong. Not a year ago he was saying that I wasn't ready to see such things on an aquagraphic. Now he parades sexuality in front of my nine-year-old brother without a care? Things are changing so fast. I am changing so fast, I feel like I'm losing myself.

"Edmon, my brother, you worry so much." He shakes his head and smiles.

And you, Phaestion, my brother, are playing with us, like an orca plays with his food.

The coldness of my thoughts sting, and anger begins to burn inside me.

It is sleeping hours after the yearly Combat and Pavaka in Meridian. A champion from House Temujin has won in the arena. The Census, in their faceless masks and black robes, have claimed the unfit babes from the mothers of the city. They've marched them to the cauldrons for extermination in the Pavaka. For the first time, The Companions are old enough to attend the subsequent fertility ritual in celebration of a new year. After the killing of the Combat and the culling of the Pavaka, the orgiastic rites represent a rebirth. All men and women of reproductive age mate in a drunken haze to release the pain of the past days and begin a new generation. It is supposed to be a joyous occasion. I have refused, instead choosing to return to my quarters and sleep. I don't feel very joyous.

I turn over and curl into a ball, trying to relax, but my body is tense. I'm angry at everything—this strange surgery that was forced upon me, the behavior of these Nightsider boys, the fact I am growing and becoming more and more like them every day. It's been two years. I miss my mother and Nadia and Gorham. I miss the sunlight . . .

To the fathoms with you, Phaestion! I thought you were my friend. All you do is keep secrets. You think you're special. Well, you're not the only one. Not anymore! I rip the covers off me and throw them to the floor. A silver camglobe whisks through the air to avoid the sheets.

Damn thing! I leap off my bed and snag it midair. I hurl it against the wall, smashing it to pieces. I'm tired of being a good little cadet.

I head into the hall, crouched low like a spy. Everyone should be in the throne room, but House Julii's camglobes hover everywhere. I pad barefoot down the hallway toward the pneumovator. "Up," I whisper. The ride is a matter of seconds but feels like an eternity with the fear that I'm being watched. When the doors open, I find myself in the maze of white halls where Phaestion brought me that day a year ago. I hear a noise, and I quickly turn a corner so as not to be discovered.

"This way." The voice is Hanschen's. I peer around the edge. "I think there's an empty room over here," he says.

He is coming from the throne room where the festivities of the fertility ritual are taking place. Shirtless, his pale skin shows the lithe musculature of a boy maturing into a teenager. I can't see who is holding his hand, though, so I hold my breath, only releasing it when they've passed.

I haven't gotten what I came for yet, but I can't help myself. I have to take a look. I pad to the double doors that open to Phaestion's personal throne room. I gently push back one panel and peer in. The chamber is full of naked bodies, undulating against one another. They moan and yell, but I don't think they're in pain, or at least it's an unfamiliar kind of pain. Some are on tables, others pressed against walls. Some lie nude on the floor. I see Perdiccus and Sigurd among the throng. I even spy our teachers Michio and Croack and Commandant Vetruk, all naked and entangled with one another and the concubines of House Julii. A pair of bouncing breasts flashes across my vision. Hips grind against one another. Drums beat. This is not the gentle Eventide feasts of Bone, though. This is something different, something wild.

Phaestion sits lazily on the throne, taking in the scene with cool gray eyes, even as several naked girls fawn over him. Talousla Karr hovers behind him, his freakish blue cat eyes observing with alien detachment. Only Alberich stands fully clothed and apart. He scowls and shifts nervously through the whole endeavor. I silently close the door and take a few steps back.

At least they're occupied, I think as I take off down the hall at a sprint. I turn one corner and then another, navigating my way through the maze of white halls. Finally, I arrive at the nondescript door that I remember from a year and a half ago.

In the unadorned room stands the weapons rack and the iron suit—the Arms of Agony. I step forward, somehow knowing what I am about to do will, in my friend's mind, transgress beyond anything I've just witnessed. I enter the suit.

Instantly, I'm enveloped in a new world, a wasteland of gray sand and tumultuous clouds. Lightning sparks from the swirling nimbus above, seeming almost alive. There is some sort of structure on the distant horizon. I cannot make it out from here, but it looks like a white rose beneath the eye of the maelstrom. Lightning discharges from the storm, striking the distant rose.

This world is alien, yet it feels somehow strangely familiar . . .

"You're not Phaestion."

I whip around to identify the speaker. I find myself face-to-face with a boy. He has thick dark hair and green eyes. His skin is tanner than I've seen it lately. He stares at me kindly. I haven't seen that expression in quite some time, either. "And you're not Edmon," I reply acidly.

The boy attempts to circle me. I match his movements. It is like staring into a perverse mirror.

"Are you here to fight me?" pseudo Edmon asks. Suddenly, a sword is in his hand. It is beautiful, silver, with a hollow pommel and a leviathan bisecting the empty space.

"No," I reply.

"Are you here for other things?" the boy asks.

"What other things?" I remember the weapons rack. Through my peripheral vision, I spy it a few meters away in the wasteland. I sidle to it, and my hand grips a sword.

"Sometimes we war. Sometimes we touch," the boy says and smiles. "Like Chilleus and Cuillan."

I'm betraying Phaestion by being here, but is it any worse than the way he's betrayed me? I haven't seen him for months. Now, I come to find that all this time he's been training, not alone, but with me—a corruption of me. If this thing's words are to be believed, Phaestion has taken liberties with this pale shadow that he knows I would never allow.

"I'm here to fight," I say, "but not you."

The boy freezes. His head cocks to the side. "Recalculating parameters," it says. "Recognize subject, Leontes, Edmon. Recalibration completed. Please specify opponent."

"Phaestion of the Julii," I say.

The boy's face melds into the perfectly symmetrical features of the red-haired prince. He stands a few centimeters taller than me, his shoulders broadened by the beginning of his maturation. His single sword has become two—rapier and dagger. The resemblance is uncanny. "Note the representation of subject Julii, Phaestion is not complete."

"Why?" I ask.

"Subject's athletic creativity is beyond the scope of artificial pattern recognition," the new boy says.

"Understood."

No sooner do I say the word than the simulacrum leaps toward me with blinding speed. I barely have time to move from the attack. Phaestion stutter steps, and I misjudge his feint. His dagger plunges into my thigh. I feel every inch of the blade as it slides through my flesh, even though I know it is only virtual. Our swords clash. I've improved much in the months with Alberich's tutelage and alongside the other Companions. This, however, is inhuman.

My arm is cut. I transfer my sword to my other hand to deflect his next strike. I shoulder into the boy to tackle him, only to find him easily sidestepping my blow. My face plows into the gray ash of the desert. The boy laughs. "Oh, Edmon, so silly to even think . . ."

I stand, readying myself again. The ersatz Phaestion smirks, excited for the challenge. *Well, they got that part of the simulation correct,* I think.

The way he moves, so quick, is always keeping me off-kilter. I can't time him. My belly is sliced. Then my back. It's not just that he's too fast. He's too unpredictable.

I remember something that Gorham told me once. The balance of music is defined not by the sound, but the negative space created in the absence of it. The friction between the beat and the silence is what beckons the listener. Phaestion's fighting is beyond even the improvisational songs of the Eventide feast. He's not using known patterns or even layers of patterns in his creations. It's pure chaotic noise, but there is a musicality through the negative space. If I can time that, then . . .

There! My sword strikes toward the earth where he should not step. It impales his foot and pins him in place. I grin with satisfaction.

"Not bad, Leontes," he says. He lashes out with an elbow, smacking me in the face. I'm stunned. He wraps his white arms around me in an embrace. "But not good enough."

Suddenly, my body vibrates as Phaestion's mouth opens. He releases a scream. My nose and ears bleed. My brain feels like it will liquefy. Lightning swirls around us. *The Arms of Agony,* I realize.

"What level is this?" I cry above the noise.

"Level one," the voice says almost directly into my mind.

"Is that all you've got?" I shout. "Give me more!"

"Commencing level two."

"More!" I scream.

"Initiating level three."

My body vibrates with so much energy that I feel it is disintegrating atom by atom. Then suddenly all is black. I awake panting on the floor of the practice room in a cold sweat. Phaestion, the real Phaestion, stands over me.

"Did you see that?" I gasp with giddiness. "The Arms of Agony, Phaestion. Level three."

I look up into his face. He is not smiling. All I see is the accusation of betrayal behind his gray gaze. "You think you've beaten me?" he asks. I've seen haughtiness in him before, competitiveness, yes, airs of superiority, sure, but never has he seemed truly angry. Is it because he's actually threatened by the fact that I've achieved something he hasn't? Or is it that I went behind his back to do it and used our friendship for my own gain?

Now he's not the only one who can use and manipulate friends, I think.

I slowly stand. I feel almost the same as when I awoke from Talousla Karr's twisted surgery—reborn. "I don't think I've beaten you. I know." It's the cruelest thing I can think to say to him in this moment, challenging his precious pride. I don't know why I hit him so decisively where I know he is vulnerable. Is it because I'm hurt by the fact that I'm no longer special to him, above the other Companions? Is it because I know he has secrets and plans that he doesn't share with me? Maybe it's also partly because I just want to see if I can.

Rage boils inside him; I see it in his eyes, and it is frightening. For the first time since our friendship, I'm scared that challenging him will lead to serious hurt.

Then it is gone instantly, and he walks away, saying over his shoulder, "It's just a simulation. I'll have a real test for you soon, son of Leontes."

CHAPTER 9

Banda

I await a punishment that doesn't come. Time passes more swiftly than I realize, and my dread slowly recedes as I carry on at the Julii Academy. Respite from cares comes with music lessons at the end of the day. It's the only time the camglobes are not hovering and watching everything, the only time I feel alone and truly unconfined. Even with the constant criticism . . .

"Ho-ho! Ho-ho! Ho-hey!" I sing.

"From the dan t'ian, Edmon!" The Maestro shouts.

"Schmie-de mein ham-mer ein hartes Schwert!"

"Attack the notes!"

"Ho-ho! Ha-hei! Ho-hey!"

"Sforzando! Remember, you are Siegfried reforging your father's sword!"

"Einst farb-te Blut dein fal-bes Blau!"

"Enough! Enough!" The Maestro taps the edge of the music stand with his baton.

Damn it. My ancient German was off.

The tongues of the ancestors aren't exactly intuitive. (Except maybe ancient Italian. Italian rolls off the tongue as if it were the only language ever meant to be spoken.) The Maestro didn't like my vowel tones. He didn't like the way I held the dotted quarter on the last phrase. I threw the timing off.

By the twisted star!

I've never had a tougher teacher, but every moment is worth it. I could do this forever. So I'm ready for the complaints leveled against me.

"Why did I stop you?" Maestro Bertinelli peers over his spectacles.

At fifteen, I'm already several inches taller than him. My gangly body is awkward, out of proportion. Just when I was getting coordinated enough to be able to stand against the others in Combat training, it feels like I have to relearn everything. My voice breaks, and I'm forced from my comfortable alto vocal range into tenor and baritone. My joints still ache, but the pain is starting to lessen. I don't know if it will ever go away completely.

The Maestro doesn't comment on these changes. He only proceeds to give me new music with relentless instruction. I learn to hit notes in both tenor and bass range. The Maestro makes me work harder. He's frustrated I spend time in classes other than music. If he had his way, I'd study only opera, but Commandant Vetruk makes no exceptions.

"You're lucky to be here at all," he says.

I'm ruining his perfectly homogenous student body.

"Phaestion's an exception," I point out.

Vetruk's face pinches. "Do not question me, cadet."

That's the end of that.

So I practice, practice, practice, singing whenever I can.

"You can only be truly great at something if you dedicate your life solely to that thing!" exclaims The Maestro over my singing.

I'd do music and nothing else if it were my choice, though sometimes I wonder if a life dedicated to only one thing is really that wonderful of a life.

"Why did I stop you?" he asks again.

I take a deep breath. "My pronunciation was off." He says nothing. "The tone of my vowels was not pure," I continue. "I could've attacked the first note of the second verse with more vigor."

"Edmon"—he removes his spectacles—"your performance was technical perfection."

Technical perfection? My breath catches.

"What you lack, I cannot teach."

My brow furrows.

"Edmon, do you want to do this? For your life?"

"More than anything!" I exclaim desperately.

"That!" He holds out his hands. "That's the feeling I need to hear with every note, the utter commitment to the music. I need to know with every lilt, every vibrato, that this is what you live for."

I remember once Alberich told me the same thing about fighting—desire is the undefinable element.

"Edmon," he says, and taps his conductor's baton, interrupting my train of thought. "This piece is about a hero named Siegfried, forging his sword. I chose this music because it's a youth creating a destiny. Do you believe music is your destiny?"

"I do."

"Then feel it when you sing." He stands and grips my shoulders. "You're one of the finest students I've ever taught. Including Andreas Catalano."

Maestro Bertinelli often mentions Andreas, the prodigy at the Sophia School of Music. His voice is so perfect, it's rumored that he's a designer organic, an artificially created human with special abilities. His music is so popular across the Centra Fracture he has earned the title "Voice of a Generation."

"You're going to have to make a choice, Edmon."

I nod. "I'm just afraid they won't let me."

"They may not," he says. "However, I believe that responsibility to yourself supersedes any that others place upon you."

"You don't understand." I don't know how to explain it to him.

"Would you like to record something?" he asks slyly. "Perhaps an aria or some other small piece of music?"

The offer is tantalizing. *If I record, then there will be no denying my talent. Perhaps my father would see fit to utilize those skills in some way. Maybe he'll understand how I could bring acclaim rather than shame to our family name?*

"Edmon, if music is what you want, we continue. If it's not, then I think my time with you is over."

I want to argue, but I know he's right. *If music won't be my life, then I've come as far as I can with him.* I imagine my life like a mirror fractured down the center, each showing a different future—

One reflection shows me something not unlike the celebrity of Andreas Catalano. I am a student at the Sophia Academy on Lyria, studying in great libraries and concert halls. I am walking down the great steps of the palazzo, talking with the grand masters and the other artists and musicians of the age. I am traveling the stars, singing for kings and diplomats. I see green worlds of woods and forests, I see desert palaces, and I see Nadia beside me as we stargaze from the cupola of a grand cruiser, young and free, exploring the Fracture together.

The other life shows me in an arena with the blood of underclass gladiators splashed across my skin. I wear the black Julii uniform and stand among the other Companions behind Phaestion as he addresses the Electors from a Synod podium. Edgaard is there, too, only he sits on the Synod alongside Phaestion. Our father looks at him proudly, while I remain in the background, unnoticed, barely tolerated. Nadia is nowhere to be seen, and the sun of the island is gone, but Miranda Wusong is there. I lift a wedding veil to reveal a white face and black teeth. I see myself pretending to listen as Phaestion teases me and boasts of how he accomplishes great things, Hanschen adds a sly comment, Perdiccus laughs like a hyena fish, and Sigurd threatens me. My heart beats faster because I want to scream and run from this vision, but I can't. There's nowhere to go.

I take a deep breath, calming my fears. *This is no choice at all.*

"I've made my decision, Maestro. I want to become a singer. The greatest I can be."

He smiles, pleased.

"Then I'm happy to tell you that I've actually already recorded you," he says.

My jaw drops. *He's already . . . ?*

"I had an aquagraphic mixer placed in the room to capture last week's lesson."

"Maestro!" Betrayal, elation, and excitement all comingle.

"Forgive me," he says. "I feared you would say no. Or somehow the Julii would interfere. It took some doing, but I bypassed tower security and released the recording anonymously on the nets."

"Did people listen?" I'm scared to know the answer.

"Siegfried's song is 'warrior music,'" he says. "Forging swords, fighting, a mythical dragon . . . the people of Meridian go for this sort of thing, yes? Edmon, they've gone, how does your planet say it? Wave?"

Wave! I let out a whoop.

"Practically the whole of Meridian has heard it," he continues over my excitement. "I also transferred them to binary code cylinder for shipment via UFP courier to the dean of admissions at the Sophia School of Music."

The Sophia School of Music in Lyria?

"Edmon, if you want it, I believe there will be a place for you there."

"Maestro . . ." My breath comes fast. I think back on our first lessons and The Maestro reprimanding me for merely breathing wrong. I've worked so hard, and now my dream is coming true.

Is this real? I think of Nadia. I haven't seen her in years. Still, I wish she were here to share in this moment.

"Edmon!"

We both turn at the new voice. Perdiccus stands in the doorway. Wild strands of gold hair hang in his eyes.

"I've been looking everywhere for you!"

"What is it?" I try to cover my excitement.

"It's Phaestion. He's set up a special training exercise for The Companions, the last of the season. Come on!" He grabs my arm, and all my thoughts slip away. The next thing I know, we're running down the hall, and my heart drops to the pit of my stomach.

Phaestion's test has arrived.

The wind whips my hair. I stare out my Plexiglass face mask at a searing drop. The other Companions are next to me in front of the open sondi carriage door, decked out in black body armor. The armor will unfold into a winged flight suit when we jump. And we are jumping.

I toe the edge and look down out the open door. The caps of the towers of Meridian just peek above the fog cover from the nearby sea. The moons of Chang and Hou are visible in the gloaming. Chang is a green sickle, while Hou is but a mere sliver of silver. My heart pounds.

This is too damn high.

"The rules have changed." Phaestion's voice pipes in over the helmet comms. "Over the centuries, young fighters of the Combat have grown in skill and prowess, attempting more daring feats. It is no longer enough to simply win with martial skill. You must entertain. That is what drives the economic viability of our most hallowed blood sport. It is what the people demand of their Electors. So the High Synod has decreed an advancement in the technology of the arena. No longer will the Combat simply pit fighter against fighter. The arena itself will be armed with obstacles and mechanized weaponry to murder her challengers."

I wish he'd cut the monologue, but I know he records this for the same purpose, to broadcast our feats for the latest episode of *The Exploits of The Companions.*

"You have already been well trained by Alberich and the automatons of our practice arena. Now it is time to test your skills in the real world. House Julii and the students of her academy will be second to none!"

"Aroo!" the other Companions shout in response.

"The game is simple. You each have been given coordinates in your heads-up display."

My face mask lights up with the time, date, altitude, wind speed, and information on the skyscrapers that claw from the city streets up into the sky. Then a bright red beacon blips.

"At these coordinates is a data card. Jump into the city, travel to the coordinates, and recover it. Return to the sondi that waits above the Banshee Rail. Whoever returns first with the data card in hand wins the graduation prize."

"What's the trick?" Hanschen interrupts over the headset. He smirks behind his mask. In the years since our first fight, I've grown physically stronger than him, but he's always been the cleverest of the others, the most likely to strike when my back is turned.

"The trick"—I feel Phaestion grinning over the comm—"is that the rest of the academy members wait at points throughout the district to stop you."

"Lovely," Sigurd growls.

"Easy, Sig," says Perdiccus. "This is going to be fun. Right, Ed?" He nudges me.

"We haven't heard what the prize is," I say bluntly.

"Oh, Edmon," admonishes Hanschen. "Must there always be a reason?" He winks and eyes me flirtatiously.

"Yes," I say, deadpan.

Sigurd snickers.

"Your loss, beautiful." Hanschen shrugs.

This has become routine—Hanschen flirts, and the others laugh. While I attempt to fit in, he will attempt revenge when the moment is right.

"As I said, there's a gift waiting for the Companion who returns with the data card first."

I picture the red-haired youth sitting on his posh throne in the Julii tower watching us squabble on an aquagraphic. This has also been routine—Phaestion talking to us from on high, sparingly handing out praise and affection. He'll hold celebrations where he will invite only one of us, but not the others. He'll join us in the practice arena every once in a while, holding court among the boys, but choosing to ostracize one. The constant competing for approval has started to wear thin for me. Phaestion used to be my friend unconditionally. Now we all fight for him like a pack of wolf eels.

"Approaching drop zone," the pilot's voice says, cutting in over the intercom.

"You will be competing against the plebeian cadets of the academy and against one another as well." Phaestion laughs.

Competing for him, I think angrily.

I flip my headset to a private channel. "Phaestion."

The sophistication of this point-to-point satellite transmission is quite beyond anything Tao had even a decade ago. Slowly the Pantheon has been incorporating the tech of other worlds into their arsenals.

"Edmon?"

"Why are you doing this?" I ask.

"Doing what?" he responds. He's probably cocking his head to the side in mock innocence.

"Dropping us out of a sondi, having us scavenge, pitting us against each other?"

"It's just a simulation, Edmon," he says coolly, his words the same as they were that night.

This whole thing is to punish me.

"This is how soldiers fight," he says.

"We aren't soldiers," I argue.

"We've always been warriors. That's our heritage. You haven't seen the new arena the Electors have been creating. Since the Fracture Point opened, the Pantheon has been looking to sell the broadcasts and feeds to extraterrestrial markets. They have to make it more dangerous, more exciting. It's a new world. We have to be ready."

I see the steely determination in Sigurd's eyes, Perdiccus's excitement for the challenge, and the mental calculations Hanschen's going through. All of it for Phaestion's love and approval. He has us in the palm of his hand.

"Edgaard is too young," I say with a snarl.

I turn and see my eleven-year-old brother tightening the straps of his suit. He's small but hearty, with a wide, square face. He tightens the final strap, completely capable even at this age, a miniature version of what my father must have been like as a boy. There is one crucial difference—Edric's pale eyes are cold and hard. Edgaard's soft blues are warm and kind.

"Perdiccus is right. This is going to be fun!" Edgaard beams.

"Edgaard isn't the weak seal pup you were when you first started training. He's pure Nightsider," Perdiccus gibes.

It's true. Edgaard isn't plagued with the same lack of skill, nor crippling sensitivity, but I'm not the same boy anymore, either. I'm stronger, my bones tougher than before. Physically, I'm now their equal. I've learned to show them a cold, hard side of myself. In the pit of my heart, though, it's a lie. I'm not one of them, not truly. I am half Daysider, after all. The teachers' insistence that the superiority of Nightsider instruction is the source of my achievements quells any question, yet everything from the lessons with The Maestro, to my old home Bone, to my dark hair screams to us all—*I am different.*

I shove the feeling aside. *You are who you say you are, Edmon, and you say you are one of them right now.*

Perdiccus punches me on the arm when he catches me staring at Edgaard. "You don't give your little brother enough credit."

Edgaard smiles. "I'm going to come in first. Our father will be proud."

"You think he's watching?" I ask. Even in the sondi, camglobes hover around us.

"He's always watching, Edmon." Edgaard nods solemnly.

No doubt the floating silver orbs will track the whole contest just as they've been broadcasting our program for years now. *The Exploits of The Companions* has been one of the most popular entertainment aquagraphics on the nets. Not that I've helped the ratings. I've refused to accept a concubine or allow a camglobe during my music lessons. In little ways, I've been a thorn in House Julii's attempt to create a narrative about us even as I've tried to fit in.

I don't care, I tell myself. *The Maestro said I might be able to go to Lyria—*

"Prepare to disembark," the pilot's voice says, cutting into my thoughts.

Perdiccus steps up to the open bay door. "Last one home suffers the humiliation." He sticks out his tongue and lets himself fall into the twilight.

Sigurd scowls at me. "Don't get in my way. Or do. I might enjoy that." He jumps.

Sigurd's always baiting me these days. It's his way of showing friendship, if in fact you could say he's truly friends with anyone. I can tell he doesn't like how much I've improved. It's threatening.

"They're numbskulls," Hanschen says. "But they're strong numbskulls. Neither of us could take them alone."

"But if we team up?" I already know where Hanschen's mind is going. He's faster than any of us and could outrun them, but if it comes to a fight, he's at a disadvantage. The way to win is to form an alliance.

"Great minds . . ." Hanschen leers. "Whaddya say, gorgeous?"

"You and me, stunner," I say. "They won't know—"

"What hit 'em," Hanschen finishes. He grins and steps out of the carriage door, diving toward the surface of Tao like a torpedo.

I peer over the edge. My heart leaps into my gullet.

"Edmon." My little brother's voice catches me. He looks at me with innocent blue eyes. "Did you just make a deal with Hanschen?"

"If I did?" I ask. Part of me still resents him. He has everything that should be mine. It's not his fault. He's not our father. "Only one of us can win. Hanschen will betray me as soon as he has the opportunity, but I'd rather have to deal with him at the end than Perdiccus or Sigurd."

Edgaard nods. "How do you know he hasn't already made the same kind of agreement with one of them?"

"Smart thinking. Does it make any difference if he did?"

"I guess not?"

"You first." I motion.

He steps up to the doorway but stops. "What about me? Will you betray me if you get the chance?"

Should I lie? Should I tell him I'd never betray him?

"You're my brother, Edgaard" is all I can say.

He smiles and steps into the atmo.

The rush of the wind is in my ears. I tense. My pulse quickens.

By the twisted star, I don't think I can do this.

"Drop zone window closing," the pilot's voice reverberates.

If I don't jump now, I won't ever. The thought hits me. *Maybe I shouldn't.* I've made a choice to follow my heart, to follow music. What does it matter if I don't play their games? I step away from the door, but the dirigible banks, and I lose my footing. I stumble out of the bay and tumble into twilight.

—

End over end, I flip as I fall. Cityscape alternates with sky. I struggle to right myself. The altimeter readout on my windshield scrolls furiously. I click my heels, bring my arms to my sides, and dive to the surface like a missile. Hooks spring from the sides of my armor and clasp my wrists. I spread my arms and tuck my chin, and a pair of mantalike wings deploy. The spider silk catches the air.

I'm a feather on the current, the skyline of Meridian stretched out before me. The world at this height seems still and beautiful. The red eye of the sun is to my left, the blackness of night to my right. A veil of stars waits there framed by the slivers of the moons, beckoning me, but the beacon in my windshield flashes. I bank left at its indication. The data card's homing device calls my armor like a pulse in my nervous system. The others must feel the same pull. Thoughts of quitting sift to the back of my brain. I circle to slow my descent, floating into the mist between two scrapers.

The buildings here are run down and dirt covered, the glass of their windowpanes shattered and broken. The ground gapes open, revealing the massive cylindrical shaft of an arcology. I descend into the darkness of this enormous vertical tunnel dug into the crust of the planet. Within the outer edge of the arco tube are the hundreds of levels of residences, storefronts, and power centers for the self-contained mini-city. Lights from the upper residential district glitter and fade as I fall into the lower industrial levels.

I swoop onto a landing pad that juts out from the side of the massive cylinder. The pavement comes zooming up at me, and I pull my arms and legs wide to hover. My feet hit; I drop and roll and come up in a crouched position. There's broken glass everywhere, chunks of building strewn here and there. I walk from the platform through a doorway into the heart of the arco.

A hallway leads to a run-down interior courtyard. Synthetic green turf and fabricated trees line the avenues. It feels close and oppressive, everything packed tightly into a kilometer of thickness. Flickering fireglobes illuminate walls slick with moss and condensation. Graffiti slathers their surfaces in swaths of electric pink and blue. There's not a soul in sight.

I've never been on the streets of Meridian before, let alone an arcology. This level of dilapidation is utterly foreign to me. It's almost like being in another world. Supposedly, my father grew up on streets like this.

The beacon display on my windshield lights up again, revealing that I'm maybe a kilometer from the target. I'm heading in that direction when I hear a shuffle behind me. A man, scraggly, thin, in a grayish jumpsuit looks at me with pale, hungry eyes. His dirty beard and hair splays out wildly.

I raise my hand in greeting, but he hobbles away, alarmed by my presence.

"Wait!" I call out.

I would have thought this place was uninhabited . . .

Voices sound behind me. I turn again. Several of the Julii Academy students decked out in black armor, carrying pikes, sprint toward me.

The "soldiers" sent to stop The Companions. Five, maybe more on their way.

I ready myself.

Fifty meters away, they stop short, recognizing me. I realize that they aren't running toward me. No, they're running away from something else. Spotting me has only confused them. They turn to look behind them, and I see what they've been running from—a mob with pipes, broken bottles, and pieces of shrapnel in their hands. Several other academy students are being beaten and kicked before the mob as they try to scurry away.

What by the twisted star is happening?

The academy soldiers hesitate, unsure if they should attack me or simply escape the mob. Then their heads tilt.

Someone is giving them audio directives.

They ready their pikes toward me. I surmise they've been told their mission to stop me is more important.

Phaestion. I grit my teeth. They run at me, full tilt. *I can't lose. I won't lose.*

I sidestep the first thrust of a pike with ease. I grab the shaft as it passes. I yank it, using the soldier's own momentum against him. He crashes to the ground, his helmet scraping against the pavement. I twirl the pike in my hand, making it look good for the camglobes and bring the butt end down in a sharp blow to the back of his helm. *Crack!* One out cold.

I swing the pike up to parry a blow from another soldier. A swift kick to his gut sends him sprawling. Two.

The next opponent swings his pike. I thumb the retractor on my own, shortening its length. I close the distance between us. His spear's unwieldy at short range. I bring the baton up under his chin, smashing him. Three down.

I'm grabbed from behind. I whip my head back, cracking my attacker's faceplate. He reels. I grab his arm and toss him over my hip in a classic grappling throw. Four.

I turn to face my final assailant. He raises his hands to surrender. A camglobe records us.

I've won! The grueling days of learning to walk again, returning to the gym with The Companions, the blood, sweat, and tears, have all led to this. *I am now a warrior.*

Or so I think . . .

The boy in front of me is shaking. I'm yanked from my moment of self-praise to feel pity for him and, worse, fear.

He'll be punished by his instructors if he surrenders, I realize.

"Attack me," I whisper. It's probably already too late, but I try anyway. "I'll make it look good, okay?"

He shakes his head.

The mob closes the distance between us. The single camglobe is joined by several others now, all floating near my head. The beacon for the data card flashes with an incessant pulse. Blood pounds in my neck from the exertion and adrenaline of the fight. The mob shouts and steps closer, the unruly citizens brandishing their "weapons."

Why are there people here at all? Why are they ready to fight?

I thumb the trigger on the baton, and it lengthens back into a pike.

"Edmon?" Phaestion's voice blares in my ear. "What's happening out there? This wasn't part of the scenario!"

No kidding!

"Edmon?" he shouts again, so I rip the helmet off to silence the noise.

The mob slows and halts. A hush runs through their ranks as we face one another. Neither of us makes a move.

"It's Edmon Leontes!" someone from the crowd shouts.

"He's one of them!" says another.

"No!" shouts a third voice. "He's never been one of them!"

"Look at his hair!" another adds.

My hand self-consciously brushes a dark lock out of my eye. I take in the mob of hundreds. They aren't the homogeneous blond of the Julii Academy Nightsiders. Gold is predominant, but there are other shades, too, hints of brown, chestnut, and auburn. Some even sport dark hair like my own. I retract my pike from attack position.

"Sir, what are you doing?" the academy soldier whispers behind me.

"Shut up, cadet," I spit back. Sometimes rank has its privileges.

An older man with withered, gnarled hands and a sagging face steps forward. A blond boy of maybe eight, wearing a gray jumpsuit, helps him. The old man holds a metal pipe in his hand. He's bleeding from the forehead.

"Edmon Leontes," the old man says. "I am Jorund."

"Jorund, you're injured. You need a doctor," I respond, but my eyes are on the boy. He has some kind of gap in his lip, a cleft palate. Such a defect should have marked him immediately for the Pavaka.

"I'm fine," he says offhandedly. "We're here to protest these war games on our streets. We're here to stop the theft of our sons and daughters for the Combat, the murder of our infants at the Pavaka. We're here to protest the drugs that have overrun our city. We're here—"

He stops as several rib-shattering coughs rack his body.

I had no idea the underclass of Tao lived like this. I always thought the Pantheon provided for them. That's what we do on Bone for those less fortunate. The village takes care of its own.

"Your father comes from streets like these. Now he is the Patriarch of House Leontes and sits on the High Synod," Jorund continues.

True. My father replaced Old Wusong last cycle when the old man became too feeble to attend councils.

"Talk to him. Ask him to remember where he came from. Ask him to do something," Jorund implores.

Even if I talked to my father, what would I say? Would he even listen?

Still, I nod as if I understand the old man's request.

"Who is the boy?" I ask, unable to pull my stare from the child's deformed lip.

Jorund protectively puts his arms around the boy. "My son, Alaric."

"He's . . . different," I say. "Why wasn't he given to the fires of the Pavaka?"

"A barbaric ritual!" the old man hisses. "Simply because a child isn't perfect does not mean he has no worth."

"You're a criminal, Jorund," I say. The camglobes hover around me, capturing everything.

"If it is a crime to save an innocent babe, then I would do it again, Edmon Leontes."

"We're hungry!" shouts someone from the ranks.

"There's no work!" adds another. "We need jobs!"

The crowd howls assent.

"Every house employs workers in their industries!" I shout over them, parroting Vetruk's government lectures.

"They take my father's money!" Alaric shouts. He's brave, this small boy, malnourished and weak, speaking up to me like he does.

"Reappropriation," I say. "In return, you're provided hospitals, roads, maintenance—"

"Does this look maintained to you?" The old man gestures to our surroundings. A hacking cough shakes his old frame again. Alaric supports him.

My heart grows dark as I see the truth of his words. The decay of the buildings speaks more than his voice ever could. I've been taught that those who are worthy, those who are strong, rise to the top. Those who do not are undeserving. Yet no one deserves what my eyes are showing me: squalor, filth, rubbish, and no chance to make it better.

"The Electors, the Synod, the Pantheon—they're keeping it for themselves," the old man says, sighing. "They use it to build private armies for their amusement."

"Tell the Julii to stop kidnapping our children!" a woman screeches.

What are they talking about? I thought the Julii Academy strictly took volunteers, but in truth, I really don't know. Nor do I know what the other houses of the Pantheon are doing.

"Cadets in the city being tracked by camglobes for entertainment? That must cost a pretty penny. Is that the best use of the money we earn?" asks the old man bitterly.

He kicks one of the Julii soldiers on the ground in front of him. The boy soldier grunts with pain. I warily eye the camglobes hovering around us, but the old man and the boy step forward.

"Open your eyes, Edmon!" Jorund says. "Electors are rarely made from lowborns. If they are, they forget who they were after they ascend, like your father seems to have done. They've escaped a life of servitude and have no interest in going back."

I hesitate, looking again at the camglobes. *He's always watching,* Edgaard said of our father. I need to show him I'm not the weakling he's always thought. "Then fight for yourself," I say, "become an Elector. Random violence won't solve your problem. Such actions belong in the arena, where everyone is equal."

I feel the lies on my lips even as I speak them.

What's wrong with you, Edmon? Nadia's voice screams in my head.

"Equal?" The old man laughs. "After years of fancy training to fight in rigged matches? Sure."

The crowd murmurs assent.

"Being the strongest, being rich, receiving adulation for those things, doesn't give one wisdom." Jorund shakes his head. "Look around at what that way of life has borne."

We face each other in uncomfortable silence.

"I was wrong. You're one of them. You always have been," Jorund says quietly.

I haven't asked for wealth or privilege. I am one of you! I want to shout. *I will change this!* Those are not the words I speak, however. "If you really had something to offer, your value couldn't be denied. They'd meet any fair demand because you'd deserve it, and they couldn't do without you. But that's not how it is. You don't count. You're replaceable, a cog in the structure. Why should they help you? Why should their hard work and wealth pay for your laziness?"

I say it to hurt him. Instead, I hurt myself. *I don't know who I am anymore.*

"We just want a fair chance!" someone shouts.

"We want a say in our own lives," pleads Jorund.

"Then keep protesting," I say, resigned.

"You know the penalty for dissent!" the old man shouts as I walk away.

The Wendigo. The brutal prison was established centuries ago by the Great Song in the heart of the Nightside. There, the first emperor of Tao sent the murderers and thieves and enemies of his house. It has been passed down through the ages to House Wusong. Only recently, though, my father, with the help of off-worlders, has turned the ice prison into something more—a forced labor camp. The convicted toil in the frozen tunnels to mine metals for House Wusong. Free, cheap labor. I've no doubt that after the camglobe footage today, the mines will have many added to its workforce.

When I was a child brought before the emperor, things seemed so simple. I'm only fifteen now, and the world is out of control. I can't fight them all—Phaestion, my father, The Companions, my teachers, the Pantheon. The strong devour the weak, war drives civilization, and pain is the only constant.

"If you believe what you say," I call to the old man, "then you'll have the courage to face it." I turn to the Julii Academy soldier who still stands behind me and say, "Come."

"Edmon!" Jorund shouts. "Leaders are supposed to help people. Not use them."

"Sir?" The Julii soldier catches my attention. He points out scores of other soldiers creeping from the alleys. He taps a finger to the side of his helm.

He's receiving orders. I need to get out of here. Fast.

I turn back to Jorund, trying to end the confrontation and save both sides. "I've heard your words. Please, I'll do what I can. Right now you must go home."

Cries ring out from the back of the mob. The soldier beside me runs past and plunges his pike into Jorund's chest.

Jorund wears a ghastly expression of surprise, his mouth open in the shape of a perfect circled O. His breath exhales with a hiss. Blood gurgles from his lips as he collapses.

"No!" I scream.

Run, boy, run. But I don't run. Neither does the boy with the cleft palate, Alaric. The Julii soldier grabs the child's head and twists, snapping his neck.

What have I done?

I'm a second too late as I tackle the soldier. I lift him off the ground and hurl him as far as I can. He lands on the pavement a few meters away with a sickening crunch.

Julii soldiers now plow into the crowd with Plexiglas shields and spears. Their black armor shines slick with blood in the dimness of the fireglobes.

"Stop!" I shout. "I order you, stop!"

I run into the morass. I smash my fists into their helmets. I sweep them off their feet with my pike. It is pell-mell, but soon the death throes of the crowd fade. Before long, the only sounds are my own exertions. I scream as I kick one soldier to the ground. I swing my pike in a wide arc, smacking another.

Every civilian is on the ground, dead or dying. I'm the last standing, and I'm surrounded, even as I sob with rage. Bodies are strewn everywhere. Blood flows into the gutters and drains of the arco.

The child soldiers lower their pikes toward me. Their orders to kill the mob fulfilled, I'm their prey again.

CHAPTER 10

Banda Continuo

"Should I just leave you, Edmon?" Hanschen sits on top of a fireglobe pole.

How the hell did he get there?

"It would certainly mean less competition." He laughs.

I take advantage of the academy soldiers' distraction. I sprint, breaking through their defenses, and hurtle down the avenue. I swerve left into an alley. A metal wall blocks the end of the narrow passage. I run full speed ahead anyway. I drive the point of my pike into a pile of refuse and vault off the end. I let go of the shaft and reach, my fingers barely snagging the edge of a ventilation grate. I try to tear the grate off its hinges, but I'm just not strong enough. I hang, helpless.

"Edmon!" I risk a turn and see my little brother running down the alley behind me.

Edgaard, too? Where did he come from?

Hanschen follows closely behind and, behind them both, sprint the soldiers. The jump is too high for either of them, but Edgaard jumps anyway. He leaps higher than I would have thought possible. Still, it's not enough. I swing my legs out at just the right moment, and he miraculously catches them. His small, strong hands clasp my ankles.

Then I feel the unbearable weight of Hanschen grabbing the human chain as well. I cry out.

"Let go, Hanschen!" screams Edgaard.

The soldiers crowd below and hurl their pikes to bring us down. One ricochets off the wall centimeters from my head.

"I just saved you, Edmon!" Hanschen screams.

He's right. More than that, he's not going to sacrifice himself so that we can escape. There's only one option . . .

"Climb!" I growl.

I grip the grate as tight as I can. Hanschen scrambles over us. He mashes his boot into my face as he reaches the grating. He quickly unscrews it, unblocking the duct. He hurls it at an oncoming Julii soldier like a discus, sending the boy sprawling to the pavement.

"Pull us up!" I demand. Another spear clatters against the wall near my head.

"Tell Edgaard to give me the data card first."

"What?" *Edgaard captured the data card?*

"Only if you promise not to let us fall!" Edgaard shouts.

"Don't do it, Edgaard! We have no guarantee he'll help us after you give it to him," I say.

I can't hold on much longer.

This is Phaestion's doing—pitting us against one another, holding us down. The Companions are all scions of noble houses, each with just as much claim to leadership as him. Yet, here he has us fighting one another at his whim. *How is this his vision of working together?*

My hands strain as the duct edge cuts into my skin.

All those innocent people were murdered in the street a few moments ago, I realize. I'm no leader if I couldn't do anything to stop what happened. I shouldn't be here. I should be at the Sophia Academy with The Maestro.

"Edgaard, give him the card. Hanschen, save Edgaard. He's no physical threat to you."

"Edmon, no!" Edgaard cries.

"I wasn't going to win this one anyway, brother. Hanschen?" I demand.

Hanschen nods. Edgaard tosses up a small black cube and climbs up over me. Then Hanschen, the bastard, tries to push Edgaard off. My brother is too quick, though. They struggle. I feel myself slipping. I contract my abdominal muscles and use my bloody fingers to pull myself up. I plow into them both, and we tumble down the ventilation chute.

We struggle. Falling through darkness, I'm punching and kicking. My fist connects with something. I hear a crack. Hanschen cries out. I've broken his rib. There's a light at the end of the tunnel.

"Hang on!" I scream to Edgaard. His hands wrap around my torso. We free-fall for a gut-lurching beat before we smack into a pile of garbage.

Hanschen scrambles to his feet and wades through the junk as quickly as he can.

"You all right?" I ask my brother.

Edgaard nods. I breathe, but I can't afford a moment to understand all that has happened in the last few minutes. *I have to find a way out of this.* "Come on. We've got to move. We can still catch him," I say.

"Edmon, we don't need to." Edgaard pulls from his pocket a golden ring inlaid with a glittering diamond—the data card. It's a silicon storage device, billions of yottabytes embedded in the crystal.

"By the twisted star!" I snag it from him, holding it to the dim light of the arcology fireglobes. "How?"

"I threw him an empty box. He didn't check it."

I smile and rub the top of Edgaard's helmet. He beams at me through his mask. Then his smile fades. "Edmon, give it back."

I'm the stronger of the two of us. There's nothing to stop me from keeping it. I could win. Why shouldn't I? Prove to my father that I am the better, prove to Phaestion I'm the greatest of his Companions. I'm tired of losing. Why shouldn't I triumph?

Then I remember another voice, my mother, saying, *You will forget what you saw here today.* My father made Edgaard his heir and beat my mother in front of all of Tao. He may think me unworthy of his love, but I know for fact he's unworthy of mine. I put the ring into my brother's hand.

"Sigurd and Perdiccus are still out there," I say. "Whoever has this is going to be a target."

There's a rumble in the chute above us.

"Run!" Edgaard shouts.

We jump up and pump our legs. I've lost my helmet and heads-up display, so Edgaard takes the lead.

"The pickup zone is on the surface level!" he shouts.

We swerve right down a dark avenue toward a residential district within the arco. The edifices are abandoned here, like ancient metal ghosts. We stop to catch our breath in the foyer of one apartment structure. The entire place is covered with soot, the concrete walls cracked, and the glass panes are filthy or shattered. The place looks as if it has been put to the torch.

"We have to get to the Banshee Rail," I say. "Can you map a way to the top?"

"Headset's giving a layout." Edgaard taps his helmet.

I have a moment to think again. The Julii Academy soldiers would not have slaughtered all those people without orders. *Someone told them to do what they did. Was it Phaestion? I don't want to believe it, but who else? He watches everything. It could be his father. It must be. Please let it be.*

A child's voice interrupts my reverie. "There isn't a pneumovator."

Edgaard and I whip around. Out of the darkness steps a little girl, perhaps Edgaard's age, with dark, tousled hair and a grime-covered face. She wears the tatters of a monochrome jumpsuit like the denizens I saw earlier. She stares at us with curiosity. She isn't a Nightsider, but neither is she a Daysider. She's some sort of half race like me.

"Who're you?" I ask.

"None of your business," she fires back.

"Why are you here?" Edgaard asks.

"I live here, or I used to." Her voice is sad. "Before the fire."

"Whoever you are, it isn't safe," I say.

"I can help you to the top, Edmon," she says.

My eyes narrow with suspicion. "You know my name?"

Perdiccus dives through a dirty window with a crash. He slams Edgaard to the ground. I run to help, but I'm lifted off my feet. I sail through the air. I twist my body, roll as I land, and spring up, looking for my assailant. Sigurd is barreling toward me.

"Where's the data card, snail guppy?"

I ready myself for an impact . . . which never comes. The little girl dives into Sigurd's feet, tripping him. They tumble into a pile of broken junk. The little girl extricates herself from the tangle of limbs and stands. She flashes a grin as I stare slack-jawed.

"Told you I could help." She shoots me a thumbs-up.

"Watch out!" I shout.

Sigurd stands behind her and takes a swipe at her head. The girl ducks the blow with surprising speed. Only one other person I know moves with that kind of agility and grace . . . and he's not fully human. *Who is this kid?*

"Too slow, you big bully," the girl teases. She dodges his grasp and kicks Sigurd in the shin. He grabs her. The speedy little girl isn't able to escape this time. She cries out. I hurtle myself forward, throwing my fist out with all my might. I connect with Sigurd's faceplate. It shatters. He grunts with pain and lets go of the girl. He reels, trying to find his bearings.

I don't let up. Jab, hook, uppercut. He falls back. I step into his fall and roundhouse kick him in the gut. He doubles over. I grab his head and slam it into a doorframe. He smashes to the ground. I see a massive staircase in the next room that twists and turns to the top.

That's our way out.

I look back. Edgaard holds Perdiccus in an armlock and cranks. Perdiccus screams a split second after I hear the hideous sound of snapping bone. The little girl runs and jumps into the air in a surprisingly acrobatic display. She boots Perdiccus in the head, and he's knocked unconscious.

Are there other people down in these arcologies like her?

The girl helps Edgaard up. "The stairwell leads all the way to the top of the arcology."

I nod. "Thanks. How did you know about us?"

"Are you kidding?" she asks. "The girls at the shelter are never going to believe I met you. Edmon Leontes. You're our favorite character!"

I shake my head. That's what I am to people, a character in a stupid aquagraphic.

"The others think Edgaard's kind of, well . . ." The tomboy blushes.

"What?" Edgaard asks innocently.

I cut in. "Thank you. We have to go."

Sigurd's already pushing himself up off the floor. A crash at the door hastens the end of the conversation. Julii soldiers swarm the foyer. I grab Edgaard's hand, and we run.

The last I see of the little girl is her leaping and climbing through a window much too high for any normal little girl to reach.

Whomever she is, she has Talousla Karr's fingerprints all over her, I think, but the truth will have to wait.

Flight after flight of stairs burn our legs. Perdiccus, Sigurd, and the rest of the soldiers below us are predators. We're the prey. They're gaining.

Edgaard slows. I pull him up the steps until finally we reach a door. I run at it full force, smashing into the metal that busts from the jamb. We spill out above the arcology onto the streets of Meridian.

A sondi hovers at the skyline. Our ride. *How the hell do we get to it?*

"This way!" Edgaard shouts.

We turn a corner to another flight of steps. They lead to a platform and the Banshee Rail.

Oh no, I think. *This is a terrible idea!*

The sonic-lev train car rushes into the platform station. The howl of its engine whines as it slows to a stop. Doors slide open, and we dive into the car, safe for the moment. We are surrounded by worn faces. They regard us furtively. Then I catch movement from my periphery. It's a streak of black with blond hair, diving in from the edge of my vision. Hanschen. He tackles Edgaard and wrenches the ring from his grasp.

"No!" I scream. I throw myself on top of my brother's assailant.

"It's mine!" Hanschen screams maniacally.

I draw back my fist and slam it into his nose. He howls and writhes under me. I lose my balance. Hanschen is up on his feet the next second and racing through the cars of the train.

"He has the card!" I scream.

Edgaard is already running after him. I scramble through one car, then another. I push past bystanders as I head for the back of the train. I bat a camglobe aside angrily.

We reach the last car of the train, and Hanschen crashes through the Plexiglas door. The compartment depressurizes. Wind rushes past us as the banshee engine screams. Passengers cover their ears. I'm thrown to the floor. I wish I hadn't tossed my helmet away earlier.

Hanschen swings himself outside of the train.

"Come on!" Edgaard shouts, though the words are lost in the wind. He helps me up off the floor.

Perdiccus and Sigurd crash through the door behind us, flanked by a cadre of soldiers. Edgaard and I sprint after Hanschen while Perdiccus and Sigurd run after us. Seal chases fish; shark chases seal. Out the back door, wind whips my hair. I grab a ladder bolted to the exterior of the train and climb. Hanschen is already plastered to the roof like a bug.

He punctures his retracted pike into the metal like an ice pick, pulling himself hand by hand. I duck as the train whips through a small tunnel.

I look ahead. The train approaches the sondi, which hovers in the sky above midcity. We are going to have to jump from the sonic train onto the sondi at just the right moment to win. *This is madness.*

Edgaard takes his pike and follows Hanschen. I jam my own pike into the roof, my chest pounding with fear. I use the pike to claw my way along the surface. Every time I pull the pike out, my heart skips a beat as I am free, holding on to nothing. The speed of the train threatens to dust me off and into the purple sky. Perdiccus and Sigurd follow, meters behind.

This is too slow.

I signal to Edgaard. *I'm going down.*

He shakes his head. *I know. It's too dangerous. Doesn't matter.*

I swing my body around to the side of the train and crash through a window. Passengers scream. I shove two stunned Julii soldiers to the ground, then shove my way through the throng, sprinting for the front of the train.

Not much time left.

I reach the front and push past the conductor.

"What are you—?"

I ignore him and smash my fist into the Plexiglas of the windshield. It feels like paper against my strengthened knuckles. I vault myself back onto the roof, teetering, but I manage to slam my pike into the roof again.

Steady, Edmon.

The sondi balloon hangs like a fat, bloated beetle on the horizon. We are all so close to death that it seems absurd. *You can do this!* I say to myself.

Hanschen has reached midtrain. He's sandwiched between me and the others. He stands.

He's going to jump, I realize. *I can't let it happen.*

The train rounds the bend. I let go of my pike and jump in the air. Hanschen rushes toward me as the train hurtles him forward. I smack into him, tackling him. We careen across the roof. I grab his wrist and pry the data card from it.

We slide past the others. Someone snags my ankle before I fall into the ether. Sigurd and Perdiccus pull me back onto the train, but now they're on top of me, punching me, clawing for the data card. Everyone wants to be the strongest. No one wants to lose Phaestion's favor.

I can't beat all of them, I realize.

I see Edgaard out of the corner of my eye, the only one not on top of me, clawing for the ring. He stands slowly, using his pike for support. I do the only thing that makes sense.

"Edgaard!" I scream. I toss the data card as high as I can. He catches it midair and leaps from the Banshee Rail . . . safely into the carriage of the hovering sondi in one spectacular move.

The sondi's side panels light up in an aquagraphic display of electric brilliance.

Edgaard wins!

The others let me go, and I fall. The beauty of the twilight rushes away. My stomach sinks with a weightless, floating feeling. I spin to face the earth, spread my arms, and accept death.

CHAPTER 11

Prima Donna

The wings of the suit splay out, and I glide, barely a meter above the cement. I soar. I hear the faint sound of cheers like a distant wave crashing to shore. The people watch the live stream on the nets. They cheer for me.

Later, the heavy double doors of the throne room open. I stride behind the others, my ears still ringing from the fight on the train. Perdiccus's arm is in a sling, Hanschen's torso is bandaged. Sigurd's face is bruised. Academy soldiers fill the hall. Michio, Croack, Alberich, and Commandant Vetruk stand by. I search for The Maestro's face in the crowd but cannot find him.

Chilleus Julii doesn't sit on his throne. None have seen the old Patriarch for the last half of this yearly cycle. Rumor is the old man is in ill health as he approaches his 125th year. On Tao, the only good death is a death in battle, and so the ritual of patricide was instituted. A son must kill his father in order to claim the rule of his house and be branded with a Patriarch's tattoos. While anyone who wins the Combat may ascend to the College of Electors, only a Patriarch may be elected from that body to a seat on the High Synod. Phaestion has not yet been branded, but that is only the first step along his path to rule.

The Julii prince lounges on the orca throne, leaning on one elbow. His leg lazily dangles over the other massive arm of the chair. Two gorgeous girls attend him, blonde, slender, and full breasted. One of them pets his coppery hair. He bats a camglobe out of his face.

Talousla Karr skulks in the corner, watching everything silently. I want to ask the renegade spypsy about the little girl I met on the streets of Meridian, but it will have to wait. I have more important matters to think of.

"All hail the fearless Companions!" Phaestion awakes from his whimsy.

He stands and straps a purple cape jauntily over a bare, muscular shoulder. As he descends the steps of the throne, he spreads his arms wide and embraces Perdiccus and Sigurd in a hug.

"My sea lions," he says, smiling, "you're truly fearsome!"

Perdiccus grins. Sigurd nods. The giant believes he should have won the contest, no doubt.

"Hanschen, my cousin." Phaestion hugs his lithe kinsman. "Cunning, graceful, and so, so beautiful," he teases flirtatiously. Hanschen, usually so confident, actually blushes. I wonder what other flirtations the two have partaken in behind closed doors. "Leave it to you to figure out the game. None of you could win on his own. You might have played your allies a bit longer, though," he chides.

"Sage advice, my lord." Hanschen winks.

"And little Edgaard"—Phaestion turns to my brother—"victor."

Edgaard bows. He presents then opens the small velvet box to reveal the "data card." Phaestion plucks the diamond from the box and holds it up to the sunset light.

"You are truly your father's son." Phaestion smiles. "You've earned the prize. Julii Academy will join you at House Wusong-Leontes for the duration of the next yearly cycle. You will host, and we will be *your* companions."

Edgaard grins from ear to ear. Hosting is a tremendous honor.

Edric will be so proud. Would he feel the same if I'd won? I'll never know. I gave up my chance at victory.

"Let's not forget you, Edmon." Phaestion grins wryly. "Edgaard wouldn't have been victorious if not for your help. In the Combat, you assume alliance only for it to be broken later. 'Never sacrifice yourself for another.' However, this exercise was more than the Combat. In war, victory is only achieved through self-sacrifice. You chose brother and house over yourself. That selfless act proclaims you the true winner of today."

Hovering camglobes catch every word.

You're my favorite character. I remember the orphan girl's words. *This is all show, and Phaestion is the star. We're merely players in his drama, but what story is he telling?*

"In acknowledgment of your achievement, I will grant you any wish that's within my power."

For the first time since we've known each other, Phaestion's praise means nothing. I steel myself against his warm feelings, though they radiate off him like sunshine. After today, I don't believe I could ever think of him the same way again.

"Take me home," I say.

Phaestion freezes. His eyes narrow.

"Before we travel to House Wusong-Leontes, grant me the boon of traveling back to the Isle of Bone."

"So be it," he says quietly.

Phaestion cocks his head to the side and nods. "You fought well," he says, addressing the room of academy soldiers. "There will be a feast this evening for all. You're dismissed." The teachers lead the academy soldiers out in formation. The Companions bow their heads and take their leave, but not before Hanschen grabs Phaestion and kisses him on the cheek. Phaestion pets his cousin's blond hair then pushes him off playfully.

Edgaard looks at me with a question. I nod to indicate he should go ahead.

Phaestion couldn't have been the one to order the attack. He couldn't have been. *But who else?*

Edgaard exits after the others. The double doors close with a thunderous slam. Phaestion returns to his throne. His consorts run their long slender fingers through his hair. They massage his feet. The whisk of the camglobes hovering is the only sound.

"Edmon, before we go to Bone, there's something I need to tell you—"

"I want to talk alone," I say, cutting him off, staring at the concubines, the camglobes, and Talousla Karr still in the corner. "Like before," I say. "It was you and me and the beach. We shared everything without anyone else watching."

"Not everything," Phaestion says with more venom than I expect. "I know that you saw the girl without me."

Does he mean Nadia?

"This is part of everything now." He gestures to our surroundings. "Part of who we're going to be."

"Who you're going to be," I respond angrily.

Phaestion shakes his head. "You know what our birthright destines us for."

"Your birthright." My words taste bitter.

"Do you think I love you any less than before?" he asks. "Just because we share ourselves with the world?" He steps from the throne and comes close. He holds my face in his hands.

I'm reminded of the mirror-Edmon in the Arms of Agony. *Sometimes we war. Sometimes we touch.* "I'm beginning to love you less."

A shadow crosses his smooth face. No trace of blemish mars his skin, unlike my own, which suffers the marks of transition to adulthood. The muscles of his tall, wiry form flex. He looks like a demigod, but his physical beauty is a distraction right now.

"People were murdered in the street, Phaestion. Someone gave the order." My voice is flat. It's in the open now. He won't let others hear now that he knows this is what I want to talk about.

"Leave us," he says. His voice is quiet but hard. His gray eyes hold me in place. The concubines exit through the rear of the chamber. Phaestion presses his palm against a panel on the arm of his throne. The camglobes whisk away, too. Talousla Karr flashes a scowl but slinks off into the shadows.

Phaestion takes a seat. "Those deaths were necessary."

It was him.

"They were innocent. All they wanted was to be heard. I promised I would speak for them. Now they're dead. Tell me it wasn't you."

"What they wanted was too dangerous," he says calmly.

"Dangerous?"

"I didn't make the final decision," he says evenly.

Thank the Elder Stars. He's still my friend.

"Who did?" Anger tinges my voice. "I told those people I'd help them. I don't like being made a liar."

"Our people were bred as soldiers," he says. "Soldiers obey, or the army collapses. The commanders became the Patriarchs of the Pantheon. The enlisted became our working class. Hard decisions had to be made for the first colony to survive. We had limited resources and a harsh, yet fragile environment. Too many voices, pulling in too many directions would have torn us apart. So our forefathers made sure not to repeat the mistakes of Miral or even Ancient Earth. They needed an efficient government and a way to ensure that the best among us were given the reins. The Combat was instituted not only as a way to manifest our darker impulses, to give us an outlet for the skills we had been bred with, but also to ensure that the strongest and most capable were the few with power."

"Thanks for the civics lesson." My voice drips sarcasm.

He ignores my gibe. "The most successful houses consolidated power through primogeniture. They trained us, their offspring, to master the Combat or sponsored others to win and rule on their behalf, like your father."

It's patently obvious why combatants rarely rise from the Under Circuit. Unlike the nobility, they are unable to train their whole lives for the event. It makes the success of my father an even more remarkable achievement when I think on it. His subsequent alliance with House Wusong certainly paid off. He is the old emperor's de facto heir.

"That structure still needs to be maintained, at all costs."

"Your structure is barbaric and stupid," I sneer. "Look what it wrought today—the death of dozens of innocents who were only asking that their world not fall apart."

"Tao is falling apart. It's dying."

His statement hangs in the air.

"It's not going to explode or anything dramatic like that"—Phaestion waves dismissively—"but our best scientists have determined that even with the Combat and the Pavaka, even with birth controls and plebeian law mandating only one child per healthy couple, the population will reach a maximum capacity within a generation. Tao's diminishing resources will no longer be able to sustain us, and there will be a crash."

"What kind of crash?" I ask.

"Population, economic, ecological, technological, famine, plague . . ." His voice trails off. "You name it. Total collapse."

He has that far-off look he gets when he talks about the future. It's as if he can see something beyond the edge of normal vision.

"However it begins, the end is the same—cessation of our civilization. Those that survive will be reduced to scraping life from the barren rock of this world," he says bitterly.

He leans back on his throne, a boy-king of a dying corpse. The prince of nothing.

"The Fracture." My mind races for a solution. "We can get resources from other worlds now."

"Paid for with what?" Phaestion says scornfully.

"With the wealth of the Pantheon," I reply.

"Our gold and jewels? I'll tell you one thing House Julii learned from dominating the interstellar trade, the same thing the other houses who dare to challenge our mercantile supremacy will learn when they send ships through the Fracture: the worlds of the Nine Corridors care little for our meager offerings. They care about invention, ideas, and technology. We have none to offer worlds more advanced than our own. We have no skilled labor. We've even depleted our world of arable land, which is itself a commodity."

"We still have the resources of the Nightside," I argue. "Metals and minerals. Mine them, trade them, or use them to build more starships. Become merchants, traders. Our people are skilled fighters. We can be soldiers again."

"Mercenaries?" He laughs. "Is that what you would have our people reduced to?"

I have no answer to his scorn.

"When Old Wusong dies, Edric will marry you, Edgaard, and your sisters to other noble houses to consolidate his power. He'll seek to keep Old Wusong's seat on the High Synod and rule the College of Electors himself. He will keep the houses divided and use the resources of the Wendigo for himself. He would have us be as you suggest—*traders*." Phaestion spits the word like an epithet.

If my father's greed and lust for power would save the planet and our people, maybe that's a better alternative. What an abhorrent thought—that of all the people to rule this world, it should be the man who beat my own mother.

"Edric's plans will cause the dissolution of our way of life," Phaestion continues. "Trade will maintain us for a generation, maybe two, but soon there will be an exodus. Our economy will stagnate. Our culture will be lost as more and more leave, never to return. Our race will fade with a whimper."

I remember the leviathan's words in my dreams.

The universe will die. What will it matter?

"All of us live and die. Governments, civilizations rise and fall. Things change," I say.

Red blossoms in Phaestion's face. His features contort and twist. His fists clench. Anger radiates from his eyes. "I would not have it so," he roars. "Ours is the greatest civilization that has ever been born. Our people were forged in the crucible of Combat. We must prove the superiority of our ways!"

"What do you mean?" I ask.

He sits, and the cool mask of beauty falls back into place. He cocks his head to the side, but his eyes remain hard.

"It's already in motion, Edmon."

I feel afraid. "What is?"

"You. Me. Us. The Companions," he replies. "If anyone's to save this world, it will be us."

A cadre of spoiled rich children living in an ivory tower? I laugh.

He looks at me perplexed, perhaps mildly annoyed.

"If you think we're going to save this mud ball from anything, you're living in a dream," I say. "Sigurd's a dumb brute, Perdiccus a sycophantic thrill seeker, Hanschen's a depraved sex addict. And Edgaard . . ."

"And Edgaard?" he asks.

"Edgaard's a little boy," I say.

"What about you, Edmon? What are you?" Phaestion hits a button on the panel of his armchair. Music floods the chamber.

Ho-ho! Ho-ho! Ho-hey! *Schmie-de mein ham-mer ein hartes Schwert!*

It's my voice, singing. My cheeks flush.

"The track was released across the nets last week. It's very good." He smiles. "The Maestro tried to keep our censors from intercepting it, but our filters are fairly sophisticated. Don't worry," he teases. "I don't mind if people hear. It's not me you have to fear on that account."

He's right. It's my father I'm worried about. I remember the look in his eyes the day of the christening, when people laughed at my proclamation that I would become a musician.

"The song is about forging a sword, correct?" Phaestion asks. "It was a smart choice. It paints you as a warrior, searching for a destiny. Perhaps a destiny not only for yourself but for all of Tao. Be careful. The warrior in this song thought himself invulnerable until he was stabbed in the back by a trusted friend."

Is he threatening me?

"I thought you'd given up your interest in music," I say.

"I haven't given up my interest in you. Or my interest in you being by my side. I can't do what I plan without you, Edmon."

What exactly does he plan?

"You've been to the arcologies now. You know the responsibility that we'll inherit as the Patriarchs, as Electors, as members of the Synod. The responsibility to see our people survive. You understand now more than anyone the suffering our people are enduring."

"We won't see them survive by killing them!" Anger rises in my voice again.

"You wanted to step into the Arms of Agony?" he mocks. "This is the true agony—having to make a choice between killing a few or saving many more. How does it feel now?"

So this is his punishment. That I should know the pain he assumes he will endure.

"Those people you met today, there are millions more like them across Meridian," he says. "They can be the fire against the collapse that's coming, but only if they can be harnessed. Dissonance must be crushed in order to achieve harmony. Don't you see? Yes, they are suffering. Yes, they are the cause of our planet dying, but that is necessary until the last moment when they become so destitute, so angry, that they are ready to lash out. They will trust in leaders who can direct their anger, who promise to make them great again. We will be those leaders. They will be our siren sword, our blade that will pierce the Nine Corridors and ensure our way of life not only survives, but thrives. That's why I was born. That's my purpose."

He turns toward the bay windows that overlook the city as he becomes lost in a reverie.

He really believes that what happened in the streets was just. All for a higher cause.

"It's *our* purpose." He turns. "The broadcasts of the competition were reedited, excising all footage of the event today."

"The massacre, you mean." My blood boils.

"We need the people behind us in order to save them from extinction. Their anger, their hunger, their strength, those must be turned outward, not within, and not until I'm ready. Those people are Tao's greatest resource, but the timing must be just right."

"For what?" Dread fills my bones.

Phaestion smiles. "For the thrust."

CHAPTER 12

Dissonance

The hum of the sondi pulses in my ears. I rest my head against my seat.

The Isle of Bone. My home. I'm coming.

It has been three long years since I've seen her white shores, since I've seen my mother or slept in my own bed. Since I've seen Nadia. I try to focus on my breathing as Alberich has taught for fighting, as The Maestro has taught for singing.

"Nervous, Ed?" Hanschen leers. "I'm sure your home is quite lovely, in a provincial way."

"I hear the surf's outstanding," Perdiccus adds. "I'd like to take an ocean screamer out. Maybe see a siren?"

I remember the last time a boy from Meridian wanted to see a siren.

"We won't be doing any of that," Sigurd interrupts. He folds his arms across his muscled chest. "We're going to train," he says with disdain. "We'll not be softened by lazy sun or backward people. We must maintain integrity."

"Aye-aye, Captain Puckered Nuts." Perdiccus salutes derisively.

Sigurd smirks, willing to take the gibe because he doesn't think Perdiccus is a real threat to him physically. He's overconfident.

"You trained alone here with Phaestion, didn't you, Edmon?" Edgaard asks.

"He did," a deep voice rumbles. Phaestion enters the passenger cabin from the cockpit. His timbre is no longer a boy's. His maturity has come faster than the rest of ours, perhaps because of his enhancements. He's more confident than ever, too. "We trained on the beaches before he became a companion."

The others eye me with jealousy. I'm the only one of us who has ever been with Phaestion alone. The only one who's ever seen his skill with a sword close up. They don't know that I've seen even more. I've seen how he trains in the Arms of Agony. I've seen how he stands in his little control room and watches us all. I've seen not only what his body is capable of, but what his mind can process and accomplish. The mystery around him is as intimidating as it is tantalizing for the others.

He's just a boy, like me, though. When he's wrong, he's wrong just like anybody else.

Whatever his special abilities are, his isolation has sparked a disconnect that has allowed him to view people as pawns. Love and affection are merely ways to manipulate, no matter if the feelings are true. Killing is a necessary evil to achieve his goals, too, I've learned.

And what of my feelings for him? Our friendship? Is it real or just another tool? Either way, I won't allow my friendship with Phaestion to permit him to hurt others again, I promise myself.

"Don't underestimate the heat of sun and sand when you train, Sigurd." Phaestion claps the giant's back. "Island pleasures can be delightful." He winks at Hanschen. "The surf definitely is intense." He nods at Perdiccus.

"Prepare for docking," the pilot chimes in over the speakers.

The sondi engine sighs a low hoot as it slows over the bay.

"I'm excited to see your home." Edgaard looks up at me. I tousle his hair. "Aw, come on, Edmon," he says and pulls away.

Commandant Vetruk gathers the other teachers, including Croack and Michio, at the entrance to disembark. They're in the black uniforms of House Julii. Alberich has donned the blue and silver of House Leontes in honor of Edgaard's win.

Perdiccus is smart in turquoise and white of House Mughal, while Sigurd looks ostentatious in violent red and gold of House Flanders.

Edgaard eyes me nervously. I'm not wearing Leontes colors. Instead, I've insisted on the white linens of the islanders. The teachers cast their eyes at me with disdain. I don't care. This is my mother's house, and I'll return to it as a member of her people.

Talousla Karr meanwhile skulks in shadows, watching us like lab animals from beneath his hood.

Maestro Bertinelli wears a frock coat over a doublet and britches of Lyrian origin. He glances at me over his tiny round spectacles under the wide brim of a straw hat. I smile back anxiously. He was not initially invited, being only my private tutor, but I insisted that he make the journey with us. I think he'll enjoy the music of the island. More than that, I need the support. I don't know that we'll have a chance to talk much, but I'm glad he's here. Perhaps he and I will figure out a way to announce a leave from Tao so that I may study music on Lyria. I just have to get through the next few days.

The doors open. Sunlight streams into the ship. The teachers and Companions step out of the carriage. Phaestion's hand is on my shoulder.

"Edmon, I tried to tell you before we left. There's something about your homecoming I need you to know," he says.

But I'm too impatient. As much as I appreciate his friendly demeanor, I still haven't forgiven him for what has happened. "Later," I say, shrugging him off perhaps a bit more harshly than I should.

The glare of hot light hits me. My ears are assaulted with a gigantic roar. I hold up my hand to shield my eyes, peering through the cracks in my fingers. They frame a crowd. The whole of the Isle of Bone is gathered at the docks. Their cheers ring in my ears.

"What's going on?" I turn to Phaestion.

"It's good to be home," he says, arcing an eyebrow. "They're here for you."

I turn back to the multitude. I raise my hand, and they cheer. Drummers bang a rhythm as the crowd parts, creating a pathway for me to walk through.

"What were you going to tell me just now?" I ask.

He shifts uncomfortably.

"Phaestion?"

"Go," he says. "Today's your day."

There's a look in his eye. He's proud for me, but also something more . . .

I stride down the ramp. The other Companions wander behind with looks of disbelief on their faces. I reach the bottom, and the crowd rushes me. I resist at first, not used to letting people touch me. Eventually, the onrush is too much. I give in. They lift me toward the sky. The music plays. I'm floating on hands, gliding on a sea of fingers. They carry me in their arms, on their shoulders, through the town, up the hill toward the summit. The moment is surreal.

This is what it means to come home.

Before I know it, I'm gently placed on the doorstep of the lonely white house my father built for my mother. The crowd disperses. The drums fade. Voices linger, and clasped hands part.

"Welcome home, Little Leontes. We need you," they say.

I no longer feel little. I feel stronger than ever. The pale-faced Companions and teachers of House Julii remain, confusion painting their faces. I'm the boy they've mistreated, and they've just seen me worshipped like a king. Maestro Bertinelli steps forward. He places a hand on my shoulder. "Well, Master Edmon, aren't you going to invite us in?"

I nod. The manse is barely a cottage compared to the gargantuan scrapers of Meridian, but still I'm the lord.

"Wait," Phaestion starts. "That thing I tried to tell you—"

For some reason I don't heed him. I open the double wide doors and step into the foyer. "Mother!" I call like a child. To the abyss with the decorum of noble houses. "I'm home!"

I'm greeted by a hollow silence. The summer breeze whisks through the dead building, fanning tattered curtains from an open window.

Hanschen snorts. "This is it? I expected at least a little barbarian hospitality."

"Quiet," Phaestion says, cutting him off.

"Mother?" I call again.

"Young master."

The voice is not my mother's, but rather one of her ladies in waiting. She enters, pushing a chair that hovers on a pneumolift. A decrepit thing, a rail-thin woman, sits in its seat, the ribs and clavicle at the top of her emaciated chest made visible by the v-line of the medical smock she wears. Her neck lurches forward, barely supporting a swollen head. Her eyes wander independently of each other, rolling at odd, dull angles. A red, puckered scar above her right eye zigzags over her shorn skull to the back of her neck.

She was left like this on purpose. She was left like this for me to see.

"No," I whisper. I run to her. "Mother, it's me, Edmon! What's happened to you? What's happened?" I hold her in my arms, but she's so frail. She groans like an unthinking animal. I pull away in horror as spittle runs down her chin.

"What happened?" I ask over and over. My heart threatens to pound through my chest. The servant looks away, unable to meet my gaze.

Alberich steps forward. "It was your father who did this, Edmon. I'm sorry, young lord."

Nausea envelops my stomach. My world spins.

"You knew," I whisper. "You knew and never told me—" Bile chokes the rest of the words before they reach my lips.

"When you left, she threatened revolt. She gathered a group of islanders to travel to Meridian to protest your 'abduction,' as she called it publicly," the seneschal explains.

"You promised you would protect her." I try to hold back the grief and sickness. I ball my fists as tightly as I can to fight the shock. My palms feel cold and clammy.

I should've been here to protect her. This shouldn't have happened. I collapse to my knees and vomit onto the marble floor. The retching continues until I repeatedly heave and nothing comes out.

"You promised you would protect her," I moan.

"I'm sorry, Edmon," Alberich says softly. "The Isle of Bone is a vassal state of House Wusong-Leontes. She threatened open, armed rebellion. The punishment for treason is execution, or worse, the Wendigo."

"This is better?" Rage boils in my veins. "She's lobotomized!"

"She lives," Alberich says. "She's here at home with her people to care for her."

"I could've stopped this. I would've told her to call off the revolt. You never told me!"

"Edmon, you had already tried. There was nothing more you could have done. You needed to focus on your studies," Phaestion adds gently. "We have training, preparation, a commitment to shut out the outside world in order to be ready . . ."

I turn on him, daggers in my eyes.

All those letters I wrote. He told me that I had done a great service for my people and for the Pantheon. He led me to believe that I had averted the crisis. He made me think that my mother was not able to respond because of her treason. The truth was that treason's punishment took away her words forever.

"You're a liar," I say with cold finality.

The tension between us is severed by laughter.

Sigurd guffaws from his belly. "Look at you, little snail guppy! You ask for her to be saved. And the very thing you want turns her into this. Priceless."

He's right. This is my fault. Alberich was trying to protect her life because of what I said. Phaestion was trying to protect me from the truth. This is my fault.

Hanschen smirks uneasily. Perdiccus grins. Only Phaestion doesn't join. "Sigurd, shut up," he says.

"Phaestion, it's just too good," the giant continues.

My fists clench. Hot blood rushes to my face.

"His own mother? She's just a Daysider."

I scream with rage and plunge forward. Sigurd looks up in momentary shock, then he readies himself. He cocks a fist and lets it fly. I duck the blow and plow my shoulder into his gut, pushing him against the wall. He brings a knee up under me. My forearms shield the strike. I hurl my right fist under his chin and feel his mandible crack. He swings a wild hook at my head. I block and snag his wrist with a claw technique. I yank his arm and twist, hearing it pop from his shoulder socket. He stifles a scream, but I'm not done. I don't even see a person in front of me; I see a monster. I see my father. I want him to suffer. I slam my forearm against his elbow hyperextending the joint. There is a wet breaking sound. His bones spike out of his flesh. He falls to the floor. I smash my knee into his face destroying his nose as he goes down.

"Edmon!" Phaestion yells.

I stand over Sigurd, panting as the red clears from my vision. He tries to stand and falls back down in pain.

"Stay down, monster," I hiss. "Never mock me or my family again."

I walk out the door, leaving them to clean up the mess.

I head to the beach, to the place where Alberich trained us. I stand at the shore, looking out at the vast Southern Sea as the water laps my toes. They sink into the wet sand. The waters splash the rock of Bone and over time will break it down, eventually swallowing it whole. The sun will explode. The universe will freeze. I've lost another piece of myself; I can never have it back.

How many pieces can be chipped away? What will remain when there is nothing left to carve?

I almost killed a person today, and I don't even care. I remember what my mother told me about killing. I remember what she said the first day I saw my father:

You will forget what you saw here today.

I'm becoming like the others because I feel no remorse. I feel only the desire for more violence to somehow fill the hole inside of me.

"Edmon, I'm sorry."

I turn, and he's there. His molten hair blows across his eyes in the summer wind.

How long have I been standing here?

"Alberich was trying to keep her alive. He was trying to save you the pain of her death."

"What do you know?" I cut him off. "I asked him to make sure no harm came to her. I should've known my father would discard her. I should have known."

"Here's what I know," he says gently. "There was nothing else you could have done to save her."

"You knew the whole time," I say.

His silence is all the answer I need. I stalk past him. He puts a hand on my shoulder to stop me.

"Edmon."

I belt him with my fist as hard as I can. He falls to the sand, blood streaming from his mouth. He looks at me with utter confusion. No one has ever struck him with such disdain before. Phaestion, the beautiful boy-king, the godlike prince of House Julii, has never even seen his own blood. He's so bewildered, he almost cries but doesn't. He stands and wipes the red from his chin with the back of his hand.

"If that's how you want it."

Yes. This is the violence I need.

His fists barrel into my face before I can respond. It's all I can do to cover up. I kick my leg out trying to back him off me. He's much too quick. He steps aside easily and counters with another fist. I reel but manage to grab him. I spin, hurling him into a boulder. He lands with a thud, and I jump back to gain distance. We circle, sizing each other up.

It has been years since we tried to tussle truly. There was the Arms of Agony, but this is him for real. He's as fast as ever, but I'm no longer the clumsy boy who had never wielded a sword before.

I kick, and he barely blocks. I'm on him with a flurry of my own. He moves away. I corner him against the boulder, not letting him escape. All of my training, my skills learned through losing again and again, all my capabilities come together with a blind rage.

I hit him. He bleeds. He hits me back. I bleed more. The smack of our fists becomes a rhythm. Then suddenly, he breaks it. He sweeps my feet from under me. He pins me to the earth.

"You've lost!" he says. "This is my arena, don't you understand?"

He looks down at me, panting. The strange look comes over his face.

"You'll always be my friend, won't you, Edmon?" he asks quietly, echoing our younger days.

"You lied to me." My voice cracks with pain.

He rolls off me, lies on his back, and looks up at the sky. His skin glistens from the exertion.

"Your mother demanded you leave House Julii and have your father return you. He refused. She threatened insurrection. Your father came to Bone to quell the rebellion. She was to be publicly executed. Alberich dissuaded him, but he couldn't keep her from punishment completely. The seneschal reasoned that leaving her impaired would deliver a much more powerful message."

"To whom?" My eyes burn with the salted tears.

"I'm so sorry, Edmon." His hand reaches out. He brushes the tears away gently with his thumb. "It wasn't my place to tell you. You wanted to contact your mother and let her know how you were doing. You wanted to comfort and be comforted, but she was already gone. I thought at least letting you keep writing would make you feel better. I didn't want to hurt you. I would never want to hurt you. I love you."

He leans in and gently touches his lips to mine.

I shove him away. I scramble to my feet, wiping my mouth.

"I'm sorry!" he blurts. "I thought that was what you wanted?"

I don't let him finish. I run.

CHAPTER 13

Aria

I need to get away from everything, but I'm trapped between past and future. Everyone wants to control me, use me. There isn't anywhere I can escape.

Maybe there's one place. One place I could always go and be safe. I remember . . .

The cliffs are the same. The white, smooth limestone still stands over a cerulean sea that blends seamlessly with the azure sky.

She's not anything like what I remember, though.

"I thought I might find you here eventually," she says. Nadia waits where I left her, on the edge of the world. She sits facing the blue on blue of the distance, her back to me.

Perhaps she's afraid to turn and look at who I've become?

Long, dark hair cascades down her shoulders. The outline of her body is no longer straight lines, but smooth curves begging for a hand to caress the contours.

"Nadia?" My voice catches in my throat. "I—" I sound not quite a boy, not yet a man.

"Shut up, Little Lord. Before you hurt yourself." She glances over her shoulder with a wry smile. She pats the ground next to her.

"I'd rather be alone," I respond.

She shrugs as if to say suit yourself, but she makes no attempt to move. I shuffle forward. I clumsily sit next to her. My thigh touches hers. The contact against her smooth skin floods my thoughts.

"You've seen your mother," she says. "I'm sorry."

"Me, too." I choke back tears. I wish I was stronger. I wish she wasn't here to see me like this. I'm glad she's here at the same time.

"What are you going to do?" she asks pointedly.

"I don't know" is all I can muster.

She stands.

"You'd better decide," she says, her voice hard. "You are Edmon of House Leontes. Your father may be given the deed by the High Synod, but he's an absentee landlord. Your mother may still be alive, but she can no longer fight for us. You are the lord of Bone. These are your people." She indicates the island. "We need you."

I've come back after years only to find my mother a walking corpse, made so by my father; my best friend knew about it and didn't tell me. Then he just . . . tried to kiss me? Now Nadia admonishes me.

"You can't leave us again," she says.

"I had to go!" I fire back.

She sighs. "You're more than what they want you to be."

"And what is that?" I ask.

"You're more than someone's companion. At least that's what I always thought." She leans down. She touches her lips to my forehead. Then she's gone, as if she were a dream.

I wander the winding streets of the town. The hot sun beats down. I wipe the sweat from my brow. My head throbs with every step. Fishermen take the fish from their lines and close their shops for the Eventide. Life goes on here as it always has. The people endure. The nobles of the Pantheon and their games make no difference here. People live; they get by, day to day. They're better off without us, without me.

"Water, m'lord?" An old woman huddled in the shadow of an awning motions to her pitchers. She pours the spring water into a pottery cup and holds it out with gnarled fingers.

I take the cup and sip the cool water of the isle. I reach into my pockets for a coin, but remember I no longer carry tokens for island bartering. Companions have no need of money. Everything in Meridian is paid by subdermal credit scans.

"No coins?" The woman clucks her tongue. "I used to give water to your mother, too, when she was a little girl." The crone smiles.

I smile back; her warmth almost makes me forget my troubles.

"You knew my mother?" I ask.

"Feisty girl, that one." The old woman clucks again. "Beautiful, too. She was born here, the daughter of a fish merchant like the rest of us. Her father was a wise man, her mother even wiser. They looked to your grandmother at council meetings, called her a chief. It was clear, with your mother's beauty, she'd follow, a chieftain's daughter. She was marked with inner fire, that she was."

"Instead she was taken by a Meridian lord," I remark bitterly.

"Taken?" The old woman's smile wrinkles with consternation.

"She became my father's concubine," I explain.

"She did, young Leontes, because she was desirable. That was unavoidable, but he couldn't claim her fierceness. Her mind has always been her own. Her heart was always on the isle. It couldn't have been otherwise. She's one of us. She couldn't be taken from here any more than your voice could be taken from you without you losing what makes you Edmon Leontes. Your father had the sense to realize she should stay. She served us until she passed."

"She's not passed," I say harshly. "She's a mindless vegetable."

The old woman slaps me across the face. She points a gnarled finger at me. "Your mother's a symbol of freedom. They may take everything from us, our bodies, our minds, our lives, but they do not take our spirits," she says emphatically. "Cleopatra's spirit is with the great Mother Ocean. She was true to her people. She was fulfilled at the end knowing she fought for us and for you. Don't shame her by thinking otherwise."

"I'm sorry," I murmur and hold my cheek.

"You're young. Lapses are forgivable." She waves me off. "Bone will endure. The universe will go on. Symbols give us hope, something to strive for, and that is something worth fighting for."

The faint sound of drums echoes from on high. The Eventide feast is beginning. When I turn back, the old woman is gone, her water jugs disappeared from the streets.

Was she ever there at all?

The sun blazes ceaseless, but I stride up the hill toward the manse to enter the night.

I turn the corner that leads to the front courtyard, and a shadow catches me. I start at the sudden appearance of the hairless, robed Talousla Karr, barring my way like some demonic phantasm. The pupils of his cat eyes dilate.

"Boy," his voice says, slithering. "Did you fight with Lord Phaestion?"

This strange foreigner has watched everything that's transpired in the years I have been at House Julii, but this is the first time we've spoken words since my arrival at House Julii in Meridian.

"Tell me," he commands.

"Yes." I control my fear. I stand in place and face him.

"Who was stronger?" he asks. His forehead folds where his eyebrows should be.

"He was," I admit. "This time," I add.

"Interesting." The spypsy's voice lingers on the last syllable. He makes some sort of calculation in his head. Of what, I'm not sure. "You think you could have won?"

I shrug carelessly as if the question doesn't matter.

"Are you afraid of my appearance, boy?" His slitted eyes bore into me. I force myself to gaze back.

"No," I say with a confidence I don't feel.

"You've nothing to fear from me. I've saved your life." His bluish lips curve upward.

Sometimes I wish he hadn't saved me with his strange surgery.

"Did you kiss him?" he asks. There's a lasciviousness to his tone that makes my skin crawl.

I force myself to walk past him.

"Did you kiss him?" he asks again.

"He kissed me," I spit back.

The man considers this pensively.

"Is that what you wanted?" I say acidly. "Does it make your blood hot to think of two young boys pressing lips in the sand, spypsy?"

"You resisted him. That is also interesting," he comments.

"I'm leaving now," I say flatly. I walk away.

He bows and calls after me, "You continue to surprise and impress, Lord Leontes. I look forward to more."

I enter to the rhythm of the music. The shades have been drawn, and the villagers have gathered to celebrate in faux darkness. No one notes my entrance. Phaestion sits on a makeshift throne that rests atop a dining table, the king of the proceedings as always, a glass of wine in his hand. Hanschen sits on the table at his side, doting on him.

Sigurd is in the corner, brooding. His arm is encased in a glass cast filled with fluid. He holds it close to his chest in a sling. His face is bruised but healing. I'm not sorry.

A woman dances in the center of the circle, the crowd around her shouting and unruly. The men catcall. She tries to leave the circle, but they push her back into the center.

Disrespectful. This isn't how nighttime festivals used to be. They are behaving as if this were the orgy after the Pavaka.

I look for any familiar face in the crowd. Toothless Gorham is not at his drum. He's trying to fight his way past several Julii Academy members into the circle. They shove him back. Maestro Bertinelli is shouting something to Teacher Croack and Alberich in the corner. Croack laughs in his face and pushes The Maestro to the ground. Alberich grabs Croack and holds him back from a further beating.

My mother, attended by her nurse, sits in her chair on the outskirts of the crowd. The waxy scar on her head shines in the fireglobe light. Her eyes stare, glassy and vacant, but I feel like she wants to stand and shout, only she's locked inside a paralyzed body, unable to act. Perhaps I'm just imagining her intention.

The drums bang louder. The dancer screams above the clamor. I swiftly circle the table to Phaestion. I hop onto it to get a better view.

The dancer is Nadia. Her graceful curves whirl and spin.

"I'll not dance for you!" she screams.

She's beautiful, even in her anger. The Julii soldiers are clawing at her, grabbing her. They grope her as she comes near and clutch at her breasts and buttocks. Perdiccus jumps into the circle and takes her in his arms. She shoves him, punches him, and kicks him to the rhythm of the music. He dances out of the way like a shark matador. He tears strips of her skirt away exposing her thighs. He rips a strip from her gown. She clutches at it to prevent her breasts from being exposed.

"Come on, beautiful," he calls. "I know you want it!"

I've been here before. I look at my mother. I couldn't save her. I couldn't act that day in the hall of Old Wusong. *I can act now.*

"Stop!" I scream. I feel my vocal cords rip as I bellow. Pain doesn't matter. All eyes turn to me.

"You're in my chair," I say to Phaestion coldly.

"Edmon—"

"Get out of my seat!" I cut him off.

I see shock in his eyes, hurt. It just as quickly turns to anger. "Who's going to make me?" His smile is smug and fierce. He knows that I can't beat him physically. What he doesn't know is that I don't care.

"I am." I kick the chair out from under him. He jumps out of the way as it clatters off the table to the floor. Strength is all they understand. Strength and their rules of tradition. That's what I must use.

"I am Edmon Leontes, son of the leviathan. I rule here in his stead. My word is law. You're here only by the grace and courtesy I give you. I now renounce your invitation!"

"Edmon!" Alberich steps forward.

I shout over him, "I renounce the bonds of fosterage. I renounce your presence within my hall. Leave. Now!"

"Edmon." Phaestion steps forward and puts a hand on my shoulder. "We're sorry, but we're your brothers. You cannot—"

"You are not, nor have you ever been my brothers," I interrupt. "None of you!" I spot Edgaard's face in the crowd. The words hit him like a physical blow. I'm sorry for it, but there's nothing I can do. "You believe you've a right to do as you wish because of your birth as sons of Patriarchs, but you have no right. Not here. You will all leave. Now."

"Edmon, I'm your friend." Phaestion tries to reason again, but I know that I'm more than just a friend to him. If he considers any of The Companions a true brother, it's me. "If you revoke fosterage, it's for good."

I pull my shoulder from his touch. "Leave now or face punishment."

"Punishment!" exclaims Perdiccus. "For what?" He's truly baffled. He continues to grope for Nadia even as he says this. "We've done nothing wrong. We're just having fun."

I hop off the table and walk toward him. His face registers confusion as I grab his hand, take hold of one of his fingers, and yank violently. There is a snap of bone. He cries out. He tries to hit me with his other hand, but I hit him first. He crashes to the floor.

"What's wrong with you, Ed? First Sigurd, now me? We're companions. You're going to give that up for this?" He flicks his gaze, indicating Nadia.

"Any member of House Julii still on the isle after an hour's passing forfeits his life!" I respond.

The Julii coterie gather on one side of the room. Islanders instinctively gather behind me on the other. We're not a strong group. We're not fighters, but we do outnumber them.

Phaestion takes his place at the head of his line. "You've made a terrible mistake." His voice is calm. He stands barely half a meter from me. He looks beautiful, more vivid in this moment than I've seen him before. He speaks as if his words were prepared.

In another lifetime, we could have just been ourselves together. We would always be friends, but not here or now. I can't love him like he craves. His is an unending desire to have everyone adore him—male, female, it doesn't matter. His instinct is to covet. His will is to dominate, grasp all those around him, and contain them in a bottle.

"With a word, I could sack this island and kill all of its inhabitants. End their little lives. You know this," he says calmly.

He's right. The men behind him are warriors with weapons. It would be a bloodbath.

"My father might have something to say about an attack on his property," I counter. *Two can play politics.*

"Because of our past friendship and the love I bear you, we will honor your wishes," Phaestion says, finishing with his eyes narrowed.

Our *past* friendship, he says. He reaches a hand out to me.

"Goodbye, Phaestion," I say gently before he can touch me again. He nods and turns. His group follows.

Alberich lingers, shaking his head. "Edmon, I understand, but you must also understand—this will complicate things. You've forced House Leontes into conflict with House Julii, without regard to your father's position. He will take umbrage. It may not be tomorrow, but the hammer will fall. I hope you're prepared."

So do I. "Go," I say. Alberich follows, leaving with the others. The Maestro also turns to go. "Maestro," I call out. He looks back at me. "If you stay, you will be welcome here, but you may never be able to return to Lyria again."

The old man is caught between the two groups and the choice between his old home and what he knows to be right. "My boy," he says as he steps beside me, "we'll train every day from now on if that's what you wish. And we will record. They will hear your music across the stars, I swear. Most of the galaxy's finest musicians don't have a degree from any university. Even Andreas Catalano dropped out before graduating, you know. Besides, I doubt there are any at the Sophia School who could boast having the full private instruction of Maestro Bertinelli." I put a hand on his shoulder. He smiles. "I'm proud of you, my boy. And so are they."

He gestures to the crowd of islanders remaining in the hall, who nod at me in solidarity. Nadia clutches at the torn fabric of her dress, holding it together. She stares straight ahead, defiant and proud. My mother, scarred and vacant-eyed, sits with no expression on her face at all, but I know she, too, is with me.

The breeze lifts Nadia's dark hair from her shoulders. It fans the white linen tatters of her dress. She stands at the cliffs overlooking the ocean.

"Here again?" I ask.

"We're always here, aren't we?" she replies softly as I approach.

I don't know all they did to her. I only hope I stopped it in time. I had lost sight of her when the crowd dispersed. I knew she couldn't have gone far. I knew we would come back to this place.

"You want to be alone," I say. I turn to leave, but she lunges and grabs for me, burying her face in my chest.

When did she become so much shorter than me?

"They forced me to dance for them. I fought, but they were too many and too strong. I felt helpless, Edmon. They were going to do more, if you hadn't been there . . ." Her words pour out.

"I'm sorry." I pet her hair. "I tried to be who you wanted me to be. I wasn't fast enough."

My excuses fall like Meridian twilight, never reaching their destination. She looks up at me, and her soft lips find mine, and there are no more words. She kisses again and again. She smells of the dirt and dust of the island. The clean salt of the sea. It's familiar and exotic all at once. I feel her lips part. The gentle tip of her tongue grazes mine.

How does she know to do that?

The blood rises in my face, hot and red. I feel myself stirring below. An ache and hardness and panic. I've not kissed a girl before. Not like this.

She pulls away and brushes the hair from her face. She clutches the broken strap of her dress. My eyes lock on her smooth, tanned skin, then drift down to the curve of her full breasts hinted at beneath the torn linen. She catches my look. I turn away, ashamed at my transgression.

"It's okay. You can look if you want." Her voice is husky and calming.

My body reaches forward. It's all I can do to stop myself from reaching down to hide the sight of it thrumming against my leggings.

"I should go," I say, my voice cracking.

"Wait."

I'm desperate to leave, more desperate to stay. I don't know what I should be feeling. *What would a warrior do?*

"What's happening to us, Edmon?"

She embraces me again. I turn so she can't feel my arousal. This only upsets her.

"Forget it," she says. "Go." She pulls away brusquely.

I feel terrible. I've rejected her. I'm so confused. I grab her hastily and kiss her again, hard and clumsy. She laughs. "I'm sorry," I say. I'm not sure what I've done that's funny.

"You kiss like an ox fish," she says, snorting.

I feel the red in my face. "I've never done it before," I admit.

"Liar," she teases.

"Well, Phaestion kissed me at the beach," I stammer. "But that was just today and—"

"You kissed Phaestion today?" Her brow furrows. "I didn't think you—"

"It's not like that. I mean, he's beautiful. When you get near him—"

"There's something different about him, I know," she says, cutting me off. "He has some power. Something that makes people want to be near and love him. It's intoxicating."

"Yeah," I mutter. His physical beauty is only part of it. There's something else, something chemical. "His beauty isn't natural," I say. "Not like yours." My voice cracks again. *I'm such an idiot.* "He's like a god. You're—"

She puts her finger against my lips to shush me. "Please don't keep spoiling this moment by saying something stupid." She smiles and leans in close. "Just do it like you did before."

We kiss again.

"How was that?" My voice is hoarse.

We kiss, and we kiss, and we kiss. We kneel down to the earth. I lose my balance. I fall on my butt like a lout. She laughs again. "Always so awkward. Little Lord, I'm going to have to save you from falling again."

"I remember." I pull her to me. We wrestle like we did when we were young. Now I roll on top, pinning her. "I remember you always used to beat me at this."

Then I feel her hand close around my hardness. I gasp. Our eyes lock. Neither of us breathe.

"I didn't mean to," she says, stammering now. "Does it hurt?"

I shake my head no. My pulse quickens. I want to run, but I don't.

The other Companions had concubines to experiment with. Now I wish I hadn't refused. Maybe I wouldn't feel like a colossal lump, not knowing what to do.

She gently slides a hand to the strap of her dress. She pulls it from her shoulder. Her naked breasts are bare in the sunlight like full, newly ripened fruit.

"You can close your mouth, idiot," she says mildly.

I clap my jaw shut, not realizing it was open. I try to swallow, and my throat feels so tight. The blood pounds in my neck.

"Your turn."

My mind is no longer working. I pull my shirt over my head, following her lead. The sun blazes against my bare skin for the first time in years. Nadia's eyes run along the lines of my torso. She kneels down and gently pulls my leggings to my ankles. I almost trip again trying to step out of them. My hand goes to her smooth shoulder for support.

"So clumsy." She chuckles. She sucks in her breath as she stares.

Her touch, when she holds me, is slow. I feel a tightening in my belly. I kneel down. I brush a lock of hair from her dark eyes. "I can feel your heartbeat," she says, her hands still on me. I kiss her hard. She pulls me into her, and as we roll on the white earth, entangled in each other, my hand closes around the softness of a breast. Our bodies create a drumbeat, and I feel the vibration of the strings of the universe, the song of life pulsing through us both. Waves crash between us for what seems forever and an instant all at once. All that's left is me breathing on the ground staring at the sky. In the distance, a siren calls for her mate.

I lock eyes with hers. "What did you do to me?" I whisper.

"Same thing you did to me." Her head rests in the crook of my neck, and her dark eyes look up to me. "You saved me."

I lean down and kiss her. My eyes close in the warm bliss of the summer isle sun. This contentment feels so rare.

—

I don't know how much time has passed when my eyes open. *A moment? Eternity?*

It's a rustling behind me that's woken me, the sound of a few skittered pebbles. Nadia, still deep in slumber, does not stir. I see a flash of red-copper hair behind the rocks.

"Phaestion?" I stand. "Phaestion?" I ask again.

He bursts from behind the boulder and sprints away so fast. I take a step after him, but he's gone. I can see the red hair trailing behind him like the lick of a flame. He rounds a bend out of my sight.

"What is it?" Nadia asks. She pushes herself up to sitting.

"Nothing." I return to her side. "Go back to sleep, love." The words sound new and strange on my lips, but she doesn't notice. I lie beside her, and she drifts off once again. My eyes do not close this time. A few moments pass, and I hear the blast of the sondi. The large black airship looms over us. I feel more than see a pair of cold gray eyes staring out from a porthole. The ship makes a soft bank away from the island, sailing into the sky over the Southern Sea.

CHAPTER 14

Trio

The morning of my eighteenth birthday begins the same as every other has in the last three years. I wake up, arm stretched out over Nadia's belly. My bleared vision comes into focus. Her dark eyes are already open, looking at me with playful derision.

"Happy birthday, Little Lord," she whispers. She presses her lips to mine. Very slightly, only very slightly. I want more. I grab her and pull her close for something deeper.

She pushes me off. "No!" she squeals playfully. "You need to sanitize first!" I grab her more tightly. Then I breathe the hottest, most foul-smelling breath of morning I can into her face. She struggles to turn away. "No, Little Lord! No!"

She slaps me gently across the cheek. I grab her wrist and kiss it softly. I pull her arm around my neck. Our legs intertwine. I feel myself rising to meet the softness of her body. Now she's the one grabbing me closer. We kiss and touch and caress. Her body is as familiar to me now as the blanket I was born in. My hips rise to enter her . . .

"Wait," she breathes.

The blast of a seashell horn sounds—the call to the boats. I groan as if in pain, rolling over onto my stomach. My head and arms hang off the edge of the bed.

"It's your birthday. They'll understand," she says softly.

"I have to go." I sit up. "With the embargo, we barely survive. What kind of leader would I be if I allowed others to work in my stead? We already live on top of the hill. I can't let myself be any different from any of them."

"But you are different," insists Nadia. "You're the one that will suffer if this independence from your father fails."

"That's why I need to go." I stand and call for the drawers. They pop out of the walls, and I quickly dress in the linens and large-brimmed hat of the islanders. She sits up, sweeping the sheets around her. She should get up, too. Everyone must work. That's the way of it, as much as I understand the desire to rest at least for a day.

"Meet me at the cliffs after you've held court?" she asks with a sultry gaze.

"And miss the afternoon nap?" I yawn and stretch, half teasing. Of course the sleep would be nice before the Eventide feast, but if anything is going to make me skip a few minutes of valuable sleep, it's the chance to be alone with her.

"I have something special to give you for your birthday," she says in a silky tone.

"Oh, do you?" I sweep her into my arms. The second sound of the seashell rings. "After court. I will see you then."

Work on the sea isn't easy. The sun beats down as we check our traps and our nets for hours. Today's haul isn't large, but with rationing, a day's or even several weeks' bad take should be manageable. The pod captain calls, "Pull!" We work the lines at his expert direction.

Gorham smiles at me with brown gums. The old man has become withered but seems as happy as ever working by my side. Later he'll be drumming at the feast as always.

I'm no different than anyone else on Bone, but I face the worry. There aren't many resources available here. The weather is too warm, and the isle too bare to support large forests or game. Fish and kelp are our main sources of sustenance. I'm the one to ensure everyone has enough. I listen to my fish captains, and then we set policy together. We move to different spawning grounds on a cycle to avoid overfishing. Lately we've been venturing farther and farther out to sea seeking new sources. Still, our haul has dwindled. Even if we weren't under the Pantheon embargo placed on us by my father as my punishment for disrespecting the fosterage, this planet is getting hotter and the fish are dying. I can feel it and see it daily.

The population of Meridian in the last century has boomed, and resources in the Twilight Band have dwindled, too. The opening of the new Fracture Point should have increased Tao's access to foreign resources, but as Phaestion told me once, we have little to barter with.

Add to that a Nightsider culture that has always been xenophobic. Eighty years ago, we forced all aliens to fight in the Combat or be expelled from our atmo. I've heard of only one off-worlder who stayed and survived, though he disappeared soon after his Combat triumph.

Midday comes. We row the boats into the docks, carrying our meager haul ashore. We've done all we can this day. It's time to hold court before the afternoon rest. I catch Nadia's eye as she works with the women in the kelp farms just inside the harbor. Her smile is comforting as always, but I can tell the harvest today is also thin.

It's your birthday, Little Lord, I can almost hear Nadia's voice in my head. *Don't worry so much.* I smile back at her. She's right, of course. There is her and me, our home, and that's not so bad at all.

I sit on the chair in the foyer listening to the grievance of a fisherman. He claims that his neighbor is responsible for the damage to a shared wall between their dwellings. My mother sits beside me in her chair as her handmaid attends her. She stares vacantly. I keep her beside me as a reminder of the sacrifice she has made for our freedom. I like to think I can feel her spirit by my side even in her current state. Her presence gives me comfort. Gorham stands on my other side, advising me. I am still young after all, and as a village elder, his are words of experience.

I listen as intently as I can, but the worries of the harvest, the excitement of meeting Nadia on the cliffs soon, the notion that I shouldn't have to deal with such petty things . . . all distracts me.

"A shared wall?" I ask.

"Yes, my lord," both men reply in unison.

"Has this happened before?"

"No, my lord," they reply.

I look to Gorham. "If the wall affects both, then perhaps there must be compromises from both sides," he suggests.

I nod in agreement. "Very well," I say, trying to sound formal. "You're both to mend the wall on the damaged side. Together. As recompense, Talman"—I point to the man who has damaged the property—"you shall host dinner. Break bread with each other. The only way we survive is by taking care of each other. And Jayhotep"—I refer to the fisherman who brought the grievance—"forgive."

The men bow their heads. I don't know if what I've asked them to do is fair. My word isn't binding. I've no army to enforce my decisions. They come to me as an objective party for suggestions. In turn, I ask them for their expertise.

How are we to make harvest? Can we farm the kelp more efficiently? Can we risk a communiqué with another island to smuggle in goods? The village seems to work as well as it can. On Bone, *village* is another word for family.

I call the afternoon's proceedings to a close for the traditional midday rest. The villagers bow and exit. Later, some will return for the music and feast. Right now, I'm anxious to meet Nadia, though. Anything else can wait. It's my birthday, after all.

"My lord." Maestro Bertinelli approaches me just as I'm about to slip out. His pale skin has become ruddy and freckled working on the boats with everyone. At first, he resisted the idea of joining the fishing, but eventually came to see that no one's situation on the isle would be changing soon. He accepted his lot was cast with the rest of us on Bone the day he chose me over Phaestion. Now, he's just as much a fisherman as any, but he's still a maestro of Lyria first and foremost.

"I've been wanting to record a new track to pirate out to the stations on Meridian. I know that every broadcast is a risk, but your last single, 'Tradimento del Popolo,' has over two hundred million extractions off the aquagraphic nets. I've been in touch with contacts on Lyria. We may have a broadcaster off-world if we can convince some of the Meridian jockeys to smuggle the data in photon packets through the Fracture."

I nod.

He sighs impatiently. "Do you know what this means, Edmon?"

"Maestro, I'm happy to record. It's exciting for me to share my music, but my concerns are here, on the island now."

"Edmon," he says, clucking. "The opera and your responsibilities are one and the same. Every song spreads the word of your story, the plight of your people against the oppression of the Pantheon."

I can tell he's about to lecture me.

"If your father wanted to return to the isle and take control, what would stop him? Your popularity!" he says, answering his own question. "Your struggle against the regime keeps him at bay so long as you remain publicly relevant. Killing you would make you a martyr. Music is your safety. 'Tradimento del Popolo' . . ."

"Betrayal of the People," I translate.

"Yes, the tune based on your mother's lullaby. Your fans are calling it 'The Song of Edmon'!" he exclaims. "Music is your message!"

"I never wanted to be a symbol," I insist.

He nods sadly. "That's precisely why you are." He understands my wishes, and yet he's happy to be my spinmeister, penning lyrical manifestos.

It is wrong for me to blame anyone but myself for my current situation. I knew very well what I was singing when I recorded The Maestro's songs. I also know I can't stop singing any more than I can stop breathing. If I'm as popular as he says, the songs will be a political statement regardless of their content.

I exhale, resigned. "No, you're right. We'll continue."

The Maestro skips off with an aquatablet and a stylus in hand. No doubt he's preparing a new aria of resistance. He may think my fame keeps us safe, but a tickle in the back of my brain tells me each defiance also infuriates Edric.

He won't let it continue.

She stands brown and naked in the sun. My heart catches, and the blood rushes to my skin. I resist the urge to sprint to her and grab her. No, then she will have won, and we both will have lost. She knows the power the sight of her has on me. Her erect nipples, the smooth curve of her hips, all lead my eyes to the thatch of dark hair between her two silky thighs. She is seduction pulling me slowly toward her. I meet her stare of mild derision. She beckons me. I move to her but do not acquiesce, not yet. That would be too easy. Nadia never likes it easy. My fingertips reach forward and gently graze the smooth skin of her neck. I lean in and kiss her softly. Gentle pressure, now here, now there, her neck, her finely crafted collarbone. Her nipple enters my mouth. She breaks away, then grabs me fiercely. We devour each other with mouths, eyes, and hands. We hug the contours of each other's bodies. She sighs as my mouth tastes her inner thighs, then moves closer to her center . . .

We lie entangled in each other's limbs just as we did on that day three years ago after the first time. The afternoon sun warms us, and sweat glistens on our bodies. I feel myself drifting into blissful slumber.

"We won't be able to do that again for a while, love," she whispers.

I pull myself from the brink of oblivion and prop myself on an elbow. "Are you hurt?"

She looks away, laughing, with a secret joke in her head.

"What?" I insist.

"Nothing, Little Lord," she teases.

I grab her. "Well, I know it isn't nothing!"

I kiss her in all the spots that I know torture her with pleasure. "Tell me," I growl. She yelps and pushes me away. "Tell me!" I admonish again.

"It's your birthday gift, my lord," she says.

"I thought you just gave me my gift," I say slyly.

"Oh, no. Not that." Her sentence hangs in the air. The sound of the waves crashing and the summer breeze keeps it suspended. "I am with child," she says quietly.

Everything drops to the ground. I'm numb. I'm terrified. I'm speechless. My heart pounds. I'm overjoyed. *It can't be true. What am I going to do? What's going to happen? What of my father? He can't know.*

"Hey!" She pulls my face back toward her. She looks me in the eye, and I realize it's going to be all right. Nothing matters but her and me. Not the island, not Phaestion, nor my father, nor my mother's condition. None of it. *Your life, all life, will end,* the leviathan once told me. It does not matter. Me and her and a child, whether we live another five hundred years or another five minutes, now is all we have.

"Nadia, I will never leave you," I whisper. She buries her head in my chest, and I know she feels safe. We lie that way forever.

Forever doesn't last.

I'm awoken by the sound of ships. A fleet of black sondis sails on the clouds.

Nadia and I enter the manse. Many are already gathered for the Eventide festivities, but there are only a few moments to prepare. "Ready the room to receive guests," I command. We set up a chair as a makeshift throne at the top of the foyer staircase. "My mother will be on the right, Nadia beside me on the left," I direct.

These are not servants; they are simply friends, but there is no time for familiarity. I refuse to meet the interlopers with any sign of weakness.

"Gorham?" I call out. The old musician pads alongside me as the party scrambles to construct a welcome.

"At least twenty sondis bearing the crest of the leviathan have landed. They have docked, and soldiers have disembarked. We have word they're coming through the town, making their way here. Spread the message that all townspeople are to stay inside with the doors shut. They are not to engage the invaders until they have been received by me. Send envoy to the soldiers. Make sure they arrive here for parlay." I gently grip the old man's shoulder. He nods and is off.

This is all happening too fast.

The chair is set, and my mother is brought beside me. I take my seat and reach my hand to hers. Her vacant stare doesn't register the touch, but the contact isn't for her. It's for me. My remembrance of the woman she was gives me strength.

"Are you ready?" Nadia asks me as she stands proudly at my side.

"I'll have to be," I mutter.

The double doors of the manse open. Gorham steps forward. "Lord Edric Leontes of House Wusong-Leontes, two-time champion of the

Combat." He bows and steps out of the way barely in time to avoid being hit by my father coming through. He's still tall and powerful, his pale hair now mostly silver. He strides forward, looking like a god in his flowing robes and armor. Off his left shoulder is Alberich, stout and grizzled as always. On his right is Edgaard, now at fourteen almost as tall as my father, though still lean and angular from boyhood. There's no doubt, seeing them side by side, that this is his true son and heir.

My eyes connect with my brother's for a moment. His sky-blue irises were once warm and full of wonder. Now I sense nothing, neither love nor hate. Alberich, too, holds no sign of acknowledgment. It appears I have no friends in this company. Behind them, soldiers wearing the blue and silver of House Leontes file in.

"You think to greet me as lord of the isle, do you?" Edric snarls.

I stand. "I greet you merely as I am, nothing more."

"Edmon"—his tone is soft, deadly—"it's time for this to end. You will return to House Wusong-Leontes to fulfill your duties. My governorship will be reestablished here on the isle."

"I will not leave my people," I say flatly. Edric never cared for nuance or pleasantry anyway.

I see the wave of anger pass across his face, but then, curiously, he bottles it.

He must have expected that I wouldn't acquiesce.

Edgaard and Alberich shift uncomfortably at the confrontation. They know how to fight in an arena, but they have no stomach for the war of words that is politics.

"The responsibilities are not yours," Edric says tightly. "They're mine."

"These are not your people," I answer without hesitation. "They were my mother's." I gesture to the lifeless form in her chair, anger in my voice. "Now they're mine. They need no governance from you."

Does he want a weakling son, or a son that will stand and face him? Aren't you proud, Father?

"Then they shall have none. That doesn't change the fact that you will be leaving this day."

"Shipped off to another noble house to be their training dummy while my mother is mutilated?" I ask, fists clenched.

Edgaard can no longer stand it. He steps forward, red-faced. "You're lucky you weren't imprisoned for shaming the honor our father bestowed on you!"

Edric raises his hand, signaling for his younger son to remain quiet.

Edgaard, he has twisted you far worse than he has me.

"No, Edmon," Edric says calmly. "You won't be returning to the comforts of House Julii."

I snort at the mention of the *comforts* of my former imprisonment.

"Have you forgotten? You're to be wed to the daughter of Old Wusong." He smiles cruelly.

"Miranda," I whisper.

I remember the day that Edgaard was named heir, and I was promised to the emperor's daughter.

"You're betrothed." Edric grins wolfishly.

"In order to secure the fortune and power of House Wusong for you. There is one problem, Father," I add with venom. "I'm not your heir. The emperor may have betrothed me to Lady Miranda that day, but you also disinherited me from my birthright. I'm your second illegitimate son. Is that not right?"

Edric tilts his head in acknowledgment.

"Old Wusong," I say, "is a feeble old man. He no longer even attends councils of the High Synod. You've assumed his seat and power. Change the rules. Make Edgaard, your true son, claim the honors that go with the title you gave him."

Edric grins dryly. "If Edgaard could take this burden, he would. He knows the responsibilities of family outweigh his personal desires, unlike you. The whole of Tao saw Old Wusong accept only you as consort to his daughter for reasons that pass my understanding. Even

I cannot change this outcome, much as I would like, *son.*" The word is an epithet on his lips.

Why would Old Wusong demand that it be me that marry his daughter? Most probably the withered old prune enjoys tormenting his paladin.

"Wait until Old Wusong is dead," I suggest, "then do whatever you like with his daughter and your son. Problem solved for us both. See? I do think of our family."

"Do you?" he asks sardonically.

"Of course. I think of my true family here on Bone," I add.

That was stupid, Edmon, I think. *You're facing the monster. Is it necessary to risk his wrath because you wish to cut him?*

Edric grits his teeth and continues. "Wusong is old but very much alive. He has demanded that his daughter marry before the turn of the yearly cycle so that he may still be present to see it done. So return with us and take your vows to Lady Miranda. Afterward, I don't care to think what will become of you."

"You'd wish me to return to the isle?" I ask with suspicion. I make it a point not to say *let me return to the isle.* I want it known that he doesn't *let me* do anything.

"When you acknowledge the rule of House Wusong-Leontes, you may return."

Can I trust him? His offer makes sense for him. I don't have to play actual husband to this Miranda Wusong, this stranger. Perhaps, in time, I may annul our union through the College of Electors. I'll be absolved of all responsibilities as son of Edric Leontes, but only after this duty is executed. I'll return to the island, but Bone will not ever be sovereign; my father is clear that I do not govern here. Perhaps Edgaard or maybe one of my hapless sisters will be overseer of affairs here. That's as good as it is going to get.

Perhaps it's fair. I can still live a quiet life here with Nadia and my child. I turn to my mother, who stares straight ahead, glassy-eyed. *Do I see a stirring behind her gaze? A simmer of defiance?* I turn to Nadia. Her dark eyes are as beautiful as ever, strong and proud. I survey the room. Gorham, Maestro Bertinelli, and the rest of them look on with a fire of determination.

I know what I must do.

"That will not be possible," I say calmly. "I'm already promised to another." I reach my hand out and feel Nadia's cool, slender fingers grip my own. We aren't married by the laws of Meridian, but what I've said is true enough. She's mine, and I'm hers.

"I see." My father's lips purse tightly. The room goes silent. I feel the screws being twisted in the backs of both our brains.

Who will break first?

Edric exhales and says resignedly, "This certainly changes things, doesn't it?"

He pauses. Everyone holds their breaths . . .

"Let us then put this behind us. If you're indeed already married, Old Wusong will no longer see you fit to marry his daughter. He must accept another. Perhaps Edgaard. I see no reason why we shouldn't then leave each other in peace, once and for all."

The crowd smiles nervously in response. *Is he sincere? Can I trust him?*

"There's still the matter to be settled of governance," I say firmly, not quite believing this turn of events.

"In due time, we shall discuss plans for the isle's future," Edric says calmly. "First, though, it's been a long trip. I ask that my company be allowed to rest, break bread, and enjoy the sunlight we've long been without."

My father sounds, for the first time in all the aquagraphics I've ever seen of him, beaten, tired, and unwilling to fight. I nod. I am uneasy, but it is finally over—the enmity, the fighting. I will be disinherited and forever forgotten and will remain here on the island with my true family. It would be foolish to let my guard down, but if he's making a genuine offer, time will bear it out.

"Agreed. See the guests situated. Prepare for the Eventide feast," I call out. The islanders raise their voices with a cheer.

I turn to Nadia, who meets my gaze with a solemn smile. She leans and whispers in my ear, "Is that how you plan on proposing to me, Little Lord? If you're asking to get married," she teases, "you're going to have to do much better than that if you want me to say yes."

—

The rhythm of the drums pulses through our bodies. I pull her close to me. Our eyes connect. I spin her away. The crowd surrounding us on the dance floor whoops in excitement. Nadia runs toward me. I lift her off the ground as the song reaches climax. The crowd applauds. I gently lower her to the floor where she steps on tiptoes to meet my lips.

"They aren't dancing," she whispers.

Her eyes flick to the Nightsiders—Edric, Alberich, and Edgaard sitting in chairs at the head of a feast table. Alberich is stern with his arms folded across his barrel chest. Edgaard tentatively smiles as someone fills his cup. My father, however, sits with a large grin on his face, looking as if he actually enjoys the festivities. It is unsettling.

"They don't dance in Meridian," I whisper back. "This is unfamiliar. That's all." She looks at me skeptically. "I haven't forgotten the day of my brother's christening or what he did to my mother," I whisper solemnly. My trust has not been gained. The islanders don't know what kind of danger they are in from the military might of the Pantheon. My father could wipe us out if he wanted. We'd fight back to lose just the same.

I need to make sure this pact is real.

I raise my hands, signaling for the music to cease. I stand center before where my father is seated. I grab a glass filled with ale that the islanders have fermented from kelp and toast. "To our honored guests from House Wusong-Leontes, welcome."

The crowd claps in response.

Edric stands and holds his own goblet out. "And to my son, Edmon, Lord of the Isle of Bone." He pauses as the crowd waits on his next words. If there's condescension in his tone, I don't hear it. "I am proud of you, my son."

I'm stunned. This is the last thing I expect. Edric Leontes has forever been a shadow in my life casting fear and doubt. Tyrant and fiend. Monster. Those are the names I think to describe him. He's a ruthless killer who has sought his own advancement at the expense of those around him, including his own family. Even so, to hear him say he is proud of me touches something within I didn't even know was there. I've longed to hear him say those words, in spite of all he has done. I'm not sure I ever realized it until this moment.

"Thank you, Father," I respond. "With your blessing, there is another I must toast." The crowd hushes as I stand in the center of the circle. I take Nadia's hand in mine and kneel before her. "Nadia, my love, you are my heart. You are my song. With the eyes of witnesses before us, from the Island of Bone and the Pantheon of Tao, will you make me your husband for all time?"

She brings a hand to her mouth, and though we've been together for years, though we have a child to be born, I see the tears well in her eyes. She nods yes. I stand and pull her into my embrace. I whisper, "I will always love you, Nadia."

I glance at my father. His smile fades for a split second and then returns. I have sealed our agreement before all present. It may not be what he originally intended, but it is the bargain we have made. I nod, and he returns the gesture.

The revelry continues into the evening. Musicians play. Dancers dance. We eat and drink. Nadia does not leave my side. I'm in bliss.

"Edmon," she says, pulling me from the dizziness of feeling like everything in my life is on the perfect path.

"What?" I ask, carefree, absent.

"You aren't here," she muses. "Where are you?"

"Oh." I smile. "I was thinking that for the first time in my life, I'm happy. That's all."

"No, *we* are happy," she corrects. She places my hand on her belly. We kiss. Then she pulls back for a moment. "Can you trust him?"

"I trust him to maintain his own best interests. No more, no less. Our union gives him leverage to ply Old Wusong to allow the princess to marry my brother. That will buy us time. Beyond that, we will have to see."

"Then what?"

"One step at a time, my love."

"Edmon." A hand touches my shoulder. Edgaard's square face and pale eyes loom over me. "Our father would like to have words with you." Edgaard stands a hair taller than me, though he is lanky, not bearing the full muscle of adulthood yet. I gesture for him to lead the way.

I jest to Nadia, "Perhaps there will be more surprises from Edric the Compassionate?"

She intertwines her arm in mine and whispers, "He's still dangerous, Edmon. Be careful."

"I know better than most, wife," I reply, trying out the word. She rolls her eyes at me.

We follow Edgaard to the table. My father stands, his ice-blue eyes locking onto mine.

"You would like to speak with me?" I ask.

"Not here." His eyes flick to Nadia. "I would speak with you. Alone."

I take Nadia's hand in mine. "Anything you can say to me can be said to her as well." Anger flares in his eyes at my defiance. I try to soften it with a conciliatory tone. "You're right, Father," I say. Calling him that name sounds strange to my ears. I've used it so little. "Privacy would be best."

He smiles, tight-lipped. I lead them from the hall with Nadia on my arm.

—

The screamer-skiff cruises the calm of the harbor. I point her toward the open Southern Sea with a gentle howl. Nadia and I stand on the prow. Spray hits our faces, cooling our skin against the heat of the never-setting sun. I turn the yoke and bank off a rising wave to grab more spray.

"Edmon!" she shouts in mock anger. "You'll upset the guests."

I glance back at Edric, Alberich, and Edgaard, all looking stern. Their dark robes and armor glint in the light, making them look fierce and dour.

"I'm not sure they could be any more upset," I whisper jokingly. She playfully hits me on the arm, and I acquiesce. "All right, all right." I level the skiff into a gentle angle. I slow the speed and dip her hull to rest where we bob on the blue-green brine.

I turn to the cadre of men. Their visages range from furtive to glowering.

"I want to begin by thanking you." I hope to break the tension. "By visiting Bone with respect, it goes a long way toward mending relations with Meridian."

"You're almost a man now, Edmon, and so I will treat you as such," my father growls. He addresses me politely, but somehow I don't think what he says can be good. "There has been a shift on Tao. Not in just the political climate, but in the physical climate, the emotional climate."

I nod. "I'm aware."

In truth, I've not been entirely informed of the news from Meridian. The embargo has been almost total. We receive no goods, nor supplies, nor information. My time at House Julii, however, has not been forgotten, either. Phaestion intimated my father had been maneuvering to take hold of the Synod. Phaestion had his own plans to the contrary. The common people were caught in between. Inevitably, there would be a reckoning. It's something I want no part of.

"The people are restless," Edric says. "They've lost faith in the government. The economy is depressed. Protests and crime have risen."

His eyes cast blame. *He believes I play some part in this unrest?*

"Meridian is a powder keg. If the dissidents are not controlled, if chaos reigns, it will trigger a long spiral into darkness. It will be an end to our civilization."

He, like the others, truly believes the Pantheon is the greatest human accomplishment in the universe? What a joke!

I can't help but laugh.

"Edmon, reconsider your choices." His tone is pained. It costs him to ask, and it is unlike him to ask.

I look at Nadia. "Reconsider what?" I feel my anger rising.

"Marry Lady Miranda Wusong. Secure the Leontes name to the ruling house of Tao."

His request is now a command. *Now, that's the father I know.* I take Nadia's hand in mine. I'll not leave her, and she'll not leave me, either. "I will not." I'm no longer a boy to be bullied. I can fight him now.

He moves more quickly than I would have thought possible. He shoves me aside. I hit the deck of the skiff, hard. I scramble, but Alberich plants a knee in my back, holding me down. Edgaard grabs my flailing arms. I try to get up, but someone yanks my head and slams it to the deck. My skin splits, and blood from my scalp streams into my eyes. Through the haze, I see Edric grab hold of Nadia. She screams, but the sound is cut off almost before it starts. With a quick twist of his hands, Edric breaks her neck. Bones snap. She goes limp in his arms.

"No!" I scream, my voice raw.

Edric lifts Nadia's lifeless body and gently rolls her over the railing. She tumbles into the sea. With a splash, she is gone.

"Nadia!"

His icy eyes bore into me. "I reasoned with you. You refused. I treated you with due regard. You didn't listen. I tried to spare you this, but you are an insolent child. You don't get to choose. I've already chosen for you. You want to be a man? Learn the consequences. Power is all that ever matters. Defy power and you will be broken."

"Monster!" My voice breaks into a wail. Edgaard holds my head against the deck. "She was carrying our child!"

There's no response to this, only the sound of the waves.

"Our baby. She was carrying our child! Nadia! Nadia!"

My body is racked by coughs and sobs. The men just stare. A siren calls out, lone and forlorn in the distance.

"Let him up," Edric says finally. The pressure of Edgaard's and Alberich's weight lifts from me, but I don't rise. I am pasted to the wet deck, sobbing.

"Get up," Edric commands coldly.

I push myself to my hands and knees. I look at him through blood streaming down my face.

"Coward! You claim power is all that matters? Face me, you piece of human waste! You killer of innocent women! You killer of unborn children! Champion of the Combat? No. Coward!" I spit into his face. "You are champion of filth! May all your riches fade to dust and your name pass unremembered!"

It is the ultimate insult to a man who wants to live forever and have his name written across the Elder Stars.

"Get up," he says again. Alberich and Edgaard grab my limbs and stand me upright. "I will fight you," he says simply, his voice unwavering.

I've never fought my father before. He's terrifying. I hesitate but only for a moment. Hatred outweighs fear. I charge with all my strength. I kick. I punch. I've been trained, but I am out of practice since I left House Julii. Still, I'm not helpless. Whirling, I strike, clipping him across the jaw. I see his eyes widen with a startling realization—I am a threat—the son he thought was weak and useless.

Now he exerts his full strength. He is not a boy soldier; he's no automaton. He is a seasoned pit fighter who clawed his way from the bottom of an arcology to stand triumphant over all comers. Even my fury doesn't make me equal. He is the perfect balance of strength, speed, and deadly accuracy as he blocks everything I throw at him. His hand whips out. He punches me in the throat, the only punch he even throws. One touch and I crumple.

"You're weak," he says evenly. "Your child would have been weak, too. They would have taken him in the Pavaka."

I gasp for air. I plod forward. *Don't give up,* I think. *I just need one scratch to end him. Anything. Just one. For Nadia.*

Kick. Punch. Jab. Cross. Uppercut. Jab.

He grabs my fist—actually grabs it in midair. He turns my wrist back. Snap. My bones break. Then his fist comes for me again. It slams me like a rock. My vision goes black, then starry. I can feel my cheekbones indented, crushed like a seabird's eggshell. Still I try to stand.

"Edmon." I hear my name being called. Something slams sharp and swiftly against the back of my head.

A sea monster slithers beneath the waves of my dreams.

CHAPTER 15

Elegy

I exist in glimpses: an azure island sky, the white adobe of the manse, a set of doors opening . . .

Eventually, I become aware of my weight hoisted between two people, my feet dragging on the ground.

"What is the meaning of this?" asks an outraged voice.

"Edmon Leontes has abdicated his position as your overseer," says Edric.

Edric or maybe the monster of the sea?

"Put him down or I promise—"

"Ah, yes, the music teacher." I feel the smile in my father's tone. "You've made enough promises to my son." Bones snap. A body hits the floor. The Maestro stares up at me at an odd angle, blood trickling from his mouth.

"Stop!" I recognize Gorham's voice.

My body sags as one of my supports leaves me—*Edgaard,* I think. I cannot reconcile this lanky man with the innocent-eyed memory of my brother.

A cry from Gorham is followed by a wet smacking sound against the stone floor.

"Cleopatra?" Alberich asks.

"End it. Swiftly," Edric responds.

Darkness again.

I'm strapped to a chair. Edgaard and Alberich sit across from me. My arms feel heavy. The rest of me, sore and weak. *Am I underwater? Inside a fishbowl?*

"What's wrong with me?" The words are thick on my tongue.

"You're under mild sedation," answers Alberich.

"Drugs from Nonthera make you weak, open to suggestion," adds Edgaard. "In the event that you might decide to try something foolish before the wedding."

"Wedding?"

Nadia. My mother. Maestro Bertinelli and Gorham. Murdered. All so I could marry Miranda Wusong and secure my father's position.

"The preparations are underway. You'll be married within the next diurnal cycle," Edgaard replies coolly.

I turn my eyes. It feels like they travel a kilometer before I look Alberich square in the face.

"There was never any chance for peace, was there?" I ask through numb lips.

He is silent. I rest my head against the seat back and close my eyes.

"Once you've done your duty, it will be over. Father will let you live out your days on Bone. You can return to a life of obscurity, provided you never sing of rebellion or raise a word against the Electors and High Synod again," says Edgaard.

To the depths with you, brother.

"Don't you care about your family?" he goes on. "About the future of this world?"

I summon the strength to open my eyes one last time. I stare at him with blades of hatred. I barely have the strength even for that. Sleep takes me.

—

I wake. *How long have I been here? Have I been slumbering this whole time?*

Aquagraphic images flash before my eyes.

"Edric Leontes was born in the arcologies of Tao. Through his own cunning and strength, he rose from the killing matches of the Under Circuit to gain sponsorship, fighting under the House Wusong banner in the Combat," the computerized voice drones, accompanying images of my father fighting.

Why are they showing me this? I cannot move my arms or my legs. I'm in some sort of pod, bathed in a kind of gel. The images and sound project in front of me.

"Edric's happiest moment was not his wins in the arena, but rather it was the birth of his eldest son, Edmon Leontes." My father strides from the birthing chamber to the balcony, where he holds a child to the star of Tao and proclaims, "This is Edmon, the son of Leontes. Let all behold and claim, 'The son is greater than the father! He is a leviathan!'"

My father loves me. The thought soothes me.

"Edmon grew up in House Leontes under the watchful tutelage of their loyal seneschal Alberich and guidance of his father. Even the emperor, Old Wusong, noticed the boy's intelligence and tenacity at a young age."

I didn't grow up in House Leontes. I grew up on the Isle of Bone . . . didn't I? A scene plays out. I'm a child standing before the throne of Old Wusong. I make a joke, and the entire audience laughs.

I remember that, but that's not the way it happened. Is it?

"It was on this day that he was first introduced to the woman who would become the love of his life, Princess Miranda Wusong."

Miranda Wusong? What about Nadia? Wait . . . who is Nadia?

There is a red flashing before my eyes. I hear voices from beyond the amniotic deep of this strange trance.

"He's resisting the programming, my lord."

"Then intensify the medication and procedure," says Edric.

Now I remember. Edric murdered Nadia. He murdered my unborn child. He murdered . . .

"If you push this too far, my lord, he may no longer remember who he is at all."

There is a pause. "Do it," Edric says.

Lightning shoots through my body. All my nerves are on fire. I scream, but the sounds are muffled in this liquid dream.

"Young Edmon and Miranda were betrothed, and it was not long after their fifteenth birthdays that they began a courtship in full. The two became storybook loves—he from humble origins, and she from the most powerful dynasty in the Pantheon. Even the emperor could not deny their deep connection. He admired the young warrior's courage. With his best friend and younger brother, Edgaard, at his side, Edmon quickly won the hearts of the people."

Images of us during the war games with The Companions flash. I'm fighting off Sigurd and Perdiccus.

The aquagraphic shifts. Old Wusong addresses a crowd in the throne room in some sort of royal announcement. Miranda, now older, veiled, and dressed in lavish kimonos, stands at his side.

"While there are many fine, strong youths of this new generation, there is only one who is truly worthy of my daughter's hand—Edmon Leontes."

Miranda. I've won your heart, and you've won mine. This is the story that all of Tao knows.

The image dissolves to me, standing in a dress uniform before a throne. *I remember that. The image is from the day I confronted Phaestion about the murders in the arcology. I never stood before the emperor and accepted his daughter's hand . . .*

The lightning shoots through my body again and again. I scream. The sound is muffled by the liquid I swim in. The pain is too great.

"Edmon Leontes even abdicated his place as heir to House Leontes in order to devote his time and efforts to supporting Miranda with charity work designed to heal the planet. He joined her in their humanitarian activities to rally public support against the passage of House Julii's military creation act . . ."

Miranda, my love, soon we will be married. We can help Edric and serve his plans to save this world.

The show goes on, and my heart swells with joy.

My body moves, but it's not in my control. The drugs cause me to feel outside myself, watching everything that happens. I smile with giddy satisfaction.

This is the day I've waited my whole life for. I'm floating!

"Edgaard," I say with a voice that feels like it comes from another room. "Did Father really think the drugs were necessary?"

"Father felt you were so nervous that they would help relax you. Don't worry, brother, Alberich and I are here to guide you for the camglobes."

I watch as Edgaard and Alberich accompany me to the preparation spa. My stubble is shaved. My skin is sprayed with a layer of shading paint that hides every blemish and scar. I radiate an artificial glow. My hair is styled with a glossy finish, making the dark locks shiny and lustrous. Edgaard and Alberich clothe me in ceremonial robes of midnight blue. Armor plated with silver is fitted to my wrists and shins to round out the colors of House Leontes.

The double doors to the hall of Old Wusong open, and a long aisle spreads out before me. It seems to go on for kilometers. The nobles of the Pantheon, dressed in their finery, flank either side.

"Walk," Alberich whispers in my ear.

"Thank you," I whisper back, grateful for the direction. The drugs take over, and my body moves forward.

The audience erupts in applause at my entrance. Fanfare plays on gilded trumpets. Camglobes hover in front of my face. *Edmon Leontes, the prodigal son, has returned from his self-imposed exile on the Isle of Bone!* the aquas will say. *He has been living the life of an ascetic, meditating, preparing himself for this day, when he weds the love of his life, the beautiful Miranda Wusong.*

A voice tickles the back of my brain. *Fight them, Edmon!*

Fight them? I think. *This is my proudest moment!*

Alberich takes position in the crowd. Edgaard, as best man, nudges me forward. "It's almost over, brother," he reassures me. "Move up the stairs."

I nod and lurch forward. My father stands upon the dais, looking every bit the feudal lord. I smile. *I love you, Father,* I think.

Two women also in the colors of House Leontes stand on his left. One looks like a diminutive porcelain doll with raven hair and refined features. Her perfectly arcing eyebrows frame violet irises. She's coldly beautiful. *Lavinia, my elder sister,* I realize. *I haven't seen her since I was nine . . . no, wait, I grew up with her in House Leontes. Didn't I?*

The other girl has a heart-shaped face and long, lustrous copper hair. The smile on her full lips is genuine, full of joy at the pageantry. My dull-witted younger sister. *What was her name? Phoebe?* I think. *I should know this.* She and I were constant companions before she joined Lavinia at finishing school. She's beautiful in a bland sort of way, a perfect pawn for my father to marry off to one of the other noble houses.

Pawn? I chastise myself. *Father loves us. He wouldn't deny us the marriage of our hearts.*

The crowd has the same radiant smile that I wear. Camglobes hover everywhere.

Break free, Edmon!

Why do I think that all of a sudden?

I'm tempted by an overpowering urge to flee. I don't know why. I try to run, to will my body to break free from the hold of the narcotics coursing through my blood. My foot slips, and I almost crash into the carpet. Edgaard catches me.

"Don't try to resist," he urges. "You'll only look bad. Just move forward."

Thank the ancestors for Edgaard. I'm so glad that I abdicated my position as heir. Edgaard is truly the strong warrior our house needs.

I feel a particular set of eyes upon me. They pierce through my stupor. I feel them as I ascend the dais. I feel them as I bow before Edric's cold, triumphant gaze. It takes all my strength to turn my head toward the eyes I feel on my back.

Yes! I can move my head! I smile. *I knew I was stronger than some silly drugs.*

My eyes lock with the gray gaze of Phaestion Julii. He looks back at me from the first row of guests. Perdiccus, Hanschen, and Sigurd are of course by his side, decked in the regalia of their respective houses. The sight of them stops me in my tracks. I'm flooded with images: Hanschen stabbing me with a pair of short swords. Perdiccus with a trident pinning my foot to a mat. Sigurd standing over me with a giant mace. Phaestion kissing me on a beach. A beach with white shores.

Where can I run? Do I try to fight them all? What do I do? Why am I thinking these thoughts?

Phaestion is taller, broader. His form under his black suit is muscular and powerful, yet still sleek and athletically quick. His thick red hair is shorter and coiffed beneath the silver circlet of victory.

We're eighteen now, eligible to enter the Combat, old enough to wear the forearm tattoos of a Patriarch, to bear the weight of black robes and white masks of the Census. These boys plan to rule, I realize, while I am standing here in a frozen body on my wedding day. This should be the happiest day of my life, but somehow I have a dreaded feeling that really, I've failed to save the ones I love from death. Looking around the room—my brother, Edgaard; my teacher Alberich; my sisters, Lavinia and Phoebe; and of course Phaestion—all those I'm supposed to love are alive and well.

Wait, Phaestion is an enemy of my father, right? Why is he here then? I wonder. *To gloat because I did not join him?*

I wince. My head hurts. All these thoughts are too much to sort.

On Phaestion's other side sits a decrepit old man with snow-white hair, Lord Chilleus of the Julii, Phaestion's father, still alive. Next to the Patriarch is the bald alien with the cat eyes, Talousla Karr. The hairless man attends the old lord like a nursemaid.

A scientist with a favorite lab fish, I think. *I know that man. Why do I know him?*

The spypsy glances from the old man to Phaestion, gauging their reactions to the scene. More than a century separates father and son. Even so, Phaestion bears a wonderful resemblance to the old man, though younger, taller, and more powerfully built.

This is how a father and son should be, I think. *The father old and kind, innocuous. The son the image of his father, only greater.*

Phaestion nods at me. Triumph and coldness are in his gaze.

What does that mean? I wonder.

The double doors open again. A hush falls. The veiled girl enters ahead of her father, Old Wusong, who is carried on a palanquin. The old man resembles a corpse; his eyes are black ball bearings staring blindly out of sunken and sallow cheeks. His heavy ornamental head-dress looks as if it will topple off his wrinkled eggshell-head and pull him with it, crashing to the floor. I hold my smile. *I must be respectful to my future father-in-law, the emperor of the greatest civilization in the known Fracture.*

I cannot make out Miranda's face beneath her veil. It makes no difference. *She is the only woman I have ever loved.*

It takes them what seems an eternity to arrive at the dais. Miranda helps her father step from the palanquin. Old Wusong clasps his daughter's white hands with gnarled fingers. He brings them gently to his livered lips. A retainer helps the old man into a seat alongside the other nobles. Miranda ascends the dais to stand beside me. She takes my hand in hers, knowing what's expected of us both. The oaths are administered.

"Say the words," Edgaard whispers in my ear, and I do.

"Elder Stars illuminate only because there is darkness. A warrior can know righteous cause only because there is evil. Heart to thought, thought to voice, harmony rises from discord. This is the Balance. Two are now one."

My tongue moves slowly as I say the words by rote.

I have a horrible feeling in the pit of my stomach that I can't explain. I want to break down and weep, but I don't know why. I ignore the impulse and smile. My father informs me I may kiss the bride. I watch myself from outside again as I lift the veil, revealing a painted snow-white face, a perfect moon, soft and doughy. Her thin lips pull back at the corners. Her teeth are painted black, in the ancient tradition of Old Wusong. *Who is this? This is not my love!*

I gasp suddenly. Images rush through my head—a girl with dark hair, a small mole on her cheek. She pulls me up onto white cliffs, preventing me from falling into a green sea. Now she is older, and we are making love on those same cliffs, our bodies matching the rhythm of the waves. We are in bed on a morning, my birthday, and later she is telling me a child is to be born . . .

Nadia. Her name is Nadia!

"Kiss me," Miranda hisses. She steps on her tiptoes to kiss me. I try to pull away, but she grabs my neck and pulls me in closer. "The globes are watching." She clamps her lips to mine. The crowd explodes with applause.

A reception is held upon the rooftop of the House Wusong central scraper. I sit at the head of a table next to Miranda. She smiles black-toothed and nods politely to attendees who offer congratulations and gifts. Musicians fill the air with tinny metallic tunes. Guests dance in the center of the floor.

The drugs have begun to wear off, and I reach for wine, downing a glass in one gulp. Across the twilight sky, I see the thousands of glittering skyscrapers of Tao lit up like ornaments in celebration of the auspicious occasion. *This is wrong.* I feel it. I don't know what it is, but I feel an anger boiling inside of me. I cannot get the image of the girl with dark hair out of my mind.

"More wine," I mutter to the waiter who refills my glass. I gulp it immediately. "More, I said!" I shout again. I want to break something, but I don't know what. I don't know why. I have just married the love of my life, Miranda Wusong, yet I'm filled with nameless rage.

She is not your love, a voice whispers inside me. I feel the truth of the words even though I know them to be a lie. *What is happening to me?*

"Don't you think you are overdoing it, husband?" Miranda hisses at me through hideous teeth.

I stare at her coldly. "Don't tell me what I should think or feel."

Where did that come from? That's not like me. Or is it? I drink another glass of the wine. She ignores me and returns to greeting guests from some minor noble house who have offered us a jewelry box or some other useless item.

"House Ruska's tokens of affection will be cherished for all time," Miranda politely tells the fat youth who presents the gifts.

"If I could have a moment of Lord Edmon's time?" he asks.

"My husband needs his rest at the moment," Miranda says, cutting off the boy.

"More wine!" I slam my fist down on the table. The youth blanches and moves to sit among the crowd of other fat, milky nobles.

I need to banish the thoughts in my head. I need to be happy again. I need to forget the girl with the dark hair.

"Do you think that I'm enjoying this?" Miranda whispers at me. I turn, startled. It actually didn't occur to me for a second what she thought. "I'm just as much a pawn in our fathers' games as you are, but I have the decency and intelligence to suffer through it and wait for an opportunity to make a move."

"If the opportunity never comes?" I ask.

"Then I will have bettered my position by calmly accepting the situation, rather than drinking myself into oblivion. Don't think you are the only one who chafes under the confines of tradition, Edmon Leontes. I may not be an aquagraphic star, a musical sensation, or a freedom fighter, but I am an emperor's daughter. I demand to be treated as such."

I want to strike her, and an image flashes through my mind of my father striking my mother in front of a crowd like this when I was a child. I am horrified at the memory. *What is happening to me?*

"Your arrogance presumes you know anything about my life," I sneer. "I will treat you accordingly, *wife*." The word sounds wrong. I shove myself back from the table.

Phaestion stands on the outskirts of the party, holding a court of his own. The Companions crowd around him. The rest of the young men of Tao hold him in their eyes like a god. He sees me looking from across the room and raises his glass. My head explodes with images—a haughty boy arriving at an island manse, claiming my room for his own.

I never lived in an island manse, did I?

"He's the perfect specimen, is he not?" the sly voice of the spypsy, Talousla Karr, whispers in my ear.

I don't deign to look at his hairless face beneath the hood. Somehow, I know this snake of a man.

"Depends on your definition of perfection." I sip my wine.

"Your people are so curiously fascinating," he goes on. "There are others throughout the cosmos who have used genetic manipulation as means to adapt to niche habitats . . ."

"Like space gypsies who craft hollow bones or hairless bodies?" I ask.

He nods and prattles on. "Most humans merely change the color of their hair or the shape of their eyes to suit some arbitrary beauty trend, but yours is an entire culture obsessed with physical perfection. The whole of Tao society is built around achieving it. Politics, economics, cultural behaviors, mating rituals . . ."

"The Combat, the Pavaka," I add sarcastically.

"The strong survive. The weak are cast out. Your race is remarkably resilient, all without microcellular science to achieve it. Some humans in the known cosmos may be stronger, or faster, or fit some unique function better, but the median level of physiological and mental capability here is astounding. It's a considerable achievement. Rarely do you see government becoming an environmental pressure that impacts evolution."

"You don't know your ancient history." I wash down the last of my glass. "How many warlike empires from Ancient Earth sought to control their people? How many cultures threw away a child because it was the wrong gender or because it suffered some deformity? Do you know what happened to all those cultures? Those empires? They all ended, choking on their own perfect blood and ashes." My voice is filled with venom rather than veneration. I am deeply disturbed. I am supposed to think the Nightsider way is the pinnacle of human success.

"I said it was rare, not that it's never happened," the man corrects. "I marvel at what they were able to create for their brief moments in time. Here is Tao, an entire planet dedicated to the principles of such excellence."

"We call that arête," I say bitterly. "The idea that each being should strive for perfection of the self—physically, intellectually, and morally."

"Imagine what a geneticist like myself might accomplish were they to have access to such a specimen as, say, your father? Already superior in strength, speed, and athleticism. A hormone activated, a gene transferred . . ."

"You want my father as an experiment?" I ask.

The man shrugs. "I've made do with other options."

He means me, the pale reflection of the great leviathan. I am his experiment. He did something to me, I remember.

He leans close. "In all my studies, I've come to a conclusion about what pushes humanity forward, makes us better than we are . . ."

I hang on his words.

"Pain, struggle, obstacle," he whispers. "Push a man to his limit, push him past what he thought those limits were, break him. If he's strong enough to survive, he becomes something more."

"What's that?"

"A god. A monster. Who is to say?" he answers cryptically.

For some reason, his words fire me with anger. I find my legs are not as wobbly as they should be. "The eel that devours every last minnow eventually turns to its own tail. Don't be surprised if your experiments blow up in your face." I stalk off, feeling his eyes on my back the whole way.

I grab a drink from the bar. I'm not drunk enough. Not nearly enough. If I cannot burn the images from my mind, I'll burn myself. It does no good. With each sip I imbibe, my head swims with more dark memories.

I must do something. I don't know what.

"Look at you wallowing," a voice says. I spin. "The great Edmon Leontes, voice of a generation, reduced to a blubbering drunkard."

Voice of a generation? That's what they called me.

"Or do you not remember?"

Lavinia. The delicately boned woman arcs a dark, wicked eyebrow.

"Sister, you hardly know me." I pound the liquor in the glass to the back of my throat. It tastes of fire.

"What I know is what I see in the aquagraphics." She smiles. "Someone with idealism and charisma, someone who makes others believe in something. You are a Leontes, after all." She casts her gaze to our father, who sits at the head of the feast table, concubines doting on him.

"I'm nothing like him," I answer.

She merely smiles. "You're just like him. You don't like to lose. And right now, you are losing." She grabs a drink of her own and sips. "It's ironic, really."

"What is?"

"You're the one born to the power, and you've done nothing but try to be rid of it. Me? I'm given nothing, but I would take that power gladly if I could."

"Would you?" I mutter acidly.

"I should've been born a man. But for my gender, on this planet anyway, I would have been our father's heir. After all, I am the eldest, dear brother."

"Sounds like you're the one who's losing." I smile.

"Some things can't be changed." She purses her lips tightly. "But there are more ways to fight than with a sword. Sometimes truth is enough."

"And what's the truth, dear sister?" I ask.

"I know everything that happens within these castle walls." She gestures to the surroundings of the glass skyscraper. "I manage all our house's finances. Without me, House Wusong-Leontes would be bankrupt within a year." She shakes her head. "None of that is important to you, I'm sure. This is your day. You must be so happy with your blushing bride. She's really charming, isn't she? That white, dough-painted face? Those beautiful black teeth?"

I do not love Miranda. I am supposed to love her. I'm told I love her and no other. It is a lie. I clench my fists. My head pounds. "What do you want, Lavinia?" I seethe.

Her voice drops low. "I want what you want. Father defeated . . ."

I want Father to succeed in his plans for our people.

"I want you and Edgaard absolved of all noble duties . . ."

I want to see Edgaard become the Patriarch of our family. I want to marry my beautiful wife and serve her and our charitable work for the College of Electors.

"I want to make you remember who you are so you can bring this system of patriarchy crashing down. Then only I will be left to rebuild the world in my image."

"And they say I'm the singer." I smile ruefully. "You're the one who sings so sweetly."

I'm a singer? Yes, I'm a singer.

"We use the gifts we're given," she says evenly. "Do you have the stones to use yours? For Nadia."

The glass drops from my hand and shatters on the floor. *Nadia. My love.* Memories pour into my brain like too much sand in a sieve—*Bone. My mother. Nadia. Gorham. The Maestro. All dead. My unborn child.* Pain. *He murdered them. Edric murdered them. He tried to brainwash me. He tried to make me forget. He lobotomized then murdered my mother.* I scream and collapse to the floor clutching my head in my hands.

"Edmon?" Lavinia kneels next to me.

I grab her fiercely by the arms. "Don't speak her name!"

She winces at my grip but smiles. "Now that's the brother I remember."

"I remember, too," I say. "Everything."

"Good. Then act," she whispers.

I look around at the crowd, the guards, The Companions, my father . . .

There are too many to fight physically. *Even if I could win, what would I do after?*

Lavinia points to the dozens of camglobes hovering the rooftops, broadcasting the celebration all across Tao. "You have an audience. Tell them the truth about the murders that Edric Leontes commits."

Our father may kill me. Lavinia may win. So what? Use the gifts I am given . . . I'll destroy Edric and avenge my love. Lavinia is right. There is more than one way to fight.

I walk to the orchestra, to the first chair electric viola. I rip the magnetic amplifier off his instrument and pin it to the lapel of my suit. The man protests so I punch him in the face, breaking it. There is an intense hiss of feedback as the amplifier adjusts to the new sound source. I make my way to the middle of the dance floor. I raise my arm, signaling that everyone should come to a silence. My father stands behind the wedding table. Miranda gapes like a hooked cod. The camglobes hover and converge on my location. They orbit around me like moons.

"Today we celebrate the union of two noble houses of Tao!" I toast. The guests erupt in cheers. "A bond between the long and storied, now sick and dying, behemoth of House Wusong, and the lowborn, inauspicious, young upstarts of House Leontes!" The applause now comes with a tepid pitter-patter. *Is this praise?* they wonder. "All in an attempt to consolidate power and move us forward to a new future. A blind future."

I look to The Companions. Perdiccus grins. Sigurd glowers. Hanschen rests lazily on Phaestion's arm. Phaestion's eyes flare with interest.

"People of Tao, this marriage is a farce!" Cries erupt from the audience. "I was drugged and forced; my words were not my own this day. I resist now in telling you. You, too, must resist. It is not the circumstance of our births that define us, but how we choose to live!"

My father grabs Alberich and tells him to send for the guards.

"Those born with the title, noble, have done nothing to earn that gift. I stand here before you the son of a lowborn and of mixed race, but I'm a free man who chooses to struggle against the oppression. Oppression that says one person is better than another. Oppression that says this one should live while that one dies. Oppression of brother against brother!" I look at Phaestion. "And oppression of the father against the son."

Out of the corner of my eye, I see Lavinia smile with sinister glee.

"My gift is not a Combat. My gift is an elegy for all those who have died in the struggle."

Guards hustle into the reception area. My father directs them to surround me. I look Edric square in the face, and I sing. I sing the song that The Maestro wrote the words for. I sing the song my mother sang to me as I child. I sing the song the people call "The Song of Edmon."

Edric's jaw tightens. The veins stand out like cords in his neck. His hands clench with the intention to strangle me, but now he's the one who stands frozen and impotent. As do they all. The Maestro knew this day would come—the day we lost. The words he wrote to the tune my mother taught speaks of a last glimmer of hope's light against darkness. I reach the climax, and my voice rises in the cool twilight like a beacon. I force back tears.

Nadia and my poor unborn child. I won't forget you, but I will not let them see me cry. I will not let them see me break.

Silence hangs between me and the rest of the world—a vast gulf unable to be crossed.

Lavinia smiles like a shark. Phaestion shakes his head, each of us lost to the other. Edric yells, "Seize him!" All hell breaks loose.

I stand in one of my father's bedrooms in a Wusong-Leontes scraper, several miles from the remains of the party. My hands are bound. I'm bleeding from the mouth.

"Wipe the shit-eating grin off your face," my father snarls.

"Wipe it yourself. You're the one who put it there," I retort.

He backhands me with his fist. My nose breaks, and I crash to the floor. My eyes water so that I can hardly see. Blood drips onto the marbled floor. Edgaard and Alberich stand like sentinels at the door, presumably to prevent me from making some kind of mad dash for freedom. I laugh. *I don't want freedom. I just want it all to be over.*

"Edmon, I've tried," Edric begins calmly. The throbbing in my face keeps me from a smart-ass response. My tongue feels like a thick rubber slab in my mouth. "I've showed you mercy and compassion—"

"Mercy? Is that what you showed me? Is that what you showed my mother? Is that what you showed Nadia? My unborn child?"

"A quick death is a mercy. It would be a mercy for you as well, but you are no longer deserving. There is more at stake than your petty desires and your insignificant teenage longings. A whole planet hangs in the balance. I've tried to bring you into the fold. I've tried leaving you to your own devices. Yet you will not shut up!"

His scream echoes through the chamber.

His voice drops deadly low again. "All you had to do was wait, fool. You could have stayed tucked away and forgotten. I was wrong to think you would do that. Who knows what damage you've caused here tonight. I will not be humiliated by you again. I will end you without mercy. Take him to the Wendigo."

He nods at Alberich, and I'm dragged from the room.

MOVEMENT II: INTERMEZZO

CHAPTER 16

Tremolo

My hands are bound. My head is covered. I see nothing. I feel the hum of a sondi engine and discern I'm in a passenger compartment full of bodies. We rock and bump together, packed like sarfish in a can. The dirigible banks its way over the frozen wastes of the Nightside. At least that's what I imagine. The temperature in the cabin drops perceptibly. I calm myself, breathe slowly, and try not to shiver.

"Approaching drop zone," a metallic voice cuts in over the speakers.

Then the voice of the corrections officer sounds to my left.

"Worms! We're approaching your new home. This is merely a dump of cargo. Therefore we need make no touchdown. We'll hover approximately three meters over the deposit site where each of you will disembark."

It sounds like they won't be rolling out the plush carpets. Someone whimpers underneath his hood. I hear the corrections officer kick him in the gut.

"Quiet! You will stay at the deposit site until retrieval. If you attempt escape, you will be executed. If you do not follow all instructions, you will be executed. If you cause any problem in any way that might look bad on one of my reports, you will be executed. If on the off-chance you are able to escape the shooters, you have nothing but a continent of frozen tundra and endless dark in every direction. May the Elder Stars watch you. May the ancestors pray for you. No one else cares. Welcome to the Wendigo."

The carriage door opens, and a blast of icy air slams me even through the neoprene bodysuit I've been issued. I can barely breathe. Someone pulls me to standing. Bodies around me shuffle toward the cold air. My hood is ripped off, and I find myself at the open door of the sondi. All is darkness and stars, millions of pinpricks of sapphire in the black firmament, each a sun with worlds, and those worlds full with people. I dream those people are kinder than the ones here. Someone shoves the small of my back, and I fall.

I hurtle toward the ground but don't travel far. I try to tuck my chin and roll, but with my hands bound and the disorientation of the cramped twelve-hour journey, my effort is more of a spastic flail than anything else.

"Roll, maggot!" someone yells.

I try but am quickly grabbed by the scruff of the neck. A guard yanks me away just in time to avoid another falling body as it slams into the icy hardpack.

I stand in a small pool of light next to the scaffolding of a tower. Ice and snow swirls everywhere. I curl my arms close and huddle next to the other wayward souls. A wall of darkness is all that is beyond the patch of dim light from the tower. No horizon, just a formless and impenetrable curtain stretching to eternity.

"Stop!" the armored guard who pulled me to my feet screams.

A fellow prisoner sprints into the darkness.

"Stop or we fire!" the guard yells again, but the runner is gone.

Then the red dot of a laser sight alights. *Bang!* The shot is fired from the tower above. The guard beside me holds up his wrist communicator. "You get 'em, Greelo?"

"Got 'em, Sookah," the voice chimes back.

I look to the tower. Greelo sets the high-powered sniper rifle against his shoulder calmly.

"Listen up, maggots!" Sookah holds a voice amplifier to his snow mask. "You will form a line here." He points at the ground.

We shiver and shuffle slowly into place. *Bang!* The rifle echoes again. The man behind me drops. "My leg! They shot my leg!"

"Move faster next time," Sookah says. "Or next aim is your skull."

"I prefer to blow the stones!" Greelo's voice cuts in over the communicator. Sookah guffaws.

I lift the injured man from the ground. He's small and dark-skinned, an islander like me. He can no longer walk unassisted with the bullet lodged in his thigh.

"Thank—"

"Shut up!" I hiss through my teeth. My lips crack in the freezing cold.

"Hook your bindings to the belt of the man in front of you and prepare for descent," announces Sookah.

"Descent?" the injured man whispers.

"Quiet!" I reiterate. "Or you'll get us both killed."

The man looks no older than fifteen because of his diminutive stature, but the lines on his face are etched deep, denoting a lifetime much longer than my own. I clip the chains from my wrist bindings to a loop on the belt of the man in front of me. The guard walks back to inspect the line. He stares at me as I shoulder the weight of the scrawny man behind me.

"Man can't move on his own," Sookah says. "Best leave him to drag, otherwise you're both done."

"I'll take my chances," I reply.

The guard pulls a humbaton from his belt. He cracks me across the ribs with it. I wince as I feel bone break. "I didn't say you could talk, maggot," he growls. He straps on a pair of infrared goggles as he leads our shuffle from the pool of light into black.

It feels even colder once the lamplight is absent. I'm disoriented in the pitch, as if swimming in a dark tub of ice. A cry of desperation sounds in front of me. My arms are yanked forward. My footing falls away. I tumble down an icy slope. It feels like forever as ice and rock abrade my skin. The slide finally stops, and I try to stand, but I'm bruised, my ribs broken. My foot slips on the ice. I feel myself about to fall over the edge of something and into a chasm. The scrawny man behind me pulls me back, saving me.

"Thank you," I whisper.

"Call it even," he whispers back. "I'm Toshiro Kodai. Friends call me Toshi."

"Edmon," I say in return.

"Leontes?" he questions. "I thought I recognized your face in the light a moment ago!"

There is a loud clicking sound, and lights suddenly blind us. We're standing on the edge of a hole bored into the ice about ten meters wide and far deeper than my eyes can see. *An ice arcology,* I think. A string of intense fireglobes illuminates a sheer drop into blackness. The frozen rungs of a rickety metal ladder are bolted to the side of the chasm. I kick a stone into the pit. I wait. Finally, a pop echoes back from the black.

"Start crawling, maggots!" Sookah yells, pointing at the icy ladder.

A burly, scarred man with tattoos at the front of our chain eases himself down the first of the metal rungs. I nod to Toshi. He saved me from the fall; I'll make sure he gets to the bottom alive, even with the wound in his leg. My eyes adjust to the Nightside darkness. I look up and out onto the horizon, and I can barely make out several blinking lights. They don't move, so they must be attached to some kind of structure.

"What's that?" I whisper.

The guard called Greelo, who has come down from rifle duty in the tower, sees me point. I feel rather than see him smile underneath his mask. "The Citadel, maggot. Pray you never do time there."

The lights of the Citadel blink back. I can't make out the shape of any building, so if there's something out there, it's as dark as the night.

I feel a tug on my bindings. It's my turn to descend the ladder. The guard raises his humbaton as if to strike me for my idleness. I could rush him, take the weapon from him, beat him with it, blast the sonic pulse to scramble his brain, but then what? I'd be dead. This is all a game. A game where I am the weak worm. I must make him feel powerful in order to survive.

I throw my hands in the air, feigning a desperate attempt to protect myself. Greelo laughs at the display. I crawl past him and begin the climb down the slippery rungs of the ladder.

One foot in front of the other. We follow the string of fireglobes, down and down. We go deep into the very crust of the planet. The temperature rises to just above freezing. The pain in my hands and the hurt of each breath is lessened by the sheer terror I have of falling. Toshi shakes above me, flinching every time he puts pressure on his wounded leg.

"Easy, Tosh," I say, more to comfort myself than him. *If he slips and falls, I will be right behind him.*

Then the tattooed man at the lead of our line does slip. Each man who follows comes off the ladder, pulled by the weight of the man before. I quickly snake my leg between a rung as the human chain goes taut. I yowl as the weight of at least a dozen prisoners ahead of me is suspended over the chasm by the tensile strength of my femur.

"Help!" The man's screams echo off the cavern walls.

"Cut that prisoner loose now!" Sookah commands from above.

"No!" I shout. I feel the bone in my thigh bending. My skeleton is strong, but even this strain is too much. "No one falls!" I scream out in defiance.

"Prisoner, unhook your manacles from that prisoner now, or I will come down and unhook both of you!"

"No!" I shout back. My eyes connect with the man second in line. He immediately stops trying to unhook.

"Ancestors, help me!" the tattooed man cries hysterically.

I feel my bone splintering. The guard rappels along the wall next to me. His crampons dig in, and chunks of ice wall splash as he boots off the surface. His auto-belay slows beside the tattooed prisoner. The man flails, trying to grab hold of the ladder. The guard reaches out with a pair of electrified clippers. He snips the chain connecting the man's belt to the manacles of the prisoner behind him.

"No!" I shout. Too late. The tattooed man falls. *Another death I'm unable to prevent.*

We hear screams for a long moment grow faint until they're suddenly cut off. The only sound then is the guard's auto-belay reeling him back above us. I steady myself on the slick rungs. My ribs throb. Blood rushes through my leg.

"Start moving, maggots!"

The chain of prisoners resumes its descent. Sookah doesn't take his goggled eyes off me the rest of the journey.

We climb for hours. I lose track of time in the darkness and cold. Finally, the tunnel widens, and a light at the bottom brightens. The fireglobes give off no heat, but even dim light in this winter land gives the sense of warmth. I feel that I've climbed into an abyss from which I'll never return, and I shiver.

One by one, we shuffle off the ladder, our fingers and toes numb and aching. I rub my leg. I can already feel the microfractures beginning to heal. Sookah and Greelo lead us through a dark tunnel that opens into a huge cavernous space lit by fireglobes, torches, and campfires. A shantytown of ramshackle buildings spreads out inside this massive underground cave. Prisoners, all men, are decked out in bundled rags and furs, and mill about or huddle around bonfires. They look like barbarians, faces covered thick with filth and beards.

Greelo slams a mallet into a large gong. It reverberates through the cavern, and the wooly heads of the prisoners turn to us. Suddenly, they're on their feet, and the giant crowd of strangers surrounds us. They claw at us and push us forward.

Several more guards appear. They hold the crowd back with humbatons. "Make way!" they shout occasionally, firing a sonic pulse from their humbatons into the crowd.

The stink of bodies and refuse is oppressive even in the freezing cold. A human corridor is formed. We're pressed through it like mashed waste through an intestine. Toshi holds my shoulders to keep from collapsing.

"Edmon, I'm going to be sick," he says, groaning.

"Just hang in there."

It's no use. He doubles over and pukes all over my feet.

"Keep moving, worms!" a guard shouts at us. We arrive at the center of the cavern, and the prisoner at the front of the line is shoved up onto an auction block.

"Ragnar Erlichson!" A fat man wearing a uniform with the insignia of House Wusong-Leontes names the prisoner.

"Who's that?" I whisper, pointing to the fat official.

"Quiet!" Sookah slams his humbaton into my ribs, pumping me with sonic volts. I fall to the ground, writhing. "The Warden's speaking." Sookah pulls off his mask, revealing a rotted brown smile.

The Warden is short and squat. His greased blond hair hugs his skull, and his long mustache is waxed and curled at the ends. He reminds me more of a Combat ringmaster than a corrections officer. "Convicted of four accounts of assault with a deadly weapon against a Meridian security officer. Strong and powerfully built, perfect for the copper or iron mines in twelfth dungeon. Who starts the bidding?"

Men wave their hands and yell out bids. I don't know what measure of currency they're trading in, but it seems the ones bidding are leaders because they look the largest and most brutal.

It seems all levels of Tao society revere physical might, I muse.

"Sold at five hundred iron kilos to the Smelters!"

The prisoner is kicked off the pedestal, and the next man is brought forward. This time the charge is theft of government weapons. Sold. Next is espionage, selling royal documents of House Flanders to their enemies. He's bought by the Diggers who apparently "dig" for burnable coal and precious metals. The next man? Speech violation. He led an antigovernment rally in his arcology near western Meridian.

The Wendigo is the harshest environment on Tao. These prisoners should be the harshest, too—murderers and maniacs too unstable to even let loose in the games. Yet the men being auctioned are political dissidents, traitors, and speech violators. *This is not right.*

I'm shoved onto the pedestal at the butt of a humbaton. "Edmon Leontes!" The Warden's voice rings out. The crowd hushes, not with reverence, but with predatory hunger. "You know his pedigree, young and strong. He could surely last for years in the salt, copper, or magnesium dungeons. Who wouldn't want the son of a Pantheon nobleman under his lash? Do we have an opening bid?"

The cavern erupts. Hands and fists wave. The Warden struts in front of the block like a trick dolphin. Objects start flying. Chunks of rocks and ice. A stone strikes me. The crowd erupts in laughter. I wince in pain but refuse to fall.

"That's the spirit, pretty boy!" a large bear of a man with a bent nose and wiry beard catcalls. "Stand that pretty ass up. Yes, stand that pretty ass up for my crew!" He waves to make a bid.

"Three hundred from Bruul Vaarkson and the Haulers!" The Warden shouts. "Do I hear three fifty?"

"Three fifty!" a scarred man with a shaved head and topknot cries out.

"Jinam Shank and the Pickers for three fifty! Do I hear four?"

"I want those smooth cheeks for the Haulers!" Vaarkson cries again. "Three seventy-five!"

"Four hundred!" Shank raises a hand.

"Sounds like we have a bidding war, boys!" shouts The Warden.

"Four fifty!" Vaarkson calls out. The crowd erupts with oohs.

"You're in for it, boy," The Warden hisses through his waxed mustache. "Vaarkson never gives up once he sees a piece he wants to plow." I grit my teeth at the jest. "Even if he loses the bid, the Hauler foreman's marked you, and he'll have you."

I piece things together. Foremen are leaders of each individual faction. Each faction is a group with a specific task in this place. It's just like the houses of the Pantheon, with The Warden in position of the emperor. They seem to be trading in their respective goods, ore for food, food for tools, tools for fur.

"Five hundred!" Shank makes another bid.

"Five ten!" shouts the big bearded man.

My eyes glance at the giant domed ceiling of the cavern. Stalactites drip down as if trapping us all inside a maw of razor teeth. I conjure a memory of Nadia in the warmth of the Tao star. Her dark hair cascading in the breeze, framing her face as she stands high on the cliffs above a green sea—nothing but the summer and the promise of an unborn child between us. I think of the words of an aria The Maestro once showed me: *O mio babbino caro. Oh, my beloved daddy, he's as handsome as a king . . . and if you still say no . . . I'll throw myself below . . . What shivers, what a chill, poor me, I want to die . . .* The soaring lilt of the soprano's voice in my mind silences the cacophony of this place.

"Five twenty!" Shank shouts again.

"Do I hear five twenty-five?" The Warden responds. "Five twenty going once . . . going twice . . ."

My eyes cast down from the ceiling and rest on a strange dark man standing apart at the back of the crowd. He hangs in the shadows, calm, silent, and watching everything. His skin is darker than that of any islander I've ever seen. His hair is tight and curled, tinted the oddest shade of red. His cheeks are decorated with some kind of tattooing that I cannot make out at this distance. His appearance reminds me of something from my deep past. *The audience with Old Wusong!* It suddenly clicks in my brain. I remember seeing the foreigners from off-world, a starship captain who had the same strange coloring that this man does. *Is this man, too, an off-worlder?* His stare is haunting, his eyes opaque, milky-white. *He's blind,* I realize. He stands relaxed, like a victorious fighter, but no one pays him any mind, as if he's invisible to all but me. I'm unsettled.

"Sold to Jinam Shank and the Picker Gang!" The Warden shouts.

A guard grabs me by the manacles, unlocks the cuffs, and shoves me into the crowd.

"Get along, little prince," he snarls.

I'm engulfed by the crowd. I feel pinched, prodded, and poked at by grubby, foul-smelling hands. "Settle down!" commands Jinam Shank, the foreman of the Picker Gang. "Don't shit in the crib!"

The hands reluctantly stop as Pickers turns their attention to the next auction.

"Toshiro Kodai! From Meridian, by way of the Isle of Conch!" Toshiro, skinny and wretched, shivers on the block holding his injured leg. The crowd mutters with apathy. "Toshiro is wanted for participating in a protest rally at the Hall of Electors following the Wusong-Leontes wedding. Shall we start the bidding at twenty-five kilos?"

A protest after the Wusong-Leontes wedding?

No hands go up. "All right, how about twenty kilos?"

I work my way through the crowd until I'm standing behind the scarred man with the topknot, Jinam Shank. The back of his neck is tattooed with the symbol of a pickax, denoting his status as foreman. I tap him on the shoulder. He whirls around, eyes narrowed and shiv in hand.

"Lord Shank?" I bow my head in deference, trying to play the game. "May I suggest bidding on that next prisoner?"

"Shut your hole, fish," he hisses. "I just spent more than my share of ore on you, mainly to spite Vaarkson. Your job is to wield a pick and do what I say. That's it."

I nod with as much obsequiousness as I can muster. "But, sir, I know that man. He may not look like much, but he can mine five times his weight in ore a day."

If Toshi's arrest was something to do with my marriage to Miranda Wusong, he's here because of me. Besides, I need an ally.

Shank's knuckles land in the very spot my ribs are broken. I feel them crack again. I drop to the floor, wheezing.

"I told you to shut your hole!" He bares his teeth. "Wasn't born with the name Shank. It was given to me here. I'd rather not kill something I just paid for."

I stand, pain shooting down my sides. I glance over and see Bruul Vaarkson, the grizzled foreman of the Haulers, staring at me across the crowd. He's a full head taller than anyone, so he's hard to miss. His stare is hungry. His lips curl into a sickle shape. I shudder with revulsion.

"Sold! To the Hauler Gang!" Toshi cries out in pain as he's pulled from the block and thrust into the pack of Haulers. "That ends the bidding. Return to your bunks. Work resumes at oh-four-hundred."

The Warden and his cadre of prison guards vacate the cavern, leaving us to our own devices.

"Where do they sleep?" I turn to a Picker with a scar on his lip that pulls his expression into a perpetual frown.

"Warden stays in barracks almost a mile down. Much warmer for their fat noble asses. You'd know something about that, wouldn't you?"

The man spits fully in my face. The spittle dribbles down to my chin. He smiles. The scar on his lip makes it look twisted. *He's testing me,* I realize. I need to prove myself now or forever be branded a coward in the gang's eyes. My ribs throb, and I feel the aching of my muscles after the climb from the surface. I'm not ready to fight. *Death doesn't care for ready.* Alberich's words are in my head.

When will it ever end? I wonder. *Fight after fight until they kill me. Or I kill them.*

The crowd forms a circle around us. The anticipation of bloodshed crackles in the frost like electricity.

"You don't want to do this." My warning sounds lame even to my own ears.

"Oh, I don't want to do this?" the man with the twisted mouth mocks.

"Give it to that noble ass-rag!" someone shouts.

"Show 'em, Grinner," another catcalls.

Grinner. The man's name is Grinner. Fitting.

"Make a move," he calls.

"You first." I refuse to be the one who starts this.

He charges. I twist away from his oncoming fist. The movement explodes bolts of pain through my rib cage. I deflect another blow. Grinner's momentum carries him forward, hurtling at great speed. His back foot trails behind him. I hook my own foot to his to trip him and hasten his fall. He slams to the ground full force. His temple meets a stone jutting up from the cavern floor and cracks his skull like an eggshell. The sound reverberates through the cavern. The crowd goes silent. The fight is over before it even began.

Grinner lies dying, arms and legs twitching. I try not to register the shock and horror I feel. I got lucky, but I can't show weakness. Not now. If I do nothing, he will die slowly, horrifically. *I'm here less than a day, and I have already killed a man.* I lift my foot and bring it down decisively. The man's brains are dashed onto the ice. *A quick death is a kindness,* my father once said. *Maybe he was right.*

I feel the anger radiating off the crowd. This wasn't what they wanted. They wanted me beaten slowly, humiliated. They wanted fun. I just ended the party. *This is where I deserve to be,* I think. *My father has won. I'm a killer.*

It was an accident, but it is done.

"Anyone else?" I say.

The crowd peels off one by one. One lingers. The giant foreman, Vaarkson. "You got lucky, little boy," he says. "But luck won't save you from me." He strides away.

I grab one of the Pickers skulking off. "What was his name?" I ask, pointing at the man I've just killed.

"That there was Grinner," says the Picker.

"No, his real name."

"Don't know. He had no other name than Grinner." The man yanks his arm from my grasp. I stare at the corpse, his true identity as lost as his life. Grinner had a mother.

Maybe he had a Nadia, too, who knows?

This universe doesn't care, and maybe it never did.

The crowd disperses, all except for the mysterious dark man I saw earlier. His milky eyes stare at me. I get the feeling he understands; he understands the self-hatred that passes through me. Then slowly, he, too, moves off.

I sit apart from the fires and tents of my gang. The Pickers do not consider me one of them yet. The killing of Grinner has afforded me a wide berth and respite from any hazing I see the other new fish go through. However, I know I won't be safe indefinitely.

Jinam Shank has climbed a ladder to his foreman's nest, a tiny apartment carved in the ice of the cavern wall dozens of meters above the main camp. Heat rises from the ground floor, making his shelter slightly warmer. From the alcove, the foreman can see the cavern and his gang below. The general population huddles in lion-seal skins around the fires.

Each gang seems to have its own village staked out within the larger camp. There's no plan behind the layout. It's a haphazard smattering of tents and makeshift structures that have been erected over the last few decades. I've been given no furs, so I grab my sides and shiver in my neoprene suit. I chew on a ration stick that was tossed my way during the bonfire lighting. The place is savage, recalling some ancient barbarian past.

It is two hours until lights out, then five more until the work whistle. The pain in my torso abates to a dull ache. I know I'll survive thanks to the bone grafting from Talousla Karr. Part of me wishes he had never changed me. I would be with my mother and wife and child in the great Mother Ocean by now.

I finish the last bite of the chalk-tasting ration stick, but my stomach still growls. I try to take my mind off the hunger and all that has happened by imagining the fingerings of a flute and the lessons of Gorham from when I was a child. I hear the beat of his drum in the pumping of my heart, and my fingers tap the imaginary notes. I can almost hear the melody of the Eventide feast in my mind. Music could always transport me to another world.

"Edmon?"

I turn at the whisper. Toshi has snuck into the Picker camp. I'm new to the Wendigo, but I get the impression that he definitely shouldn't be here. His presence is a risk, and I'm already not on the greatest terms with my new "friends."

"What are you doing here?" I whisper.

"You looked cold." He drops a pile of rags at my feet. "The man you killed—I'm told you get to claim his possessions."

His face looks sunken. He should be taking care of his leg, not visiting me to chat fireside.

"I didn't mean to kill him," I respond.

"Don't be a fool." Toshi's breathing is ragged.

"Shank will kill me if he finds out you're here. Does Vaarkson know?" I ask.

"Edmon—"

Whatever he's about to say no longer matters. He collapses to the ground, convulsing. "Toshi!" I shout a little too loudly. Several other Pickers look my way.

"By the twisted star, Leontes!" A thick, stocky man steps forward from the pack. "That's no Picker. Get him out of here now or Shank will skin you!"

"His name's Toshi, and he's my friend," I snarl back. "He was shot by the sniper after we were shoved out of the transport sondi."

"I don't care if his mother shot him. He's a Hauler. Shoulder goes to the cold now, Leontes, query?"

"He's a human being first and needs help. Query?" I mock his slang. "I'm not asking you to tweeze the bullet from the leg yourself. Just tell me where I can find someone who can." The men shift uncomfortably. "There must be someone here, a healer?" I ask again.

"What about Faria, Carrick?" says one next to the stocky man.

Carrick, the stocky man, hesitates.

"Carrick," I try to reason, "if you want to take sides, Pickers, Haulers, fine. But gangs are just a way to keep you from seeing the real enemy: The Warden and the guards. It's us versus them."

I only suspect this is the truth. I remember Phaestion's war games in the arcology of Meridian. It's the common people, the multitude, pitted against the few with wealth and weapons. This is a conflict they will understand, I hope.

"You're making a mistake," Carrick mutters uneasily. "Haulers don't get into our camp without someone from their side knowing. Why he's here is a question you might want to ask yourself. You want to save some scraggly grass to remind you of home, be it on your head. Seek Faria the Red."

"Faria the Red?" I ask.

"Dark as night, reddish hair." Carrick describes the dark man I saw standing on the outskirts when I was auctioned off.

"Where can I find him?"

Carrick points into the village of shanties. "Other side. Maybe a kilometer. Igloo built into the cavern wall. You won't miss it."

I waste no more words. Toshi groans in delirium as I hoist him onto my shoulders. My ribs hurt like the nuclear fires of a star, but I'll endure. Toshi may not be so lucky. His skin blazes with febrile heat. I feel it through my suit. I selfishly welcome the warmth as I trudge through the narrow, muddy-ice avenues of the camp. Tents and shacks serve as meager dwellings and storefronts for various gangs of the Wendigo—Smelters, Welders, Loaders, Sifters, Haulers, Pickers, Trainmen, Foodies . . . I draw stares from them all as I step one lumbering foot in front of the other. Finally, I arrive at the igloo. No door, only a small portal dug into the ground to crawl in and out of. The flickering of firelight emanates from within.

"Faria?" I call out. "Faria the Red?" No answer. Toshi groans. He's burning up. I lower him gently onto the ground. "Faria!" I call again. *Damn this.* I get down on my knees and crawl through the tunnel. I don't care if I'm invading his privacy. My friend is dying.

I find myself in a room with a small cabinet and a sleeping pallet against the wall. A fire crackles in the center of the chamber. The dark man kneels on a rug before the flames, his eyes closed. His skin is the color of pitch, making the tattoos of limestone-white etched into his face jump out in contrast. I've never seen such markings before. The hair on his head is so tightly curled one couldn't run a finger through it. It's a remarkable shade of red. Not quite like Phaestion's, but certainly startling. His appearance is otherworldly and frightening.

"Faria?"

He raises a hand, silencing me. I pause, pulled in by the power of his simple, wordless command. Then I remember Toshi dying outside. "Faria, listen—"

His eyes snap open, milk-white with cataract. He stares directly at me. The effect is terrifying. "You come uninvited and violate my home with a demand," he says in a rich basso. "I don't end lives on whims, but if I did, you've certainly given me cause."

"I'm sorry." I bow my head abjectly. Everyone here forces you to abase yourself or face death it seems. "My friend is dying. I was told you could heal him?"

"You must be mistaken. You have no friends, and I will not heal him," the dark man says. He closes his eyes and returns to his meditation.

I'm stunned. I've never known a healer who refuses to heal and would let the suffering of an injured man continue. Then again, he didn't say that he couldn't heal Toshi, only that he wouldn't.

What does he want in return? That's the key to everyone, isn't it? Find what they want.

"Faria, please—"

"Why do you wish to save this man?" he interrupts.

"He's my friend," I insist again. The dark man sits and stares blankly. My answer does not satisfy him. "Because he's an islander like me, like you."

Faria looks like no islander I've ever seen, but where else could he come from with his dark skin and strange appearance? Even if I'm wrong, perhaps my assumption will illuminate the truth.

"You think to save this man because he's like you. You think to appeal to me because I may be like you?"

"Yes."

"You think geographical proximity of birth or the color of a man's skin makes him worth saving?"

"No," I answer firmly.

"Then answer better," he commands.

"Because he's a human being with a life. He's suffering. I want to save him because it's the right thing to do," I say honestly.

"Be careful what you deem right and wrong. Life is suffering," he says simply. "You may do him no favors by prolonging it."

I didn't come here to debate philosophy with an old tusk walrus. I will not back down.

"I don't work for kindness," he says. "I keep prisoners healthy. I get privacy. I mend broken bones, stitch lacerations, and receive immunity from the gangs and their feuds. I soothe pestilence; I'm rewarded with food and equipment. I keep miners strong to mine the ore for the noble houses of Tao. My commission is autonomy. What do you offer, son of Leontes? Your name's not gold here."

"I have nothing, but the rags of a man I didn't mean to kill. You can have those or any debt you see fit."

"That is all? Interesting. You will give up so much more before it's done." He smiles crookedly.

A pact has been made.

"So a killer would save a man he hardly knows because life is precious?" he asks.

"I'm no killer."

"Grinner died on his own, I suppose?"

"I've not killed before today," I protest.

"All men are killers, today or tomorrow. What does it matter?" he asks.

"It was an accident."

"Yet still, he's dead." Faria rises to his feet.

His hands are outstretched like a blind man's. I reach out to guide him to the portal of his igloo. No sooner does my hand contact his arm then he grabs my wrist and twists it with incredible strength. He snaps the bones of my finger effortlessly. I'm too shocked to cry out, but I pull my hand away in flashing pain.

"Don't touch me," he says softly.

"I was trying to guide you," I say, breathing through clenched teeth.

"Guidance is not required." With that, he crawls out of the igloo.

Faria's already examining Toshi with dark and wrinkled fingers when I crawl from the porthole. It's nearly twenty degrees colder outside.

"He was shot by the tower guard in his upper right thigh," I offer.

"Greelo has excellent aim," Faria replies. "Your friend wasn't meant to survive. He was to have been left, a lesson for the rest of you."

"Why?" I ask.

Faria shrugs. "They marked him as someone who wouldn't contribute much of his weight in ore."

"That's a reason?" My cheeks flush with anger.

"They need a reason? He's a Hauler now. You're a Picker."

"So?"

"You'll learn. Let's get him inside." Together, we drag Toshi into the igloo. It hurts my ribs, and my broken finger screams with pain, but we manage to lay him by the fire.

"Leave me to work," Faria says. I look around the room. There's no antiseptic, no instruments, and no medical tools of any kind. "If you want him alive, you'll leave," the old man says again forcefully.

I grimace. I don't like this and don't want to return to the cold outside the hut, but I'm playing by his rules. I reluctantly crawl back out and stand in the freezing cold, fuming. My breath turns to puffy white clouds in front of my face. *The charlatan first refuses to help, breaks my finger, and then forces me to stand outside in the bitter freeze and wait!*

And I wait and wait . . . I huddle up to the igloo exterior. I look at my bent finger. It has to be snapped back into place soon, or it won't heal correctly.

Faria the Red? What a stupid name.

I hear chanting emanating from inside the igloo. Some sort of strange guttural language I've never heard before, if it is indeed a language at all.

What's he doing?

I clamp my jaw shut as I grab my finger. One, two, three. I snap it back straight. Nerves shoot electric fire down my arm. I pound my head against the wall of the igloo. I feel better after the initial flare passes. I already feel the bones beginning to reset of their own accord. The finger might even be better within a few hours thanks to the spypsy's bone grafts. I close my eyes and drift off to sleep, not knowing if my friend will live or die.

CHAPTER 17

Solo

I'm awoken by the scraping of knees on ice. I stand in time to see the dark-skinned healer crawl from the igloo. "The worst is past," he says. "Return here at the end of the workday and you can take your friend back to his camp."

"The workday?"

An alarm reverberates throughout the cavern. Guards enter from a tunnel that leads to the lower levels. They fan out through the village as the prisoners awaken.

"Give me your finger," Faria commands. "You'll be needing it in the mines."

"Not necessary," I reply coldly.

His hand whips out faster than lightning. He grasps my wrist with incredible strength. "This finger has been reset. It's almost completely healed. How?" His milky-white eyes narrow.

I yank my hand back. "You have your secrets. I have mine."

"Yesterday, when you fought, you were protecting your ribs. My eyes may not function, but I still see in other ways. And now . . ." His fingers jab into my sides. I wince because I'm still tender. "No longer broken, I see." He scowls.

"I have to get back." I want to end this discussion.

"Report to your foreman for the day's assignment." He crawls back into his igloo.

I haven't slept but two hours. I've eaten almost nothing for over a day. My stomach growls, my head feels light. I jog toward Picker territory. I arrive just in time to see the gang falling into line. I find a place behind the stocky man, Carrick.

"Where are we going?" I whisper.

"Quiet, fish!" someone shouts.

"I haven't eaten anything," I say, realizing I sound whiny.

Carrick shakes his head. "Perhaps you shouldn't have spent the night helping an enemy. You dumb piece of—"

"Quiet back there!" Shank yells from the front.

We all load into a train, similar to the Banshee Rail, only smaller, packing ourselves inside the cars as the sonic engine hums. The train chugs into the darkness of a tunnel. Down, down into the caverns we go for what seems forever. Finally, the train doors slide open, and we disembark into the grime and filth of an underground mining tunnel. The cacophony of machinery echoes everywhere. I barely hear Shank as he commands the men to move deeper into a tributary off the main tunnel. We pass a station marked "Dungeon Thirteen," where each member of the gang is issued a helmet with a fireglobe, a harness, and a sonic drill from a locker. Shank opens it via a DNA identification lock.

Only foremen have access to the tools, I note.

We hook our harnesses onto a massive arterial cable that has been bolted to the cavern wall. I'm told it's the Recon Gang's job to scout the caverns and set these cables so we may move into the depths. I spend my first day in darkness with only the dim light of my helmet to illuminate the labors. I hang on a vertical cliff face picking and drilling the wall, carving rock from ore. That's what Pickers do, apparently. Chunks of debris fall somewhere below for the Sifter Gang to separate ore from rock. The Haulers, the biggest and strongest of us, oversee the delivery of the material to the smelter station, where it's further refined for transport back to the upper cavern, from there through the shaft to the surface, and then picked up by a sondi for transport to Meridian.

Phaestion said our planet has little to trade, but it was House Julii who owned the largest fleet among the Pantheon and monopolized what little there was before the Fracture Point shifted. Since my father transformed the Wendigo from prison to labor camp, he has further advanced its production through a bargain with off-worlders. House Wusong-Leontes will use the metals mined here to craft rockets. Phaestion said that my father planned to save our people through becoming traders somehow. Perhaps Tao does not have significant resources of its own, but with a fleet of ships, her people could ferry the goods of other worlds. Such a plan, if successful, could change the dynamic of the Pantheon and the fabric of our culture. I think this is what Phaestion fears the most.

I have only these musings along with hatred and self-loathing in these long hours that first day. I think on what led me here.

Why didn't Edric try to marry Lavinia or Phoebe to Phaestion instead of me to Miranda Wusong? Perhaps it's not an either-or proposition, rather an "and." Why not choose to ally with a powerful rival as well as the imperial line? Maybe the choice wasn't his. Maybe the enmity is from the other side?

My mind flashes back to the day Phaestion arrived on Bone, the day he showed me his siren swords. *They were made for my brother, Augustus,* he had told me. Augustus had died in the Combat. *Who would have been strong enough to fell the brother of Phaestion Julii?* The picture suddenly seems clearer.

Edric may have been spurned for his low birth or for having killed the Julii heir. Then didn't Phaestion try to turn Edric's own sons against him by indoctrinating them as Companions? My father allowed this. Why? Perhaps he thought that if I died or turned it might be easier to rid himself of me. Then again, Edgaard was also a companion. Perhaps Edric thought that we might turn Phaestion just as well as he could turn us? Vendetta is a funny thing, I marvel.

I ache from exertion and stop for a moment to shout to the Picker on the line next to me to ask whether we stop for lunch.

"We don't break, fish."

How do they expect us to stay alive without food? I wonder.

We work hour upon hour. Finally, the arterial cable is yanked at the end of an eight-hour cycle, our signal to return to the upper caverns. We give up our harnesses, helmets, picks, and drills. We load back onto the train, which returns us to the firelight and cold of the cavern. My body no longer throbs from injury, but from sheer muscle exhaustion. I follow the line of Pickers through the village. I head for the Ration Bar, where the Foodies hand out food packs to inmates. I need sustenance, I need sleep, but I remember my friend still in the care of Faria. I secretly grab an extra pack from the counter and break away from the lines.

Toshi is waiting for me outside Faria's hut when I arrive. He stands. I see that he can't put much weight on his leg, but otherwise looks fine.

"Edmon! You made it." He smiles.

After the ordeal of the last forty-eight hours, it feels like there's finally some bit of peace that's taken hold when I see his face.

"Toshi! You okay?" I feel ready to collapse myself.

"Thanks to you. And to the old shaman." He uses the island word for medicine man. Faria is indeed a scary son of a bitch medicine man.

"What's wrong?" Toshi asks.

"Hungry, tired, freezing, in prison. By the twisted star, what *isn't* wrong with me?" I laugh, the kind of laugh that's so bone weary, I no longer can control it. "I brought you this." I hold up the food pack. We lean on each other and trudge through the village, a pair of friendless wretches. At least we have each other.

"So how was your day, dear?" he asks.

"Hanging in utter darkness. Picking all day at rocks. Who could ask for more?"

Toshi laughs, too. Then we walk in silence. He's been brought back to life from the brink of death. It's nigh a miracle.

"How did he do it, Toshi?" I ask. "You were almost dead when I brought you in. You seem almost good as new."

Toshi shrugs. "Truth is, I don't know. I was unconscious. The moments I came to . . . it's like the whole thing was a bad dream. Distant." He looks off. "Something with his hands, though. I remember that much: his hands."

He looks at me again and laughs. "Important thing is I'm better, and you need to eat more."

I can't argue. We walk back to the Ration Bar and grab trays from a stack, hoping they won't notice that I already stole an extra pack earlier. A round man with a shaved head behind the counter grins. "Enjoy, Leontes. I picked your bags especial."

"Thanks," I reply coldly as he slaps a mud-caked pack onto my tray. Aside from the grime, I wonder if the food's been pissed in, too.

Toshi and I find a table. "I have a feeling this won't taste too good," I mutter.

"Ya think?" he replies. "Does it really matter?"

"No," I admit. I'm hungry enough to eat narwhal dung. For all I know, I'm about to. I tear open the packs and dig in. Compressed, tasteless foodstuffs. They are dehydrated rations that time-release in the gut and are supposed to provide a full day's worth of nutrients. "Modern efficiency!" I exclaim.

The alarm rings, and the guards gather at their tunnel to return to their barracks. They're gone and "night" comes to the village of the Wendigo. Toshi leans across the table conspiratorially and whispers, "Edmon, I got to show you something." He stands and gestures for me to follow.

"What is it?" I whisper back.

"Today, after Faria fixed me up, I was able to explore a bit." I find it hard to believe that he was walking about for too long, but his recovery is pretty stunning. "I think it'll be useful," he says.

He heads toward a tunnel. I follow. "Isn't this where guards go?" I ask, becoming nervous. I worry my absence will be noticed by my foreman soon.

"Exactly." He pulls a small fireglobe from his pocket, shakes it, and lights up the tunnel walls with eerie incandescence. "I found a tributary from the main passage. Looks like it goes down to the planet core."

"And?" I ask, looking around warily.

"If there's a passage that leads to somewhere they don't know about, maybe we can get out of here," he says.

"You don't think they've thought of that before?" I ask.

"Don't know," he admits. "But maybe we could strike out on our own. We can sneak into the upper caverns for food."

"Survive in the freezing cold, living off scraps?" I say disdainfully.

"They put us here forever," he argues. "We're never leaving. At least maybe we can find some freedom. We've got to find out. Even if this one's a dead end, we've got to start looking."

"You're right," I say warily. "If there's opportunity, we have to take it, but the right way. We don't know enough about this place yet to escape it. We'd be better to bide our time and learn as much as we can first."

The tunnel gets darker, colder. We round the corner down the tributary he indicates. The lights off the main track fade and so does the heat. We walk for what seems like several kilometers in increasing darkness until ahead I make out a faint light as the tributary opens into a small cave. Far from being abandoned, it's full with people. They stand against the walls on all sides. Bruul Vaarkson, the big bear of a man, is in the center, waiting.

I turn quickly to make an escape, but the passage is blocked by half a dozen Haulers with ready fists. "Stay behind me, Toshi," I warn, trying to position myself between him and our attackers. He's in no condition to fight. Neither am I, for that matter.

"He's not the one you should be worrying about protecting," Vaarkson sneers.

I turn and look him dead in the eye.

"Oh, you have spirit. I like them with spirit," Vaarkson goads. "You finished off that tillyfish the other day, and I'd pit your skills man to man against almost anyone in this joint in a fair fight. But this isn't a fair fight, is it?"

I ball my fists. "Do what you're going to do to us, but quit the sweet talk."

"Us, is it? Still haven't figured it out?" The rest of the Haulers shriek like a pack of hyena eels.

Toshi is also nervously laughing. He places his hands up and slowly backs away from me. I feel the cold knife of betrayal slip in my gut. *He knew.* This must have been planned before I even took him to Faria's. *Did Faria know? Did they all?*

"I'm sorry, Edmon. They were going to kill me." He shakes his head.

"I saved you. Twice." My voice registers bewilderment more than anger.

"Now I have to save myself." He fades into the crowd. I hear him say faintly, "You said you wouldn't hurt him."

"I say a lot of things." Vaarkson shrugs. "Besides, this isn't going to be pain, but pleasure."

They rush forward. I fight. Punch, kick, and claw. It's a sea of people. There's no space to move and nowhere to go. I'm tackled to the floor of the cave and held down. My bodysuit is torn from my back. I feel the bite of the arctic cold against my bare skin. Then he's on me. Vaarkson. Large, hairy, his breath foul. I say nothing as it happens, clamp my jaw shut and bear the pain. My mind goes somewhere else.

I see my mother the day of the christening. She defied my father with every breath as he beat her. *You will forget what you saw here today,* she said.

I remember Nadia when she pulled me up from falling that day so long ago. They tried to make me forget her, too. *I am with you, Little Lord,* she whispers in my memory.

Then another voice whispers. *Remember.* It's not my mother's or Nadia's. Strangely, it's the voice of my father. *Remember.* His anger and his power, like a single intense candle flame of hatred, grow inside me. *Remember, and when the time comes, no mercy.*

I curl into a ball and bleed onto the floor.

—

The Night Queen sings. *Gli angui d'inferno, mi sento in petto, Megera, Alletto, ho intorno a me . . . Paventa il mio furore, se non osi esser crudel. Ciel! L'orendo mio voto ascolto o Ciel! Of hell the vengeance boils within my heart, death and despair are flaming all around me . . . To pieces all the ties of nature torn, Hear Gods of vengeance, hear a mother's vow!* The song plays in my head. *The Magic Flute.* A tune as old as Ancient Earth. I drag myself hand by bloody hand through the dark tunnels.

I sing words of my own to the music The Maestro taught me. *I will not die. I must not die. If I die, Nadia's death means nothing. My mother's death means nothing. My child's death means nothing. My father will win. He cannot win.*

When I'm strong enough to stand, I hobble. I wrap myself in the torn rags of my bodysuit. Blood mixes with feces and trickles down my legs. My bowels are perforated. I'm going to die without medical help.

The passage widens. Darkness slowly becomes dim firelight. I enter the shantytown and collapse to the ground. My body wants to give in. The voice of my father does not let me.

Get up, coward.

"Shut up, son of a whore!" I scream. My cries echo through the chamber. A few figures huddled by a distant fire stir. I push myself to my hands and knees and crawl. I feel light-headed. The pain is searing through my body. Soon I am groveling in front of the frozen igloo of the dark healer.

"Faria," I call out. No answer, no sign that anyone dwells here at all. Yet the flickering light of a fire dances within. *The old man would make me beg before helping, wouldn't he?*

I'm not above begging. There is no pride or dignity left. I have nothing to lose but my life, which I will lose anyway if I do nothing. I pull my body through the entrance of his dwelling. I have nothing left.

The dark man gazes into the flames. "I knew you would return," he says. "You did not heed my warning."

I collapse, utterly destroyed.

Faria drags me close to the fire.

"What's your price now, healer?" I ask.

"You have paid enough today. We'll worry about the difference tomorrow."

I cry like a babe. "When does it stop?" I ask through salted tears. "When does it stop? The pain? The suffering?"

"It never stops" is his quiet answer. Not unkind, but truthful. I feel something jab into my back, and my vision goes dark. Then I feel nothing.

I wake. I'm lying under some sort of animal hide. I feel a dull ache below, but it's not the scorching fire of before. I prop myself up on my elbows. It hurts.

The dark, painted man sits where I first found him, meditating by the fire. "Be careful." His voice is ominous. "The stitches will take some time to dissolve. Limit your activity. Your body needs to heal."

"I'm not sure Jinam Shank or Vaarkson will care," I mutter.

"Stay with your gang. Do not wander alone. Stay out of any place where you could be caught on your own." He points to the igloo exit. Rags and furs sit on the ground there. "Used garments, furs from off-world, as well as nareel and lion-seal hides from the North Sea. They come in the monthly shipments. I collect them from the backs of those I cannot save."

I dress myself in the layers of a dead man's clothes. "Thank you." I duck to leave through the crawl space but pause. "Why did you save me?" I ask.

"All the gangs use my services."

"That's no answer," I say.

"You remember why you helped your friend? Toshi, was it?" he asks.

"Maybe I shouldn't have," I say bitterly.

"Knowing he betrayed you, has your answer changed?"

I should have let him die, I think. "No," I say instead. "He would have died if I didn't help. There's no way I could have known what would happen."

"You'd do it again?"

"Of course I wouldn't do it again!" I shout. I wince. The outburst causes pain inside, but I'm sick of the shaman's enigmatic questioning. "There's no use dwelling on something that can never be," I mutter.

The old man stares into the flames.

"You should have let me die." I stare at the ground.

"I would," he says. "But you wouldn't let yourself die."

A beat passes.

"Will anything happen to Vaarkson or the Haulers?" I ask.

"That depends on you, Edmon Leontes."

I return to the Picker camp, but there's no fanfare at my arrival. I take a seat outside the circle of men around the fire. A few steal furtive glances in my direction, but no one says a word. *Perhaps I can forget it ever happened.* I pull the furs Faria has given me close and try to steal slumber before the call of the morning alarm.

"You."

I wake to the scarred visage of Jinam Shank. He's flanked by Carrick and a few others. I look at him through bloodshot eyes.

"You will never speak of what has occurred!" he hisses. "Your shame and weakness would bring danger to all of us."

I'm an object of shame and humiliation.

I want to respond that if he's too weak to protect a member of his own gang, if he would rather cover up what's happened, then he's as vulnerable as anyone would think anyway. He doesn't deserve to be foreman.

It's not the time. Yet. I keep my mouth shut, but I remember his words.

"Do you understand?" he asks.

I understand this: *There will be no justice, unless I seek it myself.*

"Do you understand?" he repeats.

I nod and roll over onto my side.

The next day's alarm sounds. I follow the line of Pickers to the tram. I feel looks of disgust whenever the men pass their eyes over me. I was singled out on the auction block because of my parentage. I was tested and forced to kill. Now I'm an object of scorn. They all know what has happened regardless of Jinam Shank's warning to never speak of it.

The day is spent in the dim light of my helmet fireglobe. Again, I pick at rocks. I move slowly, not wanting to tear any of the stitches

Faria has made internally. My haul at the end of the day is meager, and I draw more glares.

We return to the upper caverns. The crowd surges forward from the train car, and I lose track of my gang. I look for Shank, for Carrick, anyone I recognize, but the sea of people is like a rushing force of nature. I'm caught in the human current pressing through the tunnel. Soon, I realize I'm surrounded on all sides by men of the Hauler Gang. They jab legs out, trying to trip me. Someone grabs my ear. Another slaps my face. They're herding me away from the entrance to the village and toward one of the dark dead-end tributaries.

It's happening again! I need to get out. I'm hyperventilating. I'm losing all focus. I catch the eyes of one of Vaarkson's mooks, a man with a snaggletooth leering at me. Vaarkson cannot be far behind. I feel the looming presence of the big man somewhere in the pack.

Keep your head, fool, my father's voice whispers. I grit my teeth and shake out the fear. I see a guard with a humbaton ahead.

I have to act. Play the fool now to survive. "Guard!" I scream at the top of my lungs. "Help me!"

The guard looks in my direction. I shove toward him against the human river.

"Help me!" I break free from the morass and fall at the man's feet. I grab his leg like a sniveling child.

"Get off me!" he shouts contemptuously.

I cling like a mussel to a rock in the sea. It works. The Haulers who have been trying to corral me break off and head into the village cavern.

"Get off!" The guard brings the butt end of his humbaton down on my head.

I black out for a second as I hit the ground. When I look up through blurred vision, he holds the stun muzzle of the weapon in my face. I raise my hands in protection. "I'm sorry, m'lord. I'm sorry," I grovel.

"Get out of here, worm," he says, then spits.

I scurry toward the village with a sigh of relief. My head throbs, but I'm alive and safe. I follow the flow to the Ration Bar, grab a tray, and take up my place in line. I'm shoved continuously by those behind me until I reach the counter. The server slaps a ration pack onto my tray. I greedily tear the foil open, but I'm shoved again. I almost spill my only food for the day onto the icy floor.

I move through the mess tables protecting my pack like a mother seal. I pass the Haulers' table, and they snicker. Toshi eyes me nervously. He's frightened, alone, even as he's surrounded by his new gang.

Good. I think. *I've survived. You will not.*

"Leontes," Vaarkson catcalls. "They won't babysit you forever. Night comes. Guards sleep." He licks his lips.

I turn away and head for the Picker table. I move to sit on the end of the bench. A Picker bars my path. "Seat's taken, fish," he says coldly. I move to another open seat. Again: "Move along, fish."

I'm forced to sit away from the tables, alone and unprotected. Day's cycle will soon end, and I'll need to return to my camp. If they won't let me into their ranks to sleep, if I'm left to wander the village during night hours, I'll be prey. If I'm not caught this Eventide, I will be eventually. I need to think of something. *I need to change the rules of the game, but how?*

My father was right—*a swift death is a kindness.* If I were dead, I'd be with Mother. The Maestro. Gorham. I'd be with Nadia. At the very least, I'd feel the peace of oblivion. Instead, I'm here, without even a rope to hang myself. The sharks are circling.

Drums beat in my brain. *I cannot do it. I must. I won't. Survive. I wish I were dead. No, make them the dead ones.*

Then something happens I do not expect. Faria walks through the crowd to the tables, carrying a food tray. I've not seen him intermingling with the general population before. I've only witnessed him outside the crowd, like when I was on the auction block or when I accidentally killed Grinner.

No one takes notice, almost as if he's invisible. I know better. *What's his game?* I wonder.

He steps up to Vaarkson and the Hauler table. The ever-graceful dark man trips.

No, he didn't trip on anything. He did that on purpose.

His ration pack spills all over Vaarkson and Snaggletooth, who sits next to the Hauler foreman.

"Damn you!" Vaarkson barks.

"Sorry, sir, I'm sorry!" Faria blubbers, making a mockery of himself.

"Leave, you wrinkled tillyfish, before I make you leave!" Vaarkson growls.

Faria's position commands enough respect that he'll get away cleanly so long as he continues the charade of obsequious fool. "I'm terribly sorry, Foreman Vaarkson." Faria bows and scrapes.

"Yeah." Snaggletooth grabs Faria's coat. "Beat it, ya old snail, before we beat it out of you."

Faria's fingers shoot out and tap the back of Snaggletooth's hand, almost swifter than an eye can see, but my eye sees it.

"Ow! Ya freaking maggot!" cries out Snaggletooth. The wiry man pulls his hand back.

"Terribly sorry," mumbles Faria.

The blind old man picks up his tray and shuffles back toward his igloo, and the men return to their dinners. That was strange, I think. The whole incident . . . something felt off.

I've no time to ponder the interaction, though. I need to finish my food before the evening alarm. I down the thick paste in the pack quickly.

Day's end alarm rings. The guards head to their tram. The prisoners at the tables shuffle back to their camps. I stand to return my tray to the kitchen, skirting wide of the Hauler table. It still hurts to walk, and I feel the Haulers' eyes on me.

I'm hunted.

The Haulers stand from their table. I don't know if I'll be able to outpace them, but there's no other choice. I take a deep breath and ready myself to run.

A scream echoes through the cavern that curdles the blood. Snaggletooth stands back from the others, shaking violently. Blood oozes, first from his nose, then from his ears, and finally from the corners of his eyes. He coughs. A volcano of red erupts from his mouth down his chin. He collapses to the floor convulsing, then lies still. Everyone watches silently, horrified.

"He's dead," a Hauler says in disbelief. Whispers of "witchcraft" run through their ranks.

I quietly slip away toward the Picker camp. I smile. The game has changed.

CHAPTER 18

Crescendo

Have I been here six months? Nine? No, a year and a half gone by. I am almost twenty.

I've no journal, no paper with which to write. Instead, I talk to myself in my head to help recall, like a historian recording a biography of some past figure. The time Edmon Leontes found a weird chunk in his ration pack. The day Edmon Leontes tripped and fell in the tunnels and landed on the rock that split his chin. Each incident I recount makes the passage of time more bearable.

Then, Edmon Leontes's hair falls out. I wake one morning to find a tuft inside the fur lining of my hood, the next morning, more. Soon, patches of my scalp are visible to everyone. The sight draws derision from prisoners, including my own gang.

"Hey, Baldy Patch!" they holler as I pass.

I visit Faria. "What's wrong with me?" I'm desperate to know.

The shaman says the disease is genetic, triggered by stress. It was seen in some people of Ancient Earth, but rarely since. Some races, like the space gypsies, breed it purposefully into their genome, hairlessness being more efficient in the ventilated starships of the vast cold.

I think of Talousla Karr. *Did he do this?*

"The disease may progress or plateau," Faria says. "However, it's no cause for great concern."

Faria and I have spoken but once or twice since the incident in the Ration Bar. Yet there has been a shift in our relationship. He watches me, as if waiting, and I now know he has special knowledge and secrets. Learning them may help me claim revenge against my father, against Phaestion, against the whole damn Pantheon and their bloody Combat and sickening Pavaka.

How do I get those secrets when I can barely survive? When I'm decaying like this? I don't know, but I know that I must convince the old man somehow. I should look on the Dayside. Vaarkson eyes me with disgust rather than lust now, which is a welcome blessing.

"The damage," Faria tells me, "is mainly psychological."

He says this as if sanity wasn't the only thing that mattered while being imprisoned. Then again, I've come to the conclusion that Faria isn't from Tao. He can't be. On Tao, we've been taught that physical perfection is a manifestation of our superior culture. Nightsiders give disfigured children to the fire. Our people have weeded out deleterious genes and undesirable traits, like cleft palates or baldness. The ugly and physically challenged are ostracized. The likelihood they will find a mate and pass on their genes is slim.

Unless you're the daughter of the emperor, I think ironically. *Now I'm one of the uglies. Handsome Prince Leontes, banished to a prison in the cold wastes, slowly becoming a monster.* I carry this sense of self-loathing with me to the mines every morning. *If I'd been the man I should've been, none of this would've happened. My mother would be alive. I'd have been able to save Nadia. It will take a monster to escape this place and claim revenge against those who did this to me.*

My muscles become wiry, my face gaunt and haggard. My beard mostly remains, scraggly and coarse. I don't lose my eyebrows. *Thank the twisted star for that.* I know I shouldn't care about such vanities—they're wasted here in the Wendigo—but I take solace that what little shallowness I have left means I'm somehow still human.

We get news of the yearly Combat. Inmates aren't allowed to watch on aquagraphic, but guards talk, and word spreads. Hanschen of House Julii is declared victor. The news washes over me like a cold wave. He's the first of The Companions to compete. And he's won.

This year, the rotunda was transformed into a fully automated chamber that every hour filled with another meter of water. Combatants were forced to kill as they climbed an obstacle structure, or else they drowned. Hanschen's agility gave him advantage in climbing.

I overhear a conversation between Sookah and another guard as he details the drama—

The House Julii clansman had initially allied with one of the stronger combatants, a boy from House Temujin. Of course, the Julii scion betrayed his ally when they were the last two fighters left. He stabbed the boy in the back just before the massive chamber filled with water. Not the most honorable win, but a win nonetheless, and a place among the College of Electors as prize.

I'd put siren steel on one companion competing each year until they all sit in the government. When Phaestion takes his place among them, he'll have a strong block within the ranks to be voted to the High Synod.

I could have been part of it all, I realize.

One man stands in the way—Edric Leontes. He will resist. He has moved to consolidate his own allies. With old Chilleus Julii unable to attend council, there may be room to counter Phaestion's ascension to the Synod. That is if Edgaard can win a Combat and join him.

Edgaard is younger than the other Companions. If and when he is able to compete in the games, I don't know where his loyalties will lie. Phaestion has sought to make an ally of him as he did me. *Will he stand with The Companions, or will he follow my father's will?*

Friendships become plans. People become pawns. I want no part of the game. I'd rather smash the board. *Phaestion, however, is in action and so is my father. I must do the same.*

A shout comes. "Leontes!"

Survival first. I cut off my daydreaming.

"Baldy Patch!" Carrick yells from somewhere above.

"Hark!" I scream back.

"I'm working 'round a big vein here. There's a nice fissure I want to exploit. Move your ass, or it gets rained on with chossy."

I grip rock and traverse as far as my line will take me. I'm fondly reminded of Nadia's lessons from my youth. I miss her so much. Carrick's drill pulses. A cracking sound reverberates through the cavern. Rock and ore rain down. I snag the wall fiercely and gravel sails past. I suck in my breath so as not to inhale particulate. The dust settles. *Just another typical day on the rock,* I think.

"Carrick?" I call out. "Carrick?" I call again.

A scream sounds from below. I flip the switch on my auto-belay and rappel down. Sifters stand on a ledge collecting chunk we've dumped. I unhook myself from the cables and rush to a pile of rubble where several of them have crowded. A badly broken leg juts from the debris, its foot dangling at a horribly odd angle.

Carrick! I dive into the pile of rock.

"By the star!" one of the Sifters shouts. "He must be dead!"

"Not until my eyes see it," I return hotly.

"He should be left," someone responds. "That"—he indicates the leg—"might as well be a death sentence."

I ignore them and remove the rock that covers Carrick's upper half. The big man groans. "He's alive," I growl. "Help me."

"Shue just told you, Leontes—he's a dead man. Best to put him out of his misery."

I grab Carrick's stocky frame and hoist him over my shoulders.

"Get me to a tram," I say.

"The nearest lift is a kilometer up the switchback," someone says, pointing.

Ancestors, kill me now. My auto-belay can't carry both me and the big man. Carrick moans in delirium. If I do nothing, he'll die. If I get him to Faria—

He'll probably die anyway. I stop myself. *You've been here before, Edmon. Remember Toshi. Leave him.*

I lay him on the ground. Letting Carrick die would be the smart thing.

Abyss. I've already made the choice. I hook Carrick's harness to my auto-belay.

"What in the depths are you doing?" The man called Shue gets in my face.

I shove him out of the way. "Something you wouldn't understand."

He steps up to fight, but I glare the Sifter down. Shue must see something in me that makes him shrink. I move past him and continue to work. I double-check the knots and hit the auto-belay. It winches Carrick upward. I see his dangling foot wobble, hanging on by mere tendons and skin.

Stay alive, I silently pray. Then I sprint up the switchback all the way to the top. I shove past Sifters and Haulers, forcing them out of my path. They look at me with annoyance. I don't care. My arms and legs pump blood until they're burning acid. Only a few more paces to go, and I collapse at the top from the exertion. Carrick dangles as the motor of the auto-belay grinds. I scramble over the lip of the ledge and haul him to solid ground. He groans as I slip him over my shoulder and trudge toward the tram.

The engineer is in the cabin with his feet up on the control dash when I arrive. I bang my hand against the window. He startles and flips the intercom switch. "Tram doesn't leave for four hours!" he shouts.

"Open now! This man needs medical attention."

He takes a sidelong look at Carrick. "That guy needs a mortician." He resumes his posture of *Ancestors don't give a sarfish.*

"Open up now, or I open you up!" I shout.

"You and what army, worm?" He waves me off.

I lay Carrick on the tunnel floor, then slam a fist into the tram window. The first blow ricochets off. The glass is thick-paned, designed to resist scrapes of falling rock, but bone is composed of the strongest stuff in nature, and my bones are stronger than most.

It's only pain that stops us, only lack of intention. Without fear, my limits are broken. I slam my knuckles into the glass once more. The engineer sits up in his chair, startled. I concentrate, imagining the force of my fist narrowing to the pinpoint of a laser. The pain is nothing. The engineer's face pales behind the glass. I strike again and the glass spiderwebs. I cock my fist back ready to unload a final time.

"Okay, okay!" screams the engineer. He flips a switch, and the door flies open. I pick Carrick up and settle into the cabin. I pull my helmet off. The patchwork of my balding scalp revealed, the driver gasps as if I'm some sort of horrific creature. I bore my eyes into him the way my father used to bore his.

"Drive," I command. "Back to upper cavern. Now."

He nods quickly and steers the tram into locomotion.

"Faster!" I yell.

He frantically flips the gauges. His terror is palpable. Part of me is shocked I can inspire such reaction. Another part feels pure satisfaction. This man's fear makes me powerful. It makes me worth something.

We arrive at the station. "Open, now!" I shout.

"Just don't hurt me, you maniac!" he cries desperately.

I situate Carrick over my shoulder. He's no longer moaning. Not a good sign. I head straight for the healer's hut. I drag the comatose man through the igloo portal. *Formalities be damned!*

Inside, Faria stands on one hand, poised on the tips of his thumb and forefinger in a feat of balance I've only ever witnessed in one other human being.

"Faria?" I ask.

The dark man flips back to his feet soundlessly. His milky eyes pierce me. "You've interrupted me again, Leontes."

"This man is dying," I say.

Faria comes to Carrick's side and examines him. When he arrives at the tibia protruding from the skin, he stops. "This is beyond my means."

That can't be it after all I did to bring Carrick here?

"A broken bone should be rudimentary," I protest.

"The man fell. He may have internal bleeding or complications from concussion. As for the leg, the tendons are severed. Even if I repair the bone, which would take months, he would never walk again. You should have left him for dead."

"I don't accept it."

"My suspicion is that you were already told to leave him. Now you've wasted your time and mine."

"A healer heals!" I fume. "If you try and fail, you've lost nothing, but you at least try."

"Perhaps you didn't hear me." He remains still, but I feel anger radiating off him. "In this place, he's already dead."

I hold the stare of his clouded pupils. I don't know why I care so much. Maybe I just like defying challenges. Maybe I've been presented with so much pain and death I want to win against them just once.

"There's a way," I say, "though I don't know if it will work."

"Oh?" the aged man asks.

"A bone graft."

He stares as if I've suggested something out of a fairy tale. "That kind of medicine is possible," he says carefully, "but only with proper facilities. You may as well suggest a brain transplant."

"You're afraid to try?" I challenge.

"We need a donor willing to undergo the procedure and take the proper recovery time. We'd need a warden that would allow such a thing. We have neither." He turns away.

"You have a donor." I stop him in his tracks.

"You won't survive. Not with the tools I have. If you did, you wouldn't have time to recover. They would force you both to return to work immediately."

"I will recover."

"How?" His white eyes narrow.

"First, you agree." I dangle the bait. "Then you take me as your apprentice."

"No," he says flatly.

I know he wants this. Why else would he have saved me from the attentions of the Haulers? So why resist now? For show? Or do I have to pass some test?

"You want to know my secret? I'll give it to you, but you give me something in return."

"The Warden won't allow it," Faria argues.

"Whale dung," I say, calling his bluff. "I've watched you. The Warden owes you enough to grant this. You won't live forever. They'll need someone to take your place when you're gone."

"Careful, boy," he admonishes. "I'm still long for this world."

"Now who fools himself?" I retort. "I want the freedom you have. Teach me what you know, and I'll serve in whatever way you see fit. I'll even help you escape if that's what you wish."

"You've pushed too far." He laughs derisively. "If The Warden allowed me a pupil, you think he'd let it be you? Who do you think The Warden answers to, boy?"

The Wendigo is owned by House Wusong-Leontes. Edric is Patriarch of both houses now in deed if not in name.

"Nothing happens here without his consent, without his knowing."

"He'll allow it. You're going to assure The Warden that under your watch I'll receive harsher lessons in pain than I could ever get in the mines."

He stares.

"None of this is going to work anyway, right? You said I wouldn't survive. What have you got to lose?"

I've got him now.

"If you survive, I'll take you as my assistant and show you what I know." He gestures for me to lie next to Carrick. He moves to his cabinet, where he removes a small bag of sterilized instruments. "In return, you will be my servant. Now tell me how exactly do you heal so quickly?"

I take a brief exhale and relate the story of Talousla Karr.

He pulls a scalpel from a plastic pouch.

"This planet has lived so long in its own isolation that there is about to be a rude awakening," he mutters. "Whether that awakening is for Tao or the rest of the Fracture remains to be seen. Your father allowed this?" the dark shaman asks.

"What do you mean?"

"Your culture has very strong feelings regarding artificial enhancement. Genetic engineering is outlawed. You throw defective babes out with yesterday's refuse rather than fix them. It is curious your father allowed you to be experimented on."

"What are you suggesting?" I play the fool, but I've asked the same myself over the years.

He let me live on purpose. Why?

"I'm suggesting you cut yourself and take a scraping of bone so that I may heal this Picker's leg." He hands me the scalpel. "Your enhancements still allow you to feel pain?"

"Acutely," I respond.

I slowly bring the blade to the skin when a thought occurs. *I've told him my secret. It's time to expose his.*

"Perhaps you should do that thing with your hands," I suggest wryly.

His hand lashes out quick as lightning. He jams a finger into my hip. Electric pain shoots through my legs.

"By the twisted star!" I gasp.

"There are meridians throughout the body. They are like music. If one hears the sound, he may pinch off the melody or change its pattern. Do not move," he instructs. He guides my hand, holding the scalpel, and slices into the skin. Rivulets of blood flow. My eyes widen. *I feel nothing!*

"A man can divert the music or turn it off or on. He can immobilize. He can heal . . ."

His cold dark fingers peel back the skin of my shin. I want to scream at the grisly sight, but there is no pain. It's as if my leg isn't there at all.

"Or he may kill," he finishes mysteriously.

"That's how you healed Toshi, how you performed surgery on me without anesthesia!" I realize.

"It takes decades to learn, a lifetime to master. The ancients called it the Dim Mak. The death touch," he says.

"It's how you killed Snaggletooth," I say.

He takes a small bone saw from his pile of tools. "Legend says some masters could perform Dim Mak with the sound of their voice."

"Is that possible?" I ask.

He shaves a sliver of my tibia and places the specimen in a jar. He expertly sets the muscles and flesh back into place and sutures the wound shut. "Anything is possible."

"Teach me?" I implore.

"Rest," he replies. "The Warden will be here in the morning, and you would best be healed."

He diligently begins work on Carrick. I'll receive no more answers from him tonight. I close my eyes, but my mind turns over this revelation.

I awaken by dying embers. Faria attends Carrick, who rests under the cover of furs.

"How is he?" I ask. I stand, testing my leg. There's a slight twinge of pain, but nothing I can't take. I kneel beside the dark man.

"He'll live," Faria says. "Whether or not he'll walk remains to be seen. Your bones are quite remarkable. If the graft took, the cells should last to repair Carrick's injuries and eventually work their way out of his system. Whatever transformation you were put through was keyed to your specific genetics." His milky eyes stare at me. "Who knows what other traits that man's tampering may have given you."

My hand unconsciously moves to my scalp. The morning alarm sounds.

"Faria the Red!" a voice calls from outside. The Warden. "Faria!" comes the raspy bellow again.

I follow the shaman out of the hut. The Warden stands before us, thick and paunchy. He smooths his blond mustache with a gloved hand. He's flanked by several armored guards as well as my foreman, Jinam Shank. Shank glares with his ugly, scarred face.

"I've been told that you're harboring two Pickers," The Warden says.

"One Picker was injured, and his colleague brought him for healing," Faria says deferentially.

"I was told by the foreman"—The Warden looks disdainfully over his shoulder—"that the man was damaged beyond function."

"I believed that with Leontes's assistance I'd be able to save the man," says Faria.

The Warden's jowly face grows red. I can tell that he didn't expect a conversation. The fact that Faria is even responding throws him off balance. "This man"—The Warden points at me—"had no business countermanding his foreman."

"He believed he could save the life of a worker," replies Faria quietly. "Workers help make quotas. Leontes was only thinking of your needs, my lord."

The Warden folds his arms across his chest. He can smell the whale feces in Faria's words. "So where's the man? Is he ready for work this day?"

"He needs time—"

"Do not mince words! If he's not here, he's not capable." The Warden flicks his hand, and the guards step forward. They grab me forcibly by the arms.

"What are you doing?" Faria asks.

"I can't afford to punish you, healer, but this one"—The Warden indicates me—"he's another matter."

They drag me away.

"Stop!" Faria commands with a voice so penetrating that The Warden halts in his tracks. I wonder if what he said about the Dim Mak being used with sound is actually true.

The Warden puffs out his chest. "You don't govern here, healer. Quiet yourself before you lose the little grace you've earned."

One guard trots away to summon the gangs while the others drag me through the shantytown. Faria follows. We reach the auction blocks, and I'm thrown up on the platform. The guard strips me to the waist. I hold my sides and shiver from the freezing cold.

I must not let them see me bend. If I do, they win. My father will win.

A crowd gathers. I see Smelters, Pickers, Haulers, Welders . . .

The guards erect two poles and bind my wrists to them so my arms are spread wide.

The crowd's whispers grow. "Whip 'im! Yeah, whip the little prince!"

I pick out Vaarkson, smiling, rotten-toothed. Toshi cowers next to him.

"This man left his post in the middle of the workday!" The Warden shouts through a bullhorn. "Negligence on the job. Disobedience against the chain of command. The punishment—"

"Whip him! Whip him! Whip him!" the crowd chants.

The Warden signals the guard, Greelo. Greelo winds up and cracks the whip in the air for effect. The crowd hollers. He winds up again, and this time he lets loose.

The lash scathes my back. The second strike comes, and I suck in my breath. The crowd cheers. A third, I feel the skin break. The fourth, I smile as blood runs down my back in a hot river. The crowd grows quieter. A fifth and I laugh.

They can't hurt you anymore, Edmon. They think this is pain? You've endured real pain, says the voice inside.

A sixth lash. *Is that all you got?*

The crowd watches silently as the whip lands again and I don't cry out. The Warden screams, "You're not doing it hard enough!"

"I'm hitting him with all I have," Greelo argues back.

"Then what's the problem?" The Warden's piggy face is red and furious.

The lashes hurt. In fact, they're excruciating. It's just that I've flipped a switch in my brain. It's like Faria's trick with his hands. I just don't care anymore.

Do these fools know what I've been through?

A song plays through my mind. "A Tale of Ancient Earth"—a young artist named Rudolfo professes his love for a girl, Mimi. I remember my own love. Her voice sings the words to me now—

Che parlano d'amor, di primavere, di sogni e di chimere, quelle cose che han nome poesia. Lei m'intende?

"They speak to me of love, speak they of springtime; they speak of dreams, and noble thoughts that fire me, and the charms of poetry that inspire me. Understand you?

"I do," I whisper even as another strike cracks.

Ma quando vien lo sgelo, il primo sole è mio. Col novo Aprile una rosa germoglia sul davanzal ne aspire a foglia, a foglia . . . Altro di me non le saprei narrare. Sono la sua vicina che la vien fuori d'ora a importunare.

In my room live I only, high in my white-walled chamber lonely. O'er sky and housetops high glancing. When winter is advancing first sun of morn, I greet it! First kiss of April's balmy breath I meet it! . . . No more I have of my going to confess you. I am a neighbor from without, that comes with my worry to distress you.

That last line always gets me. She was only my neighbor, there to bother me. Oh, but she was so much more. Silent tears stream down my face. It's only my body they hurt. I take courage from her words. They cannot touch my spirit.

"Hang in there, Baldy Patch!" someone from the crowd calls out.

The lash comes again.

"You can do it, Leontes!"

The Warden grabs the whip from Greelo in frustration and swings. His pudgy arms can't generate even half the force that Greelo could. The crowd erupts in laughter. The Warden's face grows pink under his waxed mustache. He swings the whip, but slips on a patch of ice and falls on his ample ass. The crowd hollers with delight.

"Execute him!" The Warden screams. Greelo hesitates. "Do it now!" The Warden squeals.

Greelo draws a knife from his belt. The crowd is stunned. He raises the knife above his head. I won't give him the satisfaction of cowering, even with my last breath.

"Stop!"

Everyone turns. Carrick hobbles from the outskirts of the crowd. The gangs make a pathway for the stocky man to stride through their ranks. He limps, but he's walking, his ankle no longer broken.

"You can't kill him," says Carrick. "He saved me."

Even I'm stunned by this bold turn of events.

"I'd be dead but for Edmon Leontes. You have to let him go!"

"Insolent worm! I command here, not you!" The Warden screeches.

"Let him go!" someone calls out. The cry is echoed. "He got his lashes. Let him go!"

"Let him go! Let him go! Let him go!" The chant rises from the inmates who only moments before were calling for my head. The Warden's eyes shift nervously. The guards around the perimeter finger their humbatons, but the inmates outnumber their jailers. Here is the reason that gangs are divided, I realize—a way to keep inmates separate, so they will never rise up against their masters. I've just given them something in common. Kill me publicly and I'm a martyr.

"All right! In light of this advent, young Leontes can be let go," he says reluctantly. "Cut him down," he murmurs to Greelo.

I save him the trouble. I pull with both blood-soaked arms. The poles break loose from their moorings and crash to the ground. I'm like the mythical Samus, toppling the dome of Hyperius with his great strength. The crowd cheers, and I hobble from the auction block.

"That's it, Baldy Patch!" they shout.

I stride toward Faria's hut, feigning strength, secretly ready to fall.

I don't feel the needle. Faria's trick with his hands ensures I'm numb as he sews my lacerations.

"You'll heal." I smell the rubbing alcohol as he dabs the wounds. "If you had a Pantheon medic, you would receive skin grafts. Unfortunately, here at the edge of darkness, there will be scarring."

"Scars you see hurt the least," I mutter.

"Pithy," he returns sardonically.

"What now?" I gently put on my shirt.

"In the morning, you'll begin as my apprentice."

"Apprentice?" My eyes go wide.

"Medical assistant," he corrects.

He's not ready to give up all his secrets. Yet.

"The Warden will want to keep you out of sight after today, but you're right. I am old. The prison will need someone to carry on the healing work." He smiles. "Your father banished you here so you couldn't cause any more unrest to his plans, but one day, he'll remember the value a son has. Stay alive, and when he calls upon you, do not forget I helped you."

"How will you help me?" I ask.

"First, by teaching you to become invisible."

My brow furrows with question.

"From the day you arrived, I knew you were trouble. You stand out. You make enemies. If you want to survive, you must change. It's the great tree that is uprooted and breaks in the storm. The lowly reed bends and survives. Do not be noticed again."

"I never wanted the attention," I say.

"You didn't eschew it, either. You've met force with equal force."

"Should I have done otherwise?" I ask.

"That's not for me to decide." He shrugs. "I only teach what I know. If you want to learn, you'll follow."

I nod.

"Good," he says. "Return to camp. Make no sound. Talk to no one. Acknowledge if you're spoken to, but no more. You're not one of them anymore. You're a shadow. Forever outside. Do you understand?"

I return to the Picker camp and take a place outside the circle. Some notice and nod. One gestures for me to sit beside him. It's more friendly acknowledgment than I've ever received, but I've made a bargain. It's funny, I wouldn't have thought I'd care, but the desire to have camaraderie is overwhelming after so long without. It feels as if the old man's blind eyes are upon me, though, so I stay apart.

I'm not one of them and never will be. I'm Faria's apprentice now. I'm invisible.

CHAPTER 19

Cabaletta

The morning alarm rouses the men, and I rise. As the camp prepares, the gangs organize themselves into lines to enter the mines, and I walk through the shantytown to the igloo. I enter to find Faria seated in meditation. I take up a seat across from him, waiting for him to speak.

My impatience gets the better of me after nearly an hour of anticipation. "Well?" I ask, exasperated. His eyes snap open, and he glares. "When do we start training?"

He closes his eyes. "I have said. You do as I do. Now I am meditating."

"That's all we're going to do?" I can't believe this.

"Perhaps you'd prefer to return to the mines?" he asks.

"No," I mutter.

"Then, yes, this is all we do."

"What are we even meditating on?" I sigh. He told me mastering the flow of meridians through the body and the Dim Mak could take years to learn. I haven't any time to lose. At the very least, I thought I'd learn to set a bone or suture a wound.

"Meditate to master the self," he says. "You can master nothing until that's mastered. So that's the only end worth anything."

I exhale in frustration, but I close my eyes. "Faria?" I ask.

"Master," he corrects.

"Master," I say, gritting my teeth. "Have you mastered the self?"

"If I had," he answers, "there would be no need to meditate."

We sit in silence for the whole day. Hour upon hour, thoughts swirl like a maelstrom. My father, my brother, Nadia, my mother, my longing, my anguish, over and over. Some moments pass where I drift and think of nothing. Before long, the evening alarm has sounded.

"Return tomorrow," Faria says.

I leave, shaking my head. *Working in the mines was almost better than sitting doing nothing. Almost.* I stop at the Ration Bar before heading to the Picker camp to sleep. I take my place outside the circle.

A healer's skill is contingent upon having people in need of healing. If there are no injured or sick, then what else is there to do than sit? I don't know how I'll survive the boredom. Toiling in a dark cave doing menial labor was not what I wanted for my life. Sitting and doing nothing isn't, either. Regardless, I settle into the routine. Wake up, go to Faria's hut, sit in silence by the fire. I take food and return to camp to sleep. Wake up. Do it again. The monotony of my inane thoughts is maddening. Mastery does not come. I drop my head into my hands.

"This is it?" I bemoan. "I'm supposed to master my thoughts, but all I think on is death and the hatred I have for this godforsaken planet, the injustice. If I'm supposed to calm the storm, I can't."

"Then don't quiet the storm," Faria responds, eyes still closed.

"But isn't the point to become emotionless?" I ask.

Faria chuckles. "Why are you here, Edmon?"

"Because my father murdered my love, my family. He forced me to marry another, and I refused to play his games."

Faria nods. "Is that fair?"

"No," I say darkly.

"What do you wish to do about it?"

"Make him suffer," I growl.

"You expect to shut that feeling away?" he asks. "No, I ask that you feel it more. There's no other way to stand over your enemy and cut out his heart. Accept your hatred and you won't be rash or stupid, you'll be cold. Don't quiet the maelstrom. Become the storm."

—

A month passes. A rockslide hits Dungeon Seven, killing several Pickers and Runners and injuring many more. Faria's igloo becomes a ward for the wounded. The space fills quickly, so patients are laid outside, littering the icy ground with blood. Quiet as the last few weeks have been, the days become equally busy now.

We don't sleep. It's a whirlwind of learning as I watch Faria attend patients. The shaman smashes bone back into place and sews shut torn skin. Then it's my turn. Faria applies the Dim Mak with such skill most patients don't even realize what's happening. He's careful to make sure that even I don't fully see the technique, lest I try to replicate it. Once anesthetized, he instructs me to reset the bones and suture the wounds while he moves to the next patient.

The Warden sees fit to bring additional equipment, including urchin needles and synth-plasma packs, so that we can infuse the injured. Carrick's miraculous recovery seems to have changed his perception of Faria's capabilities. Now even extreme measures are taken to ensure workers do not die. The Wendigo has not received a shipment of prisoners from the outside in months. No one says, but I suspect that the people of Meridian are too frightened to dissent. It won't last, of course. Rebellion has a way of festering beneath the surface and then exploding like an infected boil. For now, the dearth of new inmates spurs The Warden to keep his current workforce healthy.

The week grates on, and numbers in the "infirmary" dwindle. Faria blindfolds me. I'm made to feel injuries with my fingers. He talks me through grazing injuries with touch, feeling the ebb and flow of the body's meridians. I learn to sense inner vibrations, places where blood and energy are.

"Gently," he whispers. I apply pressure to a man's nasal bones, a Hauler who took a nasty bash from a falling rock. *Snap!* The bones click into place like the pieces of a puzzle.

"Ah!" The man exhales.

"You'll have a bump on your nose, but you'll be able to breathe correctly," says Faria.

"Bump's nothing. Thanks." The man pulls himself to his feet.

"Looks like we're done for the day," I say, noting for the first time in weeks that his dwelling is empty.

"Yes." Faria sighs. "I'd like to rest. Go home, Edmon."

For once, he does not look ancient and intimidating, just tired and old. Someday, he *will* be gone. The realization, to my surprise, makes me sad. I take my leave and walk through narrow avenues of hovels and campfires. I think on Faria's words. *Go home.* I chuckle to myself. *This will never be home. I must survive and somehow return.*

At the same time, I fear I'll never leave. My mother and Nadia and Gorham and The Maestro and my unborn child will have perished for nothing. The Isle of Bone seems so long ago.

I find myself at the Ration Bar. I stand stoop-shouldered and skulking to make myself look physically unimpressive, quiet, and invisible like Faria has directed. I am given packets of food paste without incident. I take my tray to a table.

"Hey, Baldy Patch," Bruul Vaarkson catcalls. "Where do you think you're going?"

It was only a matter of time until it happened, I suppose. I turn to face the foreman, trying to control my rage and fear. *I'm invisible,* I remember.

"You don't think you can pass the Haulers' table and not pay tribute, do you?" he asks. Toshi, who sits next to the big man, snickers along with the rest. Jinam Shank glances in my direction, then returns to his meal of paste. I'll get no help from him.

"Come here, Baldy Patch," Vaarkson commands.

Half of me is ready to leap across the table and end this now. Kill or be killed. But I need to wait until the time is right, so I split the difference. I remain where I stand and calmly ask, "What do you want, Bruul?"

"What sass! I think the little scrapper doesn't remember how I once had his pretty little ass bent over and begging for mercy."

"I haven't forgotten." My voice is clipped.

"Good," he says, smirking. "Then come here and see what new presents I have for you."

"If you need medical assistance, you can take it to Faria the Red or The Warden if you prefer." I turn to leave. My way is barred by the man whose nose I fixed an hour before. A Hauler, of course.

"What I need is to make you an offer, Baldy Patch," growls Bruul.

"I've had your offers before, Bruul. No, thank you," I say acidly.

"A man of your skills can be of use. Tenshin there"—he gestures to the man with the repaired nose—"tells me that you fixed him real good. Work for the Haulers. Work for our camp and in return receive my protection and special . . . privileges."

I stifle a laugh. I remember Faria's words about attracting attention and incurring the wrath of enemies. *Wait until the time is right.* "Generous, but I decline." Again, I turn to leave, and my way is barred.

"You don't seem to understand, Baldy Patch. I'm not asking."

Rage boils inside me. I don't take my eyes off Tenshin.

"Neither my foreman nor The Warden would appreciate if I worked solely for the Haulers," I say coldly.

"They don't need to know," Vaarkson responds.

Enough talking. Fury takes me. "Drown in fathoms!"

Vaarkson's eyes go wide. Before Tenshin can move, my fist slams the center of his face. His nose splatters against my knuckles. He goes down twitching, and I smile at his blood. *I own that; it's mine.* I revel in the violence.

The next Hauler puts a hand my shoulder. I whirl with the food tray, smacking the edge against his temple. This man hurt his ribs and sprained his knee during the rockslide, so my next blow is to his ribs. The man gasps. I kick his knee. The joint melts, and the man crumples.

Vaarkson comes for me. I fling the tray like a discus. It smacks him in the mouth, sending him flipping end over end. He belly flops on the dining table, sending ration paste flying.

I turn my gaze to Toshi, who has been cowering in his seat. *You're next, tillyfish,* I say with my enraged eyes. He cringes.

The crowd at the other tables goes ballistic, screaming. Food and fists fly everywhere around me. My altercation has instigated a full-on riot. My heart sinks. *I was supposed to stay invisible.*

A klaxon blares. Black armored guards run in from the tunnels below. It's full pandemonium as humbatons fly from holsters, and sonic pulses pump into the prisoners, sending them writhing to the floor in nausea and pain.

I squirm my way through the rioters and slip quietly back to the Picker camp. I find a corner and huddle there. An hour or so later, the riot is finally quelled. I lean my head back and close my eyes, praying the cause of the disturbance will not be found. Too much to hope for, I know.

The Warden, flanked by guards, waits by Faria's hut the next morning. Faria, Jinam Shank, and Bruul Vaarkson, sporting a fat lip and a few missing teeth stand alongside him. My face remains calm—I'm not sorry for what I've done.

"Edmon Leontes," says The Warden as he strokes his mustache. "You're coming with us."

"Where are you going to put me? Prison?" I ask wryly.

The Warden's face flushes, and Faria shakes his head. I've disappointed him by aggravating the situation. "What's the charge?" I ask more seriously.

"We don't need a reason. You're ours, worm," Greelo squawks. He and Sookah step forward to bind my wrists.

Faria shakes his head again at me. *Do not try anything,* he silently indicates.

"Inciting riot," The Warden says gleefully.

"I was defending myself!" I protest.

"We have it on good authority that you attacked three members of the Hauler Gang, including the foreman. Violence is against all regulations of my prison, Leontes."

"Violence like whipping a man in front of a crowd?" I ask.

Faria purses his lips.

Just shut up, Edmon.

"One man against three, and I'm to be punished?" I ask more calmly.

Public punishment didn't go well for The Warden. Inflicting public pain again would only strengthen me and weaken his own position.

"The Citadel." The Warden smiles. "One year."

A year in darkness! "I've done nothing but help keep your workforce strong, help you bring in the haul," I say.

"We can do without your help, Leontes. You're no noble son here." He stalks forward until his face is centimeters from my own. "You're nothing."

"Let me be judged by my peers. Call witnesses. I didn't start the riot."

The Warden hoots. "This isn't the College of Electors. You aren't a Combat champion. You haven't earned judicial reprieve! If I say you go in the tower"—his laughter ends abruptly and his voice drops low and menacing—"you go."

Faria is utterly impotent to prevent this. I'm on my own, as I have always been.

"Besides, we have asked witnesses," The Warden says. "Those who did not implicate you were easily convinced of the error of their ways."

I want to spit into The Warden's smug, fat face and watch my spittle run down his chin. Yet even if he's been told by my father to keep me alive, even if he fears making me a symbol of rebellion, such an action might not stay his hand. Pride can only be diminished so much in a man before he breaks.

Death or the Citadel. I cling to my rage, shield it like a candle against the winds of the Nightside. I look The Warden in the eye. My words come slowly and deliberately. "I understand, Warden. I'm sorry for any infraction. I accept my punishment willingly." I bow in abject humbleness, just as I did to Old Wusong as a child.

The Warden's beady eyes swivel in his porcine face. "Take him away," he says.

My back stings from the caning they gave before they hauled me to the surface and into the dark tower. We walk down its corridors by torchlight. I hear the moans of prisoners from the surrounding cells as the light of the guards passes their grates. It's the only spark of illumination in the place, this black monolith that protrudes from the barren landscape of ice. Here they send the worst of the worst to live in solitary confinement. Here they've sent me.

Greelo and Sookah open a heavy metallic door and toss me inside a small stone room. I fall to the slick wet floor. "Enjoy your time in the black, worm," Greelo says, guffawing. "Goth will be by for dinners. See you in a year." The iron slams behind them, and the light of the torch fades down the hallway.

Cold. Freezing. Left in the pitch. Somehow there's at least a little heat pumping through a vent in the ceiling to warm me. I huddle close to its airstream. They need to keep us thawed just enough to live. The Citadel isn't about sending prisoners to die; it's about breaking us. Time spent in such sensory deprivation would turn anyone mad. *Almost anyone.*

My first hour passes. Then another. I crawl on all fours, circumnavigating the confines of the cell. I feel the edges, trying to discern my surroundings. Two meters or so up the wall, there's some kind of a portal, smaller than the size of my head, that looks upon the open Nightside. I stand on tiptoes to peer at utter blackness, but for sapphire pinpricks in the velvet sky. So many stars, so little light. It makes me feel more alone.

Terror creeps in. There are moments of unspeakable fear that every man feels in silence—a moment before slumber that confronts him with who he truly is in the heart; a lucid moment when he separates from his body and looks at himself from the outside. That is when he is faced with the true, pathetic ugliness of who he is, what he has become. That's the fear I feel now, the fear that stares me in the face. It is inescapable, like the monster of the sea. It is the eel that burrows into my skull with razor teeth and a malevolent laugh. I cry out in panic.

"Don't worry," the darkness whispers back. I spin, searching for the source, but see nothing. "When the light of the moons of Chang and Hou pass overhead in six months' time, you will see for a full diurnal cycle."

"Who are you?" I hiss.

I hear the scraping of metal above me. *The heating grate,* I realize. There is a sharp bang. The grate pops loose, and someone drops from above, landing softly on the dungeon floor. Startled, I fall backward onto my rear. I yelp as I still feel the sting of the caning I've recently received.

"Quiet," the man hisses. "Goth will not be on this level for a while, but I don't want to risk it."

I know that voice!

"Master?"

I can almost hear the dark man nod. Then he's beside me. His strong and gentle hands peel the rags away to examine my oozing back. "It's fortunate that I'm used to doing my work without the benefit of sight." He strikes my neck with his fingertips. I'm numbed from the neck down. He gently places me on the icy stone floor while he probes the wounds. "Not good, but not as bad as the first time," he says, clucking. "Still, with some rest and care, you'll survive. You always do."

"Faria? How did you—?"

"Part of the plan, Edmon," he reassures me. "When The Warden punished you, I was also partly responsible for your crime. The Warden needs my services to keep the camp running, but with some well-placed anger on my part, I convinced him that I'd broken the agreement to keep you out of trouble. He was unwilling to part with me for longer than a six-month stint, however, so we won't have as much time as I would've liked."

"But why do this?" At least I'm thinking a little more clearly now that my nerves are cut off from the pain streaking my back. "I failed you."

Faria laces my skin together with spider-silk sutures. "You followed my lessons. You stayed invisible, as much as you could, but I knew you'd be forced into conflict eventually. When you were, you didn't hesitate. You exploited your enemies' weaknesses. You remembered each man's injuries, their vulnerabilities. You used them in order to defend yourself. Your fighting skills are already high caliber. Now I'll teach you to be a master. No one will ever be able to harm you again. You'll need that in order to face what is coming."

"What's coming?" I ask.

The old man gives no answer.

"You were watching the whole time?" I'm not entirely surprised. Everything, from the moment I stepped into the Wendigo, has felt like some sort of test. "Bruul and the Haulers hadn't attacked me for over a year. Why did I warrant their attention again all of a sudden?"

"You already know the answer," Faria says simply.

"You put them up to it." If I had control over my body, I'd throttle him. As it is, I can only turn my head to the side. "Why?"

"We need to work out of the sights of the gangs, The Warden, and your father. I suggested to the man with the broken nose that I'd be willing to sell your services to the Haulers. He returned to Vaarkson with the offer. Vaarkson, as expected, thought he could circumvent recompense. You had been successful being invisible long enough. It was time for the next step."

"You've trapped me in darkness for a year of my life! For what?" I fume.

"You're angry?" he asks with amusement. "Good. You're going to need that, too. But first, your real training."

CHAPTER 20

Toccata

One, two, again and again. Rhythm and numbers drive my days and nights. The pulse of Gorham's drum, the tap of The Maestro's baton, now the relentless beat of the metal rod Faria stole from an air heating unit and now uses as a makeshift sword. In the pit of blackness, he trains me. One, two, ten, a hundred. Push-ups, sit-ups, squats, jumps. Seconds, minutes, hours, days. My muscles quiver; my brain is numb. Punch, kick.

Ho-ho! Ho-ho! Ho-hey! I am being forged.

"Feel my pressure, Edmon," he whispers. "Don't resist. Deflect. Keep contact. Control my center line. Use your hands. Control with your legs. A man without sight is not a man entombed. Sense with your ears. Smell changes in the air. Let your skin feel the temperature shift."

We spar. I lose again and again. I can't see, but my other senses become more attuned. My hands, feet, fingers, and toes grow strong. I spend hours punching and kicking the black obsidian of the cell. Faria calls this "iron hand." Bone is damaged, then recalcifies stronger. My cells learn to expend energy more efficiently, inuring me to cold. I balance on my hands for minutes, then hours. I take a hand away; soon

I'm on two fingers. Now one. Muscles tear. I'm broken down, but the master builds me back up, stoking my rage.

"Remember your mother. Remember Nadia. Remember your father and what he did to you. Remember Vaarkson and The Warden."

Ho-ho! Ho-ho! Ho-hey!

My mother said I should forget. She was trying to protect me. I turn her words into strength. When I'm exhausted, the master teaches me to meditate inward, to visualize my cells dividing, rushing to places of need, and with conscious effort, I will myself to heal.

"This is a deeper level of awareness," he says. "Since Ancient Earth, science has sought to transform the human. On other worlds, you will see cybernetics, narcotics like tag, or bio-mods, but evolution can occur through sheer will. Our habits determine the expression of our genes. The darkness of our surroundings will be your blindfold to heighten your other faculties. You can see them, can't you?" he asks. "See the organisms circulating through the biosphere that is you?"

At first his words mean nothing, then I catch a glimmer of something in my inner eye. I see them just out of reach, like a dream beyond my grasp.

"You're becoming aware for the first time," the shaman tells me. "It takes a lifetime to achieve full control. When you're ready, you'll be able to do things you never thought possible."

"Such as?" I ask.

"Run for hundreds of kilometers without stopping. Stay awake without sleep for weeks on end. Lift weight that many would deem inhuman. Appear dead to all but the most sensitive of instruments. Some claim that you can even stop yourself from dying."

"Are you saying I could become immortal?" I ask.

I feel him smile enigmatically in the darkness. "The body's energy is a symphony, but it is not infinite. Take a resource from your wind section, give it to percussion, and you change the sound of the orchestration. Turn the volume up on one vibration at the expense of another."

"If I divert my focus from one thing, I won't be able to do another?" I ask.

"Everything has a cost." He puts it bluntly. "Sometimes the cost is too great and where you least expect it."

Ho-ho! Ho-ho! Ho-hey!

We take respite when Goth, the lumbering, slothlike monster of the Citadel, makes his rounds to bring food. The rattle of his shackles lets us know that he's near. There are no days or evenings. It's a black abyss of an existence. I usually take rest after the meal, so I tend to think of the meal as supper. Faria returns to his own cell through the ventilation system. Otherwise time flows on unmarked and without end. Minutes, hours, days, weeks. Tick. Tick. Tick. It becomes interminable and undeterminable.

—

Through our meditations, I'm able to fully recover from intense training more quickly than ever. I push my muscles to perform greater and greater physical feats. I jump higher and move faster, but I'm forced to sleep for long stretches. I wake only to consume food.

Then Faria trains me to stay up without sleep. I feel like a zombie and cannot train with any exertion. This is how he teaches me the delicate balance of the body. I break past barriers but also learn limitations. We are hardware, and improvements are incremental but still bounded.

I learn to divert cells in my body, manipulate meridians, but I can't grow stronger without external force. Faria provides it. Evolution bred this intuition into every organic cell long ago—adapt or die. I harness this instinct through sheer will, but like so many things in nature, when the human brain interferes, there can be deadly consequences.

One day, Faria forces me into a series of agility maneuvers using his metal rods. He swings them like an expert sword dancer. I summon newfound speed to avoid the attacks, pushing beyond the point of exhaustion. Jump over this swing. Dive under the next. Faria is so unpredictable, so attuned to my rhythms and expert at challenging them that I am at my limits far more than I ever was with an automaton. It's exhilarating, stretching my body in ways I never thought possible.

This is what I'm capable of. It must be what Phaestion feels every day of his life.

Hours without a single misstep and without warning, I collapse.

Faria is by my side when I wake. I was out for almost three days, he warns me, suffering from severe breakdown of muscle tissue. Without apology or tenderness, he tells me that knowing my limits is more important than pushing them. When I'm healed, we continue.

We explore the Citadel, climbing through the ventilation system that snakes through the black tower. We hover over the cells of other inmates and listen for hours. Faria teaches me to develop true hearing and quizzes me when we return to the confines of my cell.

"Tell me," he says.

"His heartbeat was slow and weak. An older man. Perhaps seventy," I reply.

"What else?"

"A Daysider, from one of the isles. The Isle of Shell or Bird."

"How do you know?"

"His accent when he muttered."

I can hear Faria nod in the darkness.

"An islander, so dark-skinned and old. He had lost a daughter. An only child perhaps?" I make the deduction from only a single word picked up among the random groans and breaths whispered in darkness—*Lysha.* It's hard to make a more concrete conclusion.

"You heard the name, too," Faria muses. "Are you sure it was a daughter's name? Why not a boat he prized or maybe a lover from long ago."

"Lysha is a girl's name in the isles," I say, thinking out loud. "Not a name generally used over a generation ago. Islanders of Tao do not name possessions after women like other maritime cultures. The pitch of his voice was a lamentation. He said the name as he would say a child's. I know that feeling."

My words hang in the air, and Faria says nothing. Then—

"What else?" he probes.

"He had lost a leg. I could tell from the way he moved. There was also some sort of infection or sores on his skin he kept scratching," I offer.

"Where?" Faria grows intense.

"Left hand?" A guess.

"Upper forearm. The inner elbow. The vibration tells you," he says, demonstrating the subtle difference between the scratching noises. "How would you treat such sores?"

"Antibacterial and fungal ointments, mussel glue to seal any open sores, a skin graft cultured from a healthy area of his body to complete the process."

"That's how you would treat his sores. How would you treat your sores?" he asks again.

"Divert white corpuscles to the area. Stimulate the division of new red blood cells. Increase mitosis of skin and collagen to seal the wound. Total recovery time . . . two days."

"Too long for a few bedsores."

"Open wounds can lead to complications," I offer. "The extra time might be worth it."

"You should be able to heal everything in a few hours and be ready to move."

"If I wanted to be exhausted," I respond. "I was assuming ideal conditions—"

"Never assume ideal conditions." He turns to leave for the evening.

"Wait," I call, "what was the man's crime? Why was he here in the Citadel?"

Surely that was the most important question to ask me about the prisoner, wasn't it?

"Think. You already know," he says calmly.

An islander, with his leg gone, whispering a woman's name? A fishing accident could account for the missing leg or the girl's death, but that does not equal a crime punishable by exile in the Citadel. He sounded like he had a strong bone structure, physically imposing. A fighter. The Combat. Champions are made Electors, not prisoners. He was a combatant who lost his leg and survived . . .

"He asked for mercy," I whisper.

I know I am right. Alberich also asked for mercy and was spared, but was punished with a life of indentured servitude and the loss of his reproductive organs so he could never pass on his name or cowardice to future generations. My father pitied him or thought he'd still be of use to his new house. His fate was unusual. This man's existence was more likely.

"Combat is kill or be killed," agrees Faria. "There's no other choice. Especially for an islander. Anything short of death or victory is shame. So says the Pantheon." The dark man's words are bitter on his lips. His tone, personal.

Why is Faria here in the Wendigo?

"Enough." His deep basso resonates. "It's time for rest."

"Yes, Master," I say as I do before every slumber.

We climb through the cramped vents and tunnels. Today, our journey isn't to visit cells of the other inmates, but for another purpose. The vent slopes downward and ends in empty space. Faria deftly leaps into the darkness.

"Quickly, Edmon!" he whispers from below.

I take a deep breath and let myself fall through the blackness. My stomach lurches for a beat longer than I would like. Then the hard stone of the floor touches the pads of my feet, and I roll to dissipate the force of the fall. I pop up into a ready position, my senses tuned to pick up any change in the vibration of my new surroundings.

"Sloppy," Faria admonishes.

"A falling feather wouldn't have made more sound," I counter, confident in my newfound skills.

"If you made the sound of a feather, then that is too loud," he chides.

"As if your jabbering weren't noisy enough." I grin and follow him down a hallway. My hands and feet glide along the slick, cold brick of the passageway.

"If you're satisfied with fulfilling less than the maximum of your potential, life will be very easy for you, Leontes."

"Where are we, old man?" I growl back.

"A main hallway," he replies.

I stop in my tracks. "You always told me it was too dangerous for the main routes. What about Goth?"

The rumor, as Faria has told me, is that Goth is a genetic experiment. A mad scientist from decades past created him in order to show the world of Tao the benefits of genetic engineering, a technology they had outlawed. Rather than becoming a god of the Combat, however, the child was born deformed. Both scientist and his creation were exiled to the Citadel.

The true heresy, Faria had related, *was that the experiment didn't work.* If Goth had turned out as planned, if he had been physically perfect, stronger, faster, and more handsome, his fate might have been much different. It makes me pity the creature.

Now the creature's forlorn howls and rattling of his bonds reverberate as he stalks the corridors. His sense of hearing as acute as any who has lived in darkness all his life. He has a taste for flesh, feasting on the corpses of dead inmates and the occasional living, escaped prisoner.

Rumors, I think, trying to shrug off the sense of terror I feel now that I'm exposed.

"Don't worry," Faria whispers, snapping my attention back to the present. "I've timed our trip so Goth will be too far to catch us even if he does suspect something."

"You think if he was a hundred flights up he would still know something was out of place here?" I ask skeptically.

"Would you?"

Not even with my newly acquired skills of perception. Goth, however, has lived an entire life in this place. "I'd rather not take the risk," I respond.

"Blind risk is stupid, but calculated risks are worth taking."

We move quietly down the hall, careful not to alert any other occupants to our presence. The last thing we need would be the screaming of a raving lunatic calling attention to our activities. We journey down a spiraling staircase to a hallway full of more doors. Behind the seventh door on the right is a small chamber, a cell not unlike my own, only empty. Faria walks to the center and crouches. He lifts a heavy obsidian floor tile, putting it aside to reveal a secret compartment.

"See for yourself," he says.

I hunch beside him as he pulls a box from the compartment. Inside the box is a tablet reader. He hands it to me. I feel the wood, plastic, and metal of advanced but ancient technology. The screen comes alive in my hand, projecting liquid metal pins onto the surface. They stand out like rough little bumps on the otherwise smooth surface of the device.

"A tactile pad?" I ask.

"Yes," Faria says. "Perfect for the blind. Illustrated in a long forgotten text called nightscript. It contains the literature of thousands of cultures, scientific achievements of races long dead. More importantly, it contains maps."

"To where?" I ask.

"To more destinations in the Fracture than one could travel in a lifetime." He plucks the reader from my hand and keys several of the bumps with his fingers. I hear the liquid metal morph as a new pattern is generated.

"This is the one that should concern you."

He hands me the tablet again, and my fingers gloss over the surface. I've not been trained to read with touch, not yet, so I'm not sure what I am looking at. "A map of the Citadel?" I guess.

"These are the original architectural schematics," Faria tells me. "It's how I was able to learn to move about this place. The lunar equinox is almost upon us. The moons of Chang and Hou will circle the Nightside, and my sentence will end. You'll be on your own. I'll teach you to read the script, and you will explore this place alone as I once did."

"How did you find—?"

"The second map," he says, cutting me off, "will only be of use if you ever leave the planet. I share this with you, Edmon, for I have doubts I may ever see a different sky."

"You'll live a long time yet, Master," I say reassuringly.

"You don't know how old I am, boy. The genetic code contains a maximum number of cell divisions. Telomeres shorten. Division may be slowed; it may not be stopped. With the skills I've taught you, one can keep a body alive for a long time, but there are consequences. I train you so you may complete this task."

I sit in silence.

"You're Edric Leontes's son," he says. "I believe if anyone has the chance to be released from this hell, it will be you."

I'm his means of escape, and all his tests have been to ensure that I was capable of that.

"Don't be sullen," he reprimands. "I've shared with you my secrets. Don't forget—you've used me, too. You wanted to learn. I've taught. You wanted a friend. I've given. That's what humans do."

"Use each other." I understand his meaning.

"Self-interest," he agrees, "whether for power or love. I'm too greedy to teach solely for the joy of watching you grow. I don't have much time left."

"What's on the map?" I ask.

"The Citadel stood long before your father changed the Wendigo to a labor camp. When I came here, there was a man, older and wiser than I will ever be. He was a spypsy imprisoned here. How he came to be on this accursed world, I do not know. Then again, my own story is sad and strange, so perhaps I should not wonder. Like many spypsies, he was a master of genetics. In fact, he was more. He could change his own biochemistry to such a degree that, chameleon-like, he could alter his entire physical structure. This was far beyond anything he taught me, and beyond what I've now taught you. He could become shorter or taller should the need arise. He could make the lenses of his eyes capable of perceiving in the dark. He grew fibrous hairs on his hands and feet to sense the walls with touch the way a spider can. His vocal cords shifted to reach a pitch so high, his ears were able to sense its sound reflected off the walls."

"Echolocation?" I ask, astounded. "The porpoises of the Meridian Harbor do that."

"He became a master of this place and showed me all he knew before he died. I learned to travel the corridors and circumvent Goth, and he showed me this hidden compartment. In this tablet, he had recorded places he had been and things that he had seen. Do you know of Miral?" he asks me.

Miral, home of the lost empire. The home of the Great Song and his rebels. A place now of myth and legend.

"It was the most advanced world of the Second Age," I say. "Home of the Renaissance after the loss of Ancient Earth. Before it, too, fell."

Faria nods. "Its people were scattered like dust carried on currents of dark matter."

"The spypsies are their descendants."

"As are the Taoans," Faria notes. "Spypsies encourage mysteries about their origins. It's forbidden for them to leave their clans or reveal their ways to outsiders."

"Then why did this man share his knowledge with you?"

"Perhaps because he was a renegade? Perhaps because I, too, am an outsider?" Faria engages the reader screen again. I skim my fingertips over the bumps, feeling a great mystery unfold. "Miralian coordinates," he says. "The empire fell, but the riches remain. If we can find the planet, we can use this map to find the greatest treasure in the universe on its surface. I share this with you, Edmon."

"You think I'm going to leave this prison, leave this planet to go treasure hunting?"

"A dying man's fantasy," he says.

"You aren't dying, Faria," I insist again.

He waves me off. "I exact from you two promises."

I hold still in the darkness.

"The first. If you are freed, you will free me as well. We will find this treasure and take our revenge on those who brought us our fates, together."

Will the greatest treasure in the universe bring back my mother? Will it bring back Nadia?

He lunges for me and knocks me to the ground with surprising strength. He presses his fingers to my jugular. The blood flow to my brain is cut off. I feel myself growing light-headed. "Swear it, Edmon," he hisses.

"I swear it."

He taps my neck, releasing me. "Good. The second promise . . ."

A howl reverberates throughout the deep chambers of the Citadel. *Goth.*

"We've lingered too long!" Faria whispers. "Come. Quickly!"

We return the reader to the hidden floor compartment and silently run down the hallway and up the spiral staircase. Another howl shakes the tower. My whole body tingles as if a current has pulsed through it.

"Come!" Faria says through his teeth.

I hear the panting of the creature's foul breath and the beat of his hideous, misshapen heart. I hear the clicking of jagged teeth. He's several floors up, much closer than I expected. Goth has passed my cell many times before, but the thick iron door that separates my chamber from the outside has always felt like an impregnable barrier. Now I feel naked. *I never thought I'd be pining for the security of a locked jail cell!*

Faria and I reach the top of the stairs. There is a growl. *He's here.* My master puts a hand on my shoulder. He taps his index finger in a pattern on my skin, a rudimentary code we use to communicate in silence: *Go. We have no choice.*

No! I respond. *Too risky.*

He taps again. *Calculated risk. Get to the air duct.*

He takes off down the hallway. If he dies so that I may make it safely back to the air duct, I'll kill him!

It's too late. Goth has heard the sounds of Faria's running and is coming. I freeze. There's nowhere to go. I could double back to the stairwell, but there's no telling if Goth will pick up my trail instead of Faria's. The lumbering of his meaty footsteps and the rattle of his chains grows louder. He roars like a prehistoric beast.

The air duct is ahead, but now the giant creature is in between me and escape. I hug the dungeon wall and hold perfectly still. *This is my only chance.* I hold my breath and calm the frantic beating of my heart. I look inward slowing the flow of blood . . .

The creature passes. I keep only the mildest sense of outside awareness as I enter a comatose trance. I would surely appear lifeless were any medical doctor to examine me. *Will my ruse fool Goth, though?*

The creature stops and sniffs. He's big. Perhaps seven feet tall and wider than three men shoulder to shoulder. His feet are heavy slabs; their odor wafts into my nostrils, making me want to retch. Talonlike toenails scrape the stone. He reaches out a clawed hand and waves it in the air. He senses I'm near, but I don't dare break the trance. I keep myself from falling into unconsciousness, knowing that if he does contact anything, I'll need to run for my life.

The sound of a strange tune whistles through the cavern. The monster's head whips around.

It's Faria. He's trying to draw Goth away from me!

Goth growls and takes off down the hallway, feet smacking the floor as he goes. I wait and wait. I open my ears, listening for the pulsation of his heart, the pant of his breath. I awaken my body from the trance as quickly as I dare. Blood pumps through my arteries and my muscles flex. I send hormones racing through my sympathetic nervous system, preparing for flight, and spring from my hiding place to sprint down the hall.

Goth's rattling chains stop. He reverses course and barrels down the corridor after me.

Move! Damn you, Edmon, move!

There's no way he can catch me. No two-legged humanoid that big could move that fast. Yet I hear him gaining. *How is it possible?*

The vent to the air ducts is fifty meters ahead and twenty meters up. I feel my body burning through glycogen that fuels my muscles, lactic acid pumping. I don't have much more to give. Goth's hoary breath bears down on my back. A taloned finger scrapes my shoulder blade.

By the twisted star, I'm done for!

I skyrocket toward the ceiling. Everything goes blank for a moment as all thought drops away. I pull myself into the vent and climb into the duct where the huge monstrosity cannot follow. I slam the grating closed, sealing the passageway. Below, he howls with animal rage.

The whistling of the strange tune begins again. Faria still tries to pull the monster's attentions from me. He will surely die, but I must survive. *For my mother. For Nadia. For revenge.*

I climb through the vents as fast as my weary body will allow. Three levels of vertical ascent convince me that next time I leave my cell I should find a way to take the stairs. Only fifty or so more levels to go . . .

I drop from the ceiling vent onto the floor of my hold. I gather the rags around me and pull the food tray to me from underneath the door slat. I wolf down the ration paste quickly, trying to quell the burning in my dying muscles. It is irony that the very monster who keeps me fed almost murdered me.

The thought hits me—I'll never see the old man again.

I'm not ready! I don't know if I'll be able to find the reader again, much less keep my promise to find the treasure of Miral. My brain is foggy. I've expended too much energy in the escape. My body starts to cramp. I calm myself with relaxed breaths. Weariness and grief take me.

When I awake, Faria sits over me as always. I don't see him, rather I hear it. I feel it.

"Faria?"

"You expected someone else?"

"No. But I thought—ugh." I wrinkle my nose. "I could smell you ten kilometers away."

"You're one to talk, Leontes." He stands. "Five months with no bath hasn't done you any favors, either. You're welcome for saving your life. Again."

"How did you make it past Goth?" I ask.

"The mad dash you made for the vent gave me enough time to find an alternate route. You should have stayed in the trance until I had lured him away completely."

"I didn't want to be there any longer than I had to."

"Fear is no crime," he says. "But acting from fear is. Know that you're going to lose everything one day, whether you fear to lose it or not."

I nod, feeling like I've already lost everything, anyway. Revenge is all I have left.

CHAPTER 21

Arioso

"Come at me!" Faria baits. I lunge forward, swinging a metal rod. All I hear is the sound of air. "Too slow," he murmurs.

"I could divert my energy," I say, panting. "Make myself fast enough to hit you."

"You could," he says, "but then you sacrifice your balance."

Our "blades" cross. I strike, he parries, he counters, and I riposte. The music of fencing.

"Your little friend, Phaestion Julii, is a master of rapier and dagger," Faria taunts. "How do you expect to defeat him if you cannot beat me?"

I ricochet off the wall. I flip head over heels to dodge the stroke.

"Lightly, Edmon. Use your anger to give you focus," Faria commands. "Don't prevent the storm. Become it."

I twirl the blade with an abonico flourish, aiming for the man's head. He rolls, bringing up his rod for an umbrella block with one hand and clawing my sword hand with his other. He twists my wrist with numbing strength. He flips me.

Not this time, old man.

I roll with it, land on my feet, and let go of my weapon in the process. Now he wields both rods against me. "Do you yield?"

"I haven't lost yet," I fire back. I charge, and he's caught by surprise. I tackle him. He rolls expertly, but I snag my metal rod in the tumult, and our blades cross again. I poise my weapon high over my head. I slice downward with swift power to strike his head. Suddenly, he's not there, and my metal clangs against the stone floor. His weapon kisses the back of my neck.

How, by the twisted star?

"Phaestion will not ask you to yield when you face him," he says.

"If he did, it would be a mistake." I drop to the ground so fast not even Faria can catch me. I shoot out my feet in a kick that trips him. He crashes, the rod flying from his hands. Before he can scramble, I leap on top of him, pressing my blade to his throat.

"Well done, Edmon! Still, you would have lost." He pushes me off him.

"Had you not wasted time to talk," I counter.

"Perhaps," he muses. "As long as you'd make the same choice to win again."

Phaestion was the only boy I was ever close to. He saved my life, and I saved his. He's arrogant, entitled, impossibly beautiful, and utterly flawed. He loved me but couldn't own me. I don't know what it will be when we see each other again.

"Why do you keep talking about him?" I ask.

"Do I? Let us be quiet now," he says, groaning. "These tired old bones only creak. They can't see the future. What I do know is Tao is a battleground for ambition, and it's not prescience to know your loyalties are going to be tested."

"There's only one test people understand here—the Combat," I answer.

"Strength and power. Father or brother. Your choice will have consequences," he says.

I sit down next to him. "I don't think I'm going to have to worry about it anytime soon. They locked me up and threw away the key." My shadow crosses his face in the slim light. Light? "Master?"

He nods. "I sensed it almost an hour ago. A shift in the spectrum. Six months is upon us." I sense urgency in his voice. "I've saved the last lesson for now. I pass to you the secret of the Dim Mak as it was passed to me by the Zhao monks. You will be able to take life with a touch of your finger, but you must make the second promise."

His words hang between us.

"If I teach you, you will kill someone of my choosing at the time of my choosing."

Why would he need me to do the killing?

"Agree" is his only answer.

Who? The Warden? Some ruffian of the Wendigo? Some stranger I don't know who wronged him long ago? I suppose there's only one way to find out if the techniques he teaches will actually work. This is a distinct disadvantage in practicing it, I surmise.

"Take this upon yourself or don't," he says. "Either way, let us enjoy the few hours of moonlight we'll have together in honesty."

I take a deep breath. I answered in my heart long ago. "I give you my oath."

The rising moons Chang and Hou wax their pale beams through the cell window. We study. I probe with my fingers against my skin. I feel the meridians flowing. Faria instructs me to apply pressure to change their vibrations. Some pressures lead to paralysis; others stop the resonance completely. I've learned the contact reflexes and sensitivity, the ability to sense meridians within myself and others already. Now he lays out the final piece of the puzzle.

"Gentle at first, then sharp like a knife," he instructs. "The mandibular pressure point hit at the precise moment can cause bowel dysfunction. The brachial arteries staunched may cause paralysis of limbs for days or until you release it, like so." He demonstrates. "After fingers are applied to the sacrum, a man will be locked permanently upright. Applied thusly, it will break the coccyx and release spinal fluid, resulting in collapse of the brain stem."

So it goes. For hours. The first time I paralyze my own arm, I go giddy, then I panic. "I can't feel my arm! By the star, I can't feel it!"

I try to return vibration to the limb, but I'm so flustered I can't do it. Faria refuses to help. I try to calm myself. It's the better part of an hour before I'm able to replicate the technique and return the feeling.

"Emotions are energy. Love, hate, fear, panic. Focus them and you have lightning. Rage in all directions, obstacles will stand unmoved. Concentration is precision."

We don't sleep. The moons wane.

"I've shown you all I know," Faria says finally. "The rest is up to you. Remember, fighting isn't right or wrong. It is an expression of the self. The universe is energy, and you are the lens through which it passes. Do you understand?"

"Yes, Master," I reply, not totally comprehending, but I've six months alone to figure it out.

"Let us sit in our last moments," he says.

I lean against the wall. I truly take in his visage in the pale moonlight. More than old, he's dying. His oddly colored reddish hair is now dull and gray. It has sprouted fraying ends from his unkempt head. The paint of the facial tattoos is tucked deep into the crevices of his leathery skin. He looks emaciated, a skeleton with barely enough muscle to hold up his frame. His white eyes, which at one time seemed fierce in their blindness, now seem faded. It's hard to believe this is the man who beat me in a fencing match a few hours ago.

I stand tiptoed and look out the porthole of my dungeon. The world beyond is like whipping cream scraped across the landscape in mountainous, snowy swirls. It's beautiful in its pure bleakness.

"Have you been modulating your pupil dilation?" Faria asks.

"Yes," I respond. "Still it has been six months."

Faria nods. I sit back down. “Master, how did you come to Tao?” I ask.

He smiles with brown teeth. “It’s a long and tragic tale and of no concern.”

“If I wasn’t interested, I wouldn’t have asked.”

“I’m surprised you waited this long. You’ve guessed I’m not from around these parts.”

“It was your winning charm that gave you away,” I joke.

“Long ago there was a war. A war that exploded suns, extinguished millions of souls. This was hundreds of years before the generations of Nightsiders that scurry the oceans of Tao today. The historians that deign to recount it called it the Chironian Civil War.”

“Chilleus and Cuillan,” I whisper. I remember the great myth that Phaestion and I both loved as children.

“Chilleus and Cuillan were legends even to me,” Faria says, nodding. “Anjin commanders who served long before I was born into service. Chiron was a moon of the Titanus star system. My people were conscripts.”

He says the word with a bitter inflection. *There’s more to it than simply being drafted,* I think.

“Wars are petty things. They rob men of dignity, turn them into meat and guts. Never fight a war not of your choosing, Edmon Leontes,” he says. “When our great war was over, the Titanus star was no more, and the people of its worlds and moons were scattered to space.”

“You always said fighting was the truest expression of self.”

“Martial art is not war, boy,” he says sharply. “There’s nothing personal about war.”

I now wonder if Faria is any less deluded than any of my teachers.

“So, you found your way to Tao?” I ask.

“I was the last alive on a dying cruiser, the *Perseid.* My brothers, who died first, set the ship on autopilot with a trajectory for the black hole at the heart of the galaxy. I was not designed by my creators to live beyond the conflict's end. They never saw the possibility of their own demise first," he adds wryly.

"It was my duty to helm the ship past the dying embers of Titanus, through the dust of New Byzantium's remnants, and into the heart of an event horizon. I disobeyed. Call it a defect of the genetic code. I changed course and set sail for the nearest Fracture Point.

"I lived for weeks off what was left in the meager galley, then the rotting corpses of my own brothers."

I must look horrified because he stops his tale.

"Your eyes show disgust. I slaughtered many in battle, but feasting on the flesh of my own kin? How do you come back from that, Edmon Leontes?"

I have no answer.

"Such was the will to live. You would have done the same."

I nod, not knowing that I would.

"I washed ashore on a Bernal Sphere, a space station colonized by a group of ascetic monks called the Zhao. The sphere orbited a blue star the charts name as Janus. It's remote, perhaps seven or eight points from Market."

"Market?" I ask.

"A main hub of civilization. The monks nursed me to health, but they could not prevent my biology from deteriorating. My cells were reaching their maximum number of divisions, and there was not exactly a means for a full intracellular transplant." He laughs as he explains.

"Fortunately, the Zhao are anything but conventional," he continues. "They taught, and I learned quickly. The threat of failure was enough incentive. I outlived my expiration date and reached equilibrium."

"Equilibrium?" I ask.

"A place of inner peace free of earthly pains and pleasures. The monks train for that. It's what keeps them alive for centuries."

Centuries?

He waves off my incredulous stare. "There's a price. Equilibrium brings stagnation. Change is the essence of life. The existence of a monk is dull and monotonous. There is no pain, but also no love. All I had known was the life of a soldier. I was born and bred to follow orders. Go here, kill this, shoot that. The life of an ascetic is not so different. Wake up, clean this, meditate on this. I craved more. I had seen men holding women, looking at a child who shared their own eyes."

"You left."

"I gave up immortality. I took an oath never to share the knowledge that the monks imparted to me. They supplied me with my first month's passage on a cargo ferry. I rode on the backs of cruisers, sailed over the nebulae of the Calcaides. I witnessed the births of red giants and white dwarfs and floated down the tributaries of dark matter, which carried me to Market."

"Market. You named that place before," I say.

"Spacers of the Second Age met at predestined coordinates to trade. Eventually one or two had the good sense to stay put. Then one or two more. Drifting ships, cruisers, and junks of all kinds became strung together. Market is its own world now. You float through micro-g of a cargo hold turned interstellar night club, only to cross an access tube and slam to the floor of a rotating clothing shop's artificial g. It's where all those who leave atmo end up. It's just about the only place that connects this scattered tribe we call humanity."

"A city in the sky," I say wistfully.

"Dirty, garbage, rubble-bed in the black, more like." He chuckles. "Kind of like Ancient Earth, I'm told. Market can be wonderful, though. Languages, food, and accoutrement of every shade and taste exist there. Characters and lowlifes lurk around every corner, whispers of the greater cosmos far on everyone's lips. That was where I learned of Tao, in a bookshop, the Eye of the Pyramid."

"Actual books?" I ask, stunned.

"Some cultures still print on physical objects. By then, my eyesight had started to fade. So I learned to appreciate more tactile forms of communication. I was scanning some antiquities when a man entered, pale with blond hair, very strong. He wore robes of fine silk with flashes of copper armor. He looked like a feudal relic."

I nod, picturing a nobleman of Tao. It was rare our people left the planet. I wonder if he was a Julii.

"Arrogant and with eyes of judgment. But he wasn't the one who caught my eye. It was the collared woman on his arm, a Nereian goddess, all dark skin and smooth curves."

"An islander." I'm reminded of my Nadia.

"I followed them. The man sought accommodations, and I intercepted the woman for a private tête-à-tête." He smiles roguishly. "She revealed her name—Qualia. No sound ever rang so sweet in my ears. She was the man's servant, and they were from a planet called Tao. She called herself a Daysider. This sparked my curiosity of the planet's peculiar geography. I wasn't sure if the place was paradise or a backwater. Chaos and order forever contending with each other.

"I fell in love nonetheless. I convinced Qualia to abandon the lord, and we booked passage on a UFP ship. I had found myself a new wife, but she wished to return to her home in the Western Sea, the Isle of Drum."

"And?" I press him.

"Tao has always been xenophobic. Its isolation from the nearest Fracture Point by several months' trip through deep space made your people cloistered, distrustful of outsiders. The islanders welcomed me. I didn't look too different from their natives, but your noble houses—"

"Took Qualia," I say, guessing the story already.

"For every Combat competitor like your father who willingly steps from the muck to take the garland with brute strength, there's a scryling whose legs shiver as he's handed a stick and forced to face trained killers.

The government forced me, like it did others, to fight so their highborn sons could kill."

"My father—"

"Edric Leontes was expected by most to die in the arena," Faria answers. "Through skill, he clawed his way to victory."

"And dared it a second time," I add.

"That's why he's worshipped. You might want to look up who your father killed to win."

Augustus of the Julii, I suspect.

"And Qualia?" I ask, not wanting to hear any more about my father.

"The Pantheon makes volunteers where none exist. Qualia was young and strong, but the moment House Wusong guards touched her, four were dead by my hands. I used the techniques of the monks. I used them without thinking. I couldn't fight them all, though. They returned with an army, took her, and forced me in the arena."

"You refused to fight," I say.

"On the contrary," he corrects. "I wanted to bleed them. I rained death and destruction."

"Then why are you here now?" I ask.

"Four days and nights I fought in the rotunda. Those that crossed me fell to my blade. Myself and one pale Nightsider were left standing. Camglobes hovered between us. We met like storm gods. Equally matched, though in the end, I stood victorious. When I looked down upon him, however, I didn't see a warrior who had slain many in the arena that day, only a boy. Someone's child. Someone's brother. I sheathed my sword."

"You showed mercy?" I ask, shocked.

"It was the greatest humiliation I could have given him. The High Synod ordered me to take his head or forfeit my own."

"He would have killed you had he the chance. What was one more life against your love for Qualia?" I ask.

"I don't know," the dark man concedes. "The pointlessness of it? The fact that they ordered me to do it? The knowledge that it wouldn't stop there and I'd be forced to kill many more? You may find yourself in such a moment one day. I have taken life only once since that day." I remember Snaggletooth, the Hauler that he killed for me. "If I ever again kill, it won't be because someone ordered me to."

We sit for a beat, then—

"You bound me to take the life of someone of your choosing? You won't kill on anyone else's word, but you'd condemn me to kill on yours?"

"I never said it was fair, Edmon." His skeletal face smiles like a grinning death's head.

I seethe, but the bargain has already been struck.

"So you were sent to the Wendigo?" I growl.

"Directly to the Citadel," he corrects. "I humiliated Chilleus of the Julii. Death was too good for me. I was tortured. Qualia was murdered in public. She could've lived, Edmon, found another husband, had children . . ." There is a hitch in his voice as he chokes for a moment. "The following year, Chilleus Julii entered the arena again and slaughtered everyone in an attempt to wipe the stain of his loss from people's memories," the old master says with disgust. "Vengeance burned inside me. I could have died with my brothers aboard the *Perseid*. Or with the Zhao monks on their sphere. But when I imagine what's beyond this life, I don't see resolution, only a certainty I'll no longer exist. I'd fight to keep what little life I have, no matter that it fades into decrepitude, no matter that it is full of hate."

Islanders are taught all life comes from the sea. To the sea it returns. Nightsiders believe death in Combat is the only honorable death. The fallen are burned in veneration. I've never thought much of joining the ancestors beneath the waves or as sparks in the sky. Both options seem better than the truth that Faria gives. The murders of my mother and of Nadia and all the others before and since seem like such a waste. My heart grows cold.

"Dead men don't seek revenge," Faria mutters.

I've made an oath to punish those who have killed my loved ones. That's all that matters.

"You were a singer, they said," Faria says, interrupting my thoughts. "They said your songs of rebellion shook this little world."

"Once," I answer. It feels an age ago.

"Sing something now," he suggests.

I feel ridiculous. I'm bald, bearded, and a filthy, stinking, dirt-monger in rags.

"Any tune. That's all this old man's asking. Don't worry about Goth," he says. "He's frightened of the light. He'll have found a spot in the depths of the tower and won't come out until the moons have passed."

I think on it. "My mother once told me my people were here before the Great Song, before the hybrids, back to the time of the Elder Stars. This song is from that time."

Faria nods.

> "Across the stars, spread far and thin,
> The mother calls us home
> Much too late, now we begin
> To answer the call alone
> To home, to home, through black of night
> To home, to home, on edge of light,
> From all, to one, born, and live, and die again."

Silence holds memory of the final note. The light of the moons begins to fade. "Edmon," Faria says softly. "You were not meant to be caged."

The universe is littered with corpses of what's meant to be.

"The Fracture Point burst in the skies the day I was born," I say. "Nine years later, I saw some of the first off-worlders to come to Tao in decades. There was a captain that didn't look so different from you, Faria. He was dark as night, strange reddish hair. He didn't have the same tattoos or facial markings, but he looked like you. Could he have been the child of one of your brothers or . . ."

My voice trails off. Faria is disconcerted by this mention, I can tell.

"We only have a few more moments" is his only reply. The cell returns to shadows, and I'm blind again. Faria stands. "I take my leave," he says. "The guards will come, and they must find their healer waiting."

"Master, thank—"

"Not until our enemies are dead and our thirst satisfied. We meet again in six months' time," he says. As silently as the moons slipping past the window, he's gone.

CHAPTER 22

Nocturne

The next six months are dark and lonely. There's a rhythm in their passing. I wake, train, and push my body to the limit, and after the exhaustion, I meditate. I find the cells inside, push the lactic acid out of my muscles, and repair the damaged tissues. Then I begin again. It's a delicate balance.

I practice the Dim Mak. It's not easy. There are only so many times that I can make my own arm or leg go limp without becoming bored. The first tries are terrifying. If I cannot duplicate the strike to return feeling to the limb, damage will be permanent. By the twentieth time, I revel in my new powers. The five hundredth time, I might as well be asleep. I need to practice the more lethal strikes, but I can't practice on myself without permanently paralyzing my own body, so I'm decidedly against it.

I punch and kick the reinforced obsidian of the dungeon wall. My skin grows tough and calloused. Soon it's the rock that splinters under the force of my blows.

I remember when Phaestion showed me his famed siren swords. I couldn't hold them then. Now, I breathe deeply. I feel the vibrations beginning deep within my belly. I cultivate them and strengthen them.

They boil like water in a kettle; their frequency becomes fever pitch. There's nowhere for them to travel but up. Like a flash flood, the energy rushes through my thorax. I channel it as I unleash my fist. Through my shoulder, my arm, through the tips of my fingers, the current courses. I picture my father, Edric Leontes, the leviathan, leering. The vibrations release as I hit the dungeon wall.

I scream on impact, and there is an explosion, a veritable sonic boom. I'm flung back from the wall with tremendous force, slamming into the wall behind me. I wake a moment later with a throbbing headache. I hold my aching skull and take a few tentative steps to reach out and touch the wall. A giant crater divots the surface. It's like a grenade exploded. I laugh in shock. *I did that. I may not have a siren sword, but I have my body. My body is my sword!*

Goth howls several floors up. He heard me, and he's going berserk. There's a sound of twisting metal. He tears a cell door from its hinges. The crash reverberates as the creature hurls the iron door to the ground and the cell's occupant screams in desperation. I recognize the screams. It's the man with one leg who cried for mercy in the Combat, the one who had lost a daughter. He screams for mercy now.

"Ancestors! Forgive me. Help me! Someone, help!"

Do something, Edmon! I could race up several flights to the man's cell. I might make it in time. He's going to die because of me, because my noise provoked the monster.

"Please, no!" the man shouts.

I should help. I must *help.* I don't move. I can't. *If I face the beast before I've mastered this technique, before I'm ready, I'll be done for. If I die, Nadia's death, my mother's, will be in vain. I must do nothing.*

The screams escalate as Goth's talons tear open the prisoner's belly. The man calls out for his mother in his last moans of consciousness. I hear the sickening crunch of teeth on bone and the snorts of the creature's chewing as he feeds.

It is the first time that someone has been in danger and I've done nothing when I could have helped. *The man died because of me.*

That's when I realize the truth of the old saying—those who seek vengeance must dig two graves. I've started down a path from which I can't return.

—

In the "evenings," I explore, crawling through the narrow air ducts. I stop at cells and listen. The sounds of other human beings breathing and moving are comforting. They make me believe I'm not alone in my suffering. I want to speak to some of them, but I keep my mouth shut. Knowledge of my presence would only cause more problems than it would cure.

I time the patterns of Goth's wanderings. I venture into the depths of the tower to find the hidden compartment and the nightscript reader. Faria didn't teach me to read nightscript, but he showed me the primer. With it, I'm able to begin learning. It takes a few days to navigate the data banks of the thing. It's one thing to gain ability to see with touch; it's another thing to apply that ability to learning a language. Over several weeks I discern words, then phrases. Then bits and pieces form sentences, and finally thoughts.

The tablet's a trove containing everything from the postdiaspora history of humanity to myths and legends of the Miralian Empire. I reread *The Chironiad.* Chilleus and Cuillan were brothers and lovers who ended on opposite sides of the civil war. Cuillan fell in love with Penalea of Amazonia while Chilleus led the Anjins of the Miralian Empire against the Chironian rebels. In the end, they fought in single combat, and Cuillan died in his brother's arms. Penalea committed suicide as Chilleus burned Cuillan's body with his Anjin laser in a victory ceremony. Later, Chilleus went mad and sacrificed himself in an assault on a shield station, which turned the tide of the war in the empire's favor.

Phaestion once said that we were those ancient warriors reborn.

Perhaps this isn't the best story to read.

I turn to the tale of Leontes, commander of the Anjin mechs who held off a direct assault on Miral a generation later with only a single battalion. Leontes's men were slaughtered to the last man, but his sacrifice bought the empire's armada time to return from deep space and wipe out the Chironian Army. Leontes is the name my father chose for his house. I now know that Faria's people, his brothers he called them, all died at the end when the Chironians lost the war.

It seems we're all weirdly connected to this lost history, I think.

I decide I'd be better served by studying something more practical. I'm going to need more information to find Miral and Faria's lost treasure.

My visits to the room gain in frequency. Days bleed into one another. I sharpen my body during the day; I hone my mind at night.

I read the history of the Second Age. There's startlingly little. Here's what I learn—the Fracture is composed essentially of what ancients called "wormholes" or "Einstein-Rosen bridges." The bridges are tributaries of dark matter that run throughout the universe. The dark matter gives space density, which holds gravity at an equilibrium so the universe doesn't fly apart at the seams. It runs through the cosmos in great, thick veins. Dark matter, like all matter, is composed of tiny strings that vibrate like music. Ships equipped with a Fracture saw convert the matter of the ship to energy that vibrates at the precise resonance of the point of entry. Thus, ships are able to infuse into and travel along the veins of the Fracture like boats on rivers free of time dilation.

However, Fracture Points are unpredictable. Just as there is dark matter, there is dark energy that counteracts the gravitational force of the matter and causes the universe to expand. Thus the Fracture Points move and shift over the course of eons, just like a living organism would. There was once a point near Ancient Earth, but it closed. The Great Grandmother, birthplace of all humanity, was lost. It's curious to me, however, that there has been so much movement within the last ten thousand years. Cosmically speaking, that is not very long in the timescale of the universe.

Then I run across a sentence from a science text that catches my attention. *Doctor Seldon Jones of the Prospera Institute of Stellar Cartography on Lyria posits that the Fracture Points show evidence of artificial creation and stabilization.*

Jones thinks that someone created Fracture Points? Who? I wonder. The Great Song's science officers also hypothesized that the Tao solar system was not natural. *What kinds of beings would have the power to rip open the fabric of space-time, and move and create planets?* I don't have answers and neither does the tablet. The questions are too big for me to worry about now, though.

I read about Market, the intergalactic hub for trade, and its nearest jumping points, Thera and Nonthera. I read that most ships, at least since this data-bank entry was made, are rocket-fuel based and just rudimentary shells made to withstand short flights to and from Fracture Points. Artificial gravity and cryogenic sleep have been tried throughout history for longer flights but are often deemed too expensive.

Artificial intelligence isn't trusted throughout the Nine Corridors. Human pilots mechanically maneuver ships to the points along with rudimentary navigation computers. AI was prominent on Miral before the fall, but there are no longer any worlds like that. Every planet that developed self-replicating AI suffered some kind of ecological collapse or the Fracture mysteriously closed on them.

Every. Single. One.

I sit for a beat. Humanity seems doomed to plateau in its technological evolution. It burns out, soaring too high as it tries to reach the gods.

There's a finite measure of what we can be. Unless we change, I think.

I study medical journals. I need this knowledge as part of the plan to take Faria's place. The forest world of Thera has pioneered the use of purely biological healing methods and pharmaceuticals. The Barris society of the Second Star Moons sought life extension through gene parasites. Then there's the curious case of the Gamins of Malori: an entire society of children that live for hundreds of years and can never grow old.

How do they survive? A howl sounds. Goth.

I return the reader to its hiding spot. I'd take the tome with me, but it's not safe anywhere else. The next equinox will come soon, and the guards will return for me. The Warden cannot know that such a treasure exists. I climb the winding stairs that lead to the hallway. I make out the vent about fifty meters ahead when I freeze.

Something is wrong. I can see the vent with my eyes. *Moonrise! Much too soon!*

Faria has taught me many things. The lesson about judging clock time apparently didn't stick. I figured at least several hours before moonlight. *That's what I get for getting lost in a book!*

A snarl of fury raises the hairs on the back of my neck. I see the hulking pale form shifting in the shadows of the hallway before me. I can't make out his features, only his gargantuan size in the gloaming between me and escape.

Run! I send adrenaline to my muscles. The monster's feet smack the stone in chase. I feel his hot slathering breath at my back. Talons reach out. Faria's not here to save my skin this time. I stop instantly and duck as Goth passes over me. I slide between his tree-trunk legs and catch a glimpse of the muscles on his pale back rippling in newborn moonshine. Pressing the soles of my feet against the back of his knees, I push with all my might, hoping to topple him. He's so heavy the maneuver doesn't move him. Instead, I'm rocketed backward along the slick floor. The momentum propels me into a somersault, and I snap to standing with a clear path toward the vent. I leap, and my hands grip twisted metal.

The creature has already been here! He found the vent and crushed it to cut off my escape!

Laughter. Odious, inhuman laughter sounds behind me.

I drop to the floor and stand face-to-face with the beast. His pale skin glistens with a sheen of oily sweat. I see a face more simian than human with only a bare nub for a nose. One eye bulges from its socket while the other, the size of a pin, is sucked back into his skull. Fleshy pink lips curl back with a twisted smirk, revealing broken, needlelike teeth. He rattles the chains that bind his wrists and claps his hands with the glee of a child who has discovered a new toy. Then he winces as the light of the moon brightens through the window and he lets loose a bestial roar.

I'm dead, I think.

Dead men don't seek revenge, my father's voice burns in my skull.

The moons are here. That's my advantage. I must get to the higher levels, where the light will be brighter.

He swipes for me. I leap onto his muscular arms, scrambling along them to his head. I rake his face with a clawed hand as I pass over him. Skin peels under my fingernails as I go. I flip off his shoulders and take off as fast as I can.

My mind reels, recalling the schematics of the tower. The main staircase is how Goth delivers food. There's also a cargo shaft used to get supplies from outside into the Citadel. I dive into an alcove. Goth races past me as I knew he would. I open my ears. He slows at the end of the corridor, sniffs the air, but can't sense me. He snarls, his chains rattling as he turns a corner down the hall.

Once safe, I head back to the lower levels to throw my pursuer off the scent and reach the area where I know an entry to the cargo shaft will be. I take the spiraling staircase down into the Citadel furnaces. The automated machines shovel coal into a giant cauldron that heats the fortress. The glow of orange fire pulses and belches black smoke. I hold my breath as I round the blast columns. There's a small iron door on the back wall. Locked.

Damn it!

Relax.

I breathe from the belly and summon the vibration. It builds and boils like the fires of the furnaces. It bursts through my body, and I lash out a fist. The door explodes off its hinges and into the shaft. I step into a vertical tunnel barely wider than I am. I stare up into darkness. The cargo elevator must be up several stories.

I spit into my hands and rub them together as I've seen heroes of aquagraphics do. I press my palms against the walls of the shaft and, with the opposing pressure, lift my body off the ground and proceed to shimmy skyward. I move centimeters at a time, but this is the only strategy I can think of.

After six stories and about two hundred more meters, I realize I'll never make it back to my cell at this rate. I need to travel in the open even if it risks Goth.

I grip the edge of the next cargo porthole and push myself through. It's barely wide enough for me to fit. The sharp edges of the glassy rock scrape away my flesh as I drop onto the hallway floor. The moonlight's definitely brighter here, and that's good, but it also means the guards are scheduled to come for me on this day. I carefully pad down the corridor until I reach an air vent. I listen for sounds of Goth. Nothing. I can usually make out the rattling of his chains or the smack of his feet even at a distance. Now, though, it's utterly still.

Could he be hiding?

I could enter the air vents from here, but if Goth is still on the hunt, he'll watch that path. The main stairwell might be the only route fast enough, but it leaves me vulnerable. During the last equinox, Faria told me not to worry about Goth because of his hatred of the light.

It's a calculated risk. I head for the corridor's main entry and take the giant spiral stairwell that treads up and up through the entirety of the colossal tower. I take four steps at a time, but it's still too quiet, too easy for me to not feel nauseated with unease. I finally reach the level of my cell, gently shouldering the heavy iron door to the hallway. It creaks on rusty hinges. I leap into the corridor, ready to face the Goth, but I'm alone.

Feeling like a nervous fool, I tiptoe gently to my prison cell. I hear movement in the stairwell. *The guards!*

I need to get back inside. I find the nearest air duct grate. I spring up to the ceiling and gently lift myself inside the vent shaft. I quietly crawl along the tube until I'm above the cell I've called home for the last year. I glance through the grate and see everything below empty, just as I left it. I release the grate and quietly drop to the floor of my cell.

Safe. And with time to spare.

Goth's snarl near the open cell door hits just a split second before his talons grab hold and I'm scooped into a bear hug. The moonlight now affords me a look of every detail of his monstrous face. Hot, stinking breath spews from his tooth-filled maw. I scream as he gnashes his incisors into my shoulder and tears away a chunk of flesh. He chews and swallows, then licks his fat purple lips.

I kick out as violently as I can. He pulls me in tighter, and his talons puncture my back. My old wounds rip open. He laughs, the malevolent sound echoing throughout the tower.

I must not die here! I have one weapon left. I push the anger down into my belly, feeling it boil to a pitch.

Become the storm, Faria said.

The rage vibrates until I can hold it no longer. I see the face of my father laughing in the twisted features of this hideous thing.

Why run, boy? the leviathan asks in my dreams. This time, I do not run.

I let the energy burst through me as I strike. The tips of my fingers connect with Goth's skull, and I feel the vibration pass into him like an electrical charge. I drop to the floor with a thud and roll away. Goth takes one step forward, then his misshapen eyes roll back into his skull, and a sad, mournful groan escapes from his lips. For a moment, I actually pity him. Any feeling I have, however, is cut short as his head explodes like a melon showering me with chunks of bone and gray matter. The huge muscled body falls forward, slamming with a thud against the floor of my cell.

Men's voices enter the hall.

"His door is open?" someone asks.

I hear the guards pull their humbatons from their belts, ready for trouble. They round the corner into my room and find me standing over the headless creature, anointed in blood and moonlight.

"Leontes?" one of them murmurs.

"I surrender." I raise my hands in the air.

CHAPTER 23

Cadenza

My return to the Wendigo is without fanfare. I'm smuggled into camp during sleeping hours and held in the guards' barracks until morning. I'm the picture of abject humiliation when The Warden inspects me.

"Now you understand what I can do to you?"

"Yes, lord." I make my voice raw and wilted.

"The son of a nobleman bows and scrapes before me," he smugly jokes with the guards. "What have you learned in your time in darkness, Leontes?"

I squint to pretend my eyes are pained from disuse. "I'm nothing but your servant, lord."

The Warden nods, duly impressed. "And how can you serve me?"

"Once Faria teaches me all he knows, I'm yours to do with as you will."

The Warden strokes his thick, blond mustache. "I'm told that you murdered the keeper of the tower?"

"No, my lord," I say, sniveling.

"Yet Goth was found dead in your chambers?"

I shake with fear to sell the lie that escapes my lips. "He came to the cell as he did daily to feed prisoners. He was in a frenzy." I cry softly. "He tore the door from my cell. I tried to fight but couldn't. I'm so weak." I gesture to my rail-thin arms, which, though strong from training, seem malnourished.

The guards chuckle at my cowardice. "Go on," says The Warden.

"I saw the great beast in the moonlight and soiled myself with fear."

The guards laugh.

"He ripped into my shoulder"—I point to the wound Goth made—"then the beast went mad! He slammed his own head against the black stones of the walls again and again, broke his own skull open. That was when your men found me, lord, covered in blood. Thank you for saving me! Thank you!"

The Warden and his henchmen stand silent, not certain whether to believe the story, but there isn't much other explanation. The idea that I killed Goth seems implausible. I could explain how I exploded Goth's head with a swift blow of the Dim Mak, but that would seem equally ridiculous.

"He tasted your flesh and went insane. Perhaps there is something poisonous in you, Leontes," The Warden muses.

"I throw myself upon your mercy, my lord!" I grovel at his feet with pitiful whining. He's disgusted by my presence, but Faria's right, my father doesn't want me dead yet, so he won't kill me. Not until they are both sure they can do without me. Therein lies my chance.

"Clean him and return him to the healer's hut," The Warden instructs. "You're mine now. Do you understand?"

"Thank you, my lord!" I lean to take his hand.

He pulls away with loathing. "Bah!" He stalks off.

Let him mock. Dead men do not seek revenge, and I am not dead yet.

I'm shaved and scrubbed raw. I shiver when the freezing water of the pressure hose blasts me and wince when the sting of the disinfectant powder hits my face. I run my hand over the smoothness of my scalp. It's the first time I feel clean in over a year. The guards remove my bindings and lead me to Faria's hut. They shove me to the ground and walk away. I crawl through the porthole into the healer's home. The fire burns low, creating long, haunting shadows. Faria sits in the place I first met him. His face, however, is not the same. His skin sags; his cheeks are hollow. His lean frame, which once carried an essence of hard strength, looks decayed. His wrinkled lips curve inward into his mouth as if he is sucking a straw.

"Master," I whisper.

He has aged, but he's alive, so there's still hope. "You've returned," he croaks. "And you've slain the beast of the tower."

"Yes."

"Now you understand the power and what you must do with it. I'm tired and must rest." He pulls a fur over himself and lies down before the fire. "Welcome home, son of Leontes."

This isn't home. I won't be home until it's done.

I'm now master of the hut and Faria the assistant. He sleeps most of the day, conserving his strength, willing his body to survive another hour. The Warden must have seen his decline. Now I understand why I'm allowed the position as Faria's replacement so easily.

The Warden sends men to check on me. I keep them satisfied by showing off my work mending fractures and scrapes, tending minor infections, and the like. In truth, I'm waiting for my moment. Faria believes Edric needs me alive as a contingency. I believe that I can't count on my father. In his mind, I'm just a tool to be used, and the need may never arise.

I'm not the only one with designs. The yearly Combat has come and gone, and Perdiccus of House Mughal has been named champion.

The standard of the manta flies over the city of Meridian this yearly cycle. Another Pavaka and purging of unwanted babes has followed. It makes me sick to be here, waiting, but self-pity is useless. No, I must make my own destiny, so I plot and I plan.

—

Faria and I are meditating when Carrick calls. I welcome the familiar Picker inside. *It's time for the first move.*

"Hoping Faria the Red could take a look." The big man holds up his finger, swollen and purple from some accident on the day's haul.

"I'm the healer of the Wendigo now," I tell my old colleague. The dark shaman makes the most imperceptible of nods in assent.

"Okay, Leontes. Just be careful," Carrick says warily.

"Not to worry, old friend." I take hold of the man's hand. "Didn't I save your life the day you fell from the pitch? This should be relatively simple to fix, provided you help me in return."

I grab the broken finger and twist violently. The big man opens his mouth to let out a scream. My other hand flies, slamming fingers into a pressure point in his neck. Now he cannot scream. He cannot move anything but his eyes and still feels everything.

"Carrick, you're going to cause an accident. I don't care how, but within the month, Bruul Vaarkson will find his way here. I don't want him dead. I want him here, alive, in need of medical care. Do you understand?"

Carrick glares at me—*go fuck yourself, Leontes.*

I understand his reluctance so I twist his finger some more. "This is a relatively simple request. I've saved your life, and I'll save your finger now. It will be good as new. And if you help me, there will be a reward. Agree? Blink once for yes, twice for no."

He blinks once.

"Good." I tap the inside of his forearm just below the elbow, cutting off pain to his hand. "I'm going to reset the bone. You should feel nothing."

He looks scared and confused. There's an audible snap as I reset the bone. I reach into the small medical cabinet and find two small slats of coral to fashion a rudimentary splint.

"I'm going to release you. You'll have full control of your body again, but your hand will be numb for the next ten or twelve hours to help you sleep and heal. You will not speak of our conversation to anyone."

His eyes dart back and forth nervously. Then he remembers, once for yes, twice for no, and blinks.

"Good." I tap his neck.

He scrambles away from me. "Witchcraft," he mutters. "Like the old man."

"Within the month, Carrick," I say.

"It's true what they said—you killed the monster of the Citadel, didn't you?"

"Within the month," I repeat.

Carrick rushes through the porthole and out of the hut. I take a deep breath.

No going back now.

The days pass even more slowly as I wait. I stew in my anger, pressing it down, letting it simmer. *Carrick's reneged on the promise,* I think. *I'll have to kill him.* I'm ready to lash out at anyone, anything. I've taken a step, but I want the thing finished already. I want to see my father's eyes when he's forced to face me. I meditate on the image every night; I chew on it every moment while stitching a laceration or resetting a bone.

My healing gains the trust of the men and sparks their fear. Carrick has been sworn not to talk, but rumors of my stealing Faria's mysterious skills abound. Coupled with Goth's death, I've garnered a mystique. In the Wendigo, fear equals respect. Those who before would avoid me out of disgust, now do so out of a weird deference. I am not content with this, though. I want true power. My soul aches for it.

"Don't be anxious, Edmon," Faria counsels. "There's no way to hasten what's coming. The opportunity will find you."

Before the month is out, there's an accident in the mines. A small avalanche injures several Haulers, including Bruul Vaarkson, and the grizzled, stinking bear of a man slides into the healer's hut.

"Well, if it isn't old Baldy Patch and the Black Tattoo. You're moving up in the world, eh, sweet thing? You two would make a popular aquagraphic comedy duo, you know that?" The big Nightsider grins crookedly. "The boys insist I have you look at the old ankle. Just don't try nuthin' indiscreet with those delicate hands of yours, Baldy Patch. The Warden has my back and so does my gang."

I kneel and take hold of the man's knee. I press into the pressure point in his thigh.

"Hey, you . . . hey, it doesn't hurt anymore," Vaarkson says, astonished.

I gently remove his boot and roll up the pant leg, revealing the purple swollen shinbone. The fracture is not compound or broken through the skin. *Perfect. This won't be too complicated.*

"It's broken," I say. "I'm going to reset the bone." There's a crack of ligaments and tendons as I place the bone into position. I reach into the medicine cabinet and pull out a sea-sponge liniment. I wrap the thick leg in the wet cloth, which hardens into a cast upon contact with skin.

"You should take easier duty for the next few days. By then the cast should be strong enough to bear weight. It'll naturally fall off once the bone's fully healed."

Vaarkson smiles slyly. "Well done, Little Baldy."

"And now for payment." I stare back.

"Oh?" he mocks. "Little Baldy wants another roll in the ice?"

"You once asked for an alliance," I say calmly. "I accept. I'll ally with the Haulers and serve only them."

"Is that so?" His wiry eyebrows arc with interest.

"If the Haulers follow me as foreman."

His shocked face bursts into laughter.

"You'll be leader in name and wear the tattoo of the black fist on your neck, but you'll take orders from me," I say with deadly seriousness.

His face turns hot. "You insolent—"

My fingers tap a pressure point on his knee, releasing the flow of energy I'd diverted. Pain floods into his leg. He howls and grips his shin. "You son of a—"

"Give me control of the Haulers or die."

Vaarkson stands even in his pain. He's too weak to attack, but he rages just the same. "You've signed your warrant, Baldy Boy! Only one way to become foreman—kill the foreman of your assigned gang in a sanctioned duel. Wendigo code!" *The rules of Combat echo even here,* I think. "Challenge me, and you'll know pain!"

"Face me now then," I respond calmly.

Of course he does not. The disgusting lump slowly moves to the porthole.

"Coward. I'll be waiting when you're ready," I say. "By the way, Bruul," I call out as he goes. "You'll never be able to 'claim' anyone ever again. I've seen to that."

He looks at me with confusion, then spits venomously into the fire as he exits.

"Nicely done. Your next move?" Faria asks from his corner.

"Speak with Jinam Shank," I reply.

The bait has been set. The trap must be sprung.

I wait weeks. So does Vaarkson. His leg heals, and I make myself more visible in the Wendigo. I take my food from the Ration Bar, I walk among the camps at night, and I make circuitous routes through the shantytown, always taking the same path home. I'm flaunting my reputation recklessly, daring him, but I no longer see predatory hunger in the Hauler foreman's eyes. Instead, I see fear, and I smile to myself.

I've taken his sexual function from him. Men are so easily disrupted. He feels helpless and unsure without it. He'll find other ways to dominate his men, other outlets for his cruelty, but soon his terror and anger will get the better of him. I'm ready.

News of the outside world reaches us through the first shipment of "new fish" distributed on the auction block in years. Some are thieves and cutthroats. Most, however, are political dissidents, protesters against the Pantheon and College of Electors.

"Old Wusong has finally died," they say, and my father has taken his throne. A man not of the line of the Great Song sits at the head of the great houses for the first time in over seven hundred years. House Wusong-Leontes is the newest bloodline among the Pantheon, though Miranda bears no son, and her "husband" is declared indisposed.

Edric's position is precarious. The younger generation has also stepped into power. Hanschen of the Julii sits on the College of Electors. Perdiccus of Mughal has completed the rite of patricide, taken the title of Patriarch, and has been elected to his ancestral seat on the High Synod. Both oppose my father's decisions at every turn. The wheels of government have halted. The friction is mere prelude to a coming conflagration; the common people are a powder keg sitting between the sparks.

And I'm trapped in here, I think, fuming.

Planetary weather patterns become more erratic. Crops and fish die. Shortage of work leaves the food lines interminable. Lowborns suffer and are restless and angry. The ranks of dissidents swell and so does the population of the Wendigo.

"Something must be done!" the people cry.

Some still look to the broken Pantheon for hope. Others put faith in a savior to lead them from the wasteland. My name's still bandied about by some, but another bears the weight of undying adulation.

The cult of Phaestion says the heir of Julii is immortal. They say his mother is a sea goddess his father was awarded by the ancestors after his victory in the arena. (That no one has ever seen Phaestion's mother only gives this tale credence.) They say he's the greatest warrior of his generation. Others that he is the Great Song reincarnated. They say he will win the Combat and bring a new golden age to Tao. To me it seems the Julii propaganda office has done well at bolstering its heir's inevitable grab for power. Religious fervor often brings out the violence in the human soul.

I can't lose focus, I remind myself. *Keep your mind on the task at hand.*

I walk to the Ration Bar and take my seat amid the gangs. I'm alone even in a crowd. There's a tension in the air; I feel the whispers and furtive gazes as I eat. *It's happening now,* I realize.

I make my way past the Haulers' table with purpose. I glance at the gang, including Bruul Vaarkson, with an unspoken challenge. *Come and get me.*

I pass the table of Pickers and Jinam Shank. He looks nervous, his eyes shifting back and forth. I tap the table with my knuckles, the signal that was agreed upon. I can tell his stomach is churning. Shank's not the type to upset the balance of things, though he'll gladly take any reward as long as someone else does the heavy lifting.

I move through the shantytown toward my hut and wait for the voice I know will come.

"Edmon?"

"What are you doing here, Toshi?"

It's just like Vaarkson to be so stupid as to send this slithering toad eel to me. Frankly, I'm surprised the scrawny man's still alive. His strategy to survive through duplicity must be more advantageous than I thought.

"Vaarkson is coming for you, tonight," he murmurs. "Don't go back to your hut."

"Vaarkson wouldn't challenge me against The Warden's orders," I reply, brushing him aside.

"He plans to take your life and ask questions later, Edmon. You're still enough of a problem that any punishment The Warden gives won't be so severe."

Toshi might be right. My father may have told The Warden not to kill me, but it doesn't seem that he mentioned not harming me. Any way to pass my death off as unavoidable or not of his doing might be politically expedient. I've been raped and tortured since my first days here. Edric doesn't want me protected; he wants me in pain.

"The Haulers are too strong, and Vaarkson too entrenched as their leader. The Warden won't remove them from power even if they disobey," Toshi reasons.

"That's a lot of faith in one gang," I retort.

"Vaarkson has planned this for months. You won't survive without my help."

I laugh. "Why would I take your help?"

"I've betrayed you once," he admits, "so trust my betrayal now. You wouldn't have moved against Vaarkson unless you felt absolutely safe. You have something up your sleeve. I'm betting on you, but in return, I need assurance that when the storm settles—"

"You'll still be standing." I stare at him, giving nothing away—yet.

"We have a pact?" he asks.

Indeed, I trust Toshi's traitorous nature to seek the winning side, whichever he thinks that is. Unfortunately for him, I know I'm going to win.

"Listen closely." I put my arm over his shoulder. "Tonight, while the Haulers move against me, the Pickers will raid their camp, killing any left there. The Haulers will return to find corpses. The Pickers will then fall upon them unaware."

"Are you insane?" Toshi asks. "If you wipe out the Haulers completely, how will the system work? How will The Warden not seek retribution?"

"He may select scapegoats, but there will be no evidence that the Pickers or I were behind it. He can't afford to lose too many of us. The workforce will be partitioned to create a new Hauler Gang. A new foreman will be selected."

"A new foreman?" he inquires.

"Don't get ahead of yourself, Toshi," I growl menacingly, and he shrinks. "Now be of service. We need a place to lay low while the attack happens."

"I know the best hiding spots in the Wendigo."

"I remember," I agree.

"This way." He gestures. I follow him through the shantytown. We move swiftly to avoid prying eyes.

"Where are we going?" I play dumb.

"Shelter once, you shelter always." Toshi grins.

Vaarkson, you're such a fool. "That place was no shelter for me." I stop in my tracks. It isn't a stretch to feign fear of returning to the scene.

"No one will be there now. Trust me. They're preparing their attack at the healer's hut."

"No!" I walk away. *I need to make it look good.*

"Edmon, if you go anywhere else, they'll find you, and I'll be dead."

He's going to reveal he was trying to betray me again, in order to gain my trust.

"They knew that you'd refuse me. Please. I was supposed to make sure that you went to the Ration Bar, where they could beset you with their main force. They're waiting at your hut if I couldn't convince you. The cavern is the only safe place, I swear!"

I slam him to the ground. "I hear lies in your voice." I smile menacingly, and he quivers underneath my grip. The power his fear gives me is intoxicating. "Speak another word and I'll kill you."

This is why Vaarkson does what he does. It's why my father is who he is. The rush of domination. The violence within awakening. I'm self-horrified, but right now, I need to become a horror. I glare through the back of Toshi's skull.

"Your plan will fail," he says, sniveling. "There are no Haulers in camp tonight. The Pickers will find it deserted."

"Where are they?" I growl.

"The cave!" he cries. "If you don't go there, they have men ready to report on anywhere you roam. They'll kill you wherever they find you. It doesn't matter. You're dead by morning. They've bought off Shank, too. They knew you were trying to form an alliance with him. The only difference is, if I fail to bring you, my life's forfeit, too. I've no choice, Edmon. I didn't then. I don't now. I beg of you . . ."

My stomach drops. *I am alone. It doesn't matter. I wouldn't have it any other way.*

"Take me to the cave," I say. "Now."

"You're going to let me live?"

"If we survive tonight, I won't kill you," I say.

"How are we going to survive?" he asks.

"I'm not sure we are, Toshi."

The dead-end cavern. I've seen the place in my nightmares. Toshi shakes as he steps forward. The place is seemingly empty, and the silence only heightens his fear. I know we're not alone, though. I can hear heartbeats. All of them.

"The hammer falls, Baldy Patch." The snarl bounces off the walls. Toshi and I turn to see Vaarkson at the head of his gang. They flood into the cavern from behind and surround us. The bear of a man steps forward gritting brown teeth at me. "I met you here once and had my way with you. I might have been content with your humiliation, but you wouldn't leave it alone. Now I'll kill you."

"What's wrong, Bruul?" I mock. "You don't want to have me bent over for old time's sake?" The big man shifts nervously. "Oh, you haven't told the rest of your gang? Haven't told them that you can no longer get it up for anyone?"

There are murmurs within the ranks of Haulers. Vaarkson grabs me by my ragged furs. "What the hell did you do to me? I swear by the ancestors—"

"Swear all you like." I laugh. "You'll never be able to harm anyone again." I call out to the rest of his gang now. "Your foreman's a limp dick piece of whale dung." I tap my fingers against Vaarkson's forearms, and his muscles involuntarily fire, releasing me from his grip. I back away and address the crowd. "He's not fit to lead, but I am."

The crowd of Haulers bursts into laughter. "We'd never follow you as our foreman, outcast!"

"Oh?" I ask. I raise my hand. At the signal, the Pickers, hidden on their lines and cables stolen from work lockers, rappel from the shadows above. They hang over the Hauler Gang, catching them unaware. Some Haulers make for the cavern exit, which is blocked by Jinam Shank and a handful of his strongest men.

"This needn't be settled by blood," I call out. "Haulers, follow me, and you all live. All but one," I say coldly and look at Vaarkson.

"Son of a whore," Vaarkson growls. "The Haulers will never follow you!"

Nobody moves. The rivals hold shivs and chains toward one another in a deadly standoff.

"Attack this twinkfish now!" Vaarkson screams. Again, nobody moves. "Why don't you attack?" he screams.

"They haven't decided which of us is going to win," I respond casually.

It's true that Vaarkson bribed Shank to join him here. It's also true that I knew Vaarkson would do that and made an offer Shank couldn't refuse. Shank's not stupid. All the Picker leader has to do is sit back and see how this plays out. If I win, I've offered him the leadership of the Haulers and whatever payment Vaarkson was to give anyway. If I lose, Vaarkson may be mad, but he won't make a move against Shank. Shank will say that he was abiding by the social contract of the Pantheon's code duelo, which echoes even here: one never interferes in a direct challenge. He may incur Vaarkson's anger, but it's doubtful the Hauler will seek immediate retribution. Either way, Shank wins. At least that's what he thinks.

"I know how this is going to end, Bruul," I say. "You're a bully from the arcologies, always bigger and stronger. You fought in the Under Circuit, maybe won some matches. That makes you think you're a dangerous man? You've never faced what real Combat has to offer. Ask Goth of the Citadel if his size mattered. You're nothing more than a street fish. I was born for this."

"You cunt!" he says, spitting.

"Have it your way." I smile.

"You're an outcast. Only one of my gang or a fellow foreman can make a challenge," Vaarkson growls.

He's playing on technicalities, which means he's scared. If he were certain, he'd just kill me and be done with it. They all see it.

"I was a Picker once," I say nonchalantly.

"I make Leontes my second." Jinam Shank detaches from his rope and lands on the floor. "Do you accept his challenge, Vaarkson?"

"Kill him, Bruul!" hecklers from the Haulers shout. "Kill him and rape that sarfish!"

"Pipe!" Vaarkson calls for a weapon.

Challenge accepted. Might makes right on all of Tao, whether with armies or prisoners. The ability to control and kill is the only thing that allows one man to lead and others to follow.

That's how civilization was born, Phaestion once told me. It's almost a relief to accept this. *Win or die is the nature of the universe. Then why do I feel hollow inside?*

Someone, I don't know who, puts a metal pipe into my hand. I twirl it, testing the weight. Vaarkson grins. "I'm looking forward to fucking your dead corpse before I bury you."

I try to think of something witty to retort. I figure silence is probably better for effect anyway. The big man lunges forward, swinging the pipe like a club. He has no finesse but incredible power. I leap to avoid his swing, and the pipe connects with the ice of the ground. Chunks of dirt and snow explode with the blow. The sound reverberates off the cavern walls. The crowd gasps at the sheer force.

True conflicts are often decided within seconds. He who hits first usually wins. I don't even want to attempt to block one of Vaarkson's unwieldy swings lest my weapon shatter, or worse, I do.

"What's the matter, Baldy Patch?" he sneers. "Afraid to face me head-on?" He swings for my head. I duck. He unleashes again, and I sidestep. A third swing aims for my knees, and I leap and roll. I come up, my "blade" at the ready.

The circle of onlookers tightens. The backswing of Vaarkson's pipe catches one of his Haulers in the skull, smashing it like a melon. Blood spatters the crowd, and they whoop with delight. The big man lumbers forward, and his weight transfers heavily to his lead leg as he swings.

Gather intelligence. Hit hardest at the point of weakness. Never engage unless victory is assured. Faria's words come back to me.

"No clever words now, Baldy Patch?"

He steps forward again transferring all of his weight to his front foot. *My chance.* I step aside and flick my weapon at his knee, blowing it out. He crashes to the ground like a sack of bricks.

With one stroke, I've won. I stand over him, savoring the final moments of his desperate life. The crowd hoots. They're about to witness the death of the world they know. Vaarkson crawls through the muck trying to reach the pipe that has fallen from his grasp. I calmly smash my boot onto the top of his hand, breaking it. He stares up with tears of terror streaming from his black eyes.

"Mercy, Leontes," he says, gasping.

"The great Bruul Vaarkson, foreman of the Haulers, asks me for mercy?" I spread my arms wide, addressing the crowd. "Shall I give it to him?"

Vaarkson lashes out with his fist, but I feel the shift in his body before his synapses even fire. I hear his thought to strike long before he reaches me. I deflect the attempt easily, and my finger snaps downward toward the big man's jugular. I touch him at just the right point for the effect that I want and step back.

"There's your mercy," I whisper.

It's operatic, really. I remember the first time The Maestro played *Die Walkure*'s "Ride of the Valkyries." Its thundering melody plays for me now in this moment of triumph.

Vaarkson trembles. He clutches his neck as the veins in his forehead bulge and his face turns purple. He tries to scream, but no sound escapes his lips. Instead, a geyser of blood spews from his open mouth. Then his ears and eyes. He bathes the crowd in a shower of red. The crowd's chants climax with the grotesquery. I raise my fist in victory as Vaarkson collapses in a pool of his own blood.

"I am the foreman of the Haulers!" I call out. "Any who challenge me step forward!"

My words are met with silence.

"Leontes rules the Haulers, and I the Pickers!" Jinam Shank grabs my other hand and raises it to the sky, but the crowd remains quiet.

"No." I smile. "The Pickers are also mine."

Shank's eyes narrow as I continue. "I think it's time for new leadership in the Picker Gang, too. Strong leadership. Don't you agree, Shank?"

I turn to the scarred man, who shakes with anger. I've just called him out for the leadership of his gang after everyone witnessed me murder a man twice his size in a most gruesome fashion.

Before it was just an accident. Now it's just as my father wished. I've become a killer. For Nadia. For my mother. For revenge!

"Don't be stupid, Shank. Submit or suffer Vaarkson's fate," I whisper.

The scars on Shank's face pucker as he scowls. He can't beat me, but he's wrestling with pride. To submit is worse than death. His hand shakes as it hovers near his belt, where he carries a shiv. *Can he grab it and stab the plastic into my guts before I can react?* That's what he's asking himself.

I watch his eyes, his body language, but he has already made the decision. He drops to a knee. "The leadership of the Picker Gang is yours, Leontes."

The crowd cheers. I look down at Shank. Part of me would reach a hand down, stand the groveling man to his feet, clap an arm around his shoulder, and create an ally out of him. Yet Shank has just tainted himself by Tao's laws. I must have no part of the stain. I can't have a man resentful, waiting for his moment to knife me in the back, either. Soon, he'll meet with some unfortunate accident that will remove him as any future threat. I'd rather not kill anyone, but I'm also not sorry enough to stop it.

"One more thing," I call out. "Bring me the one called Toshiro Kodai." There's a rustle within the ranks and the scrawny islander, who

I once thought was to be my only friend in the frozen wastes, steps forward.

"Foreman," he says. He smiles, but his eyes show fear.

"Toshi, when I came to the Wendigo, we were friends. I saved your life." He nods, hoping I will absolve him of his crimes. "Then you betrayed my friendship. You must be punished."

"Edmon, please!" He kneels to grab ahold of my leg and beg, but I kick him in the face before he can reach me. He falls into the snow and muck. I spit on him.

"You're not worth my effort. I've promised I wouldn't kill you. I keep my word. What man will rid me of this meddlesome worm?"

Carrick steps forward.

"Carrick, I make you my second. Kill him."

Is this necessary? I ask myself. *Vaarkson was necessary. Didn't I promise myself I would be better?*

Then I realize, I don't care. "Make him suffer before it ends so all know that no one crosses Edmon Leontes, the leviathan." I turn my back on them and enter the darkness of the tunnel, the tortured screams of a dying man echoing behind me.

CHAPTER 24

Cabaletta Segunda

Months pass. Plans come to fruition. Carrick from the Pickers and a man named Korban from the Haulers sit before me. They lead the gangs publicly while I command in secret. I've beaten all challengers. It's no longer vague fear that motivates followers, but utter faith in my ruthlessness.

"The Smelters and Welders are with us," Korban says, nodding.

"And the Trainmen?" I ask.

Carrick grunts. "They'll halt the cars, but they refuse to fight. They're still afraid to go against The Warden."

"This will be for nothing if we don't unite. The Warden relies on divisions between us. It's all of us, together, or nothing."

"And if we win? Then what?" Korban asks.

"Then we rule."

"Aren't we just inviting the Pantheon to simply bury this place with soldiers?" Carrick asks.

"The nobility of Tao doesn't care who owns these mines so long as production continues. We'll make this place more profitable than The Warden ever could. If that fails, we know these tunnels better than any Meridian soldier. We'll retreat into darkness, letting cold and guerrilla warfare wear them down. They sent us here to die. Now they'll deal or die themselves."

This is the message that I bring the men over and over: *They've forgotten us, thrown away the key. We either remain on our knees as slaves or stand and fight as men.*

"If the trains are stopped, then I don't need their men," I admit. "But tell the Trainmen foreman that if he refuses to fight, he's forfeiting their right to spoils, and his right to lead. I'll challenge him if need be."

"You'd call him out?" Carrick asks.

"Is there any other way?" Thus far, I've managed to avoid having to kill every single foreman. Usually, the mere mention of challenge is enough to spur them to join. Yet I'm willing to do the killing if necessary. That's why they follow me.

Carrick nods. "It'll be done by workday's end."

I look to the old man, who sits like a statue by the fire. He no longer moves and rarely speaks. His energies are concentrated on keeping himself alive. Fear of death drives him. *Perhaps he thinks whatever it is we'd find on the lost world of Miral will save him?* I've told the men Faria's an oracle who is imbued with magical powers to predict the future, that his silence presages the final battle.

"It's time." The words croak from his leathery lips.

I nod in agreement. "We attack at dawn."

The plan is simple. Upon my signal, the Trainmen abandon their posts, bottlenecking everyone in the upper cavern before the workday begins. The Warden will vacate his private quarters to investigate. The Haulers have been slowly smuggling tools from the lockers for weeks. They'll distribute the picks and axes, ropes and cleats to the men. They're not weapons, but in the hands of the willing they'll be effective enough. Once The Warden is exposed, the gangs will overwhelm the guards, capture The Warden, and "persuade" him to pass ownership of the Wendigo to me. My father will have no choice but to meet me in person. I will challenge him to his face, and vengeance will be mine.

I finish my morning meditations, take a deep breath, and look at Faria, who's even more gaunt than ever. "Today's the day, Master," I say. "Soon I'll rule, and you'll escape."

"This is our last chance," he adds quietly, staring blindly into the pale licks of flame.

I exit the hut and walk through the shantytown of the Wendigo to meet destiny. The ramshackle buildings that line the feces-ridden alleys will be a thing of the past. We'll clean this place under my leadership and build proper domiciles. We'll encourage true shops to open and offer incentive to work, rather than the end of the whip. We'll claim our independence from the College of Electors. Faria will take a ship off-world and find his treasure. All will be well. It's a beautiful delusion.

"Edmon!" Korban runs to meet me.

"Why aren't you with the other Haulers?" I ask.

"The Warden and his men were already in the streets before the morning bell!"

They know.

"Have the weapons been distributed?" I ask.

"There was no time," he pants. "The Trainmen have been apprehended. Carrick's running interference with the Pickers, trying to delay The Warden as long as he can, but they're all looking for you. What do we do?"

The plan has been smashed, and there aren't many places to hide. *Who betrayed me?*

"The plan will proceed, but not today. If I'm taken to the Citadel or killed, the gangs must stay together. That's the only way. Do you understand?" I say vehemently.

"Without you, there's no truce. No one's strong enough to maintain your position."

"Faria will do it." I try to keep calm, but there's an edge in my voice.

"The old man?" Korban asks.

"He's stronger than you know," I fire back. "There's no time to debate." I turn back to the igloo.

"Where are you going?" Korban hisses.

"To get the healer," I respond.

"That's the first place they'll look. You'll never make it."

I wave him off and stride forward. I gather energy in my belly. They'll have stationed guards. I've kept my true abilities secret from The Warden. That will give me a temporary advantage. They won't be prepared for what I can do, and I've been itching to let loose.

I open my senses. *Heartbeats. Three of them.* The Warden has underestimated me. I'm going to look forward to this. I smell something, too. *Gas?* They're lacing the area with an irritant. I suck in my breath. I may not be able to completely protect my eyes and mucosal membranes, but I've fought without seeing before.

I round the corner and am hit with the toxic miasma. I move with the swiftness of a shark and am on the guards before they see me. The first throws a punch wildly. I hear it and duck. I slam a short fist into his gut. He collapses like a puppet whose strings have been cut. My fingers lash out and tap the back of his neck as he falls. He'll be paralyzed for the next hour.

I feel the next guard's hand grab my arm. I break it. A subtle movement of my hips and I toss the man to the ground. A quick tap to his neck and his body goes limp, too.

The third pulls his humbaton from a holster and fires. *Damn.* The sound will alert others, which means I've lost time. My foot connects with the side of his knee, destroying the joint. He falls into my hands, which close around his neck in a simple choke. He passes out. All remain alive but down for the count.

I hurry into the hut. "Master, they knew. We must go quickly." I hurry to Faria's side. I can hear the crackling of his joints as I help him off the ground.

"Boy," the old man croaks. "It's too late."

"We can still make it," I insist.

"Fool!" the dark-skinned man barks as we exit the hut.

I drag him with me through the haze, but when my eyes see again, they're confronted by the truth. The Warden stands at the head of over a hundred men wearing the colors of midnight and silver—Leontes guards. The gang foremen of the Haulers, Pickers, Smelters, and Welders are on their knees in front of him. Alberich steps from behind The Warden's bloated body.

"Alberich?" I can't hide my astonishment.

The seneschal appraises me as he addresses me. "Edgaard is dead."

I've horribly miscalculated. *I should have known the Combat was coming.*

"Who?" I ask. My thoughts are for the little boy with the square face and warm blue eyes.

"Sigurd of House Flanders in the aristeia," Alberich replies gravely. The aristeia, the final duel between the last two contestants. "It's time to come home."

I'm a child again, too frightened to move. However, I find my tongue. "Drown in the depths," I respond.

Alberich nods. "Take him." House Leontes's men step forward to bind me.

"No!" My shout erupts like volcano fire, and everything explodes in chaos around me. The entirety of the Wendigo turns on its head in riotous calamity. I'm the eye of the storm, first here then there, throwing fists in every direction. I'll not be taken ever again. I'd rather die.

My boot slams a Leontes guard's helmet, smashing his face to pudding. I feel the sting of a humbaton pulse rip my shoulder, and I drop. I snag a pickax I find on the frozen earth and hurl it in the direction of the shooter. End over end, it whirls until the point thunks into the neck of Greelo. His blood sprays like a fountain as he collapses in the snow.

I punch, I kick, I claw, and I bite. A horde piles on top of me. I can't breathe. I can't see. I don't need to see to fight. One guard goes down, then another, but there are too many. I'm buried under a hill of people. Something sharp strikes the back of my skull. All goes black for a moment. That second is all they need to subdue me. My hands and feet are bound.

"Stand back from him now!" Alberich screams.

Something is jabbed into my arm. *An urchin needle?* My body goes numb. I can see and hear, but I cannot move. Memories of my marriage to Miranda Wusong flash through my head. I look inward to try and counteract the poison, but it works through my system like wildfire. The battle is already over.

The rebellion of the Wendigo is crushed. Guards drag me away, limp and bruised. Through the slits of swollen eyes, I see the remaining foremen on their knees, bullets blasting through the backs of their heads in a spray of red mist. Faria, though, breaks free from my father's men. He stands before Alberich.

"You have what you wanted. Patriarch Leontes promised a reward?"

Faria?

"Edric Leontes thanks you for your service. That's reward enough," Alberich responds.

My father's men grab my mentor. He fights at first, but he's not the man he once was. A humbaton strike to the old man's midsection doubles him over. I lose sight of him under the beatings of my father's men as I'm pulled away.

MOVEMENT III: FINALE

CHAPTER 25

Coda

The return to Meridian is a haze. I'm shoved into a sondi, barely able to stand upright. No matter. I'll heal fast, and nothing will stop me. My rebellion was thwarted, but I'll be led to the same place—face-to-face with my father. I'm no longer the helpless youth who was held down and watched while he murdered my wife and unborn child. I'm no longer a boy who is too small to stop the beating of his mother. Edric desired that I become a killer. Now, he has his wish, and there's only one man in the whole universe I desire to kill. I summon my energies. I've little time to clear the neurotoxins from my cells. I shut out all other thoughts.

Finally, my face is shoved to the floor at the foot of what I remember as the Wusong throne. Now, however, the chair's golden sea monkeys have been replaced with resplendent silver leviathans. The man reigning is not Old Wusong, but a silver-haired titan.

"Edric," I murmur. *One strike is all I will need.* I look up, but the man on the throne is not the father I remember.

He is wrinkled and haggard. Skin sags. Thick veins like bluish worms shine through its sickly yellow hue. The lustrous silver hair now hangs lank. His frame seems flaccid and rickety. His bones pop and creak as he stands. Edric Leontes is horribly changed. In my five years of exile, he has aged more than thirty.

"Rise," he whispers.

My plans to murder fall away as I'm too shocked to react.

"Strip him," his voice rasps. Guards descend upon me tearing the rags from my body. I don't resist. Edric's pale eyes take me in from head to toe. "Alberich." He gestures to his seneschal, who lumbers forward to help the decaying skeleton down the steps. He hands Edric a cane of whale ivory, a silver leviathan head for its pommel.

My father shuffles toward me, the cane tapping eerily. He squints.

The hate I'd been so long preparing turns to ash in my mouth. All I feel is surprise and pity.

He takes in my smooth scalp and my emaciated physique. "You look terrible," he croaks.

"Take a look in the mirror," I spit back.

His lips curl into a sneer as he shuffles past me. "I'm not what you remember." Several lung-bursting coughs rack the old man. Alberich quickly returns the old man to the throne and fetches him a drink.

"Poison." Edric gestures to the flagon in his hand. "Corocona. A rare herb scoured from the depths of some Theran jungle. Highly addictive. The doctors tell me the precursor was introduced into my blood not long after you left. You see, the drug needs multiple components in order to take effect. The precursor is harmless on its own. It only becomes deadly when bonded with a catalyst, making it all the harder to trace the source. The effects were subtle at first. Headaches, dizziness, loss of equilibrium. Most victims don't know they've been dosed. Most are dead within weeks when the toxin's removed from the diet. I'm not most."

"You're one of the lucky ones?" I taunt.

"I'm a two-time champion of the—" He doubles over in a fit of coughing.

A dying two-time champion, I think.

"I consulted physicians, top pathologists from Prospera's academy on Lyria. They said removing the toxin from my body would cause instant paralysis and death. So I continue to take the contaminant and complete a slow downward spiral, watching myself wither into decrepitude."

"Your body now matches your soul." I laugh at the bitter irony. I should kill him anyway. For my mother. For Nadia. Yet I realize someone has already done the work in a far crueler fashion than I could ever have dreamed. All I have to do is nothing, and I can watch him waste away in agony.

I feel triumphant, and I feel robbed. I've lived for vengeance for so long, to have it yanked from me like this . . . I laugh to keep myself from crying.

"I need you, Edmon," he croaks. I laugh harder. "Edgaard is dead. Those who have sought to destroy our house by murdering him and poisoning me must be punished."

Tears stream down my face as I shake with amusement. "And what does that have to do with me?"

"I've watched your progress, my son. You've faced challenges. You've become strong."

My laughter ceases. "You knew what happened to me in the Wendigo. You made sure I was kept alive in the event you needed me."

"If you died, you were too weak anyway. But you didn't, and now, you're ready. Take your place as my heir. Enter the Combat. Claim your place with the Electors. Stop the madness, this cult of Phaestion."

"I'll never fight for you!" I gnash my teeth, cutting off his monologue. "You beat my mother in front of my eyes, then lobotomized her. You strangled my wife, the mother of my unborn child, while your men held me down. You slew all the people I held dear and condemned me to darkness. You think I'd raise one finger for you?"

"You've no idea what's at stake," he whispers.

"Nor do I care. I'd rather kill you right here!"

"Do it!" he challenges. "Show me what you've learned. Commit the ritual patricide!"

That's exactly what he wants, isn't it?

I shake my head. "I'd rather watch you slowly wither."

"You're still weak," he accuses. "You think I'd let you kill me, while you still don't understand?" The thick cords of his veins bulge. "You could never see past your own selfishness, Edmon, never one action further than the next—"

"Says the man who bites the very hand he asks for help," I reply.

"What choice do either of us have now, son?"

My scornful musing soars. "I've the greatest choice. I choose to do nothing." I stand before him, naked, but fearless.

"We will force you into the arena. Do nothing, you'll die, and all the people you love, their deaths will go unanswered," Alberich growls.

"No one was talking to you, servant," I snap. He still clings to his honor, and my words dare him to attack.

Instead, he flicks his eyes to signal to a guard who enters the room and lunges at me from behind. I move without thinking. The world becomes like an orchestra as the skills Faria taught me take over. The guard touches me, a note on a piano. I counter with a rhythm of breaking his wrist. A gentle lyric as I duck the blow of his fist. A rising crescendo as my fingers lift to the spot in his chest where the energy flows. The crash of a cymbal as he falls, paralyzed. Drumbeats of another throne-room guard running to his aid. I howl in time as my kick casually punctuates a pop to his solar plexus. Chimes as he sails and a bell when I tap between his helm and neck to put him to sleep. I take a deep bow before the throne. My father and his seneschal sit unmoving.

"Bravo! Bravo! Shall I delight you with an encore?" I ask. "I think not. I'll not fight for you," I answer.

"It's in your nature. It's in every living thing that crawled from the muck to reach for the stars. You may be too dull to divine the disaster that confronts our race, or my reasons for why I've done what I've done, but if the pain I've caused you was truly so great, you would've let yourself die long ago. So stop whining about your mother and dead wife. Be man enough to kill me or kill yourself and join them. Otherwise, stop wasting your breath pretending you will."

Edric nods at the men crumpled before me, now twitching. "Get them all out of my sight."

—

I'm walked down palace halls flanked by Alberich and silent guards. We stop at a med bay where some minutes in a healing tank, combined with my own abilities, mend my contusions. All around I look for avenues of escape. I'm escorted to a small, but lavish room where a feast is laid before me.

"Regain your strength so that we may resume your training tomorrow," Alberich says. "There's a uniform on the bed." He gestures to a folded navy-and-silver garment. "The funeral is in one hour. All the great houses will respect the fallen. Phaestion of the Julii will light the pyre so that Edgaard's sparks may join the ancestors among the Elder Stars."

"Phaestion? Shouldn't it be Edric?" I ask.

"Phaestion's Companions have become powerful forces within the government. Edgaard was the last credible threat to their triumph. The Julii prince insisted on this symbolic honor."

"Edric loses his preeminence. I care not. One thing I've learned, Alberich, great warriors don't necessarily make great leaders. The strongest man isn't always the better man."

"You think Phaestion is the better man?" he asks. "Put on the uniform. I'll return in an hour."

—

The purple of Meridian twilight is lit with the electric brilliance of every fireglobe in the city. I'm heralded by silver trumpets. I can almost hear the aquagraphic telecasters commenting—

Edmon Leontes, the once handsome and rebellious scion . . . what's happened to him?

"Eyes forward, Edmon," my father rasps. He leans on his cane and beckons me to stand beside him on a balcony overlooking the city.

"Hello, brother." A woman with raven hair peeks from around my father's shoulder.

"Lavinia," I mutter, meeting her violet gaze.

"You look uglier than the last time we spoke."

"Prison requires disfiguration," I allow. "I feel much more at home with you all because of it."

I lean on the railing and look to the lower balcony where Edric's concubines—Lady Tandor, Rosalind Calay, and Olympias of House Flanders—as well as my sister Phoebe and her pudgy husband, Beremon Ruska, watch the sky procession.

"Quit your bickering," Edric says, coughing. "Were I blessed with children as obedient as they are proud, I might actually enjoy the last few years of pain before me."

"If you had children like that, they'd all be like Edgaard: dead." I smile. Lavinia snickers.

"Edgaard died honorably, husband." A cold, clammy hand grasps mine from behind. I know the face to expect before I turn. The white-powdered, moon-shaped face and black teeth of Miranda Wusong, the last remnant of the imperial house, looks back at me.

"There is no honor in death," I say quietly. "Only ashes or food for worms."

Miranda doesn't bat an eye. "I'm so happy to see you." Then under her breath: "A word misspoken by an heiress out of favor quickly hastens her fall from grace. You did not better my position by incurring your father's wrath. Though you saved me from having to endure your company."

I feel a pang of guilt. This woman no more desired to be a game piece in her forebears' schemes than I did. Yet she has met the challenge with a dignity that I've rejected.

Drums beat a tattoo, reminding me of the Eventide on Bone. This beat, however, is regimented, and portends the wails of riders.

The black screamers round the avenue in trident formation, the black-and-purple capes of their riders whipping in the wind. The most handsome man you might ever see heads the pack. His smooth face looks carved of ivory, and he has high cheekbones, a square jaw, and lips perhaps just a shade too full for a man. His shock of thick, coppery hair floats behind him. A giant sondi circling above us broadcasts an enormous aquagraphic screen pasted to its flanks. I catch the close-up of Phaestion's fierce gray eyes beneath his silver diadem. Voices erupt from the scraper windows, cheering for the handsome warrior. It's beyond excitement. It's worship.

"They used to cheer for me like that," Edric rasps.

His cough turns into an uncontrollable spasm. He doubles over, trying not to spew spittle in front of the hovering camglobes. Miranda scrunches her face at the sour smell.

"They never cheered for you quite like that, Father," Lavinia says quietly.

Alberich helps Edric stand upright and regain composure. "Our ancestors worshipped dying gods. Divine martyrs." He laughs. "This boy wants to resurrect such cravenness in his own image!"

"Make a man a god and they'll do more than follow him," says Lavinia. "They'll sacrifice. Maybe Phaestion plies the very catalyst needed to galvanize our people to change."

War made civilization, Phaestion said when we were boys.

"House Julii perverts the principles of arête and the Balance," my father snaps. "They should be our only gods."

He's only jealous it's not him, I think.

"They say he's immortal, that his mother is a goddess," Miranda chimes in.

"He's no more immortal than his old crone father, who was probably put in cold storage." Edric spits blood into a handkerchief. "I doubt that old fool had the courage to truly undergo the patricide, though Phaestion now wears the orca tattoos."

The procession stops. Phaestion gracefully steps from his screamer onto a floating platform, flanked by three others wearing the black and purple.

"What do you see?" my father asks.

Phaestion's honor guard removes their helms. I look up at the aquagraphic on the sondi to view them in close-up. The first is delicately boned, has pale skin and almost-white hair, and moves with a feline sensibility. On his left breast is the silver symbol of the orca pride. *Hanschen.*

The second has hair of spun gold that hugs ruddy cheeks in tight curls. His body is tall, wiry, and athletic. His eyes flash a wild blue, and it seems he represses an insatiable grin even on this solemn occasion. He wears the symbol of the manta. *Perdiccus of House Mughal.*

The last is huge. He looks uncomfortable in the black formal suit as if his muscles were going to burst from it. His blond hair is cropped close to his skull, and his face is broad beneath pale eyes. He stalks forward, on his chest the great toothed mako. *Sigurd, of course.*

"My old friends all grown," I say with disdain.

"Did you doubt they'd be here? What else?" Edric hisses.

This reminds me of sitting with Faria in the Citadel air vents listening to prisoners and answering his quizzing. A lone screamer enters view as it careens around the Wusong building. It pulls a coffin like a chariot dragging a fallen warrior behind it. The crowd hushes. Most fallen combatants are honored. This is beyond that. Edgaard is the heir of a house. That itself might warrant such ostentation. Still . . .

"Edgaard must have put up some fight," I murmur. I note my brother's pale face, smooth behind the glass panel of the coffin. His thick blond hair is pulled into a ponytail. He's dressed in a black uniform of House Julii, the silver medal of the leviathan pinned to his chest.

"Edgaard is wearing the colors of House Julii." I speak the thought aloud.

My father's eyes turn to me like a reptile's.

"All of them—Perdiccus, Sigurd . . . all houses swear allegiance to the Julii?"

"The remarkable speed with which your brain works astonishes me, brother," Lavinia says, dripping sarcasm.

"All prominent families claim their heirs to be Companions now. House Leontes alone remains," Edric says. "A few lesser vassals join us, but Edgaard was the last. Now in death, that fiend claims my boy as his."

"What of their fealty to House Wusong?" I ask.

"Your blushing bride's the last of the bloodline. What do you think?" Edric flicks a gnarled hand in Miranda's direction. The emperor's proud daughter bears the insult with feigned ignorance. She should have been Edgaard's bride, but Old Wusong insisted that it be I who take her hand. *Poor Miranda.*

Phaestion, Hanschen, Perdiccus, and Sigurd carry my brother's coffin to a bier built on the center of the platform.

"If he aligns all houses, there will be a united government, as in the days of the first emperor," I say.

"One world under an orca flag," Lavinia muses.

"Not the whole world. There's an entire people who will not follow," I add coldly.

"You mean the mongrel islanders?" Edric laughs acidly.

"Derides the man who fathered a half-breed."

"I wasn't born noble, either, Edmon. I'm more liberal in thinking than you suppose. But islanders count little in the game of Meridian politics."

"Then why disparage unity of the Pantheon other than for the reason it's not you who's doing it?" I ask.

"If it accomplished a worthy purpose . . ." He nods.

"You hoped Edgaard would slay Sigurd and claim the glory that Phaestion plans for himself?"

"That would have been a start. At the very least, I prevented that little redhead whale shit from turning my own children to his cause."

"Did you?" I retort. "It seems that in death, Phaestion has cloaked Edgaard in his colors, not yours."

My father scowls, the corded veins of his neck writhing as he clenches his jaw. He knows I'm right. Edric's political power has diminished to the point where he can't even control the narrative of his own child's death.

"The son you bred from high blood failed," I say. I can't bring myself to truly hate Edgaard, though he was complicit in Nadia's death. He had been brainwashed. Demeaning the old man, however, and the son he loved better is the only satisfaction I have now.

"Today we honor the glorious dead!" Phaestion's voice is amplified across the skyway. Edgaard's coffin opens. Phaestion leans down and kisses Edgaard's forehead with his own in the gesture of brothers. He's not Edgaard's brother; I am. Yet I stand so far away.

"Rest now, son of Leontes."

Sigurd hands Phaestion a torch, and he lights the bier, which erupts in a blaze that smokes to the heavens. Edgaard Leontes joins the Elder Stars.

The loss of knowledge, the loss of joy. Faria's right—there is nothing beyond death. Death is the ultimate waste, and this place reeks of it. I promise myself I will never take another life from this world. Though if Father has his way, either I or Phaestion will soon be burning, too.

CHAPTER 26

Canzonetta

"Your reaction speed was point-oh-four-percent increase from standard of our last engagement," the metallic voice of Mentor, the automaton program my father has purchased to train me for the arena, follows me as I head back to my quarters. My body is exhausted from the training session, but my mind is still on fire with the possibilities.

"Thank you, Mentor." *I'm getting better, faster,* I think.

For the past several months, I've been cooped up on this level of the Wusong Palatial Towers. My days have been filled only with eating, sleeping, and training against the Mentor program. Over and over, repeat, repeat. My father knows that Phaestion has been training with the Arms of Agony since he was a boy. Mentor is Edric's countermeasure. I would refuse to comply with my father's demand that I ready myself for Combat, but the exertion keeps my body and mind sharp, and the abundance of food is a much-needed change from the meager offerings of the Wendigo.

Edric knows I've killed in prison to survive, but he doubts that I will do so at his command. He's right. I have no intention of entering the arena. My desire is escape. *Soon . . .*

I've been looking for a way out since I've returned to Meridian, but I've been under heavy lock and key. Security camglobes hover through every corridor, and I'm closely guarded by my father's men, too. I was freer in the Citadel, but if I can survive there, I can survive this. *If I'm getting faster, my chances of evasion increase.*

Yet even if I could escape Wusong Palatial Towers, where would I go? I'd not make it far on foot. I must wait for opportunity . . . What that opportunity is, I've no idea, so I stay aware and patient. My escape will not come from hidden air vents or a service pneumovator. It will not come from battle or glorious rebellion. In the world of Meridian twilight, it will come from political subterfuge.

I was never adept at employing machinations or deceit to achieve my aims, but I promised my mother and Nadia I would make their deaths have meaning. If that's the skill I must gain to do it, so be it. I originally thought that taking revenge on my father was the way to honor their memories. Now all I can think is that somehow escaping my fate is the answer. *Where to go? The golden city of Prospera on Lyria?* The Maestro would speak of its glittering spires and libraries. *Or maybe to the treasures of Miral, whatever they may be?* Faria seemed to think finding that would give his life meaning. *Will it bring meaning to mine or the memory of my family? Did Faria, my last friend, betray me to my father?* That question still gnaws at my brain.

The plump form of my younger sister, Phoebe, and her fat husband, Beremon Ruska, suddenly appear at the end of the corridor to block my path. *Here's a surprising deviation from the monotony,* I think.

"Mentor," I whisper. "Mute vocalizations."

The couple greet me with cherubic faces. I haven't seen them since the funeral, and I don't think I've ever spoken more than two words to them in my entire life.

"Brother Edmon!" Phoebe embraces me. I'm caught off guard. Phoebe has never been cunning like our sister Lavinia, but she is a Leontes, so anything is suspect.

"Phoebe?" I peel her off me. "What do you want?"

"Edmon, it's good to see you." Beremon steps forward. The bronze buttons on Ruska's house uniform threaten to burst off his coat. He trips over himself to clasp my hand in his.

"Beremon, Edmon is tired from training," Phoebe chides. "Forgive us, Edmon. We're both just glad to see you. We've been trying to get Father's permission, but he hasn't allowed anyone other than Alberich in the barracks."

"I'm not surprised," I mutter.

"Don't think ill of him, Edmon," Phoebe chides.

She suggests I should be kind to our father? Now I suspect her intentions in meeting me even more.

"He has tried to do the best for all his children in the best way he knows how."

Anger wells inside me. "What do you speak of? You've no idea what he's taken from me."

The little girl who hid behind her mother's skirts doesn't flinch at my fury. Beremon bumbles forward. "Now, Edmon, if you take that tone—"

"It's fine, Beremon." Phoebe holds up a hand to silence her husband. "Edmon is right. We don't know what he's been through. But"—she steps forward, voice dropping to a whisper—"you're not the only one who has experienced abuses. Some of us are just wise enough not to say it in this house." Her eyes flick to the walls and the ceiling, indicating listening devices.

I file away that knowledge.

"Perhaps." I smile, impressed by her intelligence and courage, neither of which I knew she had. "But Father knows what I think of him, sister."

"Maybe," Beremon says. His jocular demeanor drops. "But that doesn't mean you know your true allies or enemies."

This just got far more interesting.

"Are you my allies?"

"No." Phoebe shakes her head. "We don't trust you yet. Whatever happened to you, it's made you uncommitted to any cause other than yourself."

"Your father fights what is happening," Beremon whispers, "but does so out of desire for power. House Ruska follows because at the least he seeks survival of the planet through means other than war. But he's dying. He tries to keep the secret, but people suspect. Edgaard's public funeral didn't help. His physical deterioration is obvious. It's time for a new leader. Choices are few. House Ruska would follow someone with your father's goals, but who would serve the people who give him power."

"Me?" I ask, flabbergasted at the implication. They do not turn away, so I laugh in their faces. "Forget it." I shove past them toward my room.

Phoebe stops me. "If you don't claim your birthright, someone else will."

"Edgaard was his perfect son. He would've been father's puppet," I sneer. "Not me."

"Edgaard was a good boy who idolized you," she says bitterly, seemingly no longer concerned by the listening devices. "He was twisted by a father he was trying to please. He wasn't ready to fight The Companions on his own, but you weren't here."

"There are no options left," Beremon says. "For you, House Leontes or Tao."

Or perhaps they've been sent as part of Father's plans to twist me as well? Either way, I'm too broken for what they wish. I want no part of this.

"Father plans to pit me against Phaestion. If I survive, Edric will not leave his house to a half-breed son who won't follow his plans."

"There's no one else," Beremon repeats. "House Ruska is your friend."

Make friends with me and end up dead. It's a kindness to say, "I have no friends."

"You're one of the few in a position to do something," Phoebe pleads. "You have a duty—"

"I'm a prisoner. I owe you and this family nothing!"

Tears well in Phoebe's eyes. "The boy you were, the one who sang about freedom, he's gone, isn't he? You know, I had all your recordings, all your songs. I knew all the words. We all did."

I want to turn away, ashamed, but I steel myself. Doing what they ask will only result in my death and theirs. They say that I'm the only one who can do anything, but only by killing. When will it ever stop?

"You're getting ahead of yourselves." Lavinia's porcelain face stares at us at from the end of the hall. "First, Edmon has to win the Combat."

"You doubt I can, Lavinia?"

"We all doubt, brother," Lavinia says, smirking. "You most of all."

"Beware eels in the nest, Edmon," Beremon whispers. "Honeyed tongues hide poisoned teeth." He takes Phoebe's arm and walks past Lavinia.

I turn into my quarters, and Lavinia trails behind. "I didn't invite you in," I remark.

"I don't need permission," she replies.

I sit as the bed automatically slides out from the wall. Anxious for sleep, I close my eyes as Lavinia waits impatiently. "I'm the majordomo of House Wusong-Leontes, second only to Father. Since his illness, I lead—"

"You weaken yourself by asserting your own significance," I interrupt. "If you were so important, you wouldn't need to mention it at all. You want something. So speak."

"Mentor, recording devices on barracks level, off!" she commands. "What did our fat, little sister and her imp of a husband offer?"

"Friendship." I keep my eyes closed.

"Did you accept?"

"Acceptance isn't required if friendship's true."

"That's no answer," she says.

Annoying her is fun, but I really need to rest. *What would my mother want me to do? What would Nadia want? Would they want me to become a Nightsider and fight for Tao's better tomorrow as one of the elite? Would they want me to murder again and again, desecrate my soul to achieve a new world? How can a ruler bring peace who rises by blood? I'm a shadow of the boy I was.*

"I'll ask again, what do you want, Lavinia?"

"To remind you of who you are." She walks to the table, the only adornment in my quarters save the bed. On it, she places a glass cube. "Play," she says. Water leaps from the cube, creating a liquid screen. The image of a swarthy, bearded man fills the aquagraphic, and the room erupts with opera.

"Andreas Catalano?" I ask, my eyes opening.

"He's in his nineties now. Still middle-aged for most denizens of the Nine Corridors—"

On Tao, most die long before that because we murder one another. All except the decrepit old rulers who gain power at the expense of their one chance at glorious death in their youth.

"Get on with it," I say.

"He tours the stars playing for chairmen, CEOs, and kings. You were thought by some to have a voice as lovely as his once, weren't you? Forward," she calls out.

The voice that fills the room now is mine. I'm singing "The Song of Edmon," the lullaby my mother sang to me and The Maestro wrote words for, the song that caused my father to throw me into the Wendigo. The young face on the screen sports a shock of thick, dark hair and a look of hope.

"Your music played in the streets of Meridian and on every island from Leaf to Rock," she says.

I stand, towering over her delicate frame. "Make your move or leave. I'm on borrowed time."

She shakes her head. "I've already told you, dear brother. I'm here to make you remember who you are." She points at the aquagraphic. "You're an artist. Not some fighter. Not some Patriarch. Maybe Phoebe was right? Maybe you have changed?"

So she overheard at least some of the conversation in the hall. I should have been more aware. Faria taught me better than to be caught off guard. Phoebe was also right—I'm unfocused.

"The old Edmon would never have allowed Father to keep you trapped. I offer a way out," she says plainly.

She's trying to manipulate me, but she isn't lying. I hear her heartbeat. I watch her pupil dilation.

"I've suffered too long for this house to let it fall," she says. "Our coffers are dwindling. With Edgaard dead, we'll have no stake in the Pantheon or the College of Electors after Father's expiration. Our only chance is through my leadership and marriage to another noble house."

I laugh. "You'd be Matriarch?"

"There's precedent. Empress Boudika led all of Tao once."

"Boudika was duplicitous, treacherous, and a hedonist. The hybrids, the Pavaka—all were her doing. The difference between you and her was she fought in the Combat and earned her place to make a mess of things."

"I'm no fighter," Lavinia retorts. "Look at me."

She's right. Lavinia is fierce but in a different way. She's slender and petite. I've no doubt that she would scrap until her last breath, but fighting requires bone structure, musculature, and athleticism. Lavinia does not take after our father in this regard. Even her dark hair is an aberration.

"You're not the only disappointment Edric has had, you know," she says bitterly.

For a moment, my heart goes to her. I've always felt different, like I didn't belong. But many of my years were spent on Bone among the Daysiders, who accepted me no matter the color of my skin or hair. I was one of the tribe. Lavinia had to experience growing up the odd fish here in Meridian from the day she was born, among a ruthless and unforgiving people. Her mother would have been no great comfort to her, if memory serves. I had teachers, a mother, a lover, the support of my people at my back. She's had no one. The tune of her ambition, drive, and deceit suddenly harmonizes when played at this tempo.

"We all must know who we are, brother, and what gifts we have to offer. Mine aren't in Combat. However, I do know politics. House Wusong-Leontes holds the Wendigo, but Father hoards its resources to build a fleet, an enterprise that has exorbitant cost and thus far, no recompense. Meanwhile, the Julii have united all the other houses under their banner. They've cut off trade with House Wusong-Leontes and surrounded the Fracture Point with their existing fleet in an attempt to monopolize the port. Edric's actions alienate and bankrupt us. I'd reverse that."

"Seems to me you would sell out to the Julii, give them access to our resources, and allow them to enact whatever plans they have for Tao. Isn't that explicitly what Father doesn't want?" I ask.

"Our only path is to acquiesce and reinforce our position through political alliance."

"So our sweet Lavinia wants to wed," I mock. "Aren't you promised to another?"

"Magnus Johan of House Angkor." She scoffs. "He's weak. He didn't even enter the Combat, nor was he considered to be one of Phaestion's Companions." She stands straight-backed and proud. "Besides, as Matriarch, there's nothing to prevent me from taking more than one husband."

I laugh, fully and loudly. "Forget a second husband. Who'd want to be your first?"

"I'm not desirable because I'm a woman with ambition?" she asks with eyes of violet fire.

"No." I lie back on the cot. "Because you're a hissing siren. I was raised on the islands, Lavinia. My mother was leader. My true wife was the strongest woman you'd ever meet. In fact, I think the right woman would do a much better job of things. You're just not the right woman." She and I should have traded places. If I were a woman, Father never would have taken much interest in me. Lavinia, were she a man, would have been his heir. "I won't destroy Edric simply so you can rule."

"That's what you want, isn't it?" she asks. "Edric destroyed? I merely suggest a mutually beneficial alliance."

"Edric's already dying a painful, slow, death. There's nothing more I can contribute."

"Father has proved more resilient than the doctors first predicted," she seethes.

Interesting. Still, I need more information.

"I only ask that you consider my suggestion. I can save you from the fate Father plans."

"The last time you spoke to me like this, I spent five years in an ice prison," I say.

She turns on her heels, the sound of my voice from the aquagraphic lilting in her wake.

When she's gone, I call out, "Stop!"

The music ceases. I pick up the cube and examine it. It's a rudimentary recording device, not simply a display-only interface. A thought occurs to me—there should be plenty of room to record something else on the device should I find words worth recording. I sit back on my bed, interlace my fingers behind my head, and close my eyes, smiling for the first time in months.

CHAPTER 27

Sotto Voce

Footsteps in the hall. Multiple assailants. I'm out of bed and crouching in the shadows in less than a second. Beads of sweat perspire on my brow. I flash back to the darkness of the Citadel and Faria's training.

Count the sounds. Listen for the heartbeats.

Faria. If his reasons for taking me under his tutelage remain suspect, does that mean his training is, too?

I shut off these thoughts and concentrate.

One, two, three men wearing heavy boots. Guards in full spider-silk body armor. Another step—heavyset but deliberate and athletic—Alberich. A final pair of feet, creaking, shuffling, accompanied by an erratic heartbeat. The syncopation of something tapping the floor? A cane. Edric, too.

They're coming for me.

If they were here to kill, they could do so more easily. If it was surprise training, why bring guards? Why would they surprise me under the threat of armed guard. I've made it clear that I will not fight for Edric . . .

That's it, I realize. *They are going to force my hand. Should I try and escape?*

My gaze flicks to the ventilation system. I could easily defeat them all, but then what? I'd be on the streets, a fugitive with no means of transportation. They're at the door. At least I'll not be caught unaware.

"Lights," I call out. I stand as the door slides open. My father is silhouetted in the frame.

"You're awake," he observes.

"Let's get this over with." I brush past him and stride through the doorway.

Later. House Wusong-Leontes is in full celebration. I'm accorded the privilege of leaving the barracks to attend a banquet in the throne room in honor of my first "victory" in the arena. I don't bother. I want no part of any celebration. I run through the hallways of the Wusong-Leontes Palatial Towers instead. Running, running in circles. Sweat drips from my eyes, and I angrily wipe it from my brow. My thoughts are a cacophony, full of doubt and fury.

Grinner, Goth, Bruul Vaarkson, even Toshi—all would have ended me if I hadn't ended them first. The men of the Under Circuit who I just battled may not have been innocent, either. I could smell the faint ozone pouring from their veins, the mark of a tag user. Tag is an enhancement drug from the jungle world of Thera, the same place that originated the poison that slowly kills Edric. It makes one stronger, faster, some say even smarter at the expense of years of life and extreme addiction. If the underclass is now turning to such narcotics and fighting in death matches, it's a sign of how desperate they have become to escape their poverty. But then I remember Jorund's words from so many years ago: *We're here to stop the theft of our sons and daughters for the Combat.* The men I fought might have been conscripted, forced to fight for the amusement of others. No matter how they ended their lives, none of them started that way. Each was a child with a mother once. Somewhere at some time, someone loved them at least a little, at least once.

Now they are all dead. My stomach twists with sickness. *What happens that turns men to monsters capable of taking a life so easily?*

Why run, boy? the leviathan in my dreams speaks.

Suddenly the lights switch off, and I am in darkness. "Mentor?" I ask.

"Your father has ordered you to cease your exertions. He commands you to enjoy the celebrations or rest and recuperate for your next competition."

To the abyss, you son of a whore!

I stomp through the narrow corridors toward my room. Though I lived a year in darkness, I've no desire to return to such a state. The lights turn back on, and I find Lavinia leaning languidly against my door in a low-cut silk kimono.

"All hail the conquering hero." Her overt display of sexuality is disconcerting.

"I don't have the time, Lavinia."

She blocks me from entering. "Does it feel good?" She grabs the back of my head with a small but strong hand and pulls me close to her lips. "Does it feel good to be a killer? The hot blood of the last victim pouring over you? To know you finally have what you always wanted, Father's love."

I want to burst with laughter at her advances, but I'm too sickened. "Edric knows that I didn't win. I only didn't lose."

Lavinia leans in and kisses me with her cold lips. "You've proven your strength. We can rule, you and I together. Let me handle the politics. You can have everything and everyone else."

My hands encircle her slender hips. I lift her off the floor and gently remove her from the doorway. "Everyone I want is already dead. Go to bed," I say coldly.

"Fool!" she shouts. "I'm your only hope of escape. Otherwise, face your friend in the arena and the civil war that follows. Are you so confident now after killing in one bout?"

"I killed no one!" I roar. The ensuing beat of silence is deafening.

"What do you mean?" she asks.

"They brought me to the arcologies, to a death match in the Under Circuit. Father thought I'd at last be forced to take life in self-defense . . ."

"And you won, of course."

"No." I shake my head. "I evaded them, allowing each combatant to kill one another until only I was the last man standing."

"You cheated!"

"I used the rules against them."

"Father must be furious!" She laughs.

"I can only imagine the celebration upstairs." We laugh together with mutual hatred. It feels good, but it doesn't last.

"You can't do it indefinitely, Edmon," she insists. "You won't kill, so there's only one other choice. Escape. There's too much pain for you here. I can help, but you have to help me."

I've known that my freedom will not come from a physical battle. I've known that I would have to wait for my opportunity. Here it has arrived, and all I feel is revulsion. Lavinia's lust for control and power has spurred her to seek this alliance. She'll try any tactic to succeed our father. I reach into my pocket.

It's time to know the truth . . .

"You poisoned him, didn't you?"

She hesitates, and I know it's true.

"Mentor, deactivate all listening and recording devices on the training level," she says.

"Affirmative," Mentor's metallic voice rings out.

Lavinia holds my eyes with a dead stare. "We all poisoned him in our own ways, Edmon. Alberich, Edgaard, Phaestion, all the other houses," she says. "And you."

"I was no part of your games. Don't include me in them now," I growl.

"You are part because you refuse to play. It was a year ago, after Perdiccus of House Mughal won the Combat. Edgaard was announced to compete the following year, but Edric wanted insurance. He hedged his bets."

He feared for his perfect son's life.

"He sought conciliation with Phaestion. There was a feast following the Pavaka. Revels lasted into the night. The bargain was to be the dissolution of your nuptials, our claim to the throne of Wusong removed, and in return, I would wed the heir of House Julii."

"You and Phaestion?" I laugh with bitterness.

"Father promised to provide Wendigo resources and a new fleet of ships to the Juliis' armada. I would be placed in Phaestion's court, more spy than wife. Father would buy time."

"For?"

"For Edgaard to win, become an Elector? Who knows?" She shrugs. "It hardly matters. Phaestion refused."

"He had no reason to accept. He's sure of victory."

She shakes her head. "No, he refused because he and I had already agreed to end the great Edric Leontes. The poison had already been administered into his food and drink."

"Alberich should have been testing the food," I say.

"Alberich's always resented Father for defeating him in the Combat—an unknown peasant ruining his chances at victory? He serves loyally, but not blindly. Phaestion sealed the pact with a kiss laced with the poison's catalyst during the final couplings of the evening."

My face twists, repulsed at the thought of Edric and Phaestion together.

"Come now, Edmon, the man's quite beautiful. I'm sure you've noticed." She smiles lasciviously. "Father should be dead. I should be Matriarch. A new balance should be struck."

"But Edric didn't die so easily."

"And Phaestion reneged. And Edgaard lost. And you came back." Her voice is frosty.

"This is sickness," I say.

"You're in the game now! You've been in it from the day you were born. You rebelled against being a companion, against Father's wishes, against the marriage to Miranda. By the ancestors, what did it get you? Your mother lobotomized, your island girlfriend killed—"

"Careful of whom you speak!"

"Power rests in your hands. Stop sitting on the sidelines or get the hell out of the game." She steps toward me. "After tonight, the whole planet will be anticipating your showdown with Phaestion Julii, the greatest aristeia in our history."

"Are we done here?" I ask.

"That's not what you want, is it?" she asks again. "Father doesn't understand. No one does but me. Be my ally, and I'll help you leave this place forever." She turns and saunters down the hall back to whatever eel pit she swam out of.

When she's gone, I pull the aquagraphic cube from my pocket and confirm it captured the audio of the conversation we just had.

"Bed," I call out, stepping inside my room. The bed does not come. It's already extended from the wall with someone on it.

"My lord?" The voluminous sheets sweep around the woman as she sits up like a goddess sprung from sea foam.

"Who are you?" The confrontation with Lavinia has dulled my senses. I should have heard the woman's heartbeat before I even stepped in the room.

"Lord Edric sent me." She stands. The sheets fall away, revealing a firm, nubile body. Her hair, the color of spun gold, falls to her shoulders, just above the curve of her ample breasts. "Do I not please you?" she asks coyly.

"You're pleasing, but . . ." *Elder Stars, I've never been good at this.*

"What?" she teases. Her hips sway as she steps toward me. She is curved, but slender and athletic. The perfect Nightsider. She reaches out with a manicured fingernail and traces the contours of my chest. I suddenly feel very exposed. She bites her lower lip. She's trained for this.

"What's your name?" I ask. "No," I say just as quickly. "I don't want to know."

She smiles and presses her mouth to mine. Her breasts are warm against my chest. I feel her heart beat. My arms wrap around her. *This isn't right, but maybe this is what I need.* After years in the cold among the vile rapists of the Wendigo without love, without . . .

Nadia. Her name whispers in my memory. *Nadia. My unborn child. My mother. That was love.*

Gorham. The Maestro. Faria . . .

"No!" I shove the woman away. She crashes into the table and chairs. I'm shocked at my outburst and ashamed. I take a step toward her to help her stand.

"No, please!" She throws up her hands, terrified.

I see my reflection in her eyes—my father.

"Leave, please!" I say. "Quickly!" She grabs her clothes from the floor and flees.

I collapse onto the bed, burying my face in my hands. Lavinia's right. Play the game or get out of the arena. I pull the aquagraphic cube from my pocket once more. My thumb touches the activator indentation. Opera fills the chamber. My song.

I was once a boy of Bone. I loved music and dancing. I had a mother and someone I loved. I had a tribe and a people.

I see a way out. It may just work, but I've been wrong before. I've been very wrong before.

—

The doors of the Wusong throne room open. My father reclines on the throne like the king of death. Two sleepy whores, drunk on the evening's wine, dote on him. A stringed quartet plunks out spare notes of an electronic tune. The languid vestiges of the celebration.

"You've missed the party, my son," the dying king croaks.

"All of you, out!" I shout. "I'll speak with Lord Leontes alone!"

I grab one half-naked courtesan by her arm and shove her toward the double doors. She screams. Everyone scatters. Alberich unsheathes a ceremonial dirk.

"Really?" I sneer. He may remember the spastic little boy he tried to teach on the sands long ago, but we both know that Edmon is gone.

"It's fine, Alberich. My son, the victor, wishes to converse." Edric sounds like a gurgling old toad.

"I watched out for you, boy," Alberich warns. "Even when your father would've had you executed. Don't forget that."

"I haven't," I respond coldly. "Nor have I forgotten who made me watch as my mother was beaten. Or held me down as Nadia's neck was snapped and her body dropped into the Southern Sea. I thank you for your kindness."

Alberich files past me. The doors slam behind him.

"If you intend to kill me, I wouldn't bother. You're fast, but the automated snipers throughout the chamber are faster still. One can't be too careful these days. And you've proven you aren't ready for the patricide. You think I don't see you looking for escape? I can't have that, Edmon."

"I haven't come to kill you, Father. I've come to save you."

He sits up in his chair, and his bones creak with the effort.

"I have an offer. Take it and live. Refuse and House Leontes is ruined." *He doesn't like being ordered? Too bad.* "You wish for me to enter the Combat, kill my old friend, take my place as an Elector, and help fulfill your plans for Tao. This won't happen. Not ever. I'm not your son. I renounce you." His eyes grow hard, and his jaw sets like stone. "Don't be angry just yet. You are going to grant me my wish." I smile.

The anger boils inside him. He's about to speak.

I cut him off. "You believe my taking your place is the only way to save our planet. You believe this because you're dying and you must see your plans in place before you pass."

Coughs rack his body.

I speak over the hacking. "It's a false hope. Think, Edric! You may live for years yet, but how many? One? Five? Ten at the most? You trust me to carry forth your plans after you're gone? The son you hate? Lavinia is self-interested and conniving. She doesn't share any vision beyond her own lust for power. Edgaard was the son you dreamed of, but Edgaard is dead. Phoebe's soft and holds little value. Alberich is a servant. And I refuse. No, the only man strong enough to lead House Leontes is you."

Through his anger, I see an admiration that I've recognized his greatness.

"I haven't come to take your place. I've come to give you knowledge to help cheat death itself."

His brow furrows in confusion.

"In the Wendigo, there was a man named Faria the Red. I suspect you've heard of him. He competed in the Combat over a hundred years ago and forced Chilleus of the Julii to cry for mercy. He taught me the deadly secrets you've witnessed me use. The power was not originally created to kill. That is simply how it has been twisted by the weakness of men." I step closer, baiting him. "Your enemies have poisoned you, aging your body beyond its years. I'll give you the power to counteract this. With my knowledge, you'll live much longer, perhaps decades."

"You'd gift me this knowledge?" His eyes narrow.

"For my freedom? Yes." *The only way to destroy you is to be free of you for all time.*

"I'll teach you to tame the cells within your body. With this power, you can fight the pathogen. It will not be easy, but you are Edric the Leviathan, two-time champion of the Combat. You will do this and then supply me with passage off this world. I'll fade into the vastness of space. You'll sire a new son, a better son. In time, no one will remember Edmon Leontes. Do you accept?"

Silence hangs between us like a thick umbilical cord, waiting to be cut.

He sighs. "You've defied me at every turn, proven that you can turn my greatest hopes into my utmost shame, but House Leontes must survive. At last you are right, Edmon. Only I can do what must be done. Go." He waves his hand. "We'll begin tomorrow."

I bow and leave the withered king on his throne.

A faint pulsing twitters beyond the edge of hearing. The rhythm grows as I shift in the blackness of unconsciousness.

Wake up, Edmon!

I struggle to open my eyes from a drowsy coma. Eventually, my eyes flit open, and I take in the blurry light of a white room. *This is not my bedchamber.*

"He's returning to consciousness, lord," a voice says.

"Leave us," my father replies to a doctor in a white lab suit.

What's happened? I open my mouth to scream, and no sound comes. My view rushes into focus. I'm in a white room with healing tanks and instrument racks. I lie in bed with a monitor reading my vitals. Edric sits at the foot of my bed, his long robes trailing on the floor. He looks like a corpse in midnight blue.

The last thing I remember was lying in bed, a clicking sound from the wall, and a sudden sting at my neck, my hand quickly flying to the site of the sting.

I try to speak, and nothing but a faint whisper passes my lips. My father raises a bony hand to quiet me. "After your speech last night, you'll not be speaking again. Or singing."

What? Again, no sound emerges.

"To cheat death, if only for a few more years, what more could a man like me want? It was a clever offer. I thought about it for a long time. An hour to be exact. For a man who prides himself on split-second cunning, that was an eternity, I assure you."

No!

"I don't have years to learn as you have had. As a warrior, I accept my fate. What I do not accept is a son who refuses to understand his place or his responsibilities to his people."

He doubles over with violent hacking. I watch the old man writhe in silence until he can speak again.

"A new path must be forged, and I've already lost too many sons. You will succeed, Edmon, because I've cut off your options. You must become what I've made you, or all is lost."

My body moves slowly, anesthesia still in my system. I push through it to force my hand to my throat. I feel a smooth, waxy scar, a line that runs the length of my neck from chin to collarbone. *How long have I been under?*

"Your vocal cords are gone. You'll never sing again. You'll never speak again. You'll never disobey again."

The scream inside my head is louder than any leviathan roar. I push the air out with every ounce of my soul, and all that emerges is a gasp, the merest exhalation of breath. Silent tears batter my cheeks, more devastating than thunder as I shake, not even able to truly sob.

"When you've triumphed in the arena, maybe you'll find a way to replace what you've lost."

He's taken every person I cared for, every hope I ever had, and torn them to ribbons. Now he's taken my song. *Who am I? I am a mere shell. All the music is gone.*

The old man reaches under his robe and pulls out an elegant, white stick. It looks like an elongated bone. He hands it to me.

"It may be mistaken for a cane," he says. "But it is much more."

On closer inspection, I see the bone is a scabbard fashioned from sea coral with an ivory inlay.

"The coral was taken from the reefs near your home. The inlay from the horn of the narwhal . . ."

I slowly unsheathe a blade.

"The singing steel was tempered in the forges of Albion. If Phaestion of the Julii has a siren sword, so shall you have one, too."

I remember holding Phaestion's blade as a boy. The metal sings but not joyfully. It is the lament of a siren who has lost her home.

"It's based on an ancient Jian design. More refined than a rapier, quicker, and stealthier than a katana . . ."

The pommel is silver and hollow with a leviathan bisecting the empty space. I've seen the design before. The mirror-Edmon in the Arms of Agony held the same sword. *How is that possible?* The siren steel sends vibrations into my body.

"She will be your voice now." The old man stands. "We must see this to the end."

CHAPTER 28

Oracion

Weeks pass. I move through them lifeless. I eat mechanically. Bathe as if I'm an automaton. I fight as if I am a beast. Perhaps that's what men are when they are violent—mere animals. Even the extrasensory experiences of my other faculties, which I learned under Faria's tutelage, seem dulled. I walk in a world of shadow. Only death can end the suffering.

Twelve nobles, winners of the Upper Circuit, and twenty-four winners of the Under Circuits will enter the arena on Combat day. The nobles will have trained their whole lives for the event; the underclass competitors, some who have never held a weapon before being forced to step into the sands of the ring, will fight their way to the top by killing their opponents.

Edric wanted me to prove myself in the Under Circuit as he had done, but now that I've won my first match, he transfers me to the Upper Circuit, where bouts are determined by stun harness or first blood. He wants no chances that I will be less than perfect in the final Combat, where I will surely face my foster brother, Phaestion of the Julii.

I no longer think of escape. If I left Tao, there would be nothing for me. The music of the universe is dead. Even in my darkest moments, I could hear the music, the voices of my mother and Nadia. Even with revenge, I could go on. I have nothing now. I am bereft.

The pretty boys of lesser noble houses fall to my skill. I'm declared the "Silent Assassin." Some doubt it's truly Edmon Leontes returned from exile. Rumors persist that Edric found some lowborn from the slums to pose as his long-lost son. Gossip is beside the point because I win again and again.

At night, I wake from sleep in cold sweats, panicked because I don't know where I am or who I am.

Father glares, but he no longer terrifies. His pale eyes are faded by the inevitability of his death.

At dinner after my latest win, the others argue about the state of the Pantheon and the food lines in the arcologies while I stuff meat into my mouth. I chomp, letting bits dribble down my chin in a flagrant display of disrespect. *Edmon Leontes is no more. The animal left in his place will soon follow.*

"Come, Alberich. I've lost my appetite." The seneschal helps the hobbling old Edric from the room. The rest follow.

"Champion of the Combat?" Lavinia whispers as she passes. "A pig porpoise would be more suitable."

If any of them had hopes that my return from the Wendigo could help change the political state, they have surely become disillusioned.

"Phoebe." Beremon holds out his arm to his wife as he flicks his gaze at me then toward the balcony. He taps his wrist with his finger twice and exits. *Meet in two hours.*

I do not acknowledge the signal.

The twilight is full of faint stars, ever waiting for true night. I've seen true night. It's not wondrous.

Ruska stands in a flowing cape, overlooking the cityscape. "You think he'll come?"

Phoebe's auburn hair swirls around her plump face. "Who's to say? He's not the man he was."

I watch from a ledge above, listening to their pulses. They're nervous. They don't want to be overheard by Lavinia's or Edric's spies. Camglobes constantly hover around the Wusong-Leontes Palatial Towers; Mentor records everything on the training level. I've escaped my quarters for this brief time, but tower security will soon be alerted to my absence from the barracks. I silently drop from above to land between my sister and her husband.

"By the twisted star!" Ruska jumps back. "Edmon! You frightened the ancestors out of me."

I feel a light touch on my shoulder, and I whirl on Phoebe. "Edmon, please. We mean you no harm."

I know that. She's right, though. I'm jumpy. Years of prison and torture have turned me into a frightened, instinctual thing. *Damn them all.*

"The preliminary bouts have ended," Beremon begins. "You've been declared victor in your division—"

"Do you plan to face Phaestion in the arena?" Phoebe blurts.

"Phoebe! We agreed not to press him."

"It's the crux of everything, Beremon," she insists.

"I know." Ruska softens. They look at me expectantly.

Do I plan to kill my childhood friend? What will I do if I win? What will they do if I lose?

I shrug.

"That's no answer, Edmon!" Phoebe clenches her fists.

Ruska plays the diplomat. "Can you win?"

I'm not sure. I'm not sure I'd want to if I could.

"I see," Ruska says solemnly. "Then we make preparations."

I cock an eyebrow.

"We believe in you, Edmon, but our belief doesn't matter tomorrow. You either win or die. I'd hoped that you'd be sure of victory. As things stand, events will move quickly once Phaestion claims the garlands."

I look at Phoebe. "Beremon believes that should Phaestion gain position in the government—"

"There won't be a government," Beremon finishes.

Phaestion will have the power to claim himself supreme ruler like the Great Song.

"He may even seek to take Miranda's hand once you're out of the way," Phoebe laments.

"Some of us don't wish to serve a new dynasty." Beremon wraps his cape around his portly torso as a chill sweeps over us. "House Ruska is a minor player, but we aren't without resources. We've reached out to Lazarus Industries of Lyria to pioneer some joint ventures. The business opportunity shows there is possibility to move the base of operations of a noble house away from Tao. I'm moving House Ruska to Lyria, Edmon."

"House Ruska is wherever the Patriarch goes," Phoebe says, nodding. "Come with us, Edmon."

They are defecting!

"We'd hoped that the course of government here could be turned, but we cannot put all those hopes on you," Beremon admits.

"There's no life left for you here, but maybe out there." Phoebe looks at the sky.

That was my dream long ago, when I could sing. Now there's only one tie I've left loose, an oath to an old man who may have betrayed me, who I'm not even sure is still alive. I shake my head.

"If you change your mind, contact us," Beremon says. He places a hand on my shoulder. It's all I can do to tamp down the instinct to tear his fingers off.

Phoebe tentatively reaches out as well, but she stops just short of touching my face. "Goodbye, poor Edmon," she says. "I'm sorry for what they did to you."

They are good people, too good for this place. I finally learn I have a sister, family who might actually come to love me one day, who might be worthy of my trust. Ironically, it is too late for me to care. They leave, and the stars wait to shine.

—

The beetlelike passenger screamer twists and turns round the city high-rises. Alberich sits on my left, my father, cloaked and hooded on my right. Edric's once lustrous silver mane has thinned to mere strands. He is practically bald now, so he has taken to wearing the hood. *We actually look like father and son for once,* I muse.

He should be in a regeneration tank, but tonight is the semifinal, the last match before the yearly games. He'll be there to witness my triumph even if it means dying sooner. *I'm touched.*

I grip the hilt of my siren sword. I'm anxious. I've fought against lowlifes and addicts and the sons of lesser houses. I've yet to face the elite. And tonight, *he* will be there. I've watched the aquagraphics. I've studied him. His speed is frightening. His skills uncanny. If we confront each other, it will be death for one of us. I open my eyes as we approach the rotunda. Its round shape looks to me like a cancerous boil on the surface of the cityscape, ready to burst.

A huge throng gathers on the steps leading to the grand entrance. They clamor over statues of past champions, threatening to tear them down. A man steps from their ranks and ascends with arms outstretched. The pilot banks away, so my hand whips out and grabs Alberich's forearm.

"Edmon?"

I cast my gaze toward the rioting crowd.

“Don’t concern yourself with them,” he says.

I clamp down on the pressure points of his wrist.

“Stop! Stop the vehicle!” he cries out.

I point to a roof landing pad just above the parade.

“Lord Edmon commands that you set us down,” Alberich says to the pilot.

“What’s going on?” My father awakes from his stupor.

“Edmon, sire,” Alberich grumbles. The pilot lands, and I bolt through the hatch before the sonic wings even retract into the scarab’s carapace.

“Edmon!” my father calls after me, but I’m already racing to the roof’s edge.

I see him, Phaestion, at the top of the rotunda stairs.

“For too long your fathers and grandfathers have scrounged for scraps cast down by the nobility. For too long have they bowed their backs and thrown their hands up in what? Gratitude? While all these so-called great houses, Wusong, Flanders, Mughal, Ruska, Leontes, and yes, even Julii, have made their children fat. Is the wealth of Tao for them or for the strong?”

The crowd screams, “The strong!” Phaestion nods, his hair the color of a flame in the breeze. When he speaks, he commands the attention of the mob like a king of old.

“The Great Song founded our society on an ideal we’ve strayed from. Food lines so long that children starve? Natural resources depleted? An interstellar trade so impoverished that even a working man cannot clothe himself? What would our emperor say now?”

My father coughs as he hobbles up behind me, leaning on Alberich for support. “He denounces the very system that grants him an audience. He includes the name Leontes when it was I who climbed from the muck of the arcos.”

A fit seizes Edric as Phaestion continues.

"You may say, 'Phaestion, you're prince of the Julii,' and I will proclaim that I am. But I am not my father, or my father's father, or kin in mind to any ancestor save the founder, Bushi Tamerlane Song. I, my companions, and you—we are the new generation. Together we proclaim the Pantheon is not birthright. It's every man's right. You are the new Pantheon!"

Cheers erupt from the crowd. *I have to get closer and look him in the eye.* I jump onto the roof ledge and run along it to a drain pipe that rides the edge of the scraper all the way to the street below. I leap into the air and snag the pipe. I slide down, zooming toward the city floor.

"I'll win this Combat and claim my place among the Electors," continues Phaestion. "I'll face the challenges and defeat any opponent thrown my way. I'll fight without enhancers or off-world narcotics. I'll kill with weapons or bare-handed. I'll fight without magical techniques . . ."

I hit the pavement and push through the crowd.

"When I win, I will not be silent. I will speak for you!" Phaestion proclaims. "We'll end corruption and injustice perpetrated by these indolent blood-suckers on the Synod. These so-called Wusong-Leonteses, these Ruskas, these Angkors, these Temujins. We'll end their reign and usher in a new order of the true master race of Tao!"

I shoulder my way up to the steps.

"Workers of the shipyards, farmers of the kelp forests, you are the product of a thousand years of breeding. We'll not stop with Tao. Our armies will sweep through the Nine Corridors, Lyria, Thera, Nonthera, Albion, Eruland. We'll claim Market and the realms of the dead Miralian Empire that drove our forefathers from the stars. We will save all of humanity for the pure!"

I race to the top of the stairs amid thundering applause. It pounds in my head. I block it out, and I focus on a single heartbeat, the one that ticks like a metronome, unwavering.

"We'll cleanse humanity's blood, cull those who have diluted and deluded themselves, spliced themselves with false genes. Mutants, spypsies, all those who have fragmented humanity and weakened it. We'll make a unified galaxy carved in the pristine image of the Nightsider. We start here at home. The impurity of these Daysiders—"

I burst through the crowd, slam through two Julii shock troopers, and come face-to-face with my foster brother. The crowd gasps. The boy who taught me to use a spear, the child I played music with, and the friend I braved the leviathan with stands before me. He's an inch or so taller, which is quite tall for someone from a high gravity planet. I hate that he's taller. Then again, I'm used to being the ugly one.

He regards me with his cool gray eyes. "Edmon of House Leontes, do you join us in this holy crusade?" he shouts to the crowd. "Do you join your strength to ours to overthrow corruption?"

I stand perfectly still. Any movement I make will be seen as an answer.

He lowers his voice and says for my ears alone, "I will find a way to give you your voice back. I swear it, brother." Then he turns to the crowd. "Yours is the strength we need, Edmon. Even with your mixed blood."

I see fire. He would not find my voice; he'd replace it with another voice that would owe him.

Shame on you. Warmonger. Racist. Hypocrite. Shame on this place that made you. I condemn him with my eyes.

"War then," he whispers.

CHAPTER 29

Aristeia

Alberich massages my muscles and kneads the knots from my back, readying me for the fight. He fastens greaves to my shins and gauntlets to my arms. He holsters the siren sword in the obi around my waist. "The cape is leviathan skin," he says as he cinches the garment over one shoulder. "A sea dragon hasn't been speared for over a hundred years, but your father swears it is true."

The smooth scales do remind me of the creature. *Could the monster have appeared to Edric as well?*

"We'll be watching from the box." The seneschal smiles like a proud parent. "When you are Patriarch, my debt to your family will have been paid in full."

You helped kill my mother, helped kill Nadia, and helped poison Edric. I'll remember your service.

He stares as if he heard my thoughts spoken aloud. "I should let you alone before the fight." He leaves.

I hear sounds of the other semi bout in the rotunda above. The obstacle machinery rumbles. The crowd roars as someone falls. My skin tingles. I know that Phaestion fights now. There's no killing today, but if he wins and I win, death will be all that's between us tomorrow.

I don't know if I can do it. If I can, I don't know that I should. I don't desire the vengeance I once did. I only desire to somehow not . . . succumb. I wave my hand over the aquagraphic sensor in the middle of the room. Images of the current bout appear.

The Julii prince moves like a predator. He leaps over streams of fire, twists midair over a spear's thrust, and barely touches the ground before he flies again. He lands behind an opponent and places a palm on the man's back. Each competitor wears an undergarment outfitted with technology that registers the pressure of any strike. If a touch is delivered to a vital part of the body, the garment electrifies, shocking the opponent out of the match. Phaestion's opponent screams as the radiating stun paralyzes him and he drops.

"Brilliant, isn't he?" Talousla Karr's electric-blue eyes shine at me from the doorway. "You do remember me, Edmon of the Leontes? Of course you remember. You have the bones I gave you."

I ignore him. How the spypsy got into the competitors' room, I don't know.

Phaestion scissors his legs midair around a man's neck and sends the man spinning head over heels into an electrified pool. The combatant's stun harness activates and shocks him out of the fight.

"Flawless. I designed him that way."

I turn to him.

"So I have your attention now?" he asks. "It was inevitable that a culture so obsessed with physical prowess would eventually break its outdated moral code. An entire race that invented an entertainment based on principles of evolution, the genetics of a thousand years of environmental pressure at my fingertips. How could I say no?" The man curls his long nails in the air. "A champion gray, old, and wanting a son. A snip of adenine here, a tuck of cytosine there. I take the extraordinary and make it beyond human. The result is more than a copy. It's a demigod."

By the twisted star! The truth of what he's saying sinks in. Phaestion is a clone. He's not even human. *If the people knew the truth . . .*

"Others have tried with more and achieved less. Still, I was able to introduce a few of my own little inventions. You two were very close once. Brothers? Lovers?"

Get to the point, serpent.

"I created several of his designer genes from scratch. A pheromone that makes him all but irresistible, and a neural enhancement, a precognition of sorts." The alien smiles coldly.

Phaestion can see the future?

"Speed and agility are augmented, of course, but his mental faculty works subconsciously. He reads body language. He calculates probable outcomes without thinking."

I suspect it's more than that. Phaestion saw things that were far beyond body language. He knew our friendship would lead to disaster the day he pressed his forehead to mine. He foresaw the sword I carry now years before my father robbed me of my voice and gave me its siren steel. Whatever this alien thinks he did, the outcome is far worse than he could have imagined. I grab the man's robe and hoist him off the ground. I slam him into the wall so hard it knocks the wind from him.

"Seven Mothers!" He laughs. "You surprise me. I remember you as a boy—weak, dying. But I knew it was inside you, Edmon. I just had to unlock it."

I lower him to the ground and back away, horrified. *This strength is not strength. My mother was strong, Nadia was strong, and The Maestro who wrote songs of rebellion—he was strong. All my physical capability is nothing compared to their love.*

"All your abilities were there from the beginning. All I did was switch them on. Pain and trauma created the precise conditions. The torture you endured conditioned you beyond the limits of normal men."

You made me a freak! I want to scream.

"Because of me, you live to bear witness to the next stage of human evolution. Phaestion is the future. I envision all humanity becoming a race of such supermen like him and then perhaps even greater than him."

In the aquagraphic, Phaestion climbs to the top of a massive tower of steel pipes. He runs along girders to face his final opponent.

"You know why your Pantheon identifies themselves with sea creatures? They spliced their own DNA with those animals. Hybrids, you called them."

I know this tale. Under the rule of Empress Boudika Wusong, the Pantheon put human DNA into the creatures of the oceans and created animals with intelligence. They did it for profit but also for fun. It was a disaster. The creatures' increased intelligence caused them to turn on the humans who had created them. They wrecked harbors, hunted fishing vessels, and murdered their crews. They destroyed Meridian's kelp farms, cutting off a major food supply for years until it could be replenished. The Pantheon acted swiftly to hunt the creatures down, but politically the damage was done. The empress was forced to abdicate, and the High Synod came to power. Genetic experimentation was banned for all time.

"A people's history is written in its genetics. Tao spliced human DNA into the animals, but also spliced the genes of animals into themselves."

Edric calls himself a leviathan. Phaestion had dreams of being an orca. The monster speaks to me in my dreams . . .

"The connection has been diluted, but traces remain."

I am the leviathan.

"Is it so hard to believe? Perhaps such genes may prove key to survival in the future."

I turn back to the aquagraphic and see Phaestion standing triumphant. The crowd chants, "Phaes-tion, Phaes-tion, Phaes-tion!"

"I even tested some of your underclass with illuminating results. You met one once. A little girl. It was broadcast as part of *The Exploits of the Companions* program when you were a boy."

I remember the girl who moved so fast, who helped me and Edgaard during the war games. *How far does this man's sick machinations extend?*

"Humanity is something beyond what we were, preceding what will come. Cyborg, mutant, modified, designed, refined. I've traveled the ends of space, but seen none so beautiful as the work of art I envisioned. So I created him. Soon my new Adam will meet the rest of the Fracture."

Phaestion climbs down from the giant metal structure.

"Winner, Phaestion of the Julii!" the announcer hails. My old friend walks toward the dais and raises his arms in triumph. The garlands are placed around his neck.

"I'm your father, just as much as I'm his," he says. "Like any good father, I don't want to see my children come to harm. Join him, Edmon. You can't win."

The spypsy's face is shrouded by the hood, but I sense a tremble in his voice. *If I can't win, why is he afraid?* The announcer calls for the next trial, and I walk past him to take my turn.

The bout is over before it begins. All fifteen of my opponents, scions of noble houses or professional combatants for hire, are paralyzed within minutes of the chime. No showmanship, no acrobatics, just cold efficiency.

The crowd howls in derision. The only thing the mob prefers to cheering champions is reviling villains. I was expected to win, but not so quickly, not so dully. I flash my teeth, and I hiss back. The camglobes pick up every last detail of my flagrant disgust. Through the noise, I pick out the sound of one steady clap from the skyboxes above. Phaestion stares out a window. Our eyes meet, and he nods. Tomorrow, thirty-six finalists will enter the arena, but the number doesn't matter. It's him and me. Winner take all.

Later, I am alone in the competitor's steam showers, scrubbing the mud and sand from my body. Tomorrow, it will be blood. I sense movement beyond the entryway. Two men, heavy, strong. They're armed. Knives and something else . . . *guns?* I dive to the bathroom floor as a bullet ricochets off the tiles. I leap into a cloud of steam that obscures me from view.

"I can't see him!" one cries out.

"'Ere he is!"

I dodge the swipe of a knife. This attacker is a giant. Scarred. His eyelids have an epicanthal fold, and his hair is a violent shade of blue. This man is not from Tao. He swipes again. I intercept the blow, and my hand strikes his neck. He drops to the ground, immobilized.

A bullet rips through my thigh, and I'm hurled against the wall with the sound of smacking meat. I drive all the energy to my other leg and spring forward before the second attacker can fire again. My fists unleash fury. Knuckles smash face. He skillfully rolls and reverses our positions, pulling a knife from his belt, jamming it down like an ice pick. I block. My forearm is sliced open, but I hold it against the pain as it is the only thing keeping the knife from plunging into me. The point of the blade quakes centimeters from my eye. The man leans his body weight against me. There's no way I can resist. I'm losing blood fast.

"Time to sleep, little man." His green hair looks like blades of grass. There's an odor of ozone from his perspiration, a telltale sign that there is tag in his system. He presses down again. My forearm buckles. *This is how it ends. No glorious finish. No fanfare. Small violent lives meeting small violent ends.*

Then a siren sweetly sings. The point of a blade suddenly sprouts from the man's throat, and he gurgles on blood just before he slumps forward onto me, his giant body smothering me. I desperately push him off.

Sirens again, two of them. The long blade impales the paralyzed blue-haired giant on the floor a few meters away.

"This one wasn't dead," the haughty voice says. "Really, Edmon, you'll have to be more thorough tomorrow." I scramble with my back to the steam room wall. Phaestion picks up the pistol from the blue-haired man's lifeless hand. "You know this is still the most popular method of killing in the Nine Corridors?"

He holds the firearm like a dead fish between his thumb and forefinger. "No skill. Look what they can do to even the most invulnerable of men." He tosses the gun aside. It skitters from sight. "They'll be useless in my new world. Crusaders with spider-weave armor, riding screamers, and brandishing siren swords will cut through gunmen like oars through shallows."

I feel woozy. My legs wobble. *Why is he here?*

"Don't run, Edmon."

Did he send these attackers? Why stop them if he did? I ready myself for a fight, but he sheathes his weapons. I relax for a hair's breadth, and he leaps toward me. *By the ancestors, he's fast!*

I'm slammed against the wall.

"I could kill you now. No one would ever know." He smiles. I struggle against his inhumanly strong grip. "But there's no glory there. Don't you want that, Edmon? Your song to last through the ages?"

I clamp my teeth down against his forearm and bite. The metallic flavor of blood spurts in my mouth, but he holds on.

"My father would have let these men kill you. He learned not to trust odds after he lost in the arena. Then he lost his first son to your father, a mere plebeian. I knew The Companions would try something. Probably Hanschen. Or maybe it was your charming sister, Lavinia, who sent them? I saw it would happen, and I came to make sure they didn't succeed. You're a survivor, Edmon. You always endure. Even when I told your father about Nadia . . ."

What?

"The day I saw you together, I knew she had to die. You're mine alone. You were promised to the empress. I knew your father wouldn't abide disobedience, so I told him you had taken a wife against his wishes."

I shove him. He counters and pins my arm behind my back. Tendons and ligaments tear. *Control the anger. Don't let it control you. Become the storm.*

"But he sent you away. That wasn't what I wanted. Still, you survived and returned more beautiful, stronger. You take your pain and become something more from it. That's why I love you. Tomorrow, we'll have our aristeia. Even after I conquer the Fracture, they'll still sing of the moment when Phaestion slew the only man he ever loved in a single combat."

Chilleus and Cuillan.

He presses his forehead to mine in the gesture of brothers. It's my moment. I raise my knee full force and slam it between his legs. *If Phaestion can see the future, I must be unpredictable.* My hand strikes his neck, and Phaestion drops, gasping for air.

"Beasts of the seas! That's a trick." He struggles against the effects of the Dim Mak. *He should not be moving at all!*

I try to run, but immediately crash to the floor, my bloody leg throbbing violently. I crawl to my sword resting against the changing bench. I hear Phaestion behind me reaching for his own. My fingers graze the pommel. His rapier sings. *Damn it!* My hand grasps the handle. I whip the blade from its sheath.

Screaming blades collide. Parry, thrust, riposte. I can barely keep time with his rhythm and speed. It's as if he knows where I am going to strike or block before I do. Then I realize—he does. He sees the events play out moments before they actually do. Therein lies salvation.

The AI of the Arms of Agony once told me that it could not simulate Phaestion truly because his level of improvisation was such that generating a creative algorithm to match was impossible. Yet, the Phaestion who attacks now is so reliant on his prescience that his moves are not chaotic. They are modeled on the pattern of what he thinks I will do. I discern their beat. He may see the future. I see the music of the universe, and then I break it. I move in a way so antithetical, so discordant, the harmony of his playing is suddenly fractured.

I swiftly grab his wrist with a claw technique. The bones snap, and his sword clatters to the floor. I twirl my blade, and it gently licks the smooth skin above his jugular. His eyes go wild as he realizes, maybe for the first time in his entire life, he's not invincible. He's never accepted this as an outcome. Me? I've died a thousand times.

"Do it or you'll die tomorrow. Do it or I'll kill many more after you. Millions. Billions."

My sword song wavers. *What kind of monster are you?*

"Edmon," he says with no malice, "it's who I am. It's who you are, too."

All men are monsters. Why run, boy?

Edmon, Nadia whispers in my memory. *You can be who you want to be.* My soul for his life and the lives of all those across the stars. Here there are no camglobes, no aquagraphics, no scribes to capture my choice in verses of epic poetry.

My sword falls. I jam my fingers into Phaestion's neck again. He slumps onto the tiles. I hobble to his sword and kick it down the hall. Then I grab a towel and wrap it around my leg to stanch the bleeding. I leave him alive on the steam room floor, perhaps making the greatest mistake of my life.

CHAPTER 30

Encore

My abilities help repair my body but do little to heal my mind. I walk into my room in a daze. *There's nothing left for me here.*

"Welcome home, sir," Mentor chimes, but I know there is no home for me.

"Yes, brother. Welcome." Lavinia's raven hair cascades down her snow-white shoulders. Her pale, naked body gleams like moonlight. She stands centimeters from me. "Father's alone tonight. Only Alberich guards him. He'll admit you to the bedchamber. Enact the ritual of succession. Win tomorrow and I'll serve you as sister, wife, whatever you desire . . ."

Her hand reaches up to my face, and her heart flutters. *Wake up!* Nadia's memory saves me again. I grab Lavinia's wrist too fast for her to react.

"Edmon!" I see something underneath her long, courtesan fingernails, something writhing beneath the cuticles. I throw her to the bed. She stares back defiantly and wraps the bedsheet around herself. "Damn you," she whispers. "Only a scratch and the nanites enter your bloodstream."

Nanites?

"Microscopic robots. I spent a fortune purchasing them from an off-world trader. They would not kill but weaken, make you slow. You destroy everyone's plans!"

She meant for me to lose against Phaestion tomorrow.

"Father's still vulnerable. Listen to me. Alberich awaits. Patricide is forbidden for daughters. If you don't do it, he'll keep himself alive for decades using healing tanks. This is our chance." She stands, and I throw up my hands to ward her off. She sighs with disappointment and puts on her clothes. "I wouldn't have really harmed you."

Liar.

"We're both trapped. Unless—" A thought interrupts her. "I can use the same distraction to lower the Wusong tower defenses. Alberich has reduced the guard in preparation for my sending you to Father's chambers. Fat Beremon Ruska plans to defect this night. If you wish to go, rather than rule by my side, they'll get you off Tao by day's end. We can both have what we want. You needn't fight and you needn't rule; just leave me to it. Do we have an agreement?"

If I run from the Combat, the punishment is death or the Citadel. If I leave Tao, I can never return.

"You can disappear, just like Edric's first son," she says.

What?

"Help me. Kill Edric so that I may be sole heir to House Leontes."

Edric's first son? I grab her and hold her down as she attempts to scratch me with her deadly fingernails. I'm reminded of Edric, holding my mother down as he beat her.

"Is this all you are?" she screams. "A mindless savage?"

I look her in the eye. I slowly breathe the words *first son.*

"You may be eldest son now, but not always. When I became majordomo of House Wusong-Leontes, I delved into the records, the history of his rise, and found the aberration. Census birth lists show the first of his line. Edvaard was to be burned in the Pavaka. Birth defects."

I release her from my grasp, shocked by the revelation.

"There's no mention of the mother, but I tell you the boy didn't die by fire. Ledgers show no record of incineration. The child simply disappeared."

Edric killed the child by his own hand? Monster. Lavinia is right—I must confront him. For my mother, for Nadia, for all the atrocities he has committed.

"I ask again, do we have an agreement?"

I drop silently from the ventilation shaft to the hallway floor. *Just like the Citadel,* I think. Normally these corridors are guarded and I'd be unable to travel this route. Now that Lavinia has deactivated the security system and Alberich has lowered the guard, I have a few moments.

The lens of a camglobe swivels as it floats down the hallway. I wait just outside its scope. I snag the pearlescent ball as it floats by and crush it like an egg. The guards won't notice the missing feed for a few minutes. Over the past few months, I've used the Mentor program to study and learn security's movements. They'll not pass this part of the palace for another two point five minutes. It's more than I need.

I open the large double bronze doors inlaid with the great sea apes of House Wusong. Alberich awaits me at a security checkpoint. "You've come."

To slay the monster or be slain myself.

I jam my fingers into his neck faster than he can react. He slumps into the guard station chair and stares up, unable to speak. I want him alive and able to witness everything.

I approach my father's bed, hand on the pommel of my sword as a partition-screen rises.

"Alberich?" The withered voice cracks. My father rises in the pillows like a corpse from a billowing tomb. I draw siren steel from ivory. "Edmon." The old man coughs. "I've been waiting, my son."

He knew I was coming? Of course he did . . .

"I knew Lavinia would send you."

I leap through the air. Twenty meters from the doorway to the edge of his pallet. An impossible jump, but I'm in an impossible mood. Siren song hums as my blade casts light on Edric's throat. "Why hesitate?" he growls. An ember of strength still burns within his pale eyes. "I murdered your mother, strangled your lover, drowned her and your unborn child. Complete the rite of patricide. Defeat that Julii tomorrow and take the world. Rebuild it!"

I've no intention of giving him what he wants . . . yet. So I shake my head.

"I've failed." His voice breaks with despair. "My children, my planet, I've failed them all. Everything I've done for them . . ." The old man cries reptile tears. "Listen, my son," he implores. "I was an orphan, alone in the arcologies with only one way out—strength. I had to survive; it was the only way. I had a wife, a child. You were not the first. You had a brother. The birth went hard, and the breach could not be sealed. Freya's eyes grew cold." His voice wavers. "He was deformed. His head massive, wine-stain marks covered the side of his paralyzed, little body. I hated him. Why would the ancestors curse me so?"

It is too much. I want to silence him, end his rationalizing. I don't want him to be human to me. I want him to be a monster, that monolith I saw the day of Edgaard's christening, the one who denounced me, who struck my mother in front of the entire world. But I may never have another chance to understand him, so I stay my hand.

Tell me it was a kindness that you killed him, monster.

"The whole world lit up when my boy laughed. He was mine." His cold eyes somehow burn with regret.

He gives the love I never had to a deformity long gone?

"I hid him from the Census. If I lost the Combat, he'd be found and killed, but there was no other way to overcome my station. I took the chance and won. My ascension, however, meant casting off my old life. Edvaard could never be the heir to a new Pantheon house. He couldn't do what you must. Yet I couldn't bring myself to kill him, either. I secretly sent him off-world and infiltrated the Electors' Hall of Records to eliminate his birth from the genealogical history."

If Lavinia could find the information, so could others . . . I have a brother. This deformed Edvaard garnered his affections. Perfect Edgaard held his hopes and dreams. What have I, his middle son, inspired? Nothing but wrath.

"Edmon, learn the truth of what I discovered when I entered the Hall of Records. The nobles of Tao claim lineage from heroes of the Ancient Empire. Lies!" He laughs dryly. "Our ancestors were slaves, test-tube soldiers. Their names—Song, Julii, Angevin, Mughal—were merely genetic templates. They rebranded themselves as kings. I realized that I, a plebeian from the arcologies, must do the same if I was to stand next to them as equals. I took the sea dragon for my symbol and the name of an ancient Anjin commander. Leontes was born." He flashes a wrinkled-lipped grin. "Just as Leontes sacrificed his own life to save his people, I, too, made sacrifices. I've done what I have because it was the only way. I had to become a monster, Edmon. I loved you more than the others because you were the one born like me . . ."

Lying sack of whale dung! My knuckles go white on the hilt of my sword.

"You were born of the light and dark, low birth and high. You were not born to be a killer, but had to be fashioned into one to save this world. You and I both know the dragon of the sea . . ."

What does he know of the monster that haunts my dreams?

"We are wild, violent men, but we must both face the truth. In three generations' time, this world will die, our resources depleted, pollution too toxic, solar radiation burning through our atmosphere—the Pantheon has known this since just before the new Fracture Point opened when you were born. If the populace knew, too, there would be rioting in the streets. When I learned, my outrage was matched only by my will to act. Unfortunately, the College of Electors and High Synod were hampered by argument and indecision. Some even denied the statistics that scientists presented and said Tao was simply going through a natural depletion cycle, that this was part of the Balance. Chilleus Julii was one of these people.

"I had no authority to end the bickering and rally other Electors to the truth, not yet. I had won a Combat and entered the college, but I was not a member of the High Synod, and I was not the Patriarch of a noble house. I knew that in order to change the course of history, I had to become something more than an anomaly. I had to become a myth, someone the poets would sing of through the ages. So I did something unthinkable—I entered the Combat a second time. Opposing me was Chilleus Julii's first son, Augustus. He was young, fast, and strong, but I knew if I trained hard, I could win. Old Wusong sponsored me, allied me with his house. He feared the threat House Julii would present if both father and son should sit in power. I emerged a victorious god. For achieving a feat greater than any other warrior of Tao, I was branded the Patriarch of a new noble house.

"Suddenly, mine was the voice that was heard above the crashing waves, my sigil rising on the high tide of the Pantheon. Yet, for all my newfound glory, questions of the planet's future still had to be tabled until I could cement the legacy of my fledgling house. I needed a son."

A scuffle in the hallway. *Guards will be here soon.*

"Then you were born. Your mother was beautiful but an islander. I named you my heir to bide time, but in truth, I was content to watch you from afar, while I could turn to face the problem of the planet's decay. The opening of the Fracture meant that a definitive strategy could be pursued in earnest. I counseled we follow in the footsteps of the Great Song, build a worldship, look for a new frontier. 'We don't migrate,' Old Julii answered. 'We conquer.'"

Edric coughs and blood sprays onto the sheets.

We're warriors, Phaestion often said. I can see how my father's proposal of wandering ten years in the void like vagabonds no longer appealed to the Synod's sensibilities.

"Julii himself knew that making war was mere obfuscation, a way to turn the masses to a cause rather than focus on the realities we were facing. It hardly mattered. I'd killed his son. He would have opposed anything I suggested. If I had roared for battle, he would have sued for peace. He called me unclean and unfit to lead. His family had the pedigree of nobility stretching back to the time of the Great Song. I could not murder him outright, but I didn't need to. I was a legendary fighter and anyone who looked on us knew I would dismantle him limb from limb should he ever back his threats with a challenge.

"I slowly built my power. My fealty to House Wusong meant I had access to their resources. I expanded the Wendigo. Still, Julii had something I did not—a purebred heir. Julii's second boy was already exceeding all others. They whispered he was the greatest warrior of his generation, born of a sea goddess, the Great Song reincarnated. When my alliance to Olympias of House Flanders, also a Combat champion, produced Edgaard, I thought you would be free of the burden of inheritance, but Old Wusong chose you for his daughter. He wanted me humbled, I think. He knew you were a political embarrassment—your mixed birth, your smart mouth. He sanctioned the union of our houses, but only through you.

"Yet, you were not what you needed to be. That day of the christening you proclaimed to be a musician. When I looked on you, compared you to the son of Julii, you showed nothing of the battle prowess I knew that boy already possessed. You shamed our house in front of the entire planet. It was my own fault, but I knew what needed to be done. I survived, Edmon, because of the pain I endured. You needed the same lesson—survive or die. It was my duty to give you what had made me. So I beat your mother for all to see . . ."

Rage boils inside of me. *This is why my mother wanted me to forget. She knew he did it to turn me into a monster, like him.*

"The emperor's decree and the popularity you gained with the common folk that day made it impossible for other houses to ignore you or for me to let you go. If only you had kept your mouth shut . . . I was suspicious when Lord Julii's son requested fosterage. Training with Phaestion would accelerate your learning and perhaps friendship between you could change the course of history. Would you be turned to him or him toward you? Would one of you die suspiciously during the Combat exercises? Refusal was politically unwise. I took the chance. I sent Alberich to Bone and then as my representative instructor to the Julii Academy. He said you had fire I didn't see. Then you almost did die. I wondered if I should let you. It would have been easier for Edgaard and succession. Sometimes I wish you had . . ."

Hearing what I already know spoken aloud still hurts.

"You lived, but you were broken. It was Phaestion's request to alter you. Somehow he convinced his father that you would be an ally, not an enemy. The danger was great and the procedure illegal, but it was the only way to have you whole again. I let love cloud my judgment and allowed it. You survived. I was almost proud."

And I almost believe him. I hear the guards gathering outside to ambush me.

"You defied The Companions. Your popularity with the people grew. When I learned you had taken a lover . . ." He shakes his head and looks at me squarely. "I wouldn't have done it, Edmon, if I had known your woman was with child."

You will not speak of her! My blade sings.

"That's it, boy! I killed one unborn by accident, but billions yet unborn will be murdered if you don't kill me now and stop the Julii. You and I don't matter, nor do our loved ones in the face of this."

A single tear of blood glides down his throat.

"Your mother, your wife, your teachers, your child—all paid the price for your obduracy. You could have married Miranda, waited until Old Wusong died, waited until I died. You could have annulled the marriage when the time was right. Your stupidity forced my hand. If I couldn't teach you, I knew Faria the Red would break you."

It's true then. Faria was commissioned by my father the entire time. He betrayed me. I did not want to believe it.

"The old warrior, a legend when I was a boy for his skill, also had a vendetta against the Julii. He ensured that Bruul Vaarkson took note of you. He healed your island friend so that you could be led into a trap . . ."

Toshi . . .

"Nothing you have suffered has been without my forethought or design. I knew you'd hate me. That hate was necessary for what you have to do now."

My head spins.

"I would've saved you from it if I could. Now let your suffering be for a purpose. These shaking hands of mine can no longer grip a dagger. I could not commit suicide and blame it on you even if I wanted." He holds up his old, gnarled hands before him. "I beg you to take my life. Make a better future."

Damn him! If I kill, he succeeds. If I do not, this world is doomed.

I hear the familiar whisk of camglobes. Three silver balls hover around us, dropped from a hidden compartment in the ceiling moments ago. No doubt the globes will automatically release the broadcast the moment I complete the patricide.

"Do it!" he screams.

There are no voices in my head anymore. No monsters or memories telling me who I am. My entire life has led to this moment, this choice. All the pain, suffering, and death my father engineered so that I would transform from a boy to a monster, a leviathan. All so that I would succumb to the violence he thought I needed to kill my rival, to kill him, and take the throne of Tao. Yet, I understand that this is not balance. One does not rise honorably, as worthy, through blood. One does not save the soul of a world by desecrating his own. I see the path before me, the choice I must make to do what is right, though it may have dire consequences for the people of this planet. It breaks my heart for the future when I choose to do what I must do. *I will not take his life.*

"You'd let the universe suffer for your own selfishness! Give me your sword!" he screams. "I'll take my own life and say it was you, damn you." He tries to reach out but can't even lift his weak arms. "Edmon, please," he begs.

I've come for this final face-to-face now so that he knows, before I go, he has failed utterly. Then again, I'm not as good as I'd like to be, either. The siren sword sings. The blade cuts cleanly. Blood spurts and then oozes. Edric screams and writhes. I pick up the memento from the floor, slick with blood. I gently tuck it into my pocket and pull out the aquagraphic recording cube. I place it at the foot of the bed and depress the playback indentation. Sound blasts from the cube.

"He and I had already agreed to end the great Edric Leontes. The poison had already been administered into his food and drink."

"Bastard!" The croak escapes Edric's lips.

"There was a feast following the Pavaka. Revels lasted into the night. The bargain was to be the dissolution of your nuptials, our claim to the throne of Wusong removed, and in return, I would wed the heir of House Julii."

Security will arrive to find my father in pain, primed for a good, long stint in a regeneration tank. He'll live out his last years in slow deterioration knowing that no son will take his head or title.

"Alberich should have been testing the food."

I listen wistfully for a moment to the echo of my lost voice, then turn to leave.

"Alberich's always resented Father for defeating him in the Combat . . ." I jump to a ventilation shaft, remove the grate, and crawl in to the air duct. Security guards burst through the doors to my father's chambers as my sister's confession plays over the loudspeakers.

—

"Hurry!" Lavinia shouts.

I run toward where she stands on the roof.

"Is it done?" she asks breathlessly.

I nod. She has not heard the record of her voice implicating her in my father's poisoning.

"You won't regret this, brother." She kisses me fully on the mouth. I'm still as a statue, repulsed, but not wanting to tip my hand.

The howl of screamers pierces the night. Two transports with black carapaces strafe the Wusong towers as sonic weapons pulse from defending House Leontes sondis. The rooftop doors open behind us. Dozens of Leontes guards in silver and midnight blue pour onto the roof. I shove Lavinia behind me defensively and unsheathe my siren steel.

An explosion rocks the tower, and I'm hurled to the ground along with everyone else. I quickly turn to see one of the House Ruska screamers in flames as it sails into one of the Wusong towers. Glass explodes, and flames burst upon impact.

Phoebe!

The second Ruska screamer careens through the sondi blockade. My younger sister leans out the cargo bay door, her auburn hair whipping in the wind. "Edmon! Jump!" she screams over the engines.

I take one last look at Lavinia standing among the guards, alone and haughty, and then I run.

"Edmon!" she shouts as I leap and dive into the cargo bay of the screamer transport.

"Pilot!" Phoebe shouts. "Get us out of here." The screamer veers away, dodging fire from the sondi blockade. I look out a porthole and watch as Leontes guards swarm the rooftop. Lavinia turns to greet them and is shoved to the ground. She tries to rise, and a guard smacks her with a pike. The figures grow smaller as we pull away. Alberich, too, is carried by the guards and thrown to the ground next to her. Edric Leontes, his face bleeding from two holes where his nose should be, is carried on a palanquin toward them both.

Lavinia looks up at me in the retreating screamer, bewilderment on her face. Our eyes lock, and she realizes that I've outmaneuvered all of her betrayals, just as the sondi turns and I lose sight of them all forever.

Phoebe collapses to the cargo bay floor, racked by sobs. I go to her. "Beremon," she whispers through tears. "He was aboard the other screamer. He thought that it was better if we split our forces. If one of us didn't make it . . ."

I reach my hand out to comfort her, but she stands and strides toward the cockpit before I can.

"We have little time to prepare if we're to escape the forces of the Pantheon," Phoebe says, wiping her tears.

I raise my finger and point to an aquagraphic map display and swipe to the coordinates I want.

"Edmon, that's on the Nightside of the planet."

I trace my finger through the aquagraphic writing out the word—WENDIGO. A silence hangs thick in the air, but she nods, understanding that I need to go back. I have one last promise to keep.

CHAPTER 31

Denouement

I drop from the screamer to the snow pack below. I never thought I'd return to this place. A part of me never thought I'd leave, either.

"Stop there!" The guard in the tower fires his rifle. Too slow. I'm already on the move. I vault up the tower as the guard tries to get a bead on me for a second pull. *Bang!* His aim is wide, and I leap from the last strut into the bird's nest. He reaches for a knife, but a well-placed finger strike to his shoulder makes his limb go numb. The next blow downs him. My boot smashes his weapon into pieces. I'm in a destructive mood.

Rung by icy rung I descend the ladder. The journey's easier than the first time I made it. My feet and hands aren't bound by chains. I'm also different, stronger. I have purpose. The tunnel opens to the hollow cavern of the firelit village. Frost mixes with musty smell of bodies in furs. I've arrived during the sleep cycle so the camp remains in repose like an ancient frontier town. I remember what happened within the icy walls of this cavern, though, and remind myself: *There's no innocence here.*

I skirt the gang camps, through the alleys of covered storefronts. My focus is on the old man I once called friend. I make my way through ice and muck to the healer's hut . . . in ruins?

The carefully crafted igloo has been smashed to powder. Stains of ash from a smoldering fire, long since extinguished, streak the cavern walls. There's no sign of Faria the Red.

Perhaps I'm naive to think Faria must still be alive, that the old man wouldn't let himself die so easily. There aren't many places he could be. Scattered tents and sad, dirty men in furs huddle around fires. *Poor souls. I can't free them now,* I realize. *I can only free myself.*

This whole trip is a risk. Every moment spent is another chance for the Pantheon to prevent my escape from Tao. Fortunately, all eyes will be on the Combat, which begins within the hour. My absence in the arena will not go unnoticed, but the games must go on. I circle the outskirts of the Picker camp then cut through the sleeping bodies to the main bonfire.

"Edmon Leontes?" a hushed voice asks. I'm on the man before he speaks another word. My hand claps down on Carrick's mouth. Subtlety was never his strong suit. I put a finger to my lips, indicating the need for quiet, and slowly remove my hand from his face. I had thought Carrick dead, but everything's foggy from that last day. Apparently my old comrade survived, though he's missing an ear and a hand.

"What are you doing here?" he asks.

As response, I point to my throat and the vertical line that runs from chin to clavicle.

"Can't talk. I see," he mutters.

I draw lines on my face hoping he'll understand I'm looking for the man with the facial tattoos.

"Old Faria?" he asks. I nod. "He's . . . Edmon, he's not the same."

I don't have time for stories. I just need to know where he is. So I shake my head and mouth the word *Where?*

Carrick points to the corner of the encampment. A sickly fire flickers next to a heap of rags. I nod, thanking the big man.

"Edmon?" he asks. He searches for something else, some other word of comfort, but there's nothing. "Ancestors watch over you."

I make my way toward the figure huddled by the fire. The dark man stares into the flames. His face is skeletal, and he's rocking back and forth, whispering a language I don't understand. I kneel and take his hand. The old Faria would never have allowed me to do such a thing, but this creature is a mere shadow of what he once was. I look at his fingers. The bones have been smashed and have healed crookedly. I pull back the furs that cover his legs to reveal them similarly twisted beyond repair. This is the payment my father and his men gave him for his service training me in his mysterious arts.

"Edmon." The old voice croaks catching me off guard. "Is that you?" He turns his blank gaze toward me. I reach out and grip his shoulder. "I knew you would return," his voice rattles. He reaches beneath his furs, and his gnarled hand pulls out the nightscript reader that contains the map of Miral. "I'm beyond healing," he says. "They sent me to the Citadel after you were taken, after they broke me. It was hell moving through ventilation shafts with mutilated legs and broken hands. But I never lost hope that you would return and fulfill your oaths to me. The treasure of Miral awaits." He expects a response. "Why don't you speak?"

I take his hand in my own. I run his fingertip along the length of my throat so he can feel the scar.

"He offered me freedom, Edmon," he laments.

He lied to you, old man.

"Know that I never would have taught you, if I felt you unworthy. That was real. The treasure is real. I believe it can return your song to you, if that's what you choose . . ."

My whole life was a lie, including my friendship with Faria. It doesn't matter. The shaman once told me that I was using him just as he was using me. So I will use him now. I take the reader from him and stand.

"Wait," he croaks. "Remember the oath you made the day I gave you my knowledge?"

To take a life of his choosing when he asked it of me. All agreements are null and void now. My training was paid for long before he taught me a single thing.

I won't kill, old man. Not Phaestion. Not my father. I will not kill at the behest of another. Not now, not ever. That is the sacred oath I have made with myself.

"Take my life, Edmon of House Leontes. Please help me go, without pain," he begs. "I cared for you, watched over you. I shared my story with you. That was real. Sometimes death is kindness. End my suffering, please."

What about my suffering and all I've lost?

"Please—" he whispers.

Words The Maestro taught me echo in my memory. A story of two star-crossed lovers fated to die in the end. I think of my own star-crossed love . . .

Que fais-tu, blanche tourterelle, Dans ce nid de vautours? Quelque jour, déployant ton aile, Tu suivras les amours!

Gentle dove, wherefore art thou clinging to the wild vulture's nest? Trust me soon thou wilt be awinging to a far dearer breast.

My finger contacts his temple just as Faria taught me. I feel the spark of his life go painlessly dark. His eyelids fall, and in this last instant of life, I feel something between him and me. No words can name it, but if they could, the closest translation would be *forgiveness.* So ends Faria the Red.

The music swells.

Un ramier, loin du vert bocage, Par l'amour attiré, À l'entoure de ce nid sauvage, A, je crois, soupiré!

See you guard him safely, that they live will know! Or your dove may flutter, from his cage and go!

A day later, my boots hit sand, and I'm overcome with the urge to kick them off. I dig my toes into the grittiness of the white beach. A wave splashes my feet, leaving them buried. It has been almost six years since I left home, and this is the last stop.

I run up the twisting switchback through the lazy town. What's left of the place is ruins. The homes are broken and torn. Cracks in the stone storefronts are highlighted by the scorch marks of humbatons my father's men made the day he took me, the day he took Nadia from me . . .

A little girl walks naked down the windy cobblestone street. There's nothing in her eyes but hopelessness. She freezes when she sees me, terror stricken. I reach out a hand, but she runs down an alley between two crumbling buildings.

I walk up the crest of the hill to the manse, the house where I grew up. I don't know what else I expected. A part of me wanted to see if it still stood, the place where the villagers would gather and play music around the fire. I imagine Nadia standing in the doorway holding a child in her arms, welcoming me home. It's only a dream. All that's left are rubble and ghosts.

EPILOGUE

Sustain

Just before launch of the rocket purchased with the last wealth of House Ruska, I'm told by my sister that Phaestion of the House Julii mounted the champion's dais. He announced his ascension to the College of Electors and promised the beginning of a "Golden Age." He vowed to follow the path of the Great Song and conquer the universe.

For my part, I take a last look through my porthole at the small lonely planet hanging in space as the ship breaks the gravity well of Tao.

Why run, boy? I still feel the monster inside me. My father tried to bring it forth. Phaestion told me it was the truth of everything, but I know what it really is—suffering.

The pilot announces the ship's approach to the Fracture Point. The hull rumbles, and a tear in the fabric of space opens. Some ancients used to say that life is suffering. The only compassionate response is acceptance. I accept that violence is a part of me, but I choose to listen to the leviathan no more.

I look through my small window. I see light everywhere and a great whirling tunnel in the blackness. It surrounds me. I feel a tug on my chest as if it is being pulled apart and opened, raw and naked for the first time. I feel music beyond words. I wish Nadia were here to feel it, too. And I realize she is. She will always be a part of me.

"Elder Stars illuminate only because there is darkness. A warrior can know righteous cause only because there is evil. Heart to thought, thought to voice, harmony rises from discord. This is the Balance."

As the door of light pulls me in, I'm no longer Edmon Leontes. He was a spirit of pain. Now there is only kindness. Out there in the black, there are good people, kind people. I'm going to find them. My body sings. For a brief moment, I'm filled only with hope.

ACKNOWLEDGMENTS

Special thanks to my early readers, Sean Toohey, Navaris Darson, Michael Onofri, and Matt Ritchey. To Jackie Batston for beta reading and believing someone would want to publish this book. To Philip Eisner for his experience and wisdom as a master storyteller and inspiring the game out of which this yarn was spun.

To my agent, Andy Kifer, who gave me my shot; my publisher, 47North, and Adrienne Procacinni, who helped bring it to life; and my editor, Caitlin Alexander, who helped me make the work the best it could be.

Finally to Samantha Barrios, who saw past the finish line before I did and who lent a friendly, honest, and enraptured ear (mostly because she insisted that I read early drafts to her aloud rather than read them herself). I am in your debt.

ABOUT THE AUTHOR

Photo © 2015 Vaney Poyey

San Francisco native Adam Burch is a classically trained actor who has had one or two lines on such television series as *Scandal* as well as multiple death scenes in cult horror films such as *Nazis at the Center of the Earth*. In addition to auditioning regularly for the part of Paramedic #2 and performing in theatre, he is an accomplished martial artist, holding a Black Sash in Wing Chun Kung Fu. The Fracture Worlds series is his literary debut.